HOPE and DESTINY

Also by Niklas Natt och Dag

1793: The Wolf and the Watchman
1794: The City Between the Bridges
1795: The Order of the Furies

HOPE and DESTINY

A NOVEL

NIKLAS NATT OCH DAG

Translated from the Swedish by Alex Fleming

ATRIA PAPERBACK

New York   Amsterdam/Antwerp   London
Toronto   Sydney/Melbourne   New Delhi

ATRIA PAPERBACK

An Imprint of Simon & Schuster, LLC
1230 Avenue of the Americas
New York, NY 10020

For more than 100 years, Simon & Schuster has championed authors and the stories they create. By respecting the copyright of an author's intellectual property, you enable Simon & Schuster and the author to continue publishing exceptional books for years to come. We thank you for supporting the author's copyright by purchasing an authorized edition of this book.

No amount of this book may be reproduced or stored in any format, nor may it be uploaded to any website, database, language-learning model, or other repository, retrieval, or artificial intelligence system without express permission. All rights reserved. Inquiries may be directed to Simon & Schuster, 1230 Avenue of the Americas, New York, NY 10020 or permissions@simonandschuster.com.

This book is a work of fiction. Any references to historical events, real people, or real places are used fictitiously. Other names, characters, places, and events are products of the author's imagination, and any resemblance to actual events or places or persons, living or dead, is entirely coincidental.

Copyright © 2023 by Niklas Natt och Dag
English language translation copyright © 2025 by Alex Fleming
Originally published in Sweden in 2023 by Bokförlaget Forum as *Ödet och hoppet*
Published by arrangement with Salomonsson Agency

All rights reserved, including the right to reproduce this book or portions thereof in any form whatsoever. For information, address Atria Books Subsidiary Rights Department, 1230 Avenue of the Americas, New York, NY 10020.

First Atria Paperback edition December 2025

ATRIA PAPERBACK and colophon
are trademarks of Simon & Schuster, LLC

Simon & Schuster strongly believes in freedom of expression and stands against censorship in all its forms. For more information, visit BooksBelong.com.

For information about special discounts for bulk purchases, please contact Simon & Schuster Special Sales at 1-866-506-1949 or business@simonandschuster.com.

The Simon & Schuster Speakers Bureau can bring authors to your live event. For more information or to book an event, contact the Simon & Schuster Speakers Bureau at 1-866-248-3049 or visit our website at www.simonspeakers.com.

Interior design by Davina Mock-Maniscalco

Manufactured in the United States of America

1 3 5 7 9 10 8 6 4 2

The Library of Congress Cataloging-in-Publication Data has been applied for.

ISBN 978-1-6680-6987-5 (pbk)
ISBN 978-1-6680-6988-2 (ebook)

For Mats Linday

Regnabo.
Regno.
Regnavi.
Sum sine regno.
(I shall have power.
I have power.
I once had power.
I am without power.)

Inscription around Albertus Pictor's (ca. 1440–1509) fresco of the Wheel of Fortune in the porch of Härkeberga Church.

Prologue

1350.

With the Black Death the reaper claims half the kingdom. *King Magnus* needs silver. To fund his loans he offers his land as a pledge. *Bo Jonsson*, a nobleman of House *Gryphon*, soon holds all the land around the Baltic, from the southernmost point of Blekinge province to the Gulf of Finland.

But for Bo the Gryphon his lot is not enough.

1364.

When King Magnus refuses to repay his debts, Bo the Gryphon invites the king's nephew, *Albrekt of Mecklenburg*, to rule over Sweden. A puppet, a lapdog king intended to warm the seat of the throne in Stockholm for the Gryphon himself.

But for King Albrekt his lot is not enough.

1386.

King Albrekt asserts himself and seeks to bolster his power, wanting to restrict the nobility's estates. The Gryphon goes to an early grave, fifty-one years old and still uncrowned. Of the Gryphon's circle his cousin is the strongest, *Sten Bosson* of Oakwood Manor, of the noble line that bears a shield parted per fess in blue and gold. A knight of the Council of the Realm, one of the most powerful men in the land.

But for Sir Sten of blue and gold his lot is not enough.

1388.

Sir Sten has learned enough at the tables of the Gryphon to try his luck at the same game. He invites *Margaret*, queen of Norway and Denmark, to Sweden to take Albrekt's throne. A woman, weak and dawdling and distant to boot. Who else would she enlist to help rule her northern province, if not the one who invited her there? Sir Sten means to rule the realm in Margaret's name.

But for Queen Margaret her lot is not enough.

1390.

Queen Margaret assigns Sir Sten the task of executing the Gryphon's will and restoring all that was unlawfully taken. The queen's trap springs shut around Sir Sten. Soon every potentate in the realm flocks to Oakwood, and while the nobles bicker, Margaret plants her Danes and Germans as bailiffs in every castle. Sir Sten goes to his grave disgruntled and defeated. The queen follows him the following year, the plague succeeding where no man could. To her heir, *Bogislaw of Pomerania*, renamed *Eric* for his subjects' benefit, she leaves her three kingdoms.

But for King Eric his lot is not enough.

1410.

King Eric wants to expand his kingdom and wages war along his southern border. Young Swedes are mustered for battle and march south never to return, while the king's foreign bailiffs plunder the people, demanding higher taxes for every passing year. They shamelessly line their pockets, taking by force what is not given willingly. Swedish noblemen cast bitter glances at the position that they once held. Among them Sir Sten's many sons, heirs to the house of blue and gold: knights, members of the Council, and the most powerful men in the realm, the blood of kings coursing through their veins.

For the *sons of Sten* their lot is not enough.

1434.

PART I

JUNE 1434

A WASTELAND. WHITE CLOUDS swathe the summer sun, the air warm and sultry. A swarm of midges weaves him a mantle, and elsewhere his sister burns. Finn casts his gaze over all that lies before him: The worn furrow of road, dusted by the dry spell. Overgrown fields between copses of trees. The horizon a snare of dense woodland. He sharpens his senses to make out the world that lies beyond this one, beneath his feet and high above, but there is nothing there for any human to divine. The dirt crackles in sweaty creases as he rubs his face and carries on up the road. His thirst is dire, but it's still long till eventide, and Finn knows he should be grateful for what anguish he suffers. He wished for worse, asked the priest for a hair shirt and a useless load, but received only a shake of the head and an admonishment for his pride. Still, he carries stones in his pack, fills his shoes with gravel each morning.

Lone he wanders, meeting few. In the distance stand farmhouses, dusky and cool, their past masters long since put to soil or gone to ash. A mild wind probes their crooked shutters before departing through the gaps in the logs on the other side, finding naught inside worth tarrying for.

Finn tries to picture these tracts as his father's mother described them, bustling with folk in merriment and strife, every village ahum with broods of children, fields and meadows purring like cats under the care of the meek. He would have thought the old woman in her dotage, but all around the dead make themselves known, haunting the voids that they have left behind. Forsaken chambers and farmland in eternal fallow, neglected tools worn by generations now gone. His whole life, soon twenty years, has been spent in a world built for more, his childhood a lark on the graves of others. The day before yesterday he passed a watermill whose wheel still turned in the stream, its floorboards pale with dust from a stone with only itself left to grind. Stone dust to feed the specters, to the unheeded groans of the wood. The plague claimed them all.

Among the living, tall tales of the reaper's whims are bandied again and again. In a village not long hence all but a single man was taken; in the neighboring village, all but a single woman. Both made for their church, tolling out on each bell their soul's afflictions. And so they found each other, and from the embrace they shared in solace a new village was sprung. Always the storyteller's. In the next breath they speak of the ravenous children whom hardship had driven from homes where all grown-ups had fallen; they found no mercy on their travels but were quickly put to earth, still crying and flailing, rather than spread the pestilence to the village to which they came. A span of life has passed and more besides, but still the kingdom lies sparse. The land stretches out for miles on end, the silence like an iron hoop around the head where all too few were left to inherit soil or voice. Out here in the plains whole villages still lie deserted. Those who were spared have left, made for neighboring villages full of empty houses, and taken ownership of them, rather than go on dwelling with the wraiths. Life seeks out life. Mankind does not live well together, but they cannot get by alone.

※

Cuckoo's Roost and the shores of Lake Hjälmaren are already three days' march behind him. Finn could have walked faster, fleet of foot and no stranger to toil, but he must stop at every church he passes, ask for the reliquary, and pray the Paternoster and the Ave Maria the entire rosary around. His arrival is often ill-timed with the priest's comings and goings, and hours are wasted in wait at the church door. If he arrives late the evening steals upon him, and there is nothing to be done but wait out the dawn. He prefers to sleep outside, wrapped in his own cloth, a tussock for a pillow. The churchyards are the safest places, after all. Finn harbors little fear of others, but he doesn't view his own strength as reason enough to tempt thieves and brigands. Within the church walls there is peace. No one disturbs him there, unless one of the congregation is doing penance in the twilight hours, trudging sunwise around the consecrated earth. Slowly the night looms, long and light. The birds twitter for hours on end before settling to rest, hastening to live in this season of mercy. Only once all is at its darkest do they fall quiet, leaving the night sky to the predatory owls' bolt on winds unseen. As for Finn, he has trouble sleeping, the unease grinding away at him as unsparingly as the forsaken stream's lonely mill. He tells himself what the priest told him, that his hardships are like a cooling breeze over memories of her singed skin, a salve on her blisters and wounds, a promise of swift relief. The nights are warm, yet he knows no peace. Every moment of rest is like a thorn in his gut. She is always in his thoughts. Ylva. As children they were always one and the same, sharing in everything, the tears of both equally bitter over the bruises that marked only one. With age they grew different, disagreeing on the right path. Where he saw God's grace in their fate, she saw something else. He complied, let himself be tamed, taking as a mercy the life that they had been given. But in Ylva the charity rankled. For her it was a punishment, and rebellion was never far away.

Now she burns alone. He knows fire and what it inflicts. He remembers his hasty grip around a hot poker as a child: the sudden bite in his fingers, the pain that lingered long after. What if he had been unable to let go, not even as the skin started to smoke and the blood hissed, not until the flesh was blackened and charred like the last scraps on the spit? This is what she must have felt.

When he rouses from his slumber in the darkest hour it is as though the rest has peeled the godliness from him, flaying open a core of wrath. His heart races, pounding hate and rage with every beat. The injustice, the cruelty. Once he has regained control of his thoughts, the panic of remorse spreads in their place. He knows that he has laid bare the depths of his soul, an affront to He who sees all, knows that he has just made everything worse than it already was. When the dawn light reaches his sleeping spot, all that remains is a dint in the tussocks. He is already on his way elsewhere.

Yet as evening falls, finding only stones in his pack, he must eat, if only a little. A roadside hamlet, a church simple in its humility, a stooping tavern next to the muddy patch around which the houses were raised. His business is already done, the scraps of cloth torn from John the Baptist's garbs venerated, the prayers intoned. Bread and water stand before him on the table's rough planks, the light dusky and gray, the earthen floor cool. Finn sits there, weary and bloated now that his stomach demands so little. People gather with the twilight. Once the crowd is big enough they draw lots to choose who will chop the firewood, then persuade the keeper to light it. Long must he kneel with bent back, breathing life into the embers brought in on a spoon from some warmer hearth, but soon enough the smoldering light spreads to the birch bark and twigs. A spindly flame sprouts among the sticks. At once the room is made anew. A golden glow imparts warmth to the mind before the body can feel it. Shadow figures sweep the walls, lending depth to the narrow hall. A moment of earthly devotion. Motionless they all sit there, staring longingly at the dance of the flames, at this comforting thing that not even the learned can explain so that common folk will understand. It draws Finn's eyes, too, until he realizes that it is but a taunt. From his stool by the door an old man strikes up a droning ballad for crumbs and drinks. The song lulls Finn.

"Hush now and give us a story!"

The cry shocks him from his restless torpor, his neck stiff where his head had hung. Even more crowd onto the benches now, their congregation enough to help the fire heat the room. The old man who sang holds out the goblet he carries with him for payment beforehand. Someone fills it. He drinks, while each and every one of his listeners edges closer to the spot they feel they best deserve. He clears his throat and begins. Finn knows the words. Some tell the tale in rhyme, but back in Cuckoo's Roost few are fain to hear it. Three handsome princes are hunting in the forest in mirth and good cheer. Before long they are lost in mist. Three figures come toward them from between the trees, and they soon see that they are three corpses risen from the earth, living yet dead, reeking of the grave's embrace. The princes shrink back in disgust, but the dead command silence and calm. From our line are you sprung, they say with worm-eaten voices. As you are now, so were we once. As we are now, so shall you become. We squandered our lives on vanity and trifles, they say. Mend your ways while there is yet time. Thus their meeting ends, and the mist lifts.

The crowd nod and mumble their approval, and the old man is wetted anew. Evening grows late now, the people starting to disperse. Finn makes to follow suit when a stranger stops by his seat and raises his empty palms.

"Peace be with you."

"And also with you."

The man is young, no older than he, wearing a well-cut tunic whose hem bears the dust of the roads. A pouch on his belt. A light fringe below a summer cowl made of lightweight wool. A smile on his lips and a countenance intended to signal honor and friendship, in a face fitting for that purpose. Cautiously the stranger takes the seat opposite.

"How'd you like the tale?"

Finn shrugs.

"No one would call it new, but I've heard it told worse before."

"They call me Olaus Jonae."

Finn's eyes narrow.

"What sort of name is that? Sounds more like a bishop than a vagrant."

Olaus blushes.

"It's true that I serve the church. Olof is my given name, Jonas my father's. Will you go south at dawn?"

"What's it to you?"

The one born Olof squirms.

"To Linköping goes my path, and I have no choice but to walk it on foot. The road isn't new to me, but I've only seen it going the other way, and in a season when the trees were bare, at that."

Sheepish, his hand reaches for a fold of his tunic before he goes on.

"I've journeyed far through kingdom and country, and all around they speak of the forest of Tiveden. They say bad things happen to he who braves its shadows alone."

"You're in luck then, since Tiveden's on the other side of the lake, and not in these parts."

"The forest may well be nameless here, but the trees are the same, are they not? They cover the land in one unbroken stretch, all the way from the other side. There's no reaching Motala but by under their branches. Any outlaw sitting among us could cross the threshold tonight and rove unseen toward sunset for days."

"So it's outlaws you fear, not goblins and elves?"

Olof Jonsson leans in and lowers his voice, so that it travels no farther than it must.

"They say that a fiend has dug his den where the trees are at their darkest, and that he lives there like a beast, secluded from others, crazed with sorrow and wrath and fraught with malice toward his neighbor. A great, hulking man with limbs like iron and soot-blackened skin, too tall to stand straight under rafters. Tor the Walker they call him. He howls by night when the moon is full, the sound carries for miles around, and the wolves reply as if he was one of their own. In the twilight hours he stalks the forest paths, making prey of all he meets. If she's a woman, then he does with her what every highwayman has done with women since the dawn of time, and if she pleases him he'll keep her till he tires of her. But if it is a man he meets, then he'll take a knife to his manhood to slake his lust with violence. When the dead are found he has cut off their ears and their noses, too, for his own pleasure and to wear on his belt as an adornment."

Finn can't stifle his snigger.

"And what makes you think I'm no brigand myself? Perhaps Tor the Walker in the flesh?"

Olof nods at Finn's belt, and when he glances down he sees that the cloak he has wrapped around his shoulders has fallen open, revealing his dagger. Inwardly he swears at his own stupidity; he should never have been tempted to seek out company, even if his hunger had never been so great. Olof smiles.

"You do look enough like one. But a weapon like that tells another story."

The dagger on Finn's hip sets him apart from other small folk: embellished, though not so ornate as to belie its true purpose, in a costly sheath bearing his master's colors, gold on blue. For a while Finn sits there peering at his neighbor, trying to weigh up whether it's to his advantage that this Olof is no fool. Finally he sighs and comes to a decision.

"Finn Sigridsson is my name. I'm in the service of Sir Bengt at Cuckoo's Roost, on the shores of Lake Hjälmaren. Anyone who asks for me there will be answered. I head south at first light. If you're on the roadside then and walking the same way, I couldn't stop you if I wanted."

Olof fidgets in his seat.

"There's another matter. I carry a heavy load, more than one man can bear alone. Iron ingots, lots of them. I had a horse before, but misfortune willed it otherwise. If you'd be willing to help, I'd gladly pay you for the trouble."

Serendipity washes over Finn. This can be no happenstance. God's mercy for his sinful thoughts, a way for him to atone. He tries to steady his voice in reply, but the words come out hoarse and thick with feeling. All he can do is keep them few.

"I'll carry it, all of it. Free of wages."

Then, twisting his belt to cover his dagger, he makes for the door and outside, to find somewhere to sleep. He feels Olof's eyes on his back, their silent wonder. The setting sun, smothered in the deepest crimsons every day since his journey's beginning, dies pale that night. He wraps his mantle around himself and pulls his hood tight against his cheek and forehead. Until now the weather has been mild, but, like all who have lain in the fields, he reads what is written in the sky and knows that the next day will bring rain, rain or worse.

He dreams of his sister. And he hears his mother's voice, hoarse with sickness and muffled by the door that locked him out, repeating the final words she gave him in consolation. Words whose truth he and Ylva could never agree upon, and that in the end drove them apart.

"It is God's will. It's God's will, all that happens."

T HE SOUNDS ARE faint in the summer night, but the more her ears adjust, the clearer their song. Shrill women's voices raised in greeting at the crack of dawn. Though Stina can't hear the words, the nuns' mood carries through the stone, unless she is letting her own state of mind lead her astray, coloring their voices. A prayer for relief from suffering is what she hears, cries for salvation aimed not at the Lord God, but at the mother of the Son of Man. Here in Vadstena Abbey, Heaven itself seems purged of men, and a woman raised to godliness is what is worshipped. To Stina it scarce seems to matter, when the answer each day is the same.

For hours she has stood in the same spot by the window, at the boundary of the chapter house's empty expanse, listening to the sounds of the dormitory even though she should be sleeping now while there is yet time. But her restlessness is the greater. She was here already when the first bell was rung by the yawning sister who had kept the night watch, and she heard the sounds of bodies in motion to the constant murmur of prayer. Ave Maria, always. Another bell, then more shuffling steps, ever fainter with the distance, crossing the attic floor that leads them off toward the church and its choir of sisters. Stina knows their habits, after far too many days as a guest.

The languor is an ache in her joints, a pressure on her brow. Her youth is long behind her, and she can scarce remember when she last had strength enough to keep such a vigil. All day and almost till midnight she had sat by the birthing bed, and she would still be there had she not been driven out by the sisters with a gruff concern. Though her legs shake with weariness she has no wish for sleep, instead seeking stillness and solitude. From Margaret's chamber elsewhere in the wing all is silent. She sleeps now, awaiting delivery yet stealing what rest she can, while her body musters strength for the onslaught to come. The girl is young, only seventeen, and the child her first, the most difficult. She is thin all over, except for around her stomach, her beautiful blond locks stuck to her forehead and darkened by sweat. Narrow hips. The unease hangs like a fog around the nun who has been assigned to help, well as she may hide it behind worldly-wise resolve.

"Mother?"

Stina recoils at the word, the one that weighs on them all, and it strikes her as a portent that it should be posed as a question in the midst of such thoughts as hers. Britta was never light of foot, and that Stina's daughter was able to steal up on her unnoticed reminds her of the dangers of extended vigils. Her own firstborn. Britta is already a woman grown, and although Stina can add up the years that have passed since to two dozen, Britta's birthday still feels like a blazing scar in her mind. Before it, the drawn-out wait under a growing burden on ever weaker knees; the sudden stabs in her gut; and then, one morning, something that burst and left her cowering in a widening pool, aghast at having spilled her load on the very threshold of this new life. Not much blood though, only water. Then led to bed, to a fog of pain in a thickening mire of time. Alone, yet hemmed in by voices and touch. After a long struggle, one final battle, a rising pressure and a deliverance so abrupt it sucked the air right out of her chest with it, the sheet suddenly wet, as though the bed had been dressed with laundry fresh from the washing. A strange howl muffled by blocked ears, a wrinkly bundle in her arms, and within her a bittersweet joy that echoed through the void left behind by the little one. From dawn to midday, the midwife said with a nod of approval. Five hours, six perhaps. Pain of a kind that makes moment and eternity impossible to tell apart. Her own abyss beyond time, too distant for words to console, far from the reach of helping hands. Little Margaret now marks her third day in such a place. The child tarries. They were all to have set off back northward by now, to celebrate the newborn's first Midsummer at Cuckoo's Roost. Not at this rate. The wait is taking its toll on everyone, for it bodes ill. Stina's fingers skim her forehead and waist and sweep from shoulder to shoulder at the thought, the motion so habitual she hardly notices it. She turns and opens eyes that have been granted but a moment's rest.

"What news?"

Britta shakes her head.

"She's still asleep."

Stina doesn't know what is wrong with her daughter, for whatever it is, it doesn't show on the outside. The girl is fair enough, if she could only drop the strained face that she wears through habit, her brow furrowed, her lips pursed. Yet still she lives at home, a whole twenty-four years old, even though whoever wins her hand is promised a dowry of the sort only seen in the realm a few times each generation. One by one she rejected them all, until every last lad who could have won her father's blessing settled elsewhere. They were few to begin with, in these dark days of full graves and empty cradles. It vexes Stina to have her daughter still at Cuckoo's Roost, scarce big enough for more than one lady of the house. Britta is always at her heels, looking on as she does her rounds, a witness to every mistake. Silent. But her big, anxious eyes and their judgmental gaze are plenty loud enough.

Outside the lake lies black and still, free of ripples. Stina's clothes fit her poorly, they chafe and scratch, and suddenly she is as hot as after a run, even in the coolness of the night. She has to shake the ruffles of her dress to waft some air around her waist.

"So what do you want?"

"One of the sisters . . ."

Britta shifts weight from foot to uncertain foot, apparently at a loss as to how best to go on. Stina is too tired to do anything but wait her out.

"I left Mara's bedside to get some rest. Outside I saw a nun, in a ruffled habit and very old. I think she was watching outside the chamber door, but she took flight as soon as she heard someone coming."

"Surely you're fast enough to keep up with an old lady."

Britta nods.

"She hastened away as fast as she could, and I followed her at a distance. She went down the stairs and outside, then off around the church to the graves. She stopped at a headstone and prayed, before scurrying back to the dormitories."

"And the grave?"

"It bears our coat of arms. But the name I couldn't make out."

A mystery sprung of a girl's fancy. The last thing Stina needs. She turns back to the window, leaving Britta standing there.

"Perhaps the old woman's in her dotage. It's none of our concern, but the sisters shouldn't be wandering alone at night. I'll speak to the abbess when I next see her."

"Mother?"

"Yes?"

"The priest at home speaks only of God the Father and Jesus

Christ, and all of his saints wear beards. Why does everyone here pray to the Virgin Mary and Saint Birgitta?"

"They're wiser than the rest. Who in their right minds would follow a man when there's a woman to be had?"

Britta can't tell whether she is mocking her. She stands there with doubt in her eyes.

"Now go back to your bed."

Stina hears her daughter obey. She wishes she had been a better mother when there was yet time, wonders whether then she would have been granted a better daughter in return. The shame flares up, and she has only bile with which to meet it. Stina crosses herself again, in the absence of any better consolation, but inside her the melancholy is the same as so often this year. From the church the sisters are singing De Profundis. From the depths we cry out to you, O Lord.

SIR BENGT STENSSON opens his sluggish eyelids a crack, only to find the day had begun without him. He wrinkles his nose, startled at his own stench; he reeks of sweat, and his beard is soaked with soured wine. For a while he lies there, still rousing himself, and then with a sigh he rolls out of bed. It has been his alone for ten years, ever since he and Stina agreed that what they sometimes did in the conjugal bed they had done enough, and that the time they spent together by day passed more amiably when they had both had a good night's sleep, instead of his snores riding her like a mare all night long. He has to rock from side to side to get his belly resting evenly on his legs, limber as a dung beetle turned on its shell. His back throbs in reluctance at once again having to bear his weight, and a crack of bones at its base makes the gooseflesh rise on his arms. His head is pounding, his thirst dire. It wasn't always like this. From his youth he remembers but few such awakenings, but now they serve as the rule. Accursed age. This year he will be as old as his mother was when she parted this life, just before her half century. His father, Sir Sten, however, plodded on another dozen years, but then again his part in bringing ten babes into this world was easy by comparison.

Sir Bengt gets dressed, careful not to tempt fate by bending his back. His hose are difficult to get on, and even more difficult to lace to his shirt. His tunic on top, gracefully embroidered with golden threads on a blue base, so ornate that his many stains bear going unwashed. Then out. He grunts at his household as he meets them, a much-practiced sound that serves as both a morning greeting and confirmation that he has his eye on them, and that no lapse will go unnoticed. He makes his way through the courtyard, where the sunlight dazzles him like a clap to the face. To the bakehouse first, where they have already seen him coming from afar and have a mug of beer ready to hand to him on the threshold. He takes it with a nod, downs it, wipes his mouth, and returns it, after which it is filled again, so that he may drink more moderately while his headache eases. Torpidly he flees the morning sun, toward the castle's stone keep and its shadows, by turns smooth and jagged. On the way he waves off a small group of attendants who have been waiting for him to rise, to seek his blessing for all manner of tasks—no doubt relating to the Midsummer festivities, and no doubt at a greater cost to himself. He makes his feelings known with a quick nod: soon but not now, be patient, stay back.

The sky is blue, mirrored in the water of the lake. He squints up at the keep to check that the man hasn't dozed off at his post atop the battlements, his eyes fixed on the only road that leads this way. Cuckoo's Roost is strong, but no fortress is built well enough that it won't be lost in an instant if its men fail it; a castle is rarely taken if not through the mistakes of the landed or an ambush from the besieger. The castle walls had been widened by his father, the ramparts stacked higher, a moat dug, and better arrow slits cut, unperturbed by Stina's disgruntled looks at the childhood home that was soon rendered unrecognizable. He sets the mug down on the ground, steps over to the ramparts, and places one hand on the stones, cool as ever. He strokes the wall's rough cheek with an admiring hand, then gives it a pat to feel its solidity. The keep can be seen from far and wide, from both land and water, its gate lined with iron, battlements well placed to send a rain of arrowheads over unbidden guests. It is a sadness to him that the place can't be comfortably inhabited. A furnace in summer, a mine in winter. But since its cellar is filled with firewood and cured meats, the whole estate can be defended for months, long enough for the cold to pour frost into the blood of any assailants. Bengt raises his tunic and straddles his legs. It takes a while for him to get a stream going; only a trickle comes out, even though the pressure inside was enough to rouse him from his sleep. Like a wolf he pisses on his own house, his and no one else's. Relieved, he steps away, ready at last to take on what the day brings.

As he suspected, the pile of bills stands almost as tall as the keep itself, the sums mounting every time they add up the costs. Midsummer is approaching, and a gathering the likes of this hasn't been seen since the days of Sir Sten. Not since their childhood have so many of the brothers piled in under one roof. Bengt has mixed feelings. The sons of Sten are a motley brood, spread over three decades of nativity. Old alliances will be reforged and forgotten grudges brought to the surface, all while the drink hollows their judgment just as surely as a skilled sapper topples ramparts that recently stood strong. The youngsters against the elders, by and large, much like anywhere else. Perhaps what he most regrets are the duties that come with hosting. The lot of peacemaker will fall to him, with all of its trappings. He would probably do best to keep a clear head, but that's not easily borne out when others are slaking their thirst until their hearts are content.

"Where's Magnus?"

His scribe makes a gesture, as if to make his reply seem even more vague.

"Who knows where your son gets to? Out with his hawk, perhaps, or with bow and quiver, or rambling in the forest."

"Is Finn with him?"

The scribe hesitates, discomforted by having to remind Bengt of what he already knows.

"Finn Sigridsson is off to Vadstena to complete his sister's penance, as my lord permitted. He isn't expected back for some days."

Sir Bengt nods, reminded of what the beer had briefly blotted from his mind. Magnus may have vanished, as the lad so often does now that he is starting to grow up, but Bengt can't find it in himself to blame his son. In his own youth he himself was no different. He rarely saw the point of wasting time on the tedium of duty when the forest and land lay wide open and ripe with adventure before him. With time things will change, and if Bengt must sit here snared in the household's net, then at least he is glad that his blood can sport elsewhere. With the last sip of his mug he drinks to his son, a warmth inside better than beer alone can bestow. The boy shows good mettle, and he is quick-witted and easy on the eye. What more can a father wish for than a son worthy of the future that he will be granted? His wife's blood appears to have thinned out the worst of what flows through every branch of his own line of blue and gold: the vagaries of a foul temper. The very same thing that plagued his own father at Oakwood, and that he has seen time and again in his brothers and in himself.

Still, she should be here, Stina, for tasks such as these are hers and not his. Overseeing the household is the woman's domain, always has been, and his own shortcomings are never so manifest as when he tries his hand at her work. The right seat at the table for each guest, the slaughter of livestock for the festivities, all manner of fare. Important decisions all, though to him it still feels like a paltry waste of his time. He can feel the beer sapping his mind's stability, drawing his thoughts down foolish tracks. His own duties, the ones to which he should rather give his time, are they so much better than this? A knight. A councillor of the realm.

Well, he remembers the day, just after his tenth birthday, when Sir Sten took him to the assembly at Mora Meadow, to see King Eric elected and receive the knighthood himself. Never would he have believed that this barren kingdom could contain so many subjects. Countless lords and their retinues. His father seemed to know them all and was greeted with reverence by each and every one, each step by necessity lined with mutual marks of respect, so as not to risk sowing discord. Bengt saw their curious eyes scan his own face for signs of his lineage: here he is, shoot of Sten Bosson's seed, who with time will have to shoulder a hefty piece of the inheritance, the land and abundant riches that his father, grandfather, and great-grandfather in all their cunning, courage, and ruthlessness managed to squeeze from their proximity to the throne. Not to mention the royal blood in his veins that, though old and weak, still thrums with promise at every heartbeat, loud enough for anyone standing close enough to hear.

The day wore on and everyone drank, until dusk fell and his father woke him from his slumber on the bearskin, then hoisted him onto his shoulders so that he would be better able to see. The church's men were gone by this point, the ones who had walked among them in resplendent attire, with golden crosses borne on staffs high above everyone's heads. In their wake a pagan ritual. Mumbled psalms were abandoned in favor of older songs, to the beating of sword sheaths on shields, with words that seemed to him so ancient that their meaning escaped him. The mood instantly altered. The air close as before thunder. He felt the hair rise on the back of his neck and on his arms, Sir Sten's heavy glove on his shoulder as he was gradually led through the horde, one in a long line of men. The smell of folk thick enough to make his eyes water, the soil beneath his feet churned to a quagmire from all that the crowds had ridded themselves of. And then, in the distance, the newly chosen king himself, like a creature from a far-flung legend, crackling with color as he stood atop the largest of the meadow's stones, his boots in the twists of the runes. Lit by a ring of raised torches, with forged gold around his forehead and a bloodred mantle on his shoulders, to receive his people's praise.

With dread Bengt was led ever closer through the crowd, one

of the youngest that night to be raised from the rank of squire. His quaking legs failed him when it came his turn to kneel; his right knee landed heavily on the slope, and he had to steady himself with both hands so as not to fall. In his ears the men's roars, his own eyes squeezed shut ahead of what everyone had long warned him about: the strike of the sword, which was to land hard enough to separate the fainthearted from those worthy of a higher rank. But nothing came, and when he found courage enough to raise his head he saw before him a king who was in no way a hero of legend, but a lad not much older than himself, red pimples on his paled cheeks just as glaring as the mantle on his back, feeble-shouldered and spindly-calved. His puny arm trembled under the weight of the sword as he tapped Bengt's shoulder with its flat edge and mumbled a few words in a language that couldn't be called Swedish. The terror in his eyes at the company in which he had found himself.

Sir Bengt still serves that same feeble boy. From that day King Eric has taken few pains to learn more Swedish, but he has grown into a fractious man, choleric, fearful, and easily offended in his efforts to keep whole the patchwork of realms that his foster mother had tacked together. Others may envy Bengt his seat on the Council of the Realm, unaware of the endless muck work it entails. King Eric sits in Denmark, and in his absence everything falls to others. Last year Bengt was sent to bargain over farms on behalf of the crown. Before that, negotiations with the Hanseatic League: hour upon endless hour with a skulk of foxes in human guise, always quick to construe every word to their advantage whatever the meaning, always with misunderstanding on their side. This year he was forced to ride all the way to Lund on winter tracks to appease the archbishop himself over the king's envy and greed, the two men increasingly at each other's throats, on those borderlands where worldly and spiritual power both claim dominion. And all the while he is meant to be playing law-speaker in his own lands, where he presides over life and death, guilt and innocence. Not to mention managing all the property that has fallen to him through inheritance and ambition. All of that which will one day fall to Magnus.

His patience gives out at the thought. Bengt settles only what can't be put off till tomorrow and leaves the rest, then dictates two letters in quick succession. One to his sister-in-law, Katarina Sharp, with a request that she come as soon as possible to advise and assist in his wife's absence. The other to Stina herself, to inquire after her delay in Vadstena. He has to start again when his words come out too brusque, for he knows as well as anyone that what she is doing is a higher duty. With a sign of the cross he sends a wordless prayer for little Margaret. His thoughts move on to Nils, his brother and the father-to-be, among the younger sons of Sten always the most restless. Where he is now, rather than at his wife's confinement, no one seems to know. God grant that the child be delivered strong and healthy.

With the day's tasks done Bengt strolls back across the courtyard. He gets himself more to drink, feeling the day's imbibements start to claim their due. He lets the intoxication grow, adding to it with more mugs while the sun wanders on its western way. On unsteady legs he rises to his feet, and he must throw out an arm to catch his balance. For a while he stands as still as he can, weighing up his choices, before making for the path that leads down to the lakeshore. He tosses open the door to the washhouse with a clap so loud it sends the laundresses scattering, as though he were a fox who had breached a plank in a drowsy henhouse. They know his purpose, and the girl he seeks stays put, running her hands down her front as though to spruce up the skirt that she knows will soon be crumpled. She smiles at him, and one corner of her mouth appears to him as lewd as the other is shy. He fumbles with his belt, thick fingers lacking feeling. Beneath the cloth his member is only half bulging; it hangs slack, to little use. Her indifference sparks his anger, her forbearing smile an affront. He gives her a slap across the cheek, sees the sting draw tears to her eyes and the blush spread. A flash of fear when their gazes meet awakens his manhood, hard at last, and he turns her around with a firm grip of her waist while she hastens to raise her skirt out of his way. He wrangles to find the soft spot and then thrusts hard, again and again, spurred on by her whimpers. Though he loses track of time he suspects the bustle is over with quickly, for that which wants out has been long pent up. Breathless and seeing black, he turns to leave without further ado, his belt over his shoulder so as not to have to fuss with the buckle. He lets the evening wind from the lake fan his tunic and dry him.

He turns his feet toward the little hillock on which the keep's foundations lie, then leans back against the wall and gazes out over his estate. All of this is his, as far as the eye can see. Dark spots dance over the terrain. Another memory rises from his internal mists, unbidden: of his father, Sir Sten himself in his glory days, on one of the few times when Bengt alone among the brothers was chosen to go out with him on a ramble. Little Bengt the knight. The meadows that they had passed had been recently fertilized, the privy barrels hauled out of their pits, rolled around and their contents spread, the stench heavy over the area. At the edge of the farmland, Sir Sten got down on one knee and waved at his son to come to him.

"Come here, Bengt, I want to show you something."

He opens his palm to reveal a fistful of black earth.

"Know what this is?"

Bengt sees well enough, and he catches the smell: soil mixed with dung. But Bengt suspects those aren't the words his father wants to hear, and he knows that when Sir Sten asks a question it is usually so that he might give the answer himself.

"Treasure is what it is, Bengt. Wealth springs from the earth. Without this"—letting the soil sieve through splayed fingers—"none of these"—now pointing at the farmers at work, strewing the earth with manure from heavy carts—"and none of these." Now he holds up his left hand, to show off the gold ring engraved with their coat of arms, a parted shield, with a woven lattice to mark the bottom half. Before Bengt can shrink back, Sten smears a brown streak across his cheek, and the stench of dung catches in his nose, damp and greasy.

"To remember that by."

Bengt drains the last drops from his mug and wipes the froth from his beard. Without people to work it, his land is of little use. All around him fields lie fallow, since his old farmers died without ensuring their next in line. Fences rot and buckle, besieged by forest and weeds. The people are too few, and what work they can be coaxed into is not enough. Of the farmhands and tenant farmers, the most able are lured away to others' lands with the promise of owning property themselves. Damn them and their endless discontent. It wasn't he who cast their fates; each one's lot is drawn by Providence itself. Sir Bengt hurls his mug at the open plain with all his might, toward the thunderheads blowing in from the south. He hears it land with a thud not far away, feels the pinch of overexertion in his shoulder. This view of all that is his turns to a taunt, and he raises his voice to a roar that rankles in his throat.

"Copulate, why don't you, you damned weaklings! If I can do it, then so can you. How hard can it be?"

"NO MORE. LET'S rest."

One soon gets to know a neighbor's temperament, their being. Olof Jonsson is tender of foot, talkative, and quick to complain, ever ready to speak ill of others. Now he raises his shrill voice so that it will carry over the rain, which falls around them in clattering sheets. Finn doesn't want to listen, nothing if not pigheaded, wrapped up in his own silent torment with the weight of two saddlebags on his neck, as heavy as a grown man. A branch that he has bent out of the way seizes its revenge, slipping from his grasp and rapping him across the nose. He nods at Olof Jonsson over his shoulder, gesturing at an oak that towers above the bare ground, alone and mighty enough to assert its own dominion as far as its branches reach, each as powerful as other trees' trunks. Finn sets his load down, feeling welts sting as the blood returns. With bark at their backs and foliage for a roof they are shielded from the worst of the downpour. Finn looks around, but the view is obscured. The rain is falling heavy and hard, rustling and pattering as the drops find stone, plant, or one of the many puddles that their ilk have formed. What treetops his eyes can see dance in the storm, and when he shakes his head in response he feels the moisture whirl around him. Olof's eyes are full of reproof.

"I thought you knew the way."

Finn looks away.

"We thought the same."

Finn has walked in forests before, and he is well aware of their guiles. How gaps between the trees can make gateways for deer and wild boars, their hooves wearing paths as credible as any tracks cleared by man. How easily a wanderer can stray from his route where those tracks meet, and, prevented by vanity from retracing his steps, his wearied mind paints a path stretching out all the farther before him, between ever-denser trunks, until an hour has gone or more and he is helplessly lost in a godforsaken place with no help to be had, up to his waist in swamp and thicket.

"What now?"

Finn squints up through the sprawl of branches, in vain.

"There's no telling where the sun is. I can't make out which way is which."

"Have you got steel and flint?"

Finn has both but shakes his head, knowing that neither will be worth the trouble in weather like this. He shifts over to drier ground, sweeps off his mantle to wring out the cloth, and crouches down by the trunk to wait. Only by twilight does the sky seem emptied. What the rain did well an hour ago the darkness does better still: all visibility is gone, too late to set out anew. Both of them try to bed down for the night, without success, for hours of sitting brings no fatigue. In the dimness of the summer night they toss and turn, while all around them the forest's leaves shed their drops, the night's creatures brush against willow and bush, drying branches extend, and gnats swarm.

"You asleep?"

"No."

"Where are you heading, then?"

"Vadstena. To the abbey."

"I guessed as much. I saw you at the church even before I saw your knife. Are you a pilgrim?"

Finn sighs, weighing silence against boredom.

"I'm doing penance."

He hears Olof make a movement of sorts, and he can't blame him. Throwing in with a sinner rarely brings luck. Finn takes a deep breath to keep his voice steady.

"Three weeks ago my sister was taken by a fit of the chills. She lived in sin with a man, and chose to keep him at her deathbed instead of calling the priest. She wasn't anointed until it was too late. When it came to light, there was no one else to do her penance in her place. The priest sent me to the abbey to pray at Saint Birgitta's bones. She was kin to Sir Bengt, and she would stand by her own, saint or not. At every church along the way I must stop and pray by the relics."

"Then you were in Kumla the other day. Did you see the garb?"

"Yes."

Olof chuckles quietly to himself. It's something he often does, as though life has some amusement in store for him alone. Yet another reason for Finn to curse his choice of travel companion. Still, he can't bring himself to stifle the question that the silence invites.

"What?"

The man beside him smiles his crooked smile and shakes his head.

"I've seen many a church in my day, from Lund down south all the way up to Nidaros, and I've spoken to others who've seen even more."

"So?"

"I should probably keep my mouth shut and have less to answer for. But if every splinter I've seen in a golden case came straight from Golgotha, then the gospels are wrong, for our savior must have been crucified on a longboat and not a cross. And if every priest is telling the truth about their bit of rag from the Baptist's loincloth, then it must have been to the women of Judaea's endless sorrow that he chose the solitude of wilderness over the joys of love."

Long must silence wait before Olof has finished sniggering at his own wit. Finn is glad that his own face is hidden by the dusk, glad that Olof changes subject.

"And what of Cuckoo's Roost?"

"I serve Sir Bengt. Have done ever since I was a child, soon ten years."

"They say hard times are coming. You'll have plenty to keep you busy."

"What do you mean?"

"Haven't you heard? The men of the north are going to war, in earnest this time. Upcountry they speak of nothing else. Soon enough they'll be marching south."

Finn shrugs at this gossip, which seems to strike up every year once the summer sets in. Olof lets it lie. He watches Finn quietly for a while before patting the cover of the pouch he carries on his belt.

"I've got something here for you. But it's dark still, and you should see it with your own eyes for me to better explain. Let's try to catch a wink in the meantime."

Wishful thinking. Finn's breeches, tunic, and mantle are soaked, and the sodden leather of his footwear is hardening into a tight vise around his sore feet. He is cold and ashamed at his own discomfort, for what are his torments against hers, Ylva's? She is burning still, and can but endure and wait for the relief that only he can give. What she wouldn't give for damp and cold. He stares out into the darkness, where his senses give shape to the unfamiliar. Faces that he knows as well as his own blacken and crack. Forest spirits rove among the trees, heard but not seen. A tawny owl cries out in the midnight hour, a howl as if from some spectral being that, upon catching a glimpse of his world, cackles in glee at its wretchedness.

Slowly Stina trudges through the churchyard's rows, her hood raised to shelter her from the rain. She searches for the gravestone of which her daughter spoke. Storm clouds aside, the very daylight bears a hint of the unreal: for one who has kept vigil all night, the new day feels like a lie unmasked. Stiff joints complain in the body that would have been glad of rest. Death is all around her, its inevitability carved in stone, life so fragile by comparison. Her breath gives out and suddenly she is sweltering. She is forced to find a headstone near the wall on which to sit, certain that the nun who rests below won't begrudge her this support.

The melancholy comes over her, the one that leeches all the color from the world, a resigned whisper that questions what it's all for, what all this toil is worth. It has been coming all the more often, and Stina wonders why. Every attempt she makes to assess the life that she has lived finds little cause for disappointment. She is highborn, half lion, half lily, descended from royal blood. She wonders what her father would say if he could see her now from Heaven. He had wanted a son so dearly, but Stina was all he got. So she was raised like a son, and like a son beloved.

※

Stina rises with a stifled sigh, brought back to the present when the bite of the hard stone outweighs the respite it offers. Her mantle is made of a dense wool that lets no drops pass its stitches. She resumes her walk among the stones. There are more than one might think, given the abbey's young age. Many wish to make this their final resting place, and those with foresight begin their campaign for a tomb in this most holy of northern soils while still in the bloom of youth. The abbey thrives on this commerce, promised ever-greater gifts in all the more wills. Estates, forests, fields, farmers. When the final judgment looms, the highest in the realm see their amassed wealth bereft of its former value and would sooner pay any price to absolve themselves of their sins.

※

Just when she has started to lose heart she finds it there before her, the stone slab that Britta mentioned. Marked with the cross, of course, but below that the coat of arms belonging to her husband, clearly carved into the rugged slate, the work of a master craftsman. She bends down to better read it, but her eyes aren't what they used to be. For a moment she hesitates, but then she plunges her hand into the soil around the stone, scatters a handful of it over the slab, and brushes away the surplus. The rain turns the earth to mud. For a few instants, before it is all rinsed away, the lettering stands out more clearly with the chisel's notches filled, and now she can read it: Karin Stensdaughter, born in the Year of our Lord 1395, and laid to rest in 1414. Here also lies Märta Karinsdaughter, born and departed the same year. Stina gets to her feet to think, treading a restless trail back and forth in front of the tomb. Karin of blue and gold, a child of Sir Sten, like Stina's own husband. A dead sister. A daughter besides. The engraved years speak their own, clear tongue. Death must have come to both of them in childbirth, some twenty years before. The name Karin sparks an old memory, vague and muddled, from a time when Stina was new to the family, when all of the names around her seemed impossible to learn and even harder to pair with the right face. Karin Stensdaughter was a sister-in-law among her glut of in-laws, a woman Stina had never met, one mentioned so rarely that her passing could have happened without anyone noticing. Had Bengt traveled to attend the burial in secret, leaving Stina in Cuckoo's Roost without a word of his purpose? Stina tries to remember, but too many years have passed. They resist any attempt to tell them apart.

She bites at the skin around her nails, as she is wont to do when lost in rumination, always going too deep so that she must put up with the keen sting of it for days thereafter. Britta wasn't wrong. There is a mystery at play here, and a portent, too. It strikes her as a bad omen that this forgotten grave should have come to light on the day when another descendant of the same line is waiting to be born just a stone's throw away. Stina compares the headstone with its neighbors. The grave is tended, while others lie in neglect. Around it the weeds have been cleared, and unknown hands have scrubbed the stone of moss and lichen. Still lost in thought, Stina leaves the grave, with a whispered prayer for the dead awaiting the Rapture. The nun who led Britta here, she must be found. A task that is as easy as telling one sheep from another when you are a stranger to the flock.

WITH THE DAWN light Olof Jonsson draws a rolled-up piece of leather from his pack, smooths it out with great care, and then unfurls it to reveal a sheet of meticulously inscribed letters in swirling long lines. Though gentle of finger, he looks proud, as if he had caught the sun itself.

"Look."

At Cuckoo's Roost Finn has sat through many long hours with the priest, quickly abandoned to the relief of both parties as soon as he could read tolerably well. Now he takes the leather that holds the sheet of paper and turns his back to Olof, to hide that he must sound out the letters in order to grasp their meaning. At first he thinks he has misread the words, that the night's anxious dreams are still muddying his senses and deceiving him in the light of day. He reads it again, now with a finger over each word so as not to lose his place. Eventually he turns back, the confusion clear on his face. Olof smiles in reply.

"It's true what it says. From the bishop himself, and above him His Holiness the Pope in Rome."

Finn's very foundations quake. He feels the sweat break out on his forehead, the air he breathes no longer enough to fill his chest. With blackness falling before him he sees a hand reach out, and at first he thinks it's to help him in his moment of need, but soon he sees that its meaning is another. A palm extended, every crease black with filth, not in support but for payment.

"Shall we say one mark? My authority has been granted. With that your penance will be over."

Misjudging Finn's silence, Olof smiles a crooked smile.

"Never fear. Your sister will get her relief even if you can't pay now. God the Father will put out her blaze as easily as you'd snuff out a piece of kindling. I'll take your word for the debt on the Lord's behalf. I'll be heading back north soon, and Cuckoo's Roost isn't far out of my way. You can have the payment ready for me then."

Finn takes his hand as if to cast it away. With dread he feels his fury rising, as though he were a vessel placed beneath a torrent, one that must sink as surely as it once floated. Wrath fills him, and though he knows that it is wrong, knows where it must inevitably lead, he is powerless to resist. And so it takes possession of his body, a doll without a will of its own, reveling in its moment of power over life and death. He grabs Olof by the collar and pushes him backward, trying to knock his legs out from under him. Olof cries out in shock, but soon enough he starts to fight back, and he is stronger than he looks. They trade blows, clumsily, poorly, nothing that serves any purpose other than to spark a greater rage. Now it's Finn who must step back, Finn whose feet must flit in a dance to keep his balance. An unseen root floors him and Olof is on top of him. Now hands around his throat, choking the next breath that Finn must draw. Panic rushes in as his eyes blacken, his defense now unthinking. With his body's last ounces of strength he steels himself and lands the hardest blow he can.

He must have succeeded in slapping the fight out of Olof, for he no longer feels his weight above him. Olof has rolled off and now lies at his side. Suddenly the fight seems stupid. To think that one single mark should be the price of his sister's pain, the worth of all the penance that he has done. The thought still makes his flesh crawl, but Olof is simply doing as he has been bidden; he isn't to blame. Finn raises his arms to make peace. But as the blackness drains from his eyes he sees it: in his right hand a rock lodged between whitened fingers, slick with blood. He is lying as though he has fallen, Olof Jonsson, still and with eyes closed, as if he fell asleep in the midst of their tussle. From his forehead the blood has spurted, enough to spread beneath him a red quilt for his rest. One last exhalation comes, a deep, sniffling sigh, and then no more.

Time itself seems drawn off-kilter; in vain it twists and turns in the mire, unable to gain traction, a wheel helpless on its own axle. Finn sits among the tussocks with his back to the dead man and his arms around his knees, rocking back and forth, his face painted on his thighs in snot and tears. He gasps for air without ever getting enough, his vision mangled by black spots, bends over to spit in the grass, and lets the bile flow. Dizziness keeps him on his haunches. The rising sun brings scant consolation. For a long time he wanders back and forth, as though fettered to the body with an invisible yarn, keeping the corpse in the very corner of his eye to avoid having to see the mortal wound he inflicted. The dead man's eyelids have opened, and beneath them glimmer the whites of his eyes.

They seek his gaze to brand him with guilt. Alongside the dead man lies the load that he carried.

Finn hears a voice of reason within him, one that tells him to leave Olof's burden untouched. The less he knows, the better. That he can name the corpse is bad enough. Knowledge tugs invisible cords, goads one to act on what would otherwise go undone. Still, he cannot heed it. Other forces are stirring around them, whispering to his conscience that it would be a greater sin to the dead man to leave his business unknown. Iron, it was said, iron ingots. With shaking hands Finn undoes one buckle and tears off the cover.

What courage he had summoned fails him now, and the merciless weight of the world forces him to his knees. The words of the Son of God chide him from the depths of his memory: Do unto others as you would have them do unto you. Once a call to meekness, now a prophesy of his own future. He has slain one man, but it will cost two their lives.

Olof Jonsson's load lies exposed to him in all its derision: purse upon purse. He knows now what they must really contain, but still he must test the theory, vain in his hope. Each and every one is stuffed with silver marks and coins of lesser value, the little pouches wrapped tightly in linen rags so as not to betray their secret to curious ears. This treasure will be missed by someone, and badly.

※

Not far away the wind has felled a tree, wrenching its roots up with it out of the earth. The bedrock lies bared beneath it, dropping away into a crevice that the night's rain has filled with murky water. He carries the bags of silver there and cautiously lowers them to the bottom. Soundlessly the pool receives its gift. He stacks stones under the water in an unseen mound, then he hides the surface under branches. Soon the forest is as it was, flourishing in indifference.

※

At the scene of the murder Olof lies untouched. For a long time Finn stands in hesitation at what he must do, and even more time is lost when he takes a stone to his knife to make it as sharp as possible—as sharp as Tor the Walker would have it, with nothing else to while away the time in the lunacy of his den but to sharpen the blade that assists him in his atrocities. Finn's task forces him to touch the dead man, and he shudders at the feeling of the cooling skin that slips beneath his grip, the skin that once was human but now is not. He shuts his eyes and feels his way, doing what is required of him to place the blame with another.

※

Once his tears have run dry, Finn gets his bearings from the sun and sets off on his way. The path they had been seeking awaits him with mocking proximity, as if to drive home the needlessness of the day that has passed. When the path reaches the top of a hill, he looks back over his shoulder, to a clear view of the great oak that played host to rest and murder. With his dagger he carves a mark in a trunk by the road. Its hilt is still unwashed, his guilt imprinted in red whorls on blue and gold. He spits on his thumb to rub away the drying stains. And then on, southward, toward Motala first and Vadstena Abbey thereafter.

S IR BENGT POURS water over the hot stones, scoop upon scoop at a brisk pace, then leans back on the bench to wait for the steam to lash across his bare skin. It soon comes in a searing wave, forcing him to hold his breath. A sigh escapes him, sprung of the pain and pleasure that only the bathhouse can offer, and he lets himself sink down farther on the bench. Slumber of a sort comes over him, a stream of disjointed thoughts verging on dreams, enjoyable in their absurdity. A draft of air tugs him back to waking with a sting of ire. The farm folk should know that when he is taking his steam the house is his alone. He keeps his eyes closed for a while, in the hope that the unwelcome visitor will understand their error and make off unseen, but when the door closes he still senses the other's presence. He opens one eye, then blinks to make sure he isn't seeing things.

"Brother Bo."

Sir Bengt studies the brother who greeted the world just a year ahead of him, as naked now as the day he was born. Bo was always weak and infirm, and he was forced to spend much of his youth in bed, laid low by some sickness that would choose him alone out of the whole pack of brothers. When Bengt was knighted Bo lay bedridden with the chills, and he was forced to wait years until the queen's coronation to have his own shoulder graced by the flat of the king's sword. Bengt knows that Bo has never forgiven him the many head starts that his health has given him over birthright, and although Bo remains the brother he is closest to, theirs is a bond fraught with bitterness and old grudges. Bo Stensson's body is still marked by its trials: Thin and wiry, every rib easily counted despite the paunch beneath, slender thighs, and loose, sagging skin, his chest shallow under the drop of his beard. His head bare and bald, the wisps between his legs now gray. As an adult he has kept healthier, ever watchful of new maladies. Though thin, he seems hardened by his setbacks.

"Brother Bengt."

"If I'd known you'd be so quick to get here I'd have given you a worthier welcome."

Bo takes a seat beside him on the ledge.

"I told your people to leave it be. They're dusty inland roads you have here, and I'd like nothing more than to rinse them off. But be warned: The household you'll find upon leaving this bathhouse won't be the same one you left. A foreign power has taken over. Kari wasted no time in taking charge of your home, and immediately set about browbeating your people. If they don't heed their orders quick enough to please her, there'll be floggings all round. When I left her she was inspecting your store-chamber. Since she only looked stern and not fuming, I think the shelves were to her approval."

Bengt nods in relief.

"Thank goodness for that. Without her help we'd have a paltry Midsummer ahead of us. And little Nils, is he well?"

Sir Bo's only son is in his eighth year, hale and hearty as a weed but with a father in constant fear of having passed on his frailty.

"The boy had to stay home, though he didn't half yammer on about it. Even though I'd tried to keep it quiet, he heard there was a tourney in the offing and was keen to come cheer, but I didn't want him traveling the roads in this dry weather. May life never grant him greater disappointments. And Britta, Magnus?"

"My daughter followed her mother south. Why they're taking so long I have no idea. Magnus is here, but there's no telling where he gets to. Come summer he's like a wild beast, loath to be indoors. But he probably saw you arrive, and I suppose curiosity will draw him out sooner or later."

"So all are well. That's good to hear."

Both brothers know well the haste with which Death pays its calls. It has been some years since they last saw each other, and few reunions of this kind are exempt from tidings of sorrow. No doubt they'll come this time, too, the news that some beloved member of the household, or some cousin, father-in-law, or aunt, has departed this life, but both brothers let themselves savor the moment. Their nearest are safe, a gift worth cherishing while it lasts.

Bo reaches for the scoop and bucket, starts ladling water over the hearthstones, and with the sweat the years run off them. A game they have played many a time before, in this form and in others: who will hold out the longest; who has the harder resolve; who will be forced to crouch and bend the knee? Two old men playing at boys' games.

Neither gives in. Satisfied in their mutual affirmation that their manhood is intact, they sit for a long time in the cooling air, letting their unfamiliar dispositions scrabble back toward a rapport that was once constant and unconstrained but has long since fallen by the wayside. Bengt shifts on the bench, clears his throat, and wipes the sweat from his arms and trunk.

"How's life back home?"

"Over in the castle Henrik Styke's flaunting his wealth, that German son of a whore, while fleecing the people for coins. But at Oakwood all is well. Though it's certainly empty compared to our boyhood years."

Their father's estate fell to Bo's inheritance. Bengt remembers it being under near constant expansion in order to fit the growing brood. Their mother was often great with child or in confinement; it seemed like two new little ones came to the world for every one that had grown old enough to be sent away. It was a manor in an older state of repair, no better fortified than it had to be, for Sir Sten meant to win his glory with guiles rather than weapons. Bo furrows his brow.

"I sometimes wonder how father found time for it all. Ten children and a kingdom at his feet. Last time I was down south I even heard someone say he'd mounted the queen herself."

Bo laughs out loud.

"If anyone was on top of anyone I'd sooner say it was the other way around. It would have been a mercy had the old man got to die without seeing how badly he'd been used, but, alas, he was wise enough to see that much."

Bengt nods, recognizing thoughts that he has often mulled over himself; like his brother, he, too, has lived his adult life in the ruins of Sten Bosson's schemes.

"The queen. I wonder if death comes worse for one like her. Three kingdoms under her skirts. Riches beyond all reckoning. Every enemy on their knees with head bowed. Then one day a boil in the groin."

"We're all forced to give it all up in the end. Is it unfair that the cost seems the greater to the rich?"

Bengt shakes his head, muttering the words that have been associated with their line's blue-and-gold shield since time immemorial, a spell against all and naught.

"Hope and destiny."

Bo rubs his face, as if to be done with all matters spiritual; he'd rather return to the earthly.

"Did you ever see old man Gryphon when he came to Oakwood? It's his fault, all of it."

Bengt shakes his head and gives a shiver, in spite of the heat.

"I saw his horse once, with his coat of arms. The Gryphon's head with its hungry beak. It was as if the sun passed behind the clouds. I ran to the forest and slept in the den that night. I mean, we'd all heard the stories."

"That he had his unborn child sliced out of his wife's belly?"

"That's one of them."

"When there's no hope of the child coming out, the mother's as good as dead already. The best you can do is try to save the child."

"Believe what you will, brother. All I know is that the very instant the newborn took its first breath, it was the Gryphon who stood to inherit his wife's riches and not her family. All of her lands, his. I've heard that what came out wasn't a healthy child but a little monstrosity. A scaly clump of flesh with eyes. Dead as a doornail. I've heard that the Gryphon raised its little mouth to his and blew into its lungs, then held it up to the priest to witness as the air wheezed out. He got his nod of approval before dropping it to the ground. For one breath the child was the biggest landowner in the realm. One moment later that was the Gryphon himself."

Bengt spits, making the hot stones hiss.

"It's bad luck to speak of such things while Mara's in the birthing bed. Besides, that's not the worst I've heard. No wonder I was scared."

Bo gives him a nod.

"I was no braver. I slept in the barn that night, as far down in the hay as I could dig. I think even Father was afraid."

"And yet with time he came to follow the old Gryphon's example."

"I wonder if Mother isn't to blame, too. She was young and pliable when they married, always let him have his way. He could have spared her more children when she was starting to get on in years, but no, Sir Sten had to have heirs aplenty, one to put in every castle he coveted in the land. And she said not a word against it, even though the burden was hers alone. Perhaps he thought all women as meek as her, that the queen would give him everything he pointed at without a murmur. Margaret, give me Kalmar. Margaret, Nyköping Castle, too. Margaret, lift your skirt why don't you."

Bo gives a subdued laugh, his head tilted back and his arms crossed over his chest.

"At least that's one mistake I won't be making. My Kari's got fists of iron."

Sir Bengt grunts his agreement. His Stina is made of the same stuff. He may have struggled with it in his youth, but with age he has grown wise enough to be grateful for all that she has that he lacks. Without her Cuckoo's Roost would have fallen into disrepair, its bills neglected, his own life far worse in comparison, and his name to be remembered with reproach. Without her no son, no future. And while many women can bear a son, who else could have given him one like Magnus? When his brother speaks again his tone is another, softer, and a sense of premonition makes Bengt shudder again in the heat. Seldom has he heard Bo whisper without purpose.

"But he did try, Father—he did his best, for himself and for those of us who outlived him. That might just be worth something, after all. We're starting to get on in years, Bengt. Who among us can look back on the time we've been granted and say as much? Me for my Nils, you for your Magnus."

Bengt sits in silence, knows that no objection is capable of subduing the truth. His brother lets what has been said sink in, before leaning forward, resting his elbows on his knees, and turning to him.

"Remember Oakwood, when we were lads? Remember how we'd play together in the forest, with twigs as lances and spruce sprigs for armor? The boulders our fortress to defend one day, the enemy's to besiege the next. We built walls and tore them down like nothing at all. We were unequaled, no one could withstand us. King Bengt and King Bo. All of the realm ours, and all its glory."

Sir Bo pauses and stares into the live coals, his face red in their glow.

"Those were the days, brother, the good old days. No?"

BACK AT MARGARET'S bed, all is as it was. The girl was awake not long ago but now sleeps again, her breaths heavy against her huge belly. The midwife is steadfast in her post, a sister who has made this calling her own, having sat at a hundred such beds or more. She is old and gnarled like the stump of a highland birch, but there is an alert glint in her eye, fists that conceal an unwavering strength in her bones. She appears cast expressly for her charge. Not once has Stina seen her leave her chair, day nor night. Instead she simply sinks into a light slumber when not needed, enveloping herself in a sort of invisibility that inspires trust all the same, quick to waken as soon as anything should demand her attention. On the bed Mara lies with a blush on her cheeks, seemingly distended to her very fingertips with the life that she is keeping. Stina creeps in on tiptoe but fails in her intent, and when Mara opens her eyes her gaze falls straight on her. Stina receives a faded smile in welcome and gives the same in return.

"Mara. How are you?"

"I wish the wait would be over soon."

Stina nods in agreement, making an effort to show a confidence that she doesn't have. She hears the unfamiliar tenor in Mara's voice: fear veiled by a feigned courage. The girl does it well. A stranger wouldn't notice the difference. A wave of pride for her young sister-in-law washes over her, and she places her hand on Mara's shoulder.

"Soon your prayers will be answered."

Mara squirms on the bed, twisting her sore back. The old woman is quick to adjust her pillow, dab her forehead, and put right the woollen blanket over her bust.

"Lady Kristina, how old were you when you had Britta?"

"Older than you, but not by much."

"Were you afraid?"

Stina remembers her fear blended with astonishment at the changes in her body. The guest inside who made her presence felt with kicks and somersaults. With each passing week heavier and heavier she grew, until the load looked impossible, left her tottering around on weak legs under a weight that threatened to overcome her.

"Yes. Who could be anything else? But the life growing within is already its own. It can hear the world calling. All you can do is be patient, and remember that what you are doing now women has done ever since the Fall, in worse beds than this and with fewer to help, besides."

Mara finds some comfort on the pillow, and the sleep takes her again, quickly and benignly, from one moment to the next. For a long while they sit together in silence, Stina and the midwife, both loath to disturb her rest, and a trio of breaths is all that is heard. As if on a given signal, both change position. The girl is fast asleep. Mercy fills the room.

"Sister Eufemia?"

"Yes, child?"

"Why does it tarry so?"

Sister Eufemia makes an equivocal gesture with her hand over her lap.

"Every birth-bearing follows laws of its own. It's true that many are faster, but it would be rash to say anything with certainty. The girl is young and healthy. There's no reason to fret without need. All we can do is wait and pray."

Stina rubs her red eyes. She wishes for peace to sleep, but has little hope of finding it. The woman wants to talk.

"Young Britta I already know. Has your ladyship any other children?"

"Magnus, my son. Six years after the first. Seventeen summers he has seen."

"And the birth, if I may ask?"

"Easier."

Like everything else with him, Stina adds inwardly. The old woman nods her approval at having her belief borne out.

"As it often is."

Stina rises, not to leave but to pacify her restlessness. Her thoughts turn to the duties back at Cuckoo's Roost that she is neglecting. Midsummer. This year with more guests than ever before: brothers, Lübeckers, Bishop Knut himself, kin, and well-wishers. But she has made her choice, and what that may cost is no longer for her to decide. Mara's mother is long since buried, and a woman in confinement ought to have kin nearby, if not by blood, then by marriage. Sister Eufemia clears her throat and lowers her voice slightly, as if to intimate a change of tone in their conversation, too.

"And Lady Kristina, dare I ask how you fare yourself?"

Stina meets the old woman's eyes, all but hidden beneath the folds of wrinkles and yet still lucid and alert. Stina rarely sees good reason to receive the sacrament of confession more than once a year, but as great as the unease of exposing one's sins and shortcomings, as salutary is the absolution, and equally powerful as God's forgiveness, is the feeling of laying one's soul bare to another and receiving mercy rather than reproach in return. She has had no close friends since childhood. As the Lady of Cuckoo's Roost she stands alone. The strength she exudes is what is required to ensure obedience. Around her she has no one whom she trusts enough to burden with her doubt or weakness. Tired and weak as she is, she is amazed that the nun's question doesn't spark her indignation, but instead disarms her in its concern. She senses that Sister Eufemia means well and knows how to keep a confidence. Out comes the truth, as though it had been waiting eagerly for its summons.

"More and more I feel the weight of dejection, though my life is no worse than it was. Better, in many ways. What more could I wish for? I'm the lady of a manor, and children I have brought into this world and raised. I want for nothing. I should be content, better yet, happy. Instead I find myself all the more indifferent to the world, all the less able to see joy in it. I don't know why, and that scares me."

"May I ask, is your ladyship's own mother still of this world?"

Stina shakes her head.

"No, the Lord summoned her to his side young, and my father, too."

"Forgive an old woman for being so forthright, but I suspect your ladyship perhaps has no one older to consult with about certain things, and I would rather speak now than hold my peace for modesty's sake. We've kept vigil for some days now, you and I, and I've seen your ladyship get hot and flushed; only sometimes, but it comes on suddenly when it does. Do you still bleed with each new moon?"

Now the redness rises on Stina's cheek, and she has to look away. She wonders whether she has misjudged the old lady—whether she is in fact losing her mind and no longer knows what she is saying. But the question also strikes an unexpected chord within her, and she finds herself answering it frankly.

"Before it was always the same. I could count the days by it.

Not so now, not for a while. Sometimes it comes quickly, sometimes it falls long behind."

The old lady nods as if her reply was expected.

"Soon they'll stop, never to return. For a time your ladyship may yet feel the same sort of pains as before, but that's all, and there'll be no need for linen rags. You have reached the turn of life."

The old lady looks at Stina, to make sure that she has understood.

"There will be no more children."

So simple, and yet so great; in Stina's single-mindedness the thought hadn't even occurred to her. She feels a whirring in her chest, an icy wind through a dark void. For the sake of her dignity she turns away, hearing with distaste the bitterness in her own voice:

"I thought myself younger."

"Don't we all. It's the same for every daughter born of a mother, when youth and ripeness are passed and old age draws near. Life changes, and the body with it. Hark my words, my lady. I've seen it strike the temperament before. Sadness, gloom, and dark thoughts, just as you say. It can become an overwhelming burden. It is perhaps even more difficult for one such as yourself than for lesser folk, for you have the freedom to brood, while others seldom see an idle moment. If you would heed an old woman's advice: Teach your soul to soar above matters earthly. Seek pleasure no longer in the world that you see, but place your trust in one who is higher, in the kingdom yet to come. All that we see is but shadows and dust. That's all it ever has been, even if we were once young and gullish enough to believe otherwise."

The old lady clasps her hands and lowers her head in prayer, perhaps in the hope of company, perhaps in intercession for her. Stina makes for the exit, seeking solitude like a wounded animal, withdrawing to the chamber that has been assigned to them as guests. She covers her face with her hands. The tears fall, but it seems to her that it is not their saltiness that seeps through her fingers, but life itself escaping her. For many years she has walked this earth, more already than many whose names fade from memory, but it's not enough, not nearly enough. And what little road remains for her, will it be the same? Each day so similar to the last that the deathbed's memories of the life lived might as well be condensed to a single day, a narrow circle trodden to tedium again and again.

Discreet hands shake her gently, waking her from a slumber that must have come on unbidden, and she is wrenched from dreams that she remembers only by their lingering discomfort. Beyond the window hangs the mild twilight of the summer night, no further advanced than that the blackbirds are still warbling. It is Britta who is waking her.

"Mara's waters have broken. The pangs have started, and if God wills it the baby will be close behind."

MAGNUS GOES HIS own way, on paths otherwise known only to hares and roebucks. Having turned from the shores of Lake Hjälmaren, named for the howl of its storms, he roams up and down through the maze of trees, heading farther inland, where gray boughs spread their leaves over soils that are fertile and soft. Bark hides faces in the hundreds, but not for one who can see: a nose of a snapped branch, eyes of knotholes and moss, cavities hollowed by squirrels and woodpeckers for mouths. He knows each one of them, childhood friends who have cradled him in their embrace since he was tall enough to reach the lowest branch. The forest belongs to his father, and it will one day fall to him, but already he feels it is more his than it was ever his father's. Time and again he stops and hides from view to make sure that no one is trailing him, half for sport and half in earnest. His father has business enough to see to, and his mother is in Vadstena. If anyone were to send servants to keep an eye on him it would be she, but he takes no risks with his privacy.

When he is nearing his goal he climbs up into a maple tree whose every branch is marked by the tracks of his feet, all the way up to heights where they threaten to snap under his weight. The tree stands on a hill, crowned higher than its peers. From here he can see all the way to the forest's edge and beyond, over the open fields that have been cleared around the estate, and on to Cuckoo's Roost itself, the brown timber houses dotted around the keep, fortified by ramparts and a moat. The people scurry like ants around their hill, but he is too far away to tell them apart. Nowhere does he see any sign that he is missed or needed. A wind wafts in from the water, carrying on it scents from the estate: freshly baked bread, beer fermenting in barrels, animals in their pens. It rocks him on his branch, strokes his cheek, and ruffles his hair.

Deeper in lies the glade that he has chosen, a secret of the kind that every forest harbors, a patch of bare ground dappled with flowers and slender blades of grass. What makes places like this one special Magnus can't say, but there must be something that holds the trees in check, reverently still in their circle: perhaps a site of sacrifice from the time of heathens, or a resting place for long-fallen warriors, or a dancing ground for elves under the full moon. An unknown power courses up from the earth, scrabbling up his calves and tickling the crooks of his knees. From late morning to early afternoon in summer the sun roams unobstructed above the canopy, filling the glade with light, a single bright spot amidst the shadows of the forest.

Magnus has learned to measure time by the light in the glade. By morning a murkiness at its eastern verge, fleeing the sun. By midday no shade at all. With afternoon, twilight creeps in from the west, marking the time when he should head back to Cuckoo's Roost, if not to seek out others' company then at least to be seen, to still the worries that might otherwise betray his secrets.

Under some leafy branches lies a roll of leather, the hide painstakingly wrapped to keep tight from the rain. Magnus brings it out into the sun and unfurls it, as gently as a prayer but as quickly as he can, for time is short and every moment precious. A sword, short for a fully grown man but big enough for him. The edge is dull and full of nicks, the point blunt, and although Magnus has tried to remedy both with a flat stone by the stream, the futility of the task soon became undeniable. The weapon has had its day. Nor does he need its sharpness, only its weight, its essence, for a sword it is still. He knows its grip well now, ever since last spring, and he cannot say for sure whether his hand has molded itself to the leather wrap of the hilt or the other way around. He raises it, and as always he is unprepared for the feeling it imparts, its jurisdiction over life and death, enough to make a boy's soul sing. Soon the sword will feel lighter, once he is used to it, once it has become more an extension of his arm than a foreign object; once it starts to hum a whispered tale as it cleaves the air around him.

His opponent is a puppet that he has wound together from birch twigs and cloth wrappings, dressed in rags and with pine-branch limbs, all raised up on a post. A root crowned with a wreath for a head, its arms open as if in a motionless embrace. Magnus fixes the post in the hole that he has reinforced with stones, then loosens the tie that binds his shirt and hose together. He slips off both until he is standing in only his smallclothes and folds the rest over a spruce branch, to keep them free of sweat and stains. Then he begins his dance around the puppet. In his mind he arms it and imbues it with movement, until it offers the resistance he craves. Finn is still away and would have made for a better teacher, but those days are gone and he must now be his own apprentice. Quick he is of both mind and foot, and he knows how to find weak spots. He moves in circles, thrusting and stabbing. His jabs pierce the twisted twigs again and again, its chest and neck, shoulder and arm. He dodges the ripostes he imagines, trying to conserve his energy even though his thighs are burning, his sword arm aching.

An hour passes, judging by the sun. Eventually his strength wanes and he allows himself to squat down and catch his breath, wipe the wet hair from his eyes. He has trained a great deal this summer, ever since the spring made the forest passable, and his pains show. New meat adorns his slender limbs, the ones that had grown so rapidly from one year to the next, always appearing to stretch out what flesh he had to new lengths without ever adding more. Now he is another. There is new strength in his shoulders and arms, his thighs and calves twists of muscle under taut skin, his palms leathery and hard.

He sinks back onto a bed of tussocks in the sunshine while his lungs and heart slow, his mind empty, as it always is after exercise. His eyelids aren't enough to block out the light. Before his eyes, strange shapes swirl in a singular dance. Light slumber steals upon him as the sun dries his skin. Shadows stretch out toward him and reach his resting hand. He jerks in his sleep, his fingers and legs twitching when his rest is disturbed. In his dream the fight is another, and he is faring worse than while waking. He speaks in his sleep, as he is wont to do, but there is no one to hear the words. He wakes as if with a jolt, then sits up, breathless again. All that remains is a fickle memory of adversity. He gets up and shakes it off, then steps between the trees to where a brook awaits, with clear, clean water from an unknown source, to quench his thirst and rinse himself clean.

Britta kneads two bits of wax between her fingers. The stone walls of the abbey retain the cool air even in heat, and her hands are cold. It takes time for what warmth she has to spread and for the lumps to soften, allowing her to roll them into the right shape between thumb and forefinger. Once she is satisfied she stuffs them in her ears. The silence is instantaneous. Only the most piercing of Mara's howls still break through, but Britta discovers that if she hums quietly to herself, then she hears only the notes that seem trapped inside, echoing in her head. She feels ashamed to avoid even this small share in Mara's torment, but she can bear no more. Even worse is her shame at the relief that she feels, her joy not to be the one lying there in agony, her belly stretched taut like skin on a drum. She mumbles a wordless prayer for forgiveness, but this place dampens not only the summer heat but also the solace of the prayer. For a week now they have been guests of the abbey, witnesses to the nuns' self-imposed thralldom, their virtue manifest in patterns as strict and monotonous as they are difficult for outsiders to comprehend. Every hour devoted to its purpose, each day begun with six hours of worship, where only the constant rising and sitting can keep the novices awake in the pews. Matins and lauds; prime, terce, and sext; then after none comes vespers, and with twilight, compline's promise of sleep and its brief respite from prayers and Latin. Saint Birgitta's angelic dictations are recited in a constant stream across all seven days of the week, as are the Psalms, time and again, like the tuning peg of a stringed instrument, stretching the younger sisters tighter and tighter until they are driven to the brink of madness and beyond, stripping them of their humanity until only the sacred remains. The older sisters endure it better; within them all resistance has already crumbled, their submission perfected with the insight that everything they had ever had of the worldly is now long gone. Old age has come, every desire now out of reach. With their youth wasted their future is also curtailed, and all that remains to them is to walk the path that they have chosen until the peace of the tomb rewards them with open arms. And, on the other side, the Kingdom of Heaven, the payment promised for all of their pains.

Britta shudders as she walks. The same track through the

same corridors, the ones that lead to Mara's chamber. Back and forth. At each corner she stops and waits by the wall, then, holding her breath, she peers around to see whether anyone is there. No one. With weary feet she leans back against the wall where she is standing. She wonders what it is like for them, those who said yes to the bridegroom who hangs bloodied on His cross. So different from her own suitors. As a girl she was promised a prince like those of legend, one who would come and rescue her from her tower, fair and handsome. But the ones who did come looked different. First there were the overgrown boys, either shy and timid or boisterous in their feigned manhood. When they stopped coming they were replaced by the old men, widowers who had already made a tomb for their young wives in the form of a birthing bed, now wanton in their hopes of winning all that is hers: young flesh to warm their sheets, a dowry and hopes of a greater inheritance, all her time to care for what children they already had, and soon more of their own mixed blood. A chamber for her like the one that is now Mara's. Every single man who has asked her she has refused. Sir Bengt has berated her for it, gruffly singing the praises of each rejected suitor until he, too, hears the absurdity of his own embellishments and is forced to come to his senses. Her mother simply makes do with a look, though it is as cold and withering as the rap of a hazel switch, worse than any words.

Well does she know that her mother wants her out of Cuckoo's Roost, past marrying age as she is. But she sees nothing of what Britta does. Not how she helps Father to bed when he has sat too long over his tankard, and washes him so that he might wake up clean and fragrant. Nor how it takes all of her ingenuity to make excuses for Magnus, so that he might roam freely without suffering reproach at the table. And, although Bengt rarely asks after his wife, whenever Britta sees her mother take the path down to the forest's edge of an evening, she invents a reason to give should the need arise. With sleight of hand she keeps the peace, thanked by no one.

One of the wax plugs slips out, melted by the heat of her body. She is about to knead it and put it back in place when she hears an unfamiliar voice through Mara's moans. Gabbled prayers, a brittle voice. Cautiously Britta peers around the corner, and there, at the door of the birthing chamber, she stands: the old woman, hands clasped and head bowed. Britta considers confronting the nun herself, but a part of her fears this old woman who roves between cradle and grave, and another is loath to interrupt what good any prayer may do. For a few moments she is at a loss as to what to do, but then she turns and runs.

"MOTHER, COME, MOTHER, make haste! She's at it again."

Britta's voice wakens Stina from her slumber, as it always does in these days that all sing the same tune: bedside vigil at a fruitless delivery until the fatigue is overwhelming; then back to a hard bed to snatch a few moments' rest. Her eyes smart when she opens them, the weariness a yoke on her shoulders. She struggles up onto her elbows. Her mind is racing, and she lies there mute and perplexed.

"The nun, the one by the door."

Stina sees black when she gets to her feet. Her daughter's helping hand scalds her self-esteem. She shakes it off as soon as she is able and waves Britta on with a vague gesture, then totters across the stone floor until she finds her balance. Together they hasten out under the shadows of the vaults. There is a half-light coming from the windows, the sky lit up by the sun even as it hangs below the edge of the world. It must be early morning, for she can't have slept a whole day away. Mara's child. Today must be its birthday. The hours have been drawn out in protracted agony, more already than for anyone Stina has heard of. Her howls carry through doors and walls, along with Sister Eufemia's voice, by turns gentle and stern. When they reach it, the corridor outside her chamber is empty.

"She was here, Mother, I saw her."

Stina forces her head to clear.

"Which way did she go last time?"

Britta points, but there is more than one route to the graves. Stina gives Britta a nudge in the opposite direction.

"Go that way. If you find her, keep her until I find you. I'll go this way. If nothing else I'll find you in the graveyard."

Even at a distance she spots her quarry, black and white, like an overgrown magpie seeking a scrap of meat among old bones. Stina slows her steps. The nun has nowhere to flee, but Stina doesn't want to scare her needlessly. The woman's frame betrays her age before Stina can even draw near. She is shrunken, bowed, and bent of knee, to better carry the curvature of her back.

"Sister?"

The old body jerks, then slowly turns on staggering feet. Over her black veil she wears the Birgittine crown with its five red marks that signify the wounds of the Son of Man, and her forehead is wrapped in white linen. Her face is ravaged, her eyes milky, and her open mouth reveals a toothless chasm. Stina must ask herself whether she has met anyone older in her lifetime, and inwardly she responds that if she has, a more placid life had preceded it. The old nun squints at her without responding, and Stina can't help but wonder whether this whole to-do has been for an old woman in her dotage, one who wanders the abbey through restless nights with neither purpose nor object. She steps closer to make sure that she is heard.

"Sister, you've been lurking by my sister-in-law's door at night. Tonight and before. My daughter followed you to the grave of our kin. I have questions."

The old woman rolls her eyes like a cow startled at the manger and starts rocking on the spot, voicing grunts that can't be understood. But before that: a moment of indecision, a glint in her eye of alertness, of choice. Stina lets the performance play out for another moment or two, before tightening the loop that will ensnare any woman of this one's kind.

"Do you swear by the Holy Virgin that you are no more than you appear? I call upon all the dead souls resting here, whose company you seek at night, to witness your oath. If you don't understand me, then your crowing will be answer enough, but if you lie it will be your damnation."

For a moment the feigned panic turns real, followed by surrender. She shakes her veil in resignation.

"I cannot make such a promise."

"Then answer me instead, Sister."

A stone bench awaits, hewn to receive the weight of those whom grief has robbed of strength. Stina takes the woman's arm, outstretched in her constant struggle for balance, and helps her along the way. Beneath the rough wool of her habit she is thin and stiff, with the same slow tremors often found among the aged, bones too thin for loose skin. Stina supports the old woman while guiding her across the treacherous paving stones, then helps her to lower her weight down onto the seat. This service rendered casts their meeting in a new light, support for the other forging unseen ties. The old woman sits quietly for a while, breathless in spite of the assistance, and she stares out into empty space for so long that Stina wonders whether she has forgotten where she is. Then she coughs the phlegm up out of her throat and speaks.

"Does my lady believe in curses?"

"Not since I was a child."

Stina's arms cross in disappointment. What can follow such a question, if not the confused ramblings of an old woman stricken by age? But the woman is alert enough to respond to what goes unsaid.

"A curse holds no power in itself. Its force lies in its repute, for to some extent we all believe in what no one can know for sure. We believe enough to shun one who is cursed, for fear that the evil will catch. And since all that takes root in the human mind, good and evil alike, finds ways of spreading its branches into the world, the curse becomes real even in the absence of witchcraft."

"Now you speak, but of what I asked you say nothing."

"Could I make the choice for you, I would choose silence. In your ignorance the evil cannot reach you. But once aware, you cannot forget."

It has been a long time since anyone spoke to Stina in such a manner, as though at a child who is demanding a summer shift in the rain, or who wants to frolic barefoot in fresh snow. The anger comes on quickly, chasing away any further reflection.

"Tell me what you know while I still have the patience. I'm this close to fetching the abbess."

The old woman shuts her eyes, and her toothless jaw chews wrinkled lips. Eventually she nods. She points at the grave from which they came, and only now does Stina realize that it is not the same, not the grave of Karin Stensdaughter and little Märta: it bears no parted shield with a latticed lower half. She gets up and walks closer to it, to read a different name: Ingegerd. Ingegerd Knutsdaughter.

"Fifty years have passed since Saint Birgitta ended her days in distant Rome. On her deathbed, God the Father promised her that she would be allowed to await the Rapture here in the convent that she had founded, and it fell to her companions to fulfill that promise. She was brought back home to us one summer, much to our delight, though the stench was equally great. Soon after that, her granddaughter came to take the vow as our sister. Her name was Ingegerd. Many saw it as God's token to his faithful. With her, the holy blood was restored to us."

She shudders in her seat.

"Not everyone seeks the sisterhood of their own volition. There are those who are given no choice. Ingegerd was eighteen when she arrived, younger than I was. Others watched over her, night and day, taking great pains to ensure she never set foot outside the walls. It was as though she slowly wasted away, one day at a time. She hardly ate at the table, didn't sing in choir, didn't answer when spoken to by elders. She was given to such raging headaches, she told me, that lightning would flash in her eyes and thunder would peal through her ears. One winter she was laid low by sickness. By spring she could speak again, but when she left her bed it was as though she was a different person. She said that the Lord had sent his angels to speak to her. She was of Birgitta's blood, and now the revelations, too, had been passed on. When a new abbess was to be chosen, the votes fell in favor of Ingegerd."

Her courage dwindles for a moment. The old woman closes her eyes, as if the words would come more easily in the face of an unseen listener.

"The angels would come to her by night, and the visits grew all the louder, echoing far into the convent. One night I was lying awake, and I listened to the sounds until I couldn't contain myself anymore. I crept up to Ingegerd's chamber and peered through the crack in the door."

The old woman falls silent, her jaw churning to form words that are loath to be spoken. Her voice quakes.

"She had two monks with her, and a novice sister. They were unclothed, but Ingegerd was still wearing her veil and Birgittine crown, the cross of her office around her neck. She lay down on her back on the floor and told them to pass their waters over her, and then she laughed as they did. No more did I want to see, but the sounds they made hounded me away, such sounds as I have heard from the boar and the sow when spring is come and the earth is to be enriched. I heard Ingegerd egging them on with words that were vile and worldly."

She pauses, and her relief at being able to share what she has long concealed is like a gentle breeze over them both. When she goes on, her voice is steadier.

"A convent can house few secrets. In the end, too many people knew. They wrote to the Bishop of Linköping, but he wouldn't listen. So then they wrote to Rome. At long last an answer came from the Pope himself. Bishop Peter of Strängnäs was sent to investigate. He listened to them all and found Ingegerd guilty. She was removed from office. When she returned the keys, they found the abbey's coffers empty. It was as though she had done everything in her power to destroy what her grandmother had built."

"And then? What happened to Ingegerd?"

"She shrouded herself in silence and withdrew within. Mostly she lay sick with her arms clasped around her head, complaining of pain. She would often weep with despair. I sat with her when I could, bathed her forehead and wiped her chin clean, brought her soup and a spoon, but I could never induce her to speak, not until she started to fade and we called the priest for the last rites. Her last words were a curse on the family that bears a shield of blue and gold."

"What exactly were her words?"

"All your love shall end in blood, to pay for the one I never had."

Never has Stina been the superstitious kind, but the words cut deeper than she could have imagined. Even worse while sitting here at the dead woman's grave.

"The year after her death, Karin Stensdaughter of blue and gold came to us great with child for help with the birth, as so many women of the nobility choose to do. We seldom fare ill, for what we do we have done many a time before, and we have the Holy Mother of God here to guide our hands with hers. But Karin bled until her heart gave out, and although her little Märta seemed hale and hearty at first, two days later she lay cold in the cradle. Both were healthy, and no reason could be found for why it should have gone as it did. But we knew of Ingegerd's curse. In blue and gold they had come to us, and the father was forced from this place alone, their love ended in blood. Now another girl has come to challenge the same fate. That is why I pray at her door."

"Who was Ingegerd and why did she come here? Do you know of her parentage?"

The old woman shakes her head.

"My world is no larger than what you see around you. I know naught of Ingegerd's line. Nor could I say why she chose to paint the blame for her life's misfortune in the colors of your family."

The truth of the old woman's warning finally descends upon Stina. All this knowledge is now hers, but to no good end. She knows a little, but not all, and her ignorance of the reasons seems to her as ruinous as having inflicted upon herself a forever festering wound. Yet the old woman appears to have more to say.

"May the Blessed Virgin forgive me for the liberties I take, but I might know the name of one who does know."

A hope after all.

"Bishop Knut; Knut Bosson of Linköping. He, too, is of blue and gold, but he bore the bishop's mitre and crosier then, as he does still. They say that when he first came to Vadstena, the abbey was rich and the bishop poor, and now it is the other way around. And there was no one closer to Ingegerd, though he was of the very blood that she so despised."

WITH EVERY STEP Finn takes the proximity of the town reveals itself all the more clearly. Between the trees the road widens, trudged by feet in greater numbers and plowed by carts' wheels. Through the trunks he glimpses flashes of fields as the landscape opens up, the path's ruts and roots no longer shaded by leafy branches. The smells in the air change as the wind shifts, the scent of burnt logs suddenly encroaching on the forest's rotting earthiness, likewise those of meat roasting on a spit, of bread on the rise, timber cut and sawn, and cleared land drying and steaming under the sun. Only then does Finn see the first houses, built low, with logs that cross at the corners, their roofs sealed with birch bark. Behind them the abbey's arches and church spire soar upward, gray stone stacked majestically above the village. And, beyond that, the open waters of the lake stretching southward, farther than the eye can see, until it disappears into blue mists where sky and lake blend together, as if the very world has found its end. By the shore stand a handful of tents in neat rows.

Finn remembers this feeling from before, but it is one that he has never grown used to: the feeling of stepping out of the wilderness and back into mankind's domain, a stranger who startles at every sound, unused to being addressed and slow to respond. Put out by noise and riled by the crowds. For the hundredth time he checks his clothes for stains, and for the hundredth time he finds none. Still, the guilt weighs on him like a wet mantle. Within him, his entire being is bellowing that it is preposterous to imagine that a deed such as his can remain hidden for any length of time behind silence, washed skin, and a face feigning innocence. Heaven knows and Heaven sees, and above the clouds an unseen finger is pointed straight at him, ready to separate him from the flock just as surely as an ailing sheep.

He finds a taphouse and gets himself a mug, then sits down on a log outside to take in all the new. The beer is cold enough, better than he remembers it. In one measured sweep he slakes days of thirst, and a faint intoxication swiftly follows. It comforts him, alleviates the loneliness that is sharpened by the presence of others, reminding him of his place among them: he is marked as one of their kind by his clothes, the way he carries himself, the dagger on his belt. His mug is empty and he needs another, now ready to answer the question that the keeper asks each new guest.

"What news of the north?"

Finn shrugs.

"I've seen little. If what others have told me will satisfy I'd be happy to oblige, though how much truth there is to it you'll have to decide for yourself."

"That'll have to do."

"There's talk of men on the march, that the men of the mountains are sharpening their pickaxes to see if they'll make as much of a dent in the bailiffs' castles as they do down the mines."

The man beside him pours himself a drink, fills Finn's mug without asking for payment.

"Same story as last year, and the year before that. Yet peace still reigns, and the people meekly pay what they owe. Your good health."

They drink as if they had practiced the movement together.

"Are those the bishop's men I've seen down by the water?"

"Indeed. They raised their tents yesterday, but they'll set off again any one of these days. Some of his lads were in here last night, and they said they're headed to the Hjälmaren's shores, for Midsummer drinking with the bishop's nephew at Cuckoo's Roost."

Finn squints at the sun as it rolls over the ridge of the abbey.

"I'd have thought the bishop would be welcome under the eaves of the abbey."

The keeper observes him for a while with wariness in his eye, looking out for a trap.

"I'm not one to speak ill of my neighbor, but there you'd be wrong. An old grudge runs deep between them. I'll say no more. You'll have little trouble finding others more talkative should it please you."

※

The abbey church at Vadstena is unlike any that Finn has seen before. From the outside it is wide and squat, but when he steps through the open door it is as though he is back in the forest, in a grove of petrified trees all grown in straight lines, spreading their crowns so high up above his head that the ceiling within seems loftier than the sky without. Between them the pillars bear arch upon arch, in a space so vast it makes him dizzy. By tall windows the sunlight fills the church with light, a great and brilliant lantern of grace and beauty. Mouth agape, Finn stares upward until his neck aches and his eyes fill with tears, running his hand over the stone pillars to assure himself of their reality. His knees quake, and he feels the air thick with all the splendor that is God's alone, the power to judge the living and the dead, redemption and damnation in one.

The worshippers are few, and he needn't wait to find a spot at the reliquary. It is larger than others he has seen, angular and red and laden with gold medallions. Journey's end for him. On hesitant legs he approaches the resting place of Saint Birgitta, chosen by the Lord, she who was allowed to gaze upon His angels, she who performed wonders in His name. The chest may be thick, but even through it he can feel her sacred bones glowing. From this close they bring a pressure on his ears, raising the hairs on his arms and the back of his neck. He kneels, pulls out his rosary, wraps it around his hand, and begins to say his prayers, while the wooden beads sift through his fingers in turn. He knows that any prayer said half-heartedly has little chance of reaching Heaven, but still he finds it difficult to keep his thoughts steady. His penance is complete, and Ylva Sigridsdaughter's soul, held in pledge by Purgatory, shall finally be redeemed. But now he prays with another's life on his conscience, one slain in wrath, outside of the exclusions that apply to justified combat. What punishment could be graver for him than for his sister to be left to burn? But surely the Lord wouldn't torment one to make the other suffer? He cannot know for sure, but he is seized by doubt. He prays the rosary around a second time for good measure, and then a third, and when the vaults are cast in shadow above him he prays still.

"What a strange thing it must be to be a saint."

A female voice. Finn sees her when he turns his head. Either her footsteps are featherlight, or his attention has waned in his hours of prayer. Her clothes are those of a peasant, and she is neither young nor old. He cannot be sure that it is a dullness of mind he reads in her face, but her voice does have a singular tone to it, not to mention her readiness to interrupt a stranger in discourse with the Most High. She rocks slowly from foot to foot, appears not to mind going unanswered.

"For half a century she's lain in her case, and for as long as I can remember, priests and monks have come from far and wide, and when they go home they do so with a piece of her in their packs as a gift, a toe, perhaps, or a shard of her hip, to put in gilded cases of their own for their people to worship. Her rest can hardly be peaceful."

She frowns, as if troubled by the thought.

"And at the Rapture all the dead shall rise and appear before the Lord. But however will Birgitta? Scattered all over the country she is, no doubt with plenty more left along the wayside from Rome. Who will put her back together? Must she do it herself, crawl from church to church and piece together all that is missing? Will the Lord send an angel to help her as she limps along? She'll likely be late to the heavenly throne otherwise. And what if it goes wrong somewhere, and she must stand before God the Father on odd feet or uneven legs?"

The woman shakes her head and clicks her tongue.

"I may not have lived the life of a saint, but at least my bones will lie undisturbed in their pit. That is a comfort."

Finn gets up, unsteady on numb legs. He has to rub his thighs before he can walk without disgrace. In vain he tries to detect the change that he was promised in a world beyond the flesh, but he is just as soon repentant for having claims above his station. Even fewer are praying now that night is falling, but among them is one he recognizes: Britta, Britta Bengtsdaughter of Cuckoo's Roost. He rushes to her side, happy to see a familiar face after so many days abroad. She turns around as his steps draw nearer, her hands clasped around her own rosary, weariness and fear written on her face.

Bengt Stensson walks before his brother, showing him all that Cuckoo's Roost has become since his wife bore it to him in dowry. The moat that runs around the great house lies deep and filled, while ditches dug to and from the lake ensure the water's flow, thus hindering the gnats' efforts to multiply. Dam gates are in place, to choke the tide and fill it to the brim on the day that necessity should call for it. The bridge lies in place, but it hasn't been allowed to champ down into the embankment; it rests freely, ready to be retracted for unwelcome guests. The buildings are well-kept and the roofs solid, new logs and boards gleaming fresh where rotting ones have been replaced.

The best is saved till last. The keep itself, the stone tower that raises its jagged battlements up to meet the sky. Sir Bo surveys the width of its walls, the position of the arrow slits, and the armory brimming with halberds and spears, bowstrings and arrows by the bushel, enough to arm all the householders who are of age. Sir Bo inspects the arms at random: he lifts an arrow here and finds the point sharpened, then pulls a sword by chance from its sheath to test its blade and finds its surface oiled and free of rust, and the axe handles are cut neither too long nor too short for the weight of the iron. Nowhere does he find cause for reproach. Never before was his brother this conscientious. Bo knows well enough that such a feat is the work of his sister-in-law, but on this he keeps his own counsel. Then onward up the stairs, all the way to the roof.

Behind them lie the blue waters of the Hjälmaren, still but for the odd ripple from a playful summer wind. To the west the line of the shore points to Örebro, while to the east the view is obscured by headland. Beyond that point the lake's waters open up wider and darker, an insidious calm that has a tendency to lash out in sudden storms and drag the ships of the unversed down into unplumbed depths. A treacherous lake, one with no mercy for the careless. Far off in the east, the lake pares back into a narrow inlet, before finally spilling its waters into the rivulet that bears off to Eskilstuna. Looking back from the lake, the plains lie wide. Forest, meadow, and farmland, with soils black and fertile. On the other side of the drawbridge the grass has been trimmed, and a Midsummer pavilion is being raised on freshly cut willows. Where the ground lies at its most level the men are beating the soil as best they can, to make a flat surface for the dance.

"Isn't that your lad yonder?"

Sir Bo nudges his brother in the side and points. Sir Bengt leans over the keep's battlements, squints, and nods in agreement.

"Indeed it is Magnus. He's out flying his bird."

"I've tracked deer that are less shy than that boy. When will I get to see my own nephew at closer than an arrow's range?"

Sir Bengt waves off the question with a resigned gesture.

"The boy's of a stubborn age, full of his own thoughts."

Sir Bo shades his eyes with one hand, trying in vain to get a better view, but Magnus is far off in the field, a shape scarce conferred with detail enough to make out the arm held at an angle and the bird above.

"What's he flying?"

"A goshawk. Made me five marks the poorer, she did, but never have I seen an animal more beautiful."

"A peregrine would have served better."

"For you at Oakwood perhaps, where the land lies open. But around here the trees grow dense, and any quarry that's startled makes straight for the forest. A hawk'll follow in between the trunks and swoop down among the thickets. But falcons fear the shadows of the branches and give up easily."

Bo grunts in response, irked to be corrected but with enough sense to hear the truth. Bengt wipes his hair off his forehead, not without some satisfaction that he still has it, while his brother is bald as a hen's egg.

"Magnus has a knack for handling her. You should hear the two of them converse. Clicking and squawking all round. You'd have sworn each understood the other. On the downside he speaks more with that bird than with his own flesh and blood these days. But rare is the day he returns empty-handed. You'll see."

They wait, feeling the tickle of the hunt in their bellies, even though it is another who is hunting, and a mile away at that.

AFTER THREE HOURS of labor, Margaret drifts off in her torments. The pain overwhelms the senses. Her belly is bulging and red, the skin pulled so tight that Stina can't fathom how it doesn't rend, sending the child bursting out of the navel. Together they have tried to feed her fluids and gruel, but she has no appetite, and where she will find strength for the final push no one can say. Sisters old and young have come by with advice, none to any avail. Intercession is all they can offer. Now Stina sees the midwife shake her head to herself, near imperceptibly yet with the weight of Doomsday; she who has been the image of calm itself, the steady nave in a pitching world.

"You'd do better to say what you're thinking, Sister."

Sister Eufemia meets her gaze with bloodshot eyes.

"She's gathering strength. When she wakens we'll try once more. But if the child doesn't come then, I fear it won't come at all."

"How long will she sleep?"

"There's no saying for sure, but from experience I'd say a few hours."

When Stina stands up the blood rushes from her head, and she must bend forward to keep her balance. When she can, she takes the few steps out into the corridor, so weary that it is as though the world is bending at its corners. She must do something, anything, and this is the only thing that seems to remain open to her. Outside, dawn draws close. The old woman has been waiting in the corridor all night, unafraid of discovery now that her errand has been brought to light. She, too, is bone-weary, all but sleeping on her feet, her lips reeling off the syllables of the prayers as if of their own accord.

"I'm not saying I believe in curses, Sister. But if there were such a thing, how could it be broken?"

Stina keeps her voice low, as if to avoid disturbing something that lurks unseen in the silence hanging over the lying-in chamber. Yet her words bear a tenor that she doesn't recognize: a shrill plea, a powerlessness, and this from her, the lady of Cuckoo's Roost, she whose every signal has been acted upon by others for as long as she can recall. Now she is ashamed at the relief she feels when she can shut the door behind her, put boards between herself and the misfortune that nothing seems able to fend off any longer.

"First you must find out what offense has caused such strife. Bring the roots of such hate to light. Then you must do the penance that would have led to reconciliation were she still alive, sincerely enough to heal whatever wound has been inflicted. If done correctly the blame will disperse in others' eyes, as well as in your own, and where once there was nothing, nothing shall return."

Steps are heard from the staircase behind her, and when Stina turns she first sees Britta, pale and dogged, leaning heavily on a young man's arm. In her fatigue it takes some time for Stina to understand who he is, and then with a chill that coils through her belly. It's Finn, Finn Sigridsson of Cuckoo's Roost. For a while she grapples with the impossibility of his presence, until the insight strikes her like a slap to the face. Magnus.

Rarely is Finn seen far from Magnus's side. Something must have happened to him, she knows it in an instant. Her knees start to buckle, her hand rises to her mouth to stopper the sounds that want out, and time seems to slow, making space for all that she can suddenly see before her. Her son has been found drowned in the stream; has fallen from a tree and broken his neck; has been taken by the plague or the chills. Already she can see the grave's freshly dug soil, a fathom of heavy earth between her and Magnus, cold and dead and prey to the worms. Fear turns to a noose around her neck, and she can't ask the question, doesn't have the strength to summon yet another defeat. Her anguish is clear to read, and Finn holds out his free hand in a gesture of reassurance.

"All was well at Cuckoo's Roost when I left. I've no reason to think that has changed."

Stina closes her eyes, feeling the gratitude wash over her, as if the sun had just come out from behind dispersing clouds. Dear Finn; steadfast, dependable, the best of the household. She staggers the few steps between them and wraps her arms around him, hiding her wet cheek against his shoulder. At first he is stiff as a post; she doesn't let go but holds him tighter, lets the cloth of his mantle stifle her sobs. She feels the tautness release when he sees what is required of him. Afterward they all stand quietly together, as reality scabs over tenderness and vulnerability. Finn is no fool; he knows how to behave, and gives Stina her dignity back with a quick bow.

"Lady Kristina, I'm here on my own behalf. My sister is dead, laid to rest with her sins unforgiven. Sir Bengt allowed me to follow the priest's order and walk to Vadstena to pray at the reliquary in penance, so that I might accompany you home, if possible as part of the bishop's entourage. The bishop will come to Cuckoo's Roost for Midsummer."

Stina feels his sadness start to catch, and is surprised that she should have the space within her to harbor any more of it. No one should die so young. And yet she is not surprised. Ylva Sigridsdaughter was always a wayward soul, even in the face of her own best interests. Those who wished to inspire obedience in her found her hard to love, and few of her kind lived to see a ripe old age. Stina places her hands on Finn's cheeks.

"I feel with you, Finn. Your sister's lucky to have a brother like you. May it please her soul to have one who shows such love."

Stina sees the pain that Finn is powerless to master, as though her praise was rather the lash of a whip. Something has changed. She wonders what has befallen him since they last met. But in the wake of her surprise comes a sudden insight, and it stretches her to her full extent as she grabs him by the arm.

"The bishop. Bishop Knut. He heads to Cuckoo's Roost, from Linköping?"

"Yes, my lady. He's here already, in Vadstena. His men have raised tents in the meadows by the shore, and he means to head north soon. Lady Britta has told me of the state of things here..."

"Lead me to him. This instant."

MAGNUS CONTEMPLATES THE bird he carries on a leather glove, bewitched as always by her beauty, her contradiction of all that reason tells him. Nothing of such power should weigh so little. Restless, she totters up and down her perch, and even through the glove lining he can feel the strength in her claws. A bell is tied around her leg, and it rings shrilly whenever she changes position. He strokes her speckled breast to let her feel the warmth of his hand, draws the air in between his lips while clicking his tongue. Once she has calmed he removes her hood. Her eyes are big and yellow, and he wonders what she sees when she looks at him. She may be as tame as a bird of prey can be, but the wild is always there. Ever since she was a fledgling he has fed her from his own hand, one scrap of meat at a time, and he has let her sleep beneath his tunic, sensing all the while that should the day come when the meat he offers her is no more tender than that which she can catch, she will fly off into the forest and never look back. A majesty she is, haughty-beaked and wrapped in a mantle of beautiful feathers, and the look she gives him is that of a queen to her cupbearer.

He walks on through the grass. The day is cooler than yesterday. High clouds dapple the sky, and a listless wind blows in from the lake, ruffling the bird's plumage. His arms, legs, and back are all sore from yesterday's exertions. He has promised himself rest, to be sure that he is restored in time.

Magnus makes for the rise of a hill, to get a better view of the tracts. He should have a dog or beater with him, perhaps, but he craves solitude, cost him what it may in hunting spoils. This meadow hosts hares in abundance, some nesting in old burrows, others vagrants who take to the soft hollows under spruces and thickets to shiver through the night. At the crest of the hill he stops and paces a slow circle in one patch to survey his surroundings, attentive to every change of color or movement in the green. He needn't wait long. A swaying dandelion reveals the hare. Magnus shouts, and the hare speeds off. He releases the hawk, feels her legs push off, and sees the plumes of her tail spread as her wings gather pace. Straight at her prey she flies, and, knowing its pursuer, the hare runs for its life, swerving sharply in its flight. Every time the bird's outstretched talons close around naught she screams in fury, lurches forward, careens around, and resumes the hunt. Soon both are out of sight, and Magnus hastens after them.

Often he must stop to listen, for only the bell betrays the hawk's position. When its tinkle reaches him it is accompanied by a thin howl. He finds her crouched with wings outstretched beside her defeated prey. The hare is still alive, lying bent on its broken back, its eyes rolling in defenseless terror. The bird seems to be wavering, unused to her first strike being anything but lethal, and now at a loss to finish what she has started. Magnus knows what he must do, though his aversion forms a lump in his belly. Still, any prey that suffers needlessly is a discredit to the hunter. He has done similar before, but he hesitates yet, for then there was always an elder close at hand, someone who knew to put a hand on his shoulder and strengthen him in his resolve, the deed done to nods of approval and looks of pride at the boy, capable of doing not only what is easy but also what is right.

He holds his breath and clenches his teeth, then closes his eyes and takes the hare by the neck. Twists it, fast and hard, and hears the fragile bones snap like a dry twig in his grip. The moment weighs on him more than it should. Alone in the meadow he stands before the dead little creature. Blood on his hand; his own. The hare must have bitten him in its dying moment, though the pain has only just made itself felt. He puts his finger in his mouth and licks it clean to better see the wound. A mere scratch, but a trifle. The wound buoys his mood slightly, as if lessening his debt to the hare. The sun is still shining, the wind gentle and the day young, and his moment of weakness is suddenly far away.

Sir Bo lowers the hand that has been shading his eyes.

"What would Father have done if he'd seen you or me falter like that?"

Sir Bengt purses his lips.

"A slap on the spot and a beating later."

"And rightly so. Doubt in the moment of truth has wrought many a man's demise."

Bengt's gaze follows Magnus away through the grass, and he is soon out of sight behind the crest of a hill.

"Magnus doesn't kill gladly. He's been at home a long time. It's Stina. She can't bear to be parted from him, fears that something will happen to him the very instant he leaves our lands. Others send their sons away to be raised, where their skins can be thickened by those who won't spare them the rod out of tenderness. We've done things differently. I've long since stopped blaming Stina for that choice. She did right to stand her ground, much as I may have blustered at the time. Tell me, did you ever feel affection for Father?"

Bo's wiry body twitches, made uneasy by the question.

"We were many sons, and Father only one. He was away more often than not. It was a rare thing to get a moment alone with him, and if he found you worth the time it was mostly to give you a chiding."

Bengt nods in agreement.

"That's how I remember it, too. And yes, he did have many sons. But I have only one. As do you. Do you mean to flog your Nils when he's big enough? Is he to learn to despise you for the sake of a dead hare?"

Bo Stensson clicks his tongue, half in rejoinder, half in concession. Bengt pats him on the shoulder to change the mood.

"Well. Magnus did the right thing, and not for his own sake, but for the hare's. I suppose that's what matters. Killing is a skill when you need it, but he who grows to like it I'd sooner keep at arm's length."

T̲HE TENTS STAND in a neat row, by the shores of the long lake where the ground lies dry and flat. There is no mistaking which one is the bishop's: taller and bigger than the others, it is draped with finer cloth, with carved battens to raise its corners and points. A man sits cross-legged outside it, whittling a stick. He leaps up and hastens over to Finn and Stina when he sees the course that they are making.

"The bishop's deep in prayer and won't be receiving visitors."

Stina straightens her back and fixes her eyes on the man, used as she is to keeping small-minded people in check.

"I am Lady Kristina Magnusdaughter of Cuckoo's Roost, kin to the bishop. It is to partake of my table that you are traveling north. Let me pass."

The man is quick to bow. Brushing the wood chips off his thighs, he seeks her gaze with a dipped head and offers a rueful smile.

"Forgive a simple man. One with more sense than I would have gleaned whom he was addressing, and I shall soon be out of your way. But your ladyship first ought to know that conversing with the Lord makes for thirsty work for the bishop, and it was to ensure that his prayers go undisturbed that he stationed me here."

Finn sweeps aside a flap of the tent to let Stina pass, and she sees from his face that the stench hits him just before it reaches her. Sour wine gone to vapor in the heat, an unwashed body in an enclosed space, the reek of a chamber pot into which bile has flowed. A leather wineskin lies flaccid in a puddle of its own making. The bishop himself is curled up on a bed made of carved beams. He is ravaged by age. Gaunt and gnarled like time itself, his beard white and sparse and the hair on his head likewise, his ears hairy and overgrown. The tent raised around him is comfortable, with a thick rug topping the earth that his men stamped flat, and a table by the bed at which to eat and write. The inkwell is out and official letters lie in disarray, some of which even used to wipe stains from the rug. Bishop Knut himself snores quietly, slurping through the phlegm that taints his beard.

Finn gives Stina a questioning look, and she nods her head in the bishop's direction. He coughs affectedly in the hope of waking the slumbering man, but in vain. The one who met them outside comes to their rescue. Stooping under the canvas with a pail of water in his arms, he shakes life into the groaning bishop and eventually succeeds in raising him to sitting. He dips a cloth in the water and places it in the bishop's hand, while whispering in his ear. Bishop Knut lowers his face into the rag, and were it not for his groans Stina would have thought that he had dozed off again and risked death by suffocation. But the bishop straightens his back, returns the cloth, and lets his servant flee. Among his creases and folds Stina makes out the wet shine of two eyes, a turbid blue on a yellowed base. The colors of his house. She notes that the bridge of his nose bears marks on either side, and around his neck hangs the cause, something that she has heard spoken of but never before seen: rounded glass in metal holders, with straps on either side to wrap around his head.

"Lady Kristina. What a pleasure to greet you even in Vadstena. I had expected only to be reunited at Cuckoo's Roost, where I imagine the preparations must be in full cry?"

"I'm here for my sister-in-law, your nephew Nils's wife, Margaret. She's in the throes of childbirth under the care of the nuns."

"God's mercy be upon her."

Once he has crossed himself, he places his talons back on his lap. He has a particular way of sitting, stock-still and staring, and she can't tell whether it's just the inertia of age or something he does by design to unsettle whomever he is addressing, to signal that the passing of time is his and his alone to command.

"Will you remind me of the last time we met?"

"We traveled to Linköping, my husband and I, so that you could baptize our son."

The bishop nods.

"Mats."

"Magnus."

"Magnus. One would think that the names of my nephews' children would be easier to recall than those of my nephews. My brother, Sten, sired offspring as though he were single-handedly trying to avenge the Black Death, but the next generation has been all the slower for it. How old is the boy now?"

"He'll see his eighteenth birthday before the year's out."

Bishop Knut rubs his nose and sighs, then places the metal pincer back in old scars and tightens the strap over the white wisps of hair that line the back of his head.

"Come closer so that I might look upon you."

The glasses enlarge his beady eyes, his face more troll-like than human. A crack cleaves one lens, making the eye behind it even more unsightly. Stina stifles a shudder while he takes his time.

"Alas, Kristina. The years go by and older we grow. But they seem to have been kinder to you. Who is that at your side?"

"Finn Sigridsson is one of our household at Cuckoo's Roost; he arrived in Vadstena this very day, to pray at the reliquary."

Before Stina can wave Finn out of the tent, the bishop beckons him closer and gives him an inspection of the same kind. Even though they have met but a handful of times, the last of which many years past, Stina, like many, knows the bishop by reputation. Kin to a saint but far from a saint himself, the mitre he wears soiled by discord. Like his brother, Sir Sten, he was among those who turned their backs on King Albrekt and welcomed Margaret as Queen of the Swedes, only to soon see their blunder. While Sir Sten sought in vain to outwit the Dane by worldly means, Knut fought her on holy ground, and he must have sung his heartfelt praise the day the queen was put to earth, burying with her a dispute that promised to end in his deposal. Under King Eric he has tried to sail a more prudent course over increasingly troubled waters, the king ceaselessly striving to fill the pulpits with his own henchmen, while the church would sooner choose from among their own. In his reluctance to take sides, Knut has lost what few friends he once had.

"From the north, you say?"

Once Knut has looked his fill upon Finn he leans back, pulls his glasses off his face, and rubs his sore nose. Stina gives Finn a look and nods at the exit.

"Go back to Mara's bedside and keep vigil there. I'll find my own way back."

※

Together the bishop and Stina listen to Finn's receding footsteps until the sounds are gone.

"So, Kristina. What can I do for you on a day as beautiful as this, now that you've wrenched me from my daily prayers for the joyous rebirth of all souls?"

"Ingegerd, once abbess here. Her last breath was a curse on your family's name. I've continued the family line; my children are of blue and gold, same as you. I have a right to know the reason."

He sits still for a long time, Bishop Knut, his scraggy hands open in his lap, then takes what support he can to get up. His nightshirt sagging over shriveled thighs, he turns his back to Stina, limps over to the chamber pot that sits in the corner of the tent, and rolls up the hem.

"Forgive me, Kristina, but if I'm to have no secrets from you, then this is as good a start as any."

It takes many a sigh before the flow begins, sluggish drops. Still, he stands there for a long time with heavy breaths, perhaps hoping for more, before shaking himself off and letting the shirt fall.

"My robe. Will you help?"

The cloth is scarlet, expensive, and beautifully stitched, with an embroidery of golden thread. She lifts it from the floor and drapes it over his shoulders while breathing through her mouth, not bothering to thread on the sleeves. He makes do with that, wraps it around his withered frame, and gestures at a stool by the wall of the tent, two interlinking trusses with cloth stretched over the top for a seat.

"She was my half sister."

He lets the words sink in.

"Bo Bosson was my father, grandfather to your husband. A knight and member of the Council of the Realm he was, as high in rank as any of our ancestors. He met a woman, and from the very first moment there was love between them. Her name was Märta. That they were both married to others was of little concern to them. To their misfortune, their coupling bore fruit. Their shame would certainly have come to light, had Märta's mother been anyone else."

He reaches for a jug, and from the disappointment on his face Stina infers that it is emptier than it should be. He drinks up the last of it, warm and sour. Red drops fleck his beard.

"Märta was the daughter of Saint Birgitta. The daughter's infidelity alone could have dashed Birgitta's courtship of the Pope in Rome, but there was worse to come: Märta and Bo were kin. Children of cousins. When Christ first found his way up to our northern tracts, the Church spread the message that every coupling of fifth-degree blood relations was incest in the eyes of the Lord. But we are easily counted up here, fewer by far than the peoples of the south. Even the most pious were compelled to see that if sin was to be sifted through such a narrow sieve as that, then few children would be born to blessedness, and so with us incest is counted differently. But Birgitta was already in Rome, and a rumor of that sort would have sent the halo she so hotly coveted slipping through her fingers. And Birgitta may well have been holy, but to the people around her she was something else, too. A walking mint. Her newly founded abbey was flourishing with alms, and everyone in touching distance became not only blessed but rich, too. Märta of Wolf Hill and Bo Bosson of blue and gold had everything to gain from their silence. Märta's husband had to let himself be persuaded that the daughter born was his own, even though his manhood wasn't nearly long enough to sow seed across borders. The newborn's name was Ingegerd, and even though her father was the same as mine she was known by another name."

Knut wipes his hand around his face.

"Our blood runs strong. Every year Ingegerd came to resemble her true father more, and she fell ever deeper into madness. No wonder, perhaps, with a mother who often flogged her in punishment for her own broken dreams, a father who rejected her, and a foster father who kept his distance. But for all of that she was no fool. It was decided that she would be sent to the abbey at Vadstena, where she would be closely guarded by sisters who knew the girl was a threat to the abbey's very foundations."

Stina can see it before her clearly. The convent's walls and community of sisters a prison full of watchful eyes, every waking moment lived under the scrutiny of others. Surely no place could better serve such a purpose.

"Märta sold her daughter short. In just a few years she had climbed from teary novice to haughty abbess. It took little time for her to uncover her true paternity, once she had acquired power over those who bore knowledge of the fact, but Bo Bosson had already made off into the grave. Instead she came to me, laid her identity bare, and demanded my support, and who was I to refuse her? My seal was stamped alongside my father's on the letter sent to Rome to petition for Birgitta's canonization. Had it all come to light I would have gone down with that ship, and with plenty of company."

"Had you treated Ingegerd with true brotherly love, then I doubt she'd have ended her life with a curse upon your house."

Knut smiles a wry smile. Yellowed teeth, well used but sharp yet. A predator's grin. He bows his head in praise.

"I've heard good things of you, Kristina Magnusdaughter, and

I'm pleased to see with my own eyes that your reputation does not mislead."

Stina shudders at this praise. Commendation from a man like the bishop stings worse than contempt, like the befouling touch of something unclean.

"Her secret would have destroyed us both. There was a constant tussle between us, with each fleeting victory won by the one who stood the least to lose at the time. I shan't deny that in the end it was probably me who benefited most. Being a bishop is expensive, I'll have you know. But I had free rein with the abbey's coffers."

"What happened then?"

"Ingegerd never found peace. I suppose she missed her father. Sought other men's approval in lieu. By the turn of the century there wasn't an inch of her that hadn't been sullied. As bishop I had to make inspections, feign impartiality before ruling in her favor. In the end it was untenable. I thought she would drag me down with her, but to my surprise that didn't happen. With her removal from office the madness took over, and since the insane are unable to bear witness I was saved. By and by she stopped speaking to others and kept to her cell, complaining of headaches and strange visions."

He stifles a belch, then pulls a face at the sour burn it leaves in his throat.

"Well. Now you know as much about Ingegerd as I do. Would you ask my servant to bring more wine on your way out? My throat is parched thanks to you. Tomorrow we resume our journey north, and if you'd like to accompany us, you and your party would be welcome in our midst."

F INN WANDERS THE road back, tracing his own steps while the bishop's yellow gaze stings in his memory; his sour wine-breath, the filth in his tent. A holy man, one of the highest in the church, deputy to the Pope himself, spent and devoid of dignity. Had the same man been found in more modest attire catching a wink against a tavern wall, he would have been shooed away before he could defile the bench and spoil the air that everyone else had to share. Finn finds himself powerless to fend off his mind's silent question of whether Bishop Knut would have fared better than Olof Jonsson in a chance meeting on the road, out of earshot of others. He spits over his shoulder and crosses himself to repel the sudden stab of conscience that he feels when his mind wanders where it should not.

At the abbey gate he is recognized and asked no questions of his business. Instead eyes are quickly turned away. Finn is marked as part of the misfortune that hangs over the abbey roofs like a cloud portending rain. For a moment he stands at a loss, searching for the right door among the countless stone edifices, before a nun who has read his mind makes a discreet gesture in the right direction. In the courtyard outside it a stallion stands grazing on the grass. Finn has tended colts for as long as he has lived and knows how to assess their value, for such gossip is the delight of stablefolk. Even though they seldom see silver coined or in bullion, they can name each steed's price down to the lot. Whoever rides this stallion is rich, as rich as anyone Finn has ever heard of, and is unafraid to leave a fortune untethered and free to wander off at will. The horse is broad, its withers high, and its coat well groomed over ample muscles, with a girth and reins of the best quality. Beneath them the corner of the saddlecloth bears a coat of arms that Finn doesn't know, a red boat on a golden background, plumes of peacock feathers fore and aft. Someone is come, a guest bearing a stranger's shield.

Finn shudders in the sun, used to taking everything unknown for a threat until proven otherwise. He draws a deep breath of the summer air, which for now carries neither the scent of a good day nor of a bad, then opens the door and climbs the stairs.

He opens the chamber door a crack without making himself

known, unsure of how best to conduct himself without Lady Kristina at his side. The birthing bed is the women's domain, and although he is of the household, he doesn't wish to intrude where he is not wanted. But a man is already there, one who has laid claim to the midwife's stool and forced the old woman to her feet. He wears the travel clothes of a nobleman: a doublet in a smooth, choice leather cut just for him, an airy tunic, a light summer wrapping around his legs and boots on his feet. The horseman no doubt. One hand is raised to Margaret's cheek, while with the other he clasps her hand. Both riding gloves lie slung on the floor. He has bent forward so that they are forehead to forehead. Both are crying, and he hushes her while her quiet whimpers sing a second part.

Finn shifts unsteadily from foot to foot. His loyalty is to blue and gold, and Margaret is the wife of Nils Stensson, brother to his master, and the child who doesn't wish to come an heir to blue and gold. Yet in her hour of need she is being caressed by another man, as close as if they were lovers. He shudders, a servant's dilemma: when left to one's own judgment, it's easy to err in the pursuit of what's right, to the detriment of oneself and others. Better to stay quiet. He makes his decision, silently retreats on light feet, and turns away to make his way back to the church, to say prayers for Margaret's successful birth as well as for his sister's soul. One who prays can hardly be caught sinning.

The hours pass. It is Britta's hand he feels on his shoulder, drawing him from the prayer's singular repose. On stiff legs he rises from the floor before the reliquary, blinking to see better in the shade that has come with the afternoon. She stands before him red-faced and bleary-eyed, her cheeks streaked with salt.

"Mother would have you come. She asks that you bring a spade."

※

Finn arrives late and sweaty to the consecrated earth where the dead are laid to rest: the monks and sisters in recognition of their service to the Lord; others in exchange for generous alms. The spade was hard to find and harder to borrow, for the sister tending to the garden was both domineering and incapable of making decisions, testy and unsure whether she could leave her tools in a stranger's hands, with no reliable assurance that they would be used to further a righteous cause. In the end he simply grabbed it with his big fists and carried it away, with a promise to return it in the same state that he had found it, deaf to her objections. A good spade, carved from a single piece of wood, with an iron-shod tip to better cleave roots and part clay; heavy enough to offer power, while light enough to spare his arm and shoulder. He hastens though loath to do so, certain of what awaits.

Lady Kristina stands with her back to him, but she is not broad enough to hide her burden. The bundle in her arms is still and silent, wrapped in white. He hovers at a distance, hesitant to draw too close to her unbidden. For a little longer she stands still, stroking a cheek that he cannot see. She doesn't turn to acknowledge his presence, simply points at an empty patch of grass, and he goes and does what he has been summoned to do. The soil is dry and intractable at first, both hard and sandy at once, but the spade fulfills its promise and pierces through the upper crust, down to a loam that still bears moisture, making it heavier yet easier to work. The day wears on but the sun is still high, and soon his sweat is streaming, though there is naught to be done to lighten his attire. Somewhere behind him stands Kristina, and her tacit grief is like a cold puff of air from an earth cellar. Finn doesn't know when to stop, and he doesn't want to ask, would rather draw what comfort there is to be found in that which he knows: silent, servile exertion. He clears spade upon spade from the hole, prizes out the stones that lie in his way and hurls them aside, widens the pit to give himself room to work, and digs deeper and deeper. The abbey walls come between him and the sun, casting the churchyard in shadow.

The ground is level with his shoulder when she tells him that it is enough and he can put the spade to one side. For another moment Kristina stands still, before folding the cloth over its little face and kneeling down to pass him the bundle. He brushes his hands as clean as he can before he receives it, wishing away their unsightliness, their calluses and blisters and scars, all clearly painted with soil and sweat. After all his effort the infant's weight is like nothing, like a wisp of cloud swathed in linen. He lays the child to rest as best he can on the ground that he has leveled at the bottom of the hole, then sweeps the soil closer to form a little nest in support of the body. He hauls himself out, then steps back and waits for her nod before stooping for the shovel again. The wood stings in his fists, but he is grateful for the pain, wishes for more of it, enough that he might forget what it is that he must do. Never has an act felt so brutal as heaping the earth over that little infant, obscured scoop by scoop until it is no longer visible. He imagines the weight of the earth with mounting panic. Still, he does as he has been bidden, until every spade of soil has been restored and nothing remains to reveal the grave but a bare patch in otherwise overgrown grass. Once again he stands, quiet and idle, his head bowed and his hands clasped in front of him.

"The sisters wouldn't have the child laid unbaptized in consecrated ground. This will cost me a whole estate and all the acreage that goes with it. But they'll never raise a stone. You can take the spade back where you found it. I'll stay here a bit."

Once Finn has left her alone with her wrath, Stina walks to Ingegerd's grave. She wishes he had left the spade with her, and that she had strength enough to unearth Ingegerd's bones and stamp them to shards, until only dust remained of her and of her spiteful words. Stina's rage seems to her greater than what her skin can contain, as if she, too, were pregnant, her burden imprisoned. A tightness inside her. Something must out. Suddenly she knows what she will do. The abbey is silent. No one hears her speak to the dead woman, and no one sees.

"This is for you, Ingegerd. May it wet your withered bones, and may every drop of it sting."

She raises her skirt high enough to wrap it around her waist and bends her knees until she is squatting, then hears a whispered stream as she lets her waters flow over the grave.

The next day they join the bishop's convoy on the road northward, home to Cuckoo's Roost and the shores of the Hjälmaren.

PART II

MIDSUMMER 1434

NILS STENSSON ARRIVES with the eventide, riding his horse through the dusk with sharper spurs than he ought, well aware that a fallen branch or insidious root could fell them both, breaking steed's legs and master's neck alike. Yet he remains undeterred, certain that such a fate is for others and not for him. The road has left its bite in his thighs and backside, the sting of sweat on his raw skin. Too many hours at too great a speed, for many days.

He has come from the north, all the way up to the highlands on the fringes of the realm, up where the men of the mountains stoke their fires against the cliffs and then drive pikes through soot-blackened rock, ever deeper underground, down to where the sun is stripped of all power and beyond the flicker of the torch where eternal darkness reigns. Beneath their feet awaits the Kingdom of the Damned, and everyone knows it's but a matter of time before their pride meets with the same fate as the angel of the morning star, when their shafts will finally pierce the roofs of Hell. And yet the air grows colder with every fathom, and so the miners suppose that one ought to feel the heat before swinging that fateful stroke. From out of the abyss they haul baskets of ore on ropes of braided leather, and from the stone heated by the bellows' blasts flow iron and copper in glowing streams, as surely as the miller grinds the farmer's grain.

Nils himself does not understand it. The sight of the furrowed brows of their guests foments the pride of the miners. The men of the north are of a different stock than those of the south, willful and used to ruling themselves, prone to both anger and merriment, toughened by the land that has been theirs to tame and by the pains taken to amass their wealth and protect their coffers. Even the lawless find welcome amongst their ranks as long as they haven't slain or violated women, but if they sin again, then justice is meted out simply and harshly.

Nils is astonished by all that is demanded of those who would be chieftains: They must be able to deal with not only the mineworks and the people, but also the river routes south, where the white waters lurking at each bend threaten to claim entire loads as their due, long before the ingots can reach Stockholm and be exchanged for coins and goods. On top of that, they must be cunning enough to claim a good sale from the merchants of the Hanseatic League, whose art of purchasing at below cost has been honed over the generations. Nils has crossed half the kingdom on his way thence, borrowing beds from peasants, kin, and bailiffs alike, his men left behind one by one as their hacks wearied. Now he is almost there. He smells the smoldering evening hearths, hears a distant bell tolling the compline that rounds off the day's canonical hours, and waits to catch sight of the abbey's church spire rising over the next crest of the path. Soon it comes, a sooty spearhead against a base of early stars.

He dismounts outside the wall, leads his horse to the stables, and throws the reins to a farmhand mucking out the stall. With the sixth sense of an experienced horseman he stops in his tracks at the sight of withers rising up over the boards, a steed that belongs in no convent. A warrior's mount. He walks closer, unable to help himself from stroking its groomed hindquarters, confirming with his hand the testimony of his eyes. The animal shrinks from this unfamiliar touch. In the language of horses he hums it calm. On a rod rests the saddle, freshly oiled and skillfully made, and beside it hangs what he seeks: the saddlecloth, embroidered with a coat of arms. The darkness dulls every color, but he has little need for them. A dark ship on a bright sea. He knows what house bears that shield, wonders which of them has come and why.

Nils hastens toward the north wing, once a hall raised for the kings of yore, where the sick house is now crammed alongside the chapter house. Where else would she be, his wife? His solicitude cankers his spirit worse than ever now that he's so close, for he knows that he is later than he should be. At every moment he hopes to hear the evening's calm pierced by a child's screams. But nothing. The languishing pulse of crickets on this summer's eve. He meets no one on his way, and where the shadows loom darkest he must run his hand along the wall to get his bearings. One floor up, a corridor, a closed door. Nils hastens toward it, but a voice stops him just as he reaches for the handle.

"Don't."

A stranger emerges from the shadows and beckons him closer, to where a slit in the wall lets in the evening light. The sun has set, but the sky still bears the memory of its rays. The moon is risen, greater than half and waxing more with every night. Its light lends the blue twilight an edge of silver. Nils knows that he has found the steed's owner. A man of his own age, perhaps a few years younger, dressed in beautiful garments and costly, too, excessively so for a horseback's wear. A face marred by a nose too small, a chin too large, an underbite. Slippery eyes and restless hands. A skinny runt in ostentatious garbs. Shorter than he, and weaker, too.

"Let her rest. She's sleeping now, at long last."

"Tell me what's happened."

"Give me your name first."

"Nils is my name, Sir Sten Bosson of Oakwood my father, our shield of blue and gold. Margaret is my wife, and the child she carries mine as well."

The stranger sighs, as though his misgivings have been borne out.

"The child came feetfirst. The navel string a noose around its neck. It never drew breath. Mara bled for a long time, but the flow has been stemmed, and she is better today than she was yesterday. The sisters have interceded for her. They say that she will live."

Around Nils the world comes to a halt. He can't tell whether the booming in his ears is silence or a roar, and all that resides within him quakes and shifts. Gone are his dreams of a son or daughter, a new budding life to bind him and Mara even more closely and cast their love into new forms. Gone all the expected pride of new fatherhood, this entry into a manhood of a new kind, its reflections in his family and friends, in praise and congratulations, his brothers clapping him on his shoulders. A future within reach but a moment ago. Just a breath away; the one that was never drawn. All thwarted by a cruel fate and a stranger's words, one without sense enough to even offer consolation. Anger flares up within him, and he clutches on to it like a drowning man a piece of driftwood, anything to avoid the emptiness that now threatens to envelop him.

"And you? Who are you and what business have you here?"

"Karl is my name, son of Knut. Crofter is my line, and land have we owned since time immemorial. It is we who ride the red boat over golden waves. Birdsfirth is my home."

Unraveling thorny family ties is an art that Nils has had to learn from a young age, but right now his memories are slick, and in its paralysis his mind can find no grip. Still, the name he does know. Karl Crofter. His wife's half brother, her elder. The same mother, the father another. The man's eyes are devoid of all sympathy, bright as spring water and just as cold.

"Karl Crofter. I know your name well enough. You come now, and all the way from Birdsfirth to boot, but when I married your sister you refused to be our guest. What sort of man are you to choose joy as your enemy and grief as your friend?"

Nils hears the unfairness of his words, and he would have fain welcomed a response in kind. A quarrel is what he needs. Instead Crofter shifts uneasily from foot to foot, his gaze fixed on the wall. Even in light as dim as this Nils can see the color rise in Karl Crofter's face, until the tears start to stream down his cheeks and he bows his head to hide the heavy drops that fall from his fair lashes. Nils regrets his heated words to one so feeble. Never before has he had to comfort a grown man, and he places a wavering hand on Crofter's shoulder. But then the man's response comes. Crofter's voice is weak and shaky, and when Nils hears his words he jerks his hand away, as if from a crevice where a snake has made its nest.

"I did everything in my power to prevent your marriage. Mara was too young, and you too old for her. Your line's glory days are numbered. But my mother was wont to listen to her husband, who thought blue and gold a good match. See now what fruit it has borne. Had she listened to me Mara wouldn't be lying here, all but ripped in two, a hair's breadth from death. For three days she fought to deliver a living child, before she burst and spilled a corpse. For two days she has cried while I've sat by her side. And only now comes the father, when all is too late."

The blows meet their mark, each word sharpened on the whetstone of truth. Yet it is the astonishment that Nils feels more keenly, that a man he barely knows could bear him such malice. Never has he met Karl before, only Karl's wife, Mara's cousin, who was one of the bride's party when they were married.

"Why..."

A child's question. He checks himself. Instead he observes Karl, who raises his slender fingers to cover his still-tear-stricken face. His voice is abject, brittle in its laments.

"She should never have chosen you."

He remembers Crofter's wife more clearly now. So like Mara that they could have been sisters, similar enough to be mistaken from afar. This grief. Suddenly the answer comes, its starkness so glaring that Nils must step back and gasp.

"You wanted Mara for yourself, your own half sister. You couldn't make her your bride, so you took the next best thing."

Karl Crofter raises his pale serpent's eyes, red-rimmed. His reply comes as a cracked whisper, the hatred naked now.

"You asked why I would seek grief instead of joy, but you are mistaken. What feast could be more joyous to me than this? She shall live, but your child is dead. A daughter. I was among the first to see her, and the last. She was pale and cold, her turgid little tongue swollen in her mouth. Inside I was laughing."

Silence reigns between them as they look upon each other with new eyes, Karl Crofter and Nils Stensson. Words have been spoken that cut wounds beyond all healing. This is no dispute over boundaries or inheritance, no matter that any third party can mediate, brokering peace with a silver tongue. This is something else, something in which grown men should know better than to engage. Both men have gained a mortal enemy this night, and the gravity of the moment extends far beyond just them. These are men of the nobility, able to muster horsemen and raise sharp weapons, both with wiles enough to strike where the greatest pain will be inflicted. This grudge between them promises devastation, in a world too narrow for them to steer clear of each other. Nils would sooner have them step away from these hallowed grounds, retreat to a grove out of sight and earshot, and remain there until only one is able to walk the road home. But he knows that now is not that time.

"Ride home to Birdsfirth, Karl Crofter. I'll keep your secret from my wife, to spare her the disgust of thinking back over her childhood and racking her brain over every time she stood unclothed before your lustful eyes, and because I want you to know that from this day forth every single gracious word exchanged with your sister is thanks to my mercy. May that temper your pride."

Karl Crofter licks his thin lips and opens his mouth to answer rashly, but masters himself. He starts again while treading restlessly on the spot, strokes the hem of his tunic with anxious fingers.

"I doubt it shall be long before our paths cross again, Nils Stensson, and that meeting will be but the first of many. So be it. This can remain our business alone. But one of these days we shall meet in the proper place to continue the exchange we've had this night, and on that day it will be you who fares the worse."

Karl Crofter turns to leave, across the stone floor to the staircase that leads down toward the stables. Nils raises his voice after him, lured by pride into claiming the last word.

"I've been upcountry. There's change brewing there, change

that promises new times. I shall harness them. When next we meet, Karl Crofter, I'll be so far above you and yours that a puddle of horse's piss will have a better chance of waging war on the sun reflected in it. Under my beams you'll parch and shrivel, until only streaks of salt remain."

※

Nils is sitting at Margaret's bedside when she wakens, to the sun's pallid first rays. All night she has lain deep in slumber, and all night he has kept watch over her, searching for traces of the happiness that was once theirs in a face marked by anguish. She is haggard, with lines previously invisible now manifest around the mouth that screamed in pain, the forehead that furrowed in struggle. Eyes sunken with bleariness. Her hand rests feebly in his, devoid of strength, and the stench of iron still hangs as heavily in the chamber as ever on a battlefield after a clash. With gratitude he listens to her every shallow breath. She is alive now, and will yet live. The words of his family spring to mind, the ones that he has heard so oft repeated in hard times as well as good. *Hope and destiny*. Destiny has spared her in the hope of a tomorrow. With the dawn light she opens her blue eyes, and when she sees that it is he sitting next to her and not her half brother, they fill with tears, her first words a sob.

"Forgive me."

Whatever words he was expecting, they were not these. Never has he wanted to reply so quickly, but nor has he ever wished so much to weigh his words.

"We've not been married long, Mara, but if I've ever given you cause to believe I'm the sort of man who would blame you for this, then it is I who should be asking your forgiveness."

Her grip on his hand tightens as she pulls him closer and holds him in a quivering embrace. Her slender shoulders remind him of her youth, and Karl Crofter's words are once more a drop of poison in his bitter chalice.

"The blame is mine. It was too early for children. We should have waited, one year, two."

He feels her chin against his shoulder when she shakes her head.

"No. I wanted it as much as you did, I couldn't carry our child fast enough. If God is punishing us for lust, then we share the guilt."

"Why would he? We took the sacrament. Everything was done right."

"Not everything."

She speaks the truth. There were times when they would see each other alone, stolen moments away from watchful eyes, on forest verges and around the backs of houses. Her hands under his tunic, eager to test their grip on a hardening manhood. His own hands under her skirt. Their lips together, tongues at play. A summer's day on her father's land: Walking hand in hand on an aimless wander, the sun high in skies of blue. Around them oats taller than an arm's reach, swaying undisturbed in a wind too mild to be felt, ripe for the harvest. Mara lets go of his hand and raises her skirt to jump across a ditch. A few more steps and she's in among the lilting ears. She slips a long glove from one arm and drops it to the ground behind her. Then the second, with both an invitation and a challenge in her eyes. Then she turns and is gone, leaving him with a laugh and the rustle of stalks tracing her flight. And him after her, his heart pounding in his ears. Strewn garments lead his way. In the middle of the field she lies waiting, the ground already cleared to form a bed, in a golden room with the sky for a ceiling. The last of her clothes but blandishments for her nakedness, for him to loosen. In her welcoming smile there is joy but also triumph, at the power that she wields over him. He loves her for both, loves her for the moment when her clear laughter turns to a sharp intake of breath and game to gravity; when she lets merriment's mask fall and shows him a face that is his only to see. For days afterward they are prickled by straws and oat husks, exchanging glances as they itch at dinner tables in the company of others.

"Children born out of wedlock are raised strong and healthy in every village."

The words don't have the intended effect. New tears spill down her cheeks, toward a lower lip that is curled as if in spasm.

"Then why not ours?"

In his mind he gropes for the right adage, the words that promise to make everything right. He grabs her by the shoulders, harder than intended, for fear that the Mara he knew will be lost in grief and self-reproach.

"No mortal is granted leave to interpret God's will. We can but act on our own. Let's stand strong together, Margaret, you and I.

There's a time for grief, but only so that joy may be offered anew. You're alive, as am I, and life lies long before us."

For a time they sit together thus, passing the hours in an embrace. It is a closeness of a kind that he has never experienced before, wordless and sincere. With the morning the sisters come to feed and wash her, ending the moment and driving them apart, but Nils knows that they have both taken their first steps toward reconciliation with their fate. They will never be rid of their grief, she much less so than he, but she will make it her own and not let it master her. It will always be near, though not as an all-consuming scourge, but rather in her love for the child who was not allowed to live. And between them no discord will fester.

He gets up to let the sisters wash her and lay new dressings, leans back heavily against the wall. Fatigue of various kinds lay siege to his being, his body tired after a long day's ride and a long night's vigil, his legs stiff and back aching, his soul all the wearier still. He lets her eat, a meager breakfast without appetite, and quench her thirst with the creamy milk that the sisters coax down her one spoonful at a time.

"Mara, I can't stay. I wish I could."

Quick as a knife cut, his betrayal is visible on her face, before she restrains herself. He places his hand on her cheek, feels her steel herself so as not to shrink away.

"I must go north. To Cuckoo's Roost, where the family is gathered. It hasn't happened in many years, and this opportunity won't strike again. It's for our future, Mara, yours and mine, and for that of our children to come."

At Cuckoo's Roost all is astir from the crack of dawn. The last tasks are completed in a flurry of industry, every free pair of arms put in the service of the lady of the house, in honor of the occasion. Men who fare better with spear or spade in their fists tread a path down to where the festivities are to be held, their arms piled high with jugs, pewter dishes, tablecloths, bowls, and tankards. Others have been put to braiding birch twigs with flower stalks, for down in the meadow a pavilion has been raised that is to be festooned, spacious enough to fit every guest. The carpenters are still surveying their handiwork with an air of authority, holding their arms up to supports, checking the sureness of their work for the hundredth time, while maids and servants sit high on shoulders in order to dress the maypole in flowers wherever the wood is exposed. In the center of the pavilion stands a long table made of planed boards on trestles, its humble nature concealed by a velvet tablecloth on which Kristina Magnusdaughter's embroidered lion and lily is combined with Sir Bengt's shield of blue and gold. The kitchen has burst its banks and overflowed into the yard by the bakehouse, where the ground has been cleared and men are tending to a bonfire that has been smoldering all night so that the wood will be charred by morning, when they can start roasting the suckling pig that hangs, butchered and ready, in the storehouse. Soon only a bed of embers will remain, long enough for Beelzebub himself to recline on. Then the rack will be raised and the pig bound to a spit to be slowly spun till evening, when the meat will be tender enough to pinch off with bare fingers. Smaller fires have been set up nearby, around which every last cook from here to Örebro is jostling for space over soups and stews. Both happy cries and curses ring out when the fresh batch of beer that has long been fermenting in barrels is to be moved and tasted. There is enough for everyone, as custom demands, for Midsummer's Day and the night that follows bow to a law higher than all the rest, and on this day much is permitted that would otherwise be frowned upon. Sir Bengt himself stands by the barrel alongside Kari, wife to his brother, Bo, drinking deep gulps and sighing with satisfaction.

"Here's to you, Kari Sharp. I can't thank you enough for all that you've done."

Sir Bengt has always held Kari Sharp in high regard, and he struggles to do otherwise even when the mood so takes him. She is the daughter of a pirate, and Sir Bengt remembers her father well, old Sven Sharp who flew the red arrowhead of his house among the Victual Brothers of the Baltic, a squat man with a paunch so great that one could easily imagine him floating even without a ship, his face cleft from forehead to cheek by a poorly healed scar. Eyes that shared equally in jest and murder, a beard dashed with gray, and a constant waft of salt and iron around Sven Sharp, the mark of a life lived with sword in hand; first for Queen Margaret, then against her; once against King Eric, now for him. Sven Sharp was forced to flee the stronghold of Visby when the queen's mercenaries crossed the sea toward it from the south, and never again did he raise their battle cry over the waves, the cry that he had earned more than anyone: *Friends to God and enemies to all.* Sven Sharp had often poked fun at Sir Bengt, for Bengt was dubbed a knight before him, despite being but a boy. *Come sit on my lap, little knight, and I'll tell you how babies are made.* Now here stands that very same knight, before the only child Sir Sven ever made. Kari is some years younger than his Stina, and though she is tough and wiry as if to contradict her patrimony, Sir Bengt can still catch glimpses of Sven Sharp, dead and buried for a decade, peering out at him through his daughter's face. Her eyes are the same, gray-green as the sea where it's at its deepest, as is her gaze: as though Sir Bengt were a bundle of fish found to weigh too little for the price claimed.

"Cheers, Bengt Stensson. I hope I'll get to see my sister-in-law soon, and that she will be just as satisfied. Managing another's household is like borrowing another's clothes, and until I have her blessing I shan't be able to enjoy even beer as good as yours."

Bengt bows his head at the compliment.

"Stina ought to be with us any moment now. A runner from the village was waiting for me when I awoke, to tell me that the bishop's people had arrived in Mellösa late last night. If I know Stina, then we can expect her soon, and the rest of the company in time for the feast."

"No word from Vadstena, of Margaret and the child?"

Bengt shakes his head and looks down, and Kari Sharp stands in silence, too. No news may well be good news, but when tidings are expected the good ones tend to be sent ahead, while the bad are left to wait. Both of them know as much. News of at least one death is in the offing, as surely as one can sense approaching thunder, or a looming autumn on a late summer's wind. They clink their tankards and drink in large gulps. Bengt jerks his head to the north, where blue clouds are brooding on the horizon.

"There's rain up there."

Kari Sharp turns her face to better feel which way the wind is blowing.

"The wind's with us yet. We might just make it through the day dry-shod. Hope and destiny, no?"

They both pretend that they are still speaking of the weather when Kari lowers her voice.

"My Bo will want to have a word with you, by and by. I urge you to listen well."

Bengt nods.

"Listen I shall, though with the matter unheard I'll promise no more."

Kari finishes her beer and hands her empty tankard to her husband when he comes to take her place. Bengt pours for himself and his brother, then drinks in silence until he can no longer hold his peace.

"What devilry have you gone and cooked up this time?"

Bo Stensson drains his tankard in one motion, then wipes his beard on his sleeve with a sigh of satisfaction.

"Not yet, brother. Let's wait for our brother Nils. He's the better with words."

Bengt is not surprised. If there's iron in the furnace, then it's Nils Stensson who put it there, he who always sees to it that the bellows are blowing, though preferably at another's expense. Among the elder of the sons of Sten, Bo and Bengt are the ones to be reckoned with, the only two who were dubbed into knighthood, councilmen of the realm, lords the both of them. Karl, though the eldest of the brothers, is feeble-minded. Firstborn as he is, he was originally christened Bo for his grandfather, but his baptismal name was stripped from him when it was found that he suffered from the falling sickness. Knut was born blind to perpetual darkness, the world he moves in known to him alone. Birger died a man of the cloth. It is said that he haunts the side chapel of Strängnäs Cathedral, that he moans while fumbling his skeleton hands through the hair of nighttime visitors, scrabbling for the mitre that he so coveted but that death placed eternally out of reach. Finally Magnus and Eric came last and together, the ones who in the end cost their mother her life, crowning off her tenth stay in the birthing bed. Two hulking twins, strong and surly the pair of them, and few who see them together can wonder that they were too much for the woman who bore them. To this day both Bo and Bengt blame them for her death. Any invitation sent to their youngest brothers is usually hollow, a no by return little cause for sorrow. Which leaves Nils Stensson, the eldest of the younger brood. Spiteful tongues call him Landless Nils. Despite being more than ten years their junior, Nils has kept Bo and Bengt on their toes ever since childhood, not least because he was a precocious tyke who felt most at home in the company of older children. Not without bitterness have they both had to learn that things often go well when Nils is on their side, and badly when he is on the other. A restless man, and quick-thinking, too, he always knows the best way to see his will done. The apple of their mother Ingeborg's eye, besides. It was said that all the love she had went to Nils, and that if there was any to spare, then the others would have to share it between them.

Sir Bengt gives his brother a sour look, certain now that all that Sir Bo said in the bathhouse was but a way of saddling him up for the ride that awaits.

"Nils, of course. Devil take him."

He whistles through his beard at a maid, then hands her the empty tankard.

"Back in the bathhouse you tried to grease me up with childhood memories. Let me repay you in kind. Do you remember, back at Oakwood, all the times when Nils found occasion for us to sneak into the store-chamber without anyone seeing? We could take whatever we wanted, sausages and jams, buns and dried apples, all of it so delicious that all time would disappear and our vigilance would melt away. Every time we got caught we'd be standing there, you and I, with sticky fingers and honey dripping from our mouths, while Nils would be nowhere to be found, and the blame would land on us alone when Father reached for the switch."

THE SUN IS at its highest when Kristina Magnusdaughter of the lion and the lily returns to Cuckoo's Roost, on a borrowed horse in the company of Finn. She could have arrived sooner, but weariness and vanity willed otherwise. To return in the midst of the preparations that she had been unable to oversee would simply have made matters more difficult than needed, and nor did she wish to return with dust in her hair and stains on her dress. She has washed in the cold waters of the priest in Mellösa's little bathhouse, and now rides a freshly groomed mount. Finn, too, she has compelled to shave and to wash. He has ridden with his clothes still drying on his body, having wrung them out as best he could. Even from a distance she can see all that Katarina Sharp has accomplished, observing as much with both satisfaction at how good everything looks and disappointment at how readily she has been replaced.

She pulls at the reins to slow the bishop's mare on the drawbridge, her desire for a dignified arrival suddenly waning. A servant sees her and approaches with his head bowed in welcome, taking the horse's muzzle with calming words while she dismounts. She gives Finn a nod over her shoulder to relieve him of further duties, then makes her way toward the outbuildings. Few take notice of her; in part because the courtyard is full of strangers, called in from near and far to assist in the preparations for the Midsummer festivities, and in part because their toil is such that every face is bowed over their task. Unused to solitude, she is left hovering in the yard in the puddle of her own shadow. It is as though Cuckoo's Roost is no longer her ancestral home but a foreign place, the life that she has lived there no longer hers. Despair and relief tussle for dominion within her, and she is unable to tell which turns her stomach more. A nausea comes on suddenly, but just as her eyes seem about to blacken she feels a hand on her arm, and when she turns around Katarina Sharp is standing before her.

"Stina."

"Kari."

Yet again the feelings come in conflicting pairs: the simple gratitude over another's touch, and the shame of being so exposed, so weak. She is glad that it is Kari, best among her sisters-in-law, wise enough not to give voice to her thoughts until the time is ripe, neither flippant nor dull. Kari is some years younger than Stina, her gray-green eyes and hard face little tarnished by the time that has passed since their last meeting, at Midsummer the previous year. Sven Sharp's daughter, her cradle a blood-spattered hull. Stina wonders, not for the first time, what marks are left on a girl of four years of age when she is led by her father down a road lined by German soldiers, the heads of their kin on spikes, all the way down to the ship that is to sail her away from the only home she has ever known. Kari shifts her grip, taking Stina's hand with such ease that it is as though she has read her every thought.

"Come."

Together they walk down to the garlanded pavilion in the meadow, all but deserted now that everything is ready. Stina finds a seat, and Kari sits down beside her rather than opposite. A maid emerges with a jug of beer and two mugs. Kari pours and hands one to her. The weight and ruggedness of the clay feel familiar in Stina's hand, its sort baked in a nearby kiln and identical to hundreds of others at Cuckoo's Roost. The beer tastes as it always has, fresh and bitter at once. The comfort fills her eyes with tears. A sob slips out before she can stifle it.

"Mara lost the baby."

Both women hold Margaret in high esteem, though she is closer in age to a daughter than a sister-in-law. So carefree, her laughter frequent and contagious: at a butterfly in spring, magpies on a roof, a cat turning a somersault. The sorts of things that they had long since stopped taking note of themselves, but had come to see again through her eyes. Now that same woman will hear a voice inside her endlessly questioning whether the guilt is hers, a voice that will never be silenced. The day she gives birth to a healthy babe will bring some solace, but a mark has been made that will not wash. Kari nods, saying nothing where there is little that can be said. She empties her mug and fills both again, and they drink, as if they were one and the same, reflections in still water. The drink's warmth imparts Stina with courage anew.

"There's something else, too. One of the sisters of the abbey glimpsed something in me and put words to what I should have seen before. My years of youth are passed, Kari. I'm to become a crone."

"That's a road we all must walk, if luck is with us."

Easy for you to say, Stina thinks before she can stop herself, *you whose youth will still be intact for a decade or more.* It would seem that not even time itself can bear to wither Katarina Sharp's stark beauty. The shame sparks up in Stina, her thanklessness toward the one in whom she confides. If age is worth anything, let it at least be the good sense not to mistake friend for foe. Stina raises her gaze up toward the keep of Cuckoo's Roost, where it is visible through the brocade of flowers.

"Not long ago I was a girl born of the lion and the lily, and then I grew up and was found a husband I could endure. Cuckoo's Roost became my dowry, and I've been content here. I had Britta, and Magnus, and I couldn't ask for more. But it always seemed to me that I was waiting for something else, as though more life than what I've lived still lay ahead, so much so that the choices I made hardly bore any weight. Now that it's too late I doubt them all. All those years passed that I'll never get back, and so little I have to show for them."

Kari sits quietly for a moment before leaning in.

"Of all my sisters-in-law in this endless family, I've always revered you the most: 'Now there's a woman with dignity, one who knows how to carry herself,' I've thought to myself more times than I care to count. Me, who starts pacing spraddle-legged as soon as the wind kicks up, like on a ship's deck in rough seas. When Bengt Stensson sent word asking me to handle Midsummer in your absence I quaked at the thought. The expectation gave me no peace, to the extent that I took to straddling Bo rather than toss and turn all night long. How could I ever live up to all that you achieve, and without ever betraying the slightest strain, at that? But you made it easy for me. Never have I seen a household in better order. Everything is where you look for it. No one I know has excelled more than you."

This is a rare grace, to be given a glimpse of oneself as seen by another, and with such kindness at that. Stina's words fail her, and she can but smile, not in joy but in gratitude. She receives one in return from Kari Sharp, who rarely turns her lips. And yet in the wake of this emotion, a deceitful voice still whispers from within that this is scant praise. Overseeing the household, working the land, keeping the servants in check, ensuring that everything has its place, that crops are harvested and the store-chamber is stocked: all are paltry things that Stina has never found difficult. A waste of gifts such as hers, perfection the least that could be demanded of her.

She turns her head so as not to bare a face that could be misconstrued. Out on the meadow's stamped earth she sees her son, Magnus, talking next to Finn. The sight makes it easier for her to shake the wicked thoughts. Now it is Stina's turn to pour, and they clink mugs before they drink. Their eyes meet over the clay rims, and, as if by prior agreement, they raise their mugs even higher and let the beer drain down their throats until nothing remains, the gravity of the moment washed away. In the silence that follows a thought strikes Stina with sudden clarity.

"Mara's loss. You already knew."

"Aye."

"How?"

"Nils Stensson. He came galloping in from Vadstena two hours ago, his horse in a lather. He must have passed you unnoticed in Mellösa."

"Where is he now?"

"With our men, together up in the keep."

"To what end?"

Kari's eyes meet hers. Gray-green, grave.

"What else? The same thing their house has always sought. As has yours. As has mine."

M AGNUS, EVER ALERT, hears the footsteps even at a distance, and turns to see Finn striding over the grass that has just been cut to clear space. He goes to meet him. They stop a few feet from each other, both timid all of a sudden. Mere days have passed since their last meeting, but other things have come to pass that have turned Finn's journey into one greater than time alone can measure, and that now make him look upon Magnus with a stranger's eyes. The face that is no longer a boy's, the tenderness of childhood present only when he smiles, which he does more seldom with each passing year. What once lay soft and open now sits hardened and concealed, gradually stiffening into an expression of dogged resolve, veiled secrecy. His sun-darkened skin makes the blue of his eyes gleam, while his long, wild hair that fades more toward brown each year has been lightened by the sun that burns deep into the night. It is Magnus who speaks first.

"Good to have you back."

"I'm just arrived from Mellösa, with your mother."

Finn falls silent, his gaze locked on the ground, uncertain of what to say next. Magnus beats him to it.

"I saw my uncle Nils not long ago. He'd come the same way, though not in your company. He told us of Mara."

Finn can do no more but nod, glad at least that the burden of the bad tidings has been lifted from his shoulders. On the ground he sees a wide ring of woven willow branches. The grass within the ring has been cleared, the bare earth stamped flat. Together they start circling the ring, slowly and side by side.

"What's wrong, Finn? You should be glad. Her penance is done now, and you're finally home."

The memories come, of the kind that Finn sees every night in unrelenting dreams: a red stone between pale fingers, blood-spattered foliage, and a knife on soft flesh, blood beneath his nails. He is another now, and a fool he would be if he thought Magnus wouldn't see. The sin is his alone to bear in silence, a confidence too heavy even for a friendship such as theirs. But there's something else, too.

"I've done everything the priest asked of me for my sister's sake. If what he said is true, then her debt is paid, her time in the flames of Purgatory lessened."

Magnus frowns at a the strange tone in his friend's voice.

"Do you doubt?"

The pair have long been close. Finn has been one of the household ever since he was a child, and though with age his duties have grown in number, it's no secret that Bengt Stensson chose him for the sake of Magnus; at just a few years his senior, he was halfway between guardian and foster brother, playfellow and guard dog all in one. Sir Bengt had found him in a plague-ravaged village farther south, a feral, raggedy little thing with neither mother nor father nor anyone to claim him, he who hovered at the edge of the hearth's light one evening, in the hopes of begging a crust of bread for himself and his sister. Two healthy children in a village laid waste by the plague: a miracle of God. Finn and Ylva. Bengt had fed them from his own hand, as though taming animals of the forest; had given them enough to still their hunger while coaxing shy, taciturn responses from them, until he eventually placed brother and sister on horseback behind two of his servants and brought them back to Cuckoo's Roost, to a future that promised more than mere starvation. Company for his own children.

At least one of them was an apt choice, for ever since those very first days Finn and Magnus have been inseparable. Finn's gratitude to Sir Bengt has never dimmed, so unlike the father whom Finn scarce remembers, a habitual drunkard till the day he fell asleep by a ditch and was loaded in error onto the cart of the plague's dead. Already sick when he awoke with a groan just before he was to be dumped into the open grave with the other dead, he nevertheless lived long enough to pass the malady to his wife, having staggered home and tumbled down beside her in bed, thirsty and with lust to slake. Finn's loyalty to Magnus may have begun as service, but it has grown stronger with the passing of each year. Without instruction he has taken on new duties, more than anyone ever asked of him. From his castle keep Sir Bengt has watched their friendship flourish, thus far without disfavor, for in youth bonds are tied beyond the limits of common sense. One day they will be forced to part ways, when Magnus comes to see that they are cut from different cloths, he and his friend, however much they may will it otherwise; life has placed a distance between them that cannot be bridged. The world is not equal. It is home to those who pray, those who farm, and those who fight. The noble has his place, the serf another. Such is the way of the Lord.

Finn shakes his head, searching for the words that escape him.

"Even the bishop chooses drink over prayers."

Magnus tilts his head to one side, waiting for Finn to go on, but Finn changes the subject.

"What's new here at Cuckoo's Roost?"

Magnus gestures up at the stone keep atop its mound.

"When Uncle Nils arrived he wasn't dressed for any feast, and he had no luggage, either. Something's brewing; what I don't know. But I don't believe it's for festivity's sake that the whole clan is gathered here this Midsummer."

"And you? How have you been?"

Magnus shows Finn his right hand, cracked and callused from the sword's grip. It takes a while for Finn to grasp what he means to tell him. Then he sees where they are standing. Willow branches and stamped earth. He stops abruptly, grabs Magnus by the arm.

"We were going to practice together. Surely you can't mean to go ahead, in spite of everything? You told me you'd sooner bide your time till next year."

"Would you have gone if I'd told you otherwise? Your sister's penance couldn't go undone for my sake. But I didn't tell you the truth. For that I ask your forgiveness."

"Alone you can't get the only kind of practice that counts. This'll end badly for you, Magnus."

Magnus looks him in the eye, the blue darkening to black, and Finn needs no more. He bows his head, aware that the decision has been made beyond all return, and that part of the blame is his.

"We don't have much time. Would you show me what you've learned? Perhaps we can improve your chances yet."

Magnus hesitates, but then nods in response. Together they take the road up to the forest.

B ENGT STENSSON PEERS at his two brothers from under furrowed brows. The conspiracy is brought to light. Nils and Bo have conspired, that much is clear, and it's a tactic Sir Bengt knows well. It's what Nils always does. United his elder brothers have strength enough to resist him, but scarce each on his own. When Nils wins one he's as good as won both, and then everything goes his way. Sir Bengt curses inwardly at the mere sight of his brother, who despite several days on horseback still has the air of someone who has but strolled in from a morning walk. As Bengt himself might well have looked, were he thirteen years the younger and still in the prime of manhood, unlike now, when at every turn he is confronted by death's portents: spongy flesh around a waist that once was firm; bony buttocks vexed by the saddle; his scalp visible through the wisps of hair that fade more with each passing year. Besides, he knows he flatters himself: in all his days he has never looked as good as Nils does now. In search of the best consolation at hand he turns to Bo, whose head is so bald and shiny he had to let his beard grow long and grizzled to avoid looking like a plucked chicken. Bengt feels his blood seethe with impatience now that the family matters are dealt with: Nils has told them about Margaret, whom they all hold in high regard, and the child lost to a cruel fate. Together they have mourned, without wasting any time. They have said what little there is to be said and what custom advises, only too aware of the paltriness of their words. They have hugged, shed tears, and wiped their cheeks. The emotion has left Bengt weary and peevish.

"So, is this when I get to hear what mischief you've been brewing?"

"All in good time, brother. First I have something to show you. And you, too, Bo."

Nils picks up a bundle that he has lugged all the way up into the great hall of the keep, where the height and stone walls shut out prying eyes and ears. He carefully unfolds the cloth to unveil its contents. Bengt snorts at the sight. A bow mounted on a wooden stock.

"Well, look at that, a crossbow. Is a Midsummer hunt in the offing?"

"This is a new kind. I won it playing dice up north in Norberg."

Bengt shrugs and exchanges a meaningful look with his older brother, who is equally perplexed.

"It looks the same."

"Well, it isn't. Here, let it speak for itself."

Nils lifts the crossbow off the table and carefully rests its steel-tipped stock on the stone floor. This is not the kind of weapon that Bengt has seen before, the kind that he has used to fell deer and roebucks. Normally the stock would be fitted with a stirrup, where the crossbowman can place his foot while using both hands to draw the string to its full span. This weapon is stub-nosed, furnished instead with a toothed wheel, a crank to turn it, and a bar of notched iron between string and wheel. Nils starts to wind the crank, the teeth latch, and with every click the string is forced farther and farther back, until the entire room is suffused with the menace of its latent power. Still, he goes on, and Bengt wonders that the stock, lathe, and string don't snap on the spot. Finally it stops, and when Nils carefully lifts the crossbow, the lathe catches a flash of sunlight from the window with a sweeping glint. Steel, hammered and tempered into a fatal half-moon with no yew nor whalebone.

Nils takes a bolt from his sack, short and squat where arrows are usually slender, its ugliness fitting for its purpose. Before either of the brothers can protest, he places it in the groove and slides it to the notch, then rests the weapon against his shoulder to take aim. On the wall hangs their father's armor, the breastplate Sten Bosson wore in his years as warden of Oakwood, fashioned with the most splendid craftsmanship that silver could buy. A mere stroke is all it takes to fire the shot. The twang of the string and clap of the bolt merge into a single sound, followed by the clatter of metal falling to the floor. The noise gives way to a deafening echo between the stone walls. In the ensuing silence Bo and Bengt stand cowering mutely, their hands clasped to their ears. The color soon rises in Sir Bengt's face.

"For fuck's sake, Nils."

His brother raises a finger for patience, then lifts the fallen breastplate off the floor and places it on the table. Bo whistles, drawing Bengt closer, too. The wide tip of the bolt has punched a hole straight through the armor, as easily as through a scrap of threadbare linen. Bengt walks over to the wall and runs his nail over the point where the bolt struck, a white speck marking where the stone has split and shards have flown. He shudders at its force.

"How far will it go?"

"Four hundred yards and then some. A sure kill within a hundred, if the shooter has a passable aim. This is what it does to steel. Where it meets chain mail, the bolt will go straight through and out the other side, leaving the wearer to cough up iron rings with his dying breaths."

Bengt sighs while running his finger around the hole in their father's breastplate.

"Few smiths can mend armor like this nowadays."

"My point exactly. Times are changing, brother."

Nils puts the crossbow down on the table, and his brothers are both drawn to it like flies to honey, to weigh it, feel it, pluck the string. Nils clears his throat, and Bengt lets out a sigh at what he suspects is a speech that his brother has long been crafting.

"In Father's day, a knight clad in iron could subdue a whole village alone. With the sun glinting off his armor and helmet, the peasantry would mistrust that it was even a man they saw before them, and any fool who dared test the knight's steel with pitchfork or spit would soon find his opponent just as invulnerable as he looked. If the knight knew how to carry himself, his mere presence would be enough. Little did anyone suspect that a deferment of their taxes could be as simply achieved as by charging forth in their numbers, knocking the man off his hack and chucking him into the nearest millpond. But folk are habitually henhearted and simpleminded, each one looking out only for himself. With reverence, fear, and ignorance a kingdom is quelled. But no more."

He pats the crossbow.

"The men of the mountains already have these in their scores. Their smiths and carpenters have been toiling all winter long to get them ready. In Father's day it would take a lifetime to learn how best to kill. Back then combat was an art; nowadays it's enough to simply aim and squeeze. That clatter you just heard was the last bugle blast of a dying era. Twilight has fallen on the age of the knights of legend."

The door groans on creaking hinges when it opens, and three heads turn in wait. Kari is the first to enter, Stina behind her.

The brothers exchange glances, Nils the most confounded. Bengt holds out one hand toward his wife in invitation.

"Go on, Nils. Whatever you have to say you can just as well say it to Stina. Nothing we decide here goes ahead without her blessing."

Bo nods in agreement, making space for his own wife at his side. Nils fidgets, straining to find where he left off.

"The northmen are on the move. The rebellion is coming."

Sir Bengt throws out his arms in exasperation.

"Again? I thought calm had been restored. I wore out my own saddle riding from Västerås to Copenhagen on their account just last year. I was in Västerås on the Council's behalf, to see how Jösse Eriksson was managing his bailiwick. That Danish pig was elbow-deep in every money pouch in town, and it would take a crooked man indeed not to see that his subjects had good cause for complaint. I said as much to King Eric, and Jösse got sent back to Denmark. Now you're telling me that all that strife was for nothing?"

"It's not just a question of bailiffs anymore. King Eric seems to have grown bored of the peace. He's put up with it for two whole years, after all. If the war starts up again, everyone knows the Hansa will side with Holstein, and when their cogs stop mooring in Stockholm the miners will have nowhere to sell their iron."

Bengt crosses his arms and shakes his head.

"I can't believe that."

"Rumor has it that Eric's privateers are already pursuing merchant ships from here to the Kattegat Sea."

Sir Bengt curses under his breath, feels his pulse pounding in his temples. His stomach turns at the thought of the cost of that war, the one that everyone believed was over. As a nobleman he is exempt from tax, but when war is to be waged every coin he has in reserve must be cashed in favor of the king's vanity. Horses and saddles, weapons and armaments, men with strength in their arms—all must he pay for, he and his peers. The young men of the local parishes must be mustered, armed, and paid before being sent south. Rarely do they return, and those who do come back as broken men, burdens to their kin until their dying day, which is eagerly awaited like a tardy guest. He closes his eyes to count up what expenses he can expect if his brother is speaking the truth. Nils lets the gravity sink in for a moment before going on.

"Do you know Engelbrekt Engelbrektsson?"

Bengt abandons the figures he has started stacking up, almost grateful to be able to push that sum into the future. He scratches his beard in thought.

"By name and reputation. A nobleman from Norberg, he is, his coat of arms a triangle of three half-lilies. He spoke for the people of the mountains in their case against Jösse Eriksson, but the king turned a deaf ear until I bore out their complaints."

Nils nods in agreement at every word.

"He's a warrior, too. He served on the German border, where he made a name for himself. They say he took a wound there to his trunk that still troubles him, and that's why he's childless. When I was up in the north I met him face-to-face. We've spoken. A man to be reckoned with, he is."

"Then I suppose there's a chance he'll listen to reason if we try to talk sense into him on behalf of the Council."

Nils and Bo exchange glances over the table, then Bo and Katarina. Nils clears his throat.

"No, brother. That's exactly what we won't do."

At last, here it comes. Bengt feels a momentary qualm at what is about to be laid bare, but chooses to wait it out in silence rather than betray his curiosity by anything but merely waving the speech on.

"I've seen the northmen, felt their fervor. The rest of the country may well be devoid of people, but they number in the hundreds. Last year they laid siege to Burg Hill Castle, and it was only with costly promises from the king that they could be sent back home. They know their might, and they have no fear. One in ten has his own crossbow now, just like this one. The uprising will grow and move south, emptying every village of its men along the way, and this time there'll be no fine words to quash it, for why make do with promises when you can just as well take matters into your own hands?"

"Sooner or later it'll end. That's always the way. The bailiffs just need to sit out the summer behind their ramparts, till snowflakes mix with the rain and cool the northmen's wrath. One by one they'll be reminded of the warmth of their own hearths, the food waiting on their tables, a willing lass in their beds, and the retreat will begin."

"Not if we join forces."

This leap seems to Sir Bengt too great a stretch even for Nils, and his first response is to snort with laughter, as if at some unexpected japery. No one shares in his mirth. Bo stands with his arms crossed and waits. Nils steps closer.

"Is King Eric really such a good friend, Bengt? Are you so content with how he rules this kingdom? Our castles brimming with Germans and Danes, while of us he demands blood spilled on foreign soils, the fruits of which we shall never enjoy? If we make the northerners' cause our own he'll have no means of resistance. Let's arm our men and ready them—not to march to Schleswig but to walk alongside Engelbrekt. Alone he will shake the realm. With us he can't lose."

Bengt raises the forefinger and middle finger of his clenched left hand.

"Twice before have we done this. Grandfather betrayed his king to back the German Albrekt, and Father did the same with Queen Margaret. It went badly for the both of them."

"Alone they were weak. Now it's you, me, and Bo. Together we're all that remains of blue and gold, and with our combined strength few can contend. Father and Grandfather overreckoned their own power. They thought that they would be able to control foreign majesties simply because they better knew the lay of our lands. But don't mistake northern mining folk for wily southerners: well may they know how to swing an axe, but these men know little of the Council's ways. Let us show the peasants how to wage war in earnest."

Bengt feels the color rise in his face, his lungs pumping as though the very air in the room has thickened. He leans in toward the tabletop, grateful that that at least is constant in its solidity, even when everything else appears to be reeling. A pimpled young lad atop the stone at Mora Meadow rises up out of his memory, his arm so weak it quakes under the weight of the sword, his head crowned with gold. And there, amidst the wonder and the confusion, comes a flutter in his belly from something else.

"And then? Are we to make him king, too, this Engelbrekt?"

The voice that replies belongs to Bo Stensson.

"Before the crown can be placed on anyone's head it must fall from he who now wears it. The fight ahead will demand much of us all, but let's find the time to discuss that matter in due course."

He smiles, and Nils smiles, and Kari Sharp, too, and old habit also tugs at the corners of Bengt's mouth. He takes a deep breath, his gaze wandering from one face to the next, then puts his arms over his chest.

"I want a go with the crossbow."

B RITTA SEES THEM disappear into the forest, Finn and Magnus. While they are gone she makes herself helpful as best she can, biding her time. Neither Mother nor Father sees her, nor even Kari Sharp, and time and time again it is to her the household flock with their questions. Where do the barrels go? And the tables? She answers to the best of her ability, tries to imagine the evening unfurling before her and make whatever decisions will prompt the least trouble. For a while these tasks stave off her melancholy, enclosing her within a greater whole in which she can forget herself. As a result she is slow to see her brother on his return, and she must make haste to catch up with him, come close enough that he can't feign blindness and deafness.

"Magnus!"

She draws level with him, and they stand face-to-face, Magnus with his head bowed, sheepishly hiding his gaze under his fringe like a child caught playing truant. And yet it is he who speaks first.

"I heard about Vadstena."

Britta nods, and in the absence of fitting words they both stand in silence, their gazes crossing on their way to the ground rather than meeting each other's. It has been a long time since they were close. Six years separate them, too many to have ever been playmates. Once Magnus was old enough and Britta still sufficiently young they would bicker and tease, each blaming the other for their own disobedience. Then other things came between them. Britta's duties multiplied, and Magnus grew too restless, constantly roving forest and field with Finn at his side. Their paths crossed ever more seldom.

"I went to Vadstena not for Mara's sake, but for mine. I didn't intend to come home. I meant to stay in the abbey."

Magnus gives an astonished laugh.

"You, a nun?"

"But then I saw how they lived. It frightened me. Not even there could I find sanctuary. It was worse, worse even than here."

He opens his mouth to say something but changes his mind. Britta wipes a tear from the corner of her eye.

"It was Ylva that made me go. Her death."

Her brother looks on, uncomprehending.

"It's years since you two were close."

"You don't remember. You were too young. Father had intended Ylva Sigridsdaughter to be for me what Finn is to you. But it wasn't to be. I was older, and she was difficult. She didn't like it here, wasn't made for a life of servitude. She refused to see that the rules that applied to me were different from the ones that she had to obey. As she grew older there was no keeping her on. I pleaded with Father, and he let her go. Rather than be my companion in beautiful chambers, she chose to live in sin with a man in Mellösa under a leaky turf roof. I didn't think her death would hurt me so much. But it did. She had so much life in her, more than Cuckoo's Roost could contain. And now she is no more."

Magnus is still bewildered, the same look on his face that he would get as a child when faced with a riddle beyond his wits. Suddenly she is angry, Britta, hardens her voice.

"You see nothing, Magnus. You're so taken up with yourself. Mother's ailing, and Father does nothing but drink. They want to marry me off, but you they want to keep forever. And both of us dig our heels in."

She falls silent, takes a breath, and starts again.

"Magnus, I know what you mean to do. I know that you've been practicing. I've been to your clearing, opened your bundle. With Finn away I'd hoped you'd think better of it."

For a moment Magnus stands unmoving, his astonishment souring to bitterness.

"There's no hiding anything from you. Not even a shrew can scamper across the attic floor without you needing to know where it's headed. And now you'll go tell on me to Mother. As always."

Britta steps forward, catching him before he can recoil, then wraps her arms around him and holds him tightly, her face hidden in the nape of his neck, where hair meets skin. He exudes the scents of the forest, grass and resin and fresh leaves. Although her junior, he stands as tall as she, if not taller. He is stiff at first, until he feels her breaths turn to sobs and places his arms around her. In the embrace she can feel his confusion.

"Nils, wait."

Stina has purposely kept her distance in order to follow him to where they won't be heard. He stops and turns in the shade behind the keep, and she looks around to make sure they are alone. Now that she must speak, the words catch. Custom wills it that she offer him her condolences over what happened to Mara, but it wasn't Nils who sat by her side, holding her hand as the pains tore through her, but Stina. She stands there wordlessly, leaving him to break the silence.

"Stina, I can't thank you enough for all that you did for Mara. Even though it didn't end well, the child received the best help she could. What happened is God's will."

He is a well-built man, Nils, though his ways leave much to be desired. Had he been worse at what he does she would have called him fawning, but this is something else. It's as though he can sense how each person would like him to behave and quickly follows suit, so credibly that it takes seeing him dupe others to note the difference; no single person can contain so much contradiction. He plays the remorseful husband now, sorrow-stricken yet grateful.

"I should have been there, Stina. There was nowhere I'd sooner have been. My journey dragged on, my errand abroad protracted. I arrived at Vadstena too late, and I couldn't stay long, either. Mara's recuperating in the safety of the sisters' care. There's nowhere better that she could be. With any luck we'll have her here before Midsummer is passed."

Stina doesn't know what to say. He has anticipated her every reproach.

She confines herself to a nod, her lips pursed to a white line. Only when he bows and turns to be on his way does she find her tongue.

"Abbess Ingegerd."

He stops, and for a moment the mask slips. It's clear that the name is known to him, and in Stina it is as though the ground gives way beneath her, revealing a chasm that she had hoped was but a figment of her imagination. The thoughts come thick and fast, weaving up threads that had thus far hung loose.

"You knew, Nils, didn't you? A curse on your blood. Your own sister died in the childbed at Vadstena, yet you sent your wife there to give birth."

She can see the blood rise in him, sees a vein swell and throb on his forehead. Rage and vexation flare up in his culpable eyes, though he meets her gaze only for the briefest of instants before looking away. An admission of guilt.

"I'm no child, no more than you. I don't believe in curses."

"Few will claim otherwise. Yet curses still hold power, unseen power. Say you have two empty seats to choose between. Better to place yourself by the one on which no spells have been cast. No smoke without fire, as they say, and who can know for certain all the things that this world may contain. So why, Nils?"

He shakes his head, his eyes locked blankly on the distance, refusing to say a word. Stina steps closer, lowering her voice.

"You know what I believe, Nils Stensson, of blue and gold? It's only too clear now that your ambitions have come to light. The day the new king is to be chosen we'll need everything in our favor, isn't that so? That day could end badly for a house cursed by one of Saint Birgitta's blood. You sent your wife to Vadstena so that she might give birth to a healthy baby, thus proving no curse exists."

Despite his denials, the look on Nils's face is that of a child, a boy finally caught in the very store-chamber in which he would abandon his brothers. The face he makes is foolish and unthinking, and his youth vexes her. It sparks her outrage more than had he stood his ground and spoken frankly. Instead he is bereft of all authority. Her arm moves as if someone tugs at it sharply with an unseen string, and when the slap lands it is so hard that she feels it through her entire body. She has dealt cuffs aplenty before, but always with a clear purpose; never with such lack of restraint; never with a rage that no force could ever quell. Nils's head turns with the blow, and she sees its sting bring tears to his eyes. When he looks back at her she raises her hand again, but this time he catches her wrist before she can land it. They stand there for a moment, his hand around her arm. The touch calms her. Stina is no match for him in strength, and once she lets her arm go limp he releases her.

"Let's sit."

She nods without knowing why, submissive now that her judgment has returned, her knees quaking in the wake of her outburst. She lets herself be led away from the keep's shadows. Nils finds himself a tussock of dry, long grass and sits down with his legs crossed. Stina hesitates at first, then adjusts her skirts and sinks down beside him. For a while they sit without speaking, gazing down at the garlanded pavilion that has been raised for the festivities, where the preparations are almost complete and the table is now being laid.

"A person is what they are, Stina, in body and temperament and all that they take themselves to be. But they're something else, too, something both greater and more singular: the idea of them, the shadow they cast in others' minds. This shadow grows and contracts with everything others see and hear of them: honor and outrage, success and setbacks alike. Therein lies a curse's power. It's just as you say: it doesn't exist, and yet it does. Although few would indulge the words of a scorned, embittered nun in the light of day, the mind works differently in the witching hour. They are a stain upon our shield. Anyone who has their sights set on the throne won't willingly be followed if such a thing comes to light. In that much you are right. But those ambitions aren't mine alone. They were Father's first, and Grandfather's before him. Our sister, Karin, herself chose to fare to Vadstena to give birth, so that her successful delivery would prove that there was nothing to fear. If she bore a daughter she was to name her after Ingegerd's mother, Saint Birgitta's daughter, as yet another token of reconciliation. But Karin died, and little Märta, too. We who remained saw to it that the matter was kept silent. What more could we do to honor the decision our sister had made for all of our sakes?"

He runs the tips of his fingers over his red cheek, sucks in the air between clenched teeth.

"I deserved that box on the ears, and more besides. But are we so different, Stina, you and I? Do our roads not go the same way? You were born under the lion and the lily, but Magnus is of blue and gold. All that is ours concerns him, which means it concerns you, too. The good of our house is also to his favor. What do you wish for him? Anyone can see how highly you prize your son, you and Bengt, but do you really want him to sit all his days out at Cuckoo's Roost? Greater things are within reach. The aspiration that is ours, should it not be yours just as much?"

The sun is high above them, but it has turned in the sky and begun its slow descent back to the earth.

"Few of us know the name of Ingegerd, much less her secret. That burden is now also yours. But it's high time, Lady Kristina, that you decide what it is you want and where your loyalty resides."

He stands up and holds out his hand to help her to her feet. Himself again, Nils Stensson, lordly and sure of himself, as though doubt itself was no longer of this world, and the future lay bright at the end of a straight road. But Stina doesn't take his hand; she stands up on her own, and they walk their separate ways to the feast that awaits.

AND SO THEY finally take to the table, all of them: the men and women of the house and their visiting guests. Bengt Stensson of blue and gold and Lady Kristina of the lion and the lily take up the high seats, with Bishop Knut to their right, Britta Bengtsdaughter opposite. Sir Bo and his Kari to their left. Around them sit the rest of the brothers, split on either side. Nils is beside the bishop, deep in conversation. Karl, eldest of them all, sits stooped and rocking under the care of a maid, who feeds him as best she can with all that he is incapable of taking for himself. He lets anything that isn't to his liking dribble out over his chin and down his tunic, emitting now and then a tuneless hum. Their blind brother who shares the bishop's name perches straight-backed in his chair. He needs help, if only to have his food served and his goblet filled and placed in his hand. Once he has moved everything to where he wants it, his hands find their way around easily.

Other guests fill the seats toward both of the table's ends. Here gather the most eminent among the farmers who work Sir Bengt's land, those who are but a generation or two from packing their coffers full enough to buy themselves into the nobility. Viper Saltlock is in attendance, having traveled all the way from the coast with some of his privateers, those who stand at the helm of Sir Bengt's ships. A handful of German seadogs, too, sent by the Hansa with whom the house has enjoyed ties of friendship and commerce. The seamen eye each other up warily over the table, while the foreigners whisper among themselves. Born enemies, these, badger and fox, but since both are guests at this table they grope fumblingly for that which they have in common, and as it happens they find a great deal: the sea's capricious weather and winds; sails and rigs; past shipwrecks that led to a tragic demise or unexpected salvation. The table's bounties help to put any differences to rest, uniting one and all in joy at all the goodness life has to offer. There is carp and pike, sausages and ham, bread so fresh it steams when the crust is broken. The beer is the pride of the house, foaming and cold, from a barrel that has rested and cooled in the lake overnight, and there's wine from the south to boot, spiced with ginger and cloves. Around and above them, garlanded beams offer shade from the blazing sun, and their fresh scents of birch and sap cut through the pungent wafts of meat and drink. Around the pavilion, firepans are lit at a short remove, which burn solely to keep the gnats at bay, the vermin being wont to rise from the backwaters and pools with the coolness of the afternoon. Around each one stand men with buckets and leafy twigs, ready to choke any spark that takes flight on the wind.

※

Sir Bengt's laughter carries far and wide once his thirst is quenched—too far, in fact; he purposely overdoes it, in an attempt to coax out real mirth with feigned. Surely it will come. The unease from the day's discussions and the anticipation around the festivities start to release, and once he has dealt with the worst of his hunger he can drink, handpick which delicacies he most wants to savor, and make the most of his role of host. Even the weather appears to have chosen clemency. Time and again he casts furtive glances at the rain-laden clouds, which have thus far confined themselves to circling Cuckoo's Roost and left the skies above them beautifully blue. Still he can't relax. Not even the sun can earn his trust. He squints and, sensing a halo around its burning disc, prays that the approaching storm will spare them all. He drinks again, lets his gaze wander over his guests and relatives. Then he turns to Stina, she, too, surveying the rows of guests with a hostess's flitting eye, straight-backed and resolute. He reaches over to fill her mug.

"Here's to you, wife. Kari may have done the last of it, but she used nothing that you hadn't already put at her disposal. Everyone knows. This feast is one for the ages, and it's you we all have to thank."

Stina is only half listening.

"I wonder where Magnus has got to. I can't see him anywhere."

Bengt leans in closer and gives her arm a more ardent caress, seeking out her gaze.

"I'd like to give you something in return for all your toil."

Only now is she completely with him, in her surprise.

"What?"

He leans back and shrugs.

"Whatever you desire, Stina. Make a wish, and if it's within my power to grant, it's yours. It could never be more than you deserve. Now then, put your cares to rest. This feast is for all of us. Cheers!"

She smiles back at him and shrugs, too, then raises her mug in response.

※

Bengt seeks out his guests' eyes so that he might drink to them, gets up every now and then to fill seats temporarily vacated in favor of the privy, exchanging familiar words now with one, then the other. Gradually he gets used to his magnificent attire, which had felt itchy and unwieldy at first, its pearl stitching rivaling even the gold chain around his neck in luster. On his feet, his punishingly dainty shoes have started to give. What had first felt peacockish is now to his pleasing. He is, after all, a law-speaker, a man of the Council and knight of the realm, a lord. On the crown of his head he wears a garland, as is the custom, one beautifully woven from birch leaves and flowers. He wishes Stina would partake more in the mirth that he now feels. Ever since her return she has been as tightly strung as the horsehairs on Nils's crossbow. She picks at her food, her eyes constantly darting back to Magnus's chair, which has sat empty so long that others have laid claim to it. Even Bengt darkens slightly at the thought, for Magnus ought to be here. Perhaps that's enough with all the pampering, now the time come for a firmer hand. They've let the boy run wild far too long. He'll have to give him a serious talking-to before Midsummer's end, for the eldest son of the house has plenty a part to play in hosting duties. Let that be the end of his childhood. God knows he's had a better run of it than most.

The sun sinks even farther in the late afternoon, and in his fuddled state Bengt needs a servant's reminder to stand up, using the edge of the table to steady himself, and call for silence with a clap of his hands. It's time for the tournament, before dusk is upon them or the sun falls so low that one side will be blinded. The band of youths are already waiting down in the meadow, outside the rope. They have wrapped their heads with cloth, their knuckles, too, and the cudgels that will be swung in the place of swords, there being no reason to inflict more damage than needed merely to exhibit the power that each possesses and which of the fighters is best. He who holds his own can hope of a place among Bengt's own retinue at Cuckoo's Roost, with shiny weapons and a horse of his own, and food served from a steaming cauldron twice a day, washed down with beer from the barrel. Around the freshly cut willow branches laid out in a ring to mark out the battlefield,

Sir Bengt's own watchmen and some of Bishop Knut's escorts stand in wait, to step in should the blood run too hot. On the given signal the warriors form a line, raise their cudgels in salute at the high seats, and step over the foliage and into the ring, where they are split into two even ranks on either side. Bengt makes a vain attempt to count them but soon gives up, contents himself with a guess of somewhere between a dozen and a score. He raises his right hand and, with every eye on him, holds it in the air for the sake of suspense, before sweeping it downward to let the battle commence.

THUS FAR EVERYTHING has gone Magnus's way; with his face dirtied, cloth wrappings on his forehead, and his doublet padded with grass, no one has recognized him. Neither Father nor Mother have called a halt to the spectacle and forced him to step aside. The cudgel feels light in his hand, though the grip is sweaty. It's the same length as his sword, but lighter, and with a weapon like this in hand he can thrust and swing faster. Some of the others' faces seem vaguely familiar from chance meetings out in the fields, but no one takes any note of him or suspects his breeding, for that which is not expected is easily overlooked.

All are silent, in grim anticipation of what is to come. Their fears are not ungrounded. Every year the whistling cudgels crush fingers and noses, put eyes out, break arms, and shatter knees. For many of these young men there is all too much at stake, and rather than lose they are wont to strike too hard. Some turn frantic, taking flight into a mist of bloodlust and brutality that only ebbs away when the elders step in, shove them to the ground, and calm them with the weight of their bodies. For those looking on it may be mere spectacle, but within the ring of willows gravity reigns.

When Magnus takes his place in the line, his eyes are finally opened to the extent of his folly. Yes, he may have seen these youths in the meadows before, but all too often from horseback, from far away. Now that he stands beside them it's clear how much smaller he is, half a head shorter and a stone lighter at least. These men are burly-shouldered and brawny-armed, his own body slight by comparison. He had tried to build his puppet tall and stocky for practice, but now it seems far too small. He feels the sweat break out on his brow; it smarts in his eyes while his heart pounds. His gaze flits toward the long table where his father has his seat, a promise of safety. But Sir Bengt's raised arm comes down, and the cries of the men around the ring confirm the signal's meaning: it has begun. Magnus's team step forward, following the lead of their biggest fighter, a flaxen-haired giant with a crooked nose, but Magnus's legs clamp and refuse to move. His hesitation doesn't go unseen, and while his team's heads turn their leader snarls in his direction.

"Move, damn it! You shame us all."

Still Magnus stands there, numbed, while the faces turn his

way. Soon he'll be revealed; soon an elder will step over the willows and carry him off to double ignominy: disobedience first, and cowardice second. The latter is worse. He stands on the spot, shaking, until the farmhand next to him holds out his cudgel and herds him forward like a wayward calf. With this his terror's spell is broken, and he can move again. The faces turn away, looking ahead. They advance in a straight line, toward those coming from the other side. Their voices ring out almost in and of themselves, a bellow to enkindle courage and chase the fear away. With a few mere bounds the distance between the teams is closed. Soon the first rap of cudgels echoes across the meadow, wood on wood, hard enough to numb the fingers. And with that, no one sound can be made out any longer in the din. The skirmish is everyone's.

All that he has learned is forgotten, gone are all the tricks and the feints. By the skin of his teeth Magnus manages to ward off the blow that flies at him and strikes upon his cudgel so fiercely it makes his fingers throb. He sees that his own fear incites his opponent, who presses his advantage and surges ahead, swinging again and again. It is soon clear that Magnus has no resistance to offer, and in arrogance the other swipes Magnus's cudgel to the ground and raises his weapon, preparing to put him out of his misery. Magnus can but shut his eyes to avoid seeing what must come, but when he opens them again the threat is gone. The lad who had shoved him forward has felled his own opponent and taken on Magnus's, who now needs all the strength he can muster in his own defense.

In that momentary respite Magnus stands alone in battle, watching the others engaged in combat. His fear is choking his mind, he knows as much, and with some effort he forces himself to think of attack and not defense. He shakes his arms to loosen his muscles, and, taking a new grip of his cudgel, readies himself. Another fighter is on the approach, free to take on someone new. Magnus takes a few steps forward, finding that his feet now obey him. Dancing out of the way of the blow, he parries his opponent's cudgel to one side, diverting its full force down to the ground. With this small feat to his gain he now sees his challenger more clearly: the lad is clumsy and slow, and scared, too. Already Magnus feels a flutter deep in his belly, one first promise of anything but defeat. He spins his cudgel to ready himself for another strike, misses his first attempt, and jumps back out of the way of the riposte. Again. Suddenly everything slows, and amidst the slackness Magnus finds himself able to anticipate every move, each new swing so languid it is as if it were cutting through water. His terror cedes all the more, and something else courses in its place, as though his body were but a dispassionate vessel for the whims of alien feelings. By now his opponent is out of breath, gasping for air, his face as red as a crayfish out of the cauldron. Magnus fakes a charge to mislead him and then lands a blow on his forearm, upon which the lad's cudgel drops to the ground. Magnus quickly steps forward, stands on the cudgel, and raises his own in warning. He who loses his weapon and cannot retrieve it must leave the ring. In the youth's face Magnus sees the disappointment tempered by relief as he backs away, crosses the willows, and bends over to catch his breath, back in safety. Only too late does Magnus turn to his left, where he sees his neighbor take a blow to the gut. With a wheezing sob his teammate drops his weapon and falls. Magnus dives out of the way of a bat that comes whistling at his head, but in doing so collides with a knee that had been stuck out merely by chance, with no intent to harm.

It isn't the pain that he feels first but the vehemence of the blow, a knock that makes his head roil, filling his eyes with color and shapes of a kind that he has never seen before. He leaps back out of instinct, feeling the stroke of the blow on his cheek, then wipes his face on his sleeve. The knee had swiped across his cheek, covering his nose in blood. His sleeve is soaked with a mere touch, and he can taste iron in his mouth. Only now does it hurt, though the pain is less and milder than the violence of the blow. Magnus fumbles for something to aid him and finds rage alone. The rage saves him. His new enemy, misled by his sudden advantage and believing the fight already won, is wide open when Magnus reacts with blow upon blow, one to the shoulder and one to his neck, the latter landing hard enough that the boy must sit down and drop his weapon in order to grasp both hands to his throat in search of his lost breath, a look of blank astonishment on his face. He is out. Attentive hands grab him by the armpits and haul him off to safety. In the fleeting respite Magnus touches his nose. The pain rises again, and he spits red in the dirt.

Not many are left. How much time has passed? He finds the next in line, and they exchange blows. A rap meets his thigh, and he feels the blood bloom beneath his skin. Though half blinded he feels his cudgel meet its mark, and when his vision is returned his adversary is another. Gone are the weak, the hesitant. Those who remain are the ones who have prepared well, those who boast both the will to be the last man standing and the luck of kin who have experience with arms. No simple blows land anymore. And now Magnus feels something new taking hold, something he hadn't reckoned with. The weariness comes on, a stifling chokehold that leaches his resolve with each new onslaught. He scarce has will enough to defend himself, let alone attack. He sees openings come and go but is unable to strike fast enough, for his shoulders are aching and his bad leg limping, and every ounce of his being is bellowing that he can't take it anymore, has long since taken all that he can bear. The others are bigger and older, their arms and legs hardened from days in the fields and tending to beasts, days as long as the sun hangs over the earth. And with that the fear returns, crippling in its power, a brisk drumbeat at the back of his throat, counting down to the defeat that soon must come.

Sir Bengt has a hard time following the fight, even though there can't be many of them left. His head is spinning from all the wine and the beer, having eaten and drunk too much and too quickly after a long fast. All this indulgence has made him bloated. He suspects a bad bout of nausea in the offing. To crown it all, the clouds have beaten closer, driving a cool breeze upon him that makes him wrap his garments tighter with a shudder. Beside him Britta is conversing in hushed tones with the bishop, while Nils and Bo have turned on their chairs, engrossed in the young men's rough-and-tumble. Bengt does his best to follow their example; the tourney is to his honor, after all, and the lads are giving their all to gain his favor. He wipes the cold sweat from his brow, blinks to see better. Just as he thought: it will soon be settled. There are five or six left, while outside the perimeter of the willow branches those who have already been put out are licking their wounds, standing or seated, fingers fumbling in mouths in search of loose teeth. All uphold a sullen silence while observing the battles that still rage, while by contrast Sir Bengt's watchmen only grow louder, having followed the spectacle from the start and gained a better idea of the fighters still standing. He hears their cries, each lending advice to their chosen favorite. He stands up to see better. The tempest in his head seethes all the more, and for a moment his vision blackens. Some remedy is needed, and urgently at that. But just as Bengt is turning to search for a place where he might surreptitiously lighten his load, he hears a crack, one so loud it echoes across the grounds, followed by silence. It is a crack different from that of cudgel on cudgel; one uglier, swathed in flesh. He turns back. One of the fighters lies flat, felled by a blow violent enough to bring the rest to a standstill. It must have landed on his head. All of the fighters stand with their bats raised, looking on at the one who has fallen. Beside him Stina leaps to her feet and leans over the table on tiptoe, a look on her face like she has just seen an approaching army with weapons glinting. Before he can tell what's come over her she is off, almost toppling her chair. When he hears her cry at first he doesn't believe his ears, and then he, too, is on his feet, tottering in his paces, each step almost downing him.

"Magnus!"

By the time he reaches them, puffing and confounded, Stina is kneeling beside the fallen boy. Bengt misjudges his landing. He feels his knees scrape on the gravel and all but knocks her aside, but pays no heed. The garland he has been wearing flies off his head in a flurry of stalks. He tears the cloth from the boy's head; it can't be Magnus. It must be someone who looks like him, perhaps a child Sir Bengt sired down in the village whose existence has been hidden even from him. The wrappings are wet with blood, the face pale beneath all the red, but it's Magnus, sure enough; Magnus and no one else. How and why is beyond him. Bengt wipes the wet redness to one side with his bare hand to expose the wound, and makes an abject sound when he sees it: an open cleft in the temple that sends forth a gush of fresh blood with each heartbeat. He presses his fist hard against it to stem the flow, gasping for air enough to give his voice power.

"Help! Help us, damn you all to Hell!"

Before long they are at his side, his brothers and watchmen, more than one of whom skilled in the art of stemming blood. They see what has happened, and others take over while Sir Bengt helplessly looks on. The largest among them lifts Magnus up carefully in his arms while another takes over the pressing of the wound, and together they carry him up toward the great house. Bengt can't contain the nausea anymore. He takes a few aimless steps, then sinks to his knees. There, on all fours, he spews up until his belly is voided. For a few moments he sits there to ensure the cramps have eased, and when he turns his gaze upward it is just in time to feel the first drops of rain begin to fall. On his way back up to the pavilion he hears the coals in the firepans hissing in the downpour, and starts waving his arms to herd away his guests, those who have sat meekly in wait of what comes next. He ushers them up to the shelter of the keep. By the time the last of them is indoors his beautiful attire is soaked. He scarce notices.

THEY ALL CROWD into the great hall of the keep. The rain lends the place a particular air, one known to all: the heat of bodies in an unfair struggle with the wetness of garments, the smell of damp wool that hangs like a mist around them, an animal scent. What embers could be saved from the firepans are nurtured in new vessels to warm the hall, and each soon amasses its own circle of guests. Host and hostess are nowhere to be seen, and no one asks after them, for fear of the response that everyone dreads. They all saw the boy lying limp and white as a corpse, perhaps already slain. Kari Sharp knows her role and is ready to do what is required, knows whose help to enlist to see to it that her wishes are met. With a nudge in her husband's side she sends him off to tend to the hosting duties. The housefolk are ordered to retrieve everything from the pavilion that the downpour hasn't spoiled, while from the kitchen emerge the dishes that were yet to be served. She sees to it that new barrels of wine are brought up to lighten the mood, has cauldrons hung above the fires, and gets tables and benches in place to save what they can of this Midsummer of misfortune. Outside, the rain rumbles on in scorn, clattering so loudly against the roof of the keep some floors above that many choose silence over having to shout. Those who are close to the family do their best to keep up appearances, stoke what festive mood they can for the guests from afar, but their attempts can be no more than half-hearted, and few let themselves be fooled. Everyone is waiting. Whenever anyone steps through the door, all heads turn.

It is a long time before Sir Bengt returns, and when he does his face isn't easily read. In silence they watch him cross the floor, making straight for the beer barrel. He takes a mug and fills it until the foam spills over. Only once he has downed it does he turn around.

"The boy will live. The blow caught him badly, but it looked worse than it was."

A murmur of congratulations comes in response. Nils and Sir Bo cross the floor and are reunited with their brother in a three-way embrace. Relief airs the room. Many a guest who has been standing on restless feet allow themselves to sink down onto a bench, as weary as after a hard day's work. Nils lets his hand rest on his brother's shoulder.

"What got into the lad? Why would he stoop to fighting peasants, and in disguise at that?"

"Devil knows."

Sir Bengt sighs and shakes his head, pounds his fist against his thigh.

"Devil knows. But I'll tell you one thing, between brothers. Rarely have I had to lay a hand on Magnus. I can't even recall the last time it happened; it must have been when he was six or seven, when he cracked a bowl he'd been told not to touch and got a slap on the wrist so as not to forget. But this time I won't hold back. That boy's in for a flogging. Seventeen he may be, but this time he'll get such a drubbing he won't sit comfortably till Michaelmas. If my arm tires I'll have someone else take over. I'll cut the hazel first thing tomorrow."

Sir Bengt's eyes are black, and he stares blankly ahead while Nils and Bo exchange glances. Nils fills all their mugs. They knock them together without need of a toast, then Bengt takes a deep breath and stands up as tall as he can, facing his other guests.

"What's wrong with you all? Rain be damned! It's Midsummer's Eve, and my boy shall live. Let's be merry! Eat. Drink. The night is young."

Sir Bengt flings open his arms, as though he could coax joy from each of them just as easily as he herded them into his keep an hour before. Yet he is met with little response. For a while they all stand in silence. Then a lone voice is raised.

It is his blind brother, Knut Stensson. He sits on a stool by one of the firepans, his impassive face turned toward the middle of the room. Now he sings. None of the brothers have heard his voice in song in many a year, for they seldom gather and he is oft forgotten, left to steep in the darkness that is his alone, a stranger to all. But each and every one of them remembers the sound and is reminded of something they once well knew: their brother's world of shadows can also be a wellspring of beauty. Knut's memory is the stuff of legend, and no one tells stories like him. He knows every word of every song, be they childhood rhymes or solemn ballads, and grasps better than anyone else how words must be bent to yield emotion. His voice is strong still, its tone only deepened by the years. Out of their memories the song rises, returning them to their childhood, those years in distant Oakwood where they all shared a roof; a world that was small and safe and rich in dreams, with adventure waiting untried beyond its walls. The first verse Knut sings alone, but when the refrain begins the brothers join him, and then again when it returns, its words cast in new lights by each verse, endlessly shifting in meaning.

The minstrels are huddled in a corner of the hall. Until now they have kept out of the way, sat shivering with heads bowed over their instruments, unsure what to do with themselves. At the feast they had hardly struck up when the tournament cut short their playing, and then came the rain. They haven't dared play a note since, for anything merry might be taken for disdain, anything solemn for a portent. Now the most senior of them stands up, and, with a nod at his fellows, takes his symphonia and goes and sits alongside Knut. He listens in silence for another verse while gently swaying, as though needing his whole body to feel his way into the melody, then thumbs the string scarcely audibly to find the accords. At this, Knut slowly reaches out his hand and places it on the minstrel's shoulder, to make sure what he's hearing isn't a figment of his mind. Once sure, the minstrel turns the crank to sound the string, then plays a simple harmony using the keys. The other musicians take their places. The drummer starts caressing the skin of his drum in time, softly to start. The rebec player puts his bow to the strings and strikes up, and finally the flute joins in with its shrill call, finding the notes that fit in the higher spaces around Knut's voice and the drone of the symphonia. More and more people take up the refrain, women as well as men. Even the Germans attempt to sound the words but find them all too hard. One of the Hansa instead steps across the floor and offers Kari Sharp his hand. She pulls Bo with her, who brings Britta, too, and together they form a circle, to dance in the flickering light of smoldering torches. The circle widens, the tables and chairs shuffled toward the center of the hall to make space for it. All are singing, and as the chorus grows in strength Knut must raise his voice so that his lead can be heard. The last in the minstrels' ranks cracks a smile, for ever since they came indoors the piper has despaired that he would never play, but finally the music is loud enough to justify his instrument. He places the bag on his knee and blows it full, then wedges it under his arm to sift the air into chanter and drone. He runs his fingers over the holes in a playful trill. The dance gathers pace, legs and arms whirling, and those who aren't dancing turn the tables to drums under mugs and fists. With shaking arms Bengt Stensson hauls the beer barrel up onto his shoulder and pours for everyone who has thirst.

When the door opens he turns around, and many with him. Magnus is standing with Stina by his side, her hands on his shoulders, a stained wrapping around his head. He looks pale and flinty, yet with defiance in his eyes rather than regret. Sir Bengt heaves the barrel into another's arms, clears a path through the room as though there were no one there, lifts his son up in a bear hug, and places him down with a laugh on the table in the center of the circle for all to see. Then, clapping along to the beat, he shouts at Magnus to dance. Others join in the chant, and the song and din rise even more.

NIGHT COMES, TO lull the storm. Never in the year is the weather so fickle as today, that much they know of old. Midsummer's Eve is singular, so is the night to come, when the borders between the world of men and all that lurk in its fringes fray and soften. Existence itself runs its ruses. Now the sky clears, the puffs of cloud dispersing on the wind to reveal the stars in their thousands. In small groups the guests go to find their beds, made up here and there throughout the dwellings, wherever space could be bidden. The bishop requires his own room, as do a number of the other guests, but for the smaller folk beds of last year's hay have been made up in the barn. The maids and servants of the house wait in the courtyard by a fire, from which each one lights a torch to lead the guests right. Stina hears their laughter and cheery voices, and knows that Midsummer at Cuckoo's Roost came good this year, too, when they hosted more guests than ever since her father's day. In spite of it all. She stands by the entrance to the keep, at the top of the steps where the torches spread light from their holders, to thank each and every guest for attending and wish them a good night. But few remain. When she feels Kari Sharp beside her she wraps her arm around her shoulders.

"Without you all would be lost. Though I fear it's cost you what enjoyment you might have had. Thank you for all you've done for us, Kari, and forgive me."

Kari Sharp places her hand on Stina's, rests her head on her shoulder, and gives a sigh of contentment.

"If you say that you can hardly have seen me dancing."

Stina gives her a smile.

"Well. It's over now. All's well that ends well."

Kari stretches and yawns, but then rubs the sleep out of her eyes.

"It perhaps needn't be completely over. With God's help I may succeed in shaking some life into my husband yet."

Stina gives a feeble smile by return, then leans against the wall while watching Kari wave for a maid. Stina hears the hum of an unfamiliar melody, some shanty perhaps from Kari's childhood at sea. Shuffling steps echo through the hallway behind her, and Stina knows who it is long before Bengt Stensson clears his throat to make himself known. Feeling no need to turn, she goes on gazing at the fire still burning in the yard.

"Dear wife."

"Dear husband."

"What of Magnus? Is he in bed yet?"

"Ulf, who fought in Schleswig and has seen such wounds before, said that it's unwise for one stunned by a knock on the head to go to sleep too soon. Not that he believes Magnus is in any danger, but with a life so precious he'd sooner take no risks. Finn's keeping him awake. They've both gone down to the lake to bail water from the boats till morning. May that be punishment enough."

Stina senses Bengt's unease, can make it out in his restless body that fidgets from foot to foot.

"Has he said anything?"

"No."

Only now does she turn to look at him, crossing her arms as she does.

"I blame myself. I should have guessed what he was up to. Something troubles the boy, and it has done for a while. He speaks in his sleep, you know. When I struggle to sleep, it's happened that I've taken a turn through the corridors, heard him mumbling, and gone to his bed. But I've never lingered. It feels too much like listening in on something not intended for my ears."

Bengt nods.

"I've done as much. On occasion I lie awake, too. Now I wish one of us had listened; perhaps then this misfortune could have been averted. But don't take the blame on yourself, for half of it is mine. I know that's meager consolation."

"Let us do better in the future."

Sir Bengt lowers his head in accord, then places a hand on her arm in the silence that follows. They stand there. It has been a long time since Stina felt such a closeness to her husband, and his pliancy takes her by surprise. He leans in closer, now with more strength in his grip. On his breath she catches the fumes of his night's beers, and understands that he must have had more than she first thought.

"Stina, my heart, it was so long ago that you set off for Vadstena. Why don't we share a bed tonight?"

She feels her shoulders stiffen with aversion. Bengt lets go, sober enough in spite of it all not to put vain hope in a reply so slow in coming, more fain to accept rejection in silence. He scrapes his foot in the gravel that his guests have trailed inside.

"You won't mind if I lie with the milkmaid tonight?"

Stina lets him stand there for a moment, then tilts her head to one side.

"Have you ever asked her thoughts on the matter?"

※

Even long afterward she stands there, alone, watching the fire outside shrink to a glow, then fall. Nils Stensson comes next, and he gives her a stiff nod through the unease that has hung between them since they last spoke. He walks down the steps and out, and makes not for his bed but down toward the lake.

THE WATER LIES still. Only the odd ripple betrays currents at work beyond the eye's reach. The moon hovers a handsbreadth above the world's end, pouring silver on the edges of the clouds, which are mirrored on the lake. Finn and Magnus are squatting in the boats, knee-deep in liquid ingots, each wielding his own scoop. Nils follows the babble of water down toward the jetty. The sounds stop when his weight on the boards heralds his arrival. The lights from the fires still blind him, his eyes unused to darkness, and it takes him a few moments to tell them apart. Finn is the bigger of them, the older. Magnus is wearing a wrapping on his head, luminous in the moonlight, glinting like a crown. A good omen. Nils looks around for something with which to bail. He finds a pail swimming with stumps of old rope and steps onto Magnus's boat. Both brace with legs bent to keep balance.

"Nephew."

"Uncle."

"Sleep isn't calling me yet. I can just as well help you."

"They said the task was meant not only as punishment, but also to keep me on my feet, though I'd rather be asleep. The longer, the better."

"Then you'll have nothing against us having a little chat, too."

Nils sits down at the stern and makes a half-hearted attempt to bail a splash or two.

"You did well, considering. You must have practiced a lot."

Magnus gives him a long look before placing his scoop to one side and taking a seat opposite.

"Not enough."

"He helped you?"

Nils gestures at Finn, and Magnus nods in response.

"With another teacher things might well have gone differently. But a friend good enough to keep your secrets even though it could serve him better to give them up is a treasure worth far more."

Magnus looks over at Finn, who is still bailing water, and more forcefully at that, so that the sounds will drown out their conversation, excluding himself.

"What were you thinking, Magnus? What did you want to prove? You put a great deal at stake. In the end the price was no greater than you can afford, but you'll wear that scar till your dying day. And your mother and father who love you above all else will never look at you the same way."

At first Magnus glares down at his feet, and Nils sees little more than a sullen child vexed by his caper gone wrong. But then he sits up straight and looks Nils dead in the eye, calm and composed, all trace of childishness gone.

"Perhaps it's about time."

Nils picks up his pail and dips the brim into the water, making no haste.

"Perhaps we're not so different, you and I, though our childhood years could scarce be more unlike. You have but a sister, while I had brothers to spare. One can feel hemmed in for many reasons. For me it was their company, that I could hardly be alone. And yet I found a freedom in numbers, for among the sons of Sten I was but the sixth. For you it's the other way around. You have plenty of space, freedom enough to sneak off and train as a swordsman with no one to notice. But as the only son, you must shoulder not only the entirety of your parents' love, but the weight of the future to boot. All of this will one day be yours."

Nils pauses in his work, sets the pail down on his lap, and leans forward.

"At Oakwood Father taught us that all power is born of land. An invisible crop. Tell me, Magnus, have you heard what people call me when I'm not around?"

Magnus hesitates before replying.

"Landless Nils."

Nils nods in agreement with a smirk.

"They think they're naming a fate I didn't choose for myself. Listen to me, Magnus: Power isn't born of land. Power is an entity unto itself. A willful creature, one reluctant to pledge itself to an unfamiliar master. When it falls from one man's hands, it drops into the hands of he who happens to be by his side."

Magnus doesn't reply, simply sits there quietly listening, and Nils feels a flutter take root in his belly, like the wings of a butterfly; a promise from a future in a tongue he doesn't fully comprehend, but whose meaning he nevertheless gleans. His nephew has shown his courage, and now he is showing him something else, too, following his every word without confusion, patient enough to wait for their meaning to become clear. Nils leans over the edge of the boat and runs his hand through the tepid water, letting it sift through his fingers. He takes up a handful in his cupped palm and sees the moon itself shimmer within it before letting it fall back whence it came.

"My brothers tell me you fly a falcon."

"She's a goshawk."

"And a good life she has, too, no? She's beautiful, and in the safety of the cage not a jot of muck can stain those fine feathers of hers. She'll fly only at the behest of her keeper, and she's blind as long as her hood's kept on, a bell around her talons to more easily restore her to captivity. Every time she gets a taste of freedom she's enticed back into safekeeping with tender meat, so voracious that she can but choose the meal that requires the least effort. Once fed, she goes back to her cage. Her life is good, certainly, with little cause for complaint, but what do you think it is that your hawk wants most?"

Not for a moment does Magnus Bengtsson hesitate in his reply.

"She wants to fly by her own free will."

Nils puts the pail to one side and stands up, then waits with legs astride for the vessel that he has disturbed to come back to stillness on the waves. Once it does, he steps back onto the jetty.

"You'll hear no praise from me while your father and mother are in earshot, but let me tell you now: That was a brave thing you did, Magnus. You fought with heart. A few more years and not one of them would have withstood you. Good night now, nephew. I shan't risk your health by depriving you of any more work. Hold out through the night, and let's see if tomorrow proves itself worth the vigil."

A MILD SUN SIFTS down through the summer leaves, green and gold by turns. Bengt Stensson places one foot before the other, carefully, so as not to betray his presence on parched twigs or last year's leaves. After each step he stops, casting a net spun with his every sense as far as he is able. He knows that they are there, but he can't yet discern them. His forest is home to copious deer, and he knows the herd well enough to tell one animal from the next. Occasionally he will steal a glimpse of the prize stag, albeit seldom during a hunt, standing atop a hillock, outlined by the light of the rising or setting sun, his crown of antlers worthy of a king's head. For as long as Sir Bengt has been master of Cuckoo's Roost the same stag has ruled his herd, still mighty enough to fend off challengers in autumn, when strength is to be tried and the strongest proven; when their bellows echo through the forest along with the crack of antlers clashing.

In his hands he holds his brother Nils's crossbow, quickly accustomed to its unfamiliar heft. Old bolts have been summoned from his own armory and hastily cut to size for the new weapon. The quiver hangs from his belt, stuffed with moss to prevent the shafts from clinking. Nils has taken care of everything, with Sir Bo at his side, and together they have mustered many a man from the bishop's retinue to further augment Sir Bengt's own party, who know the forest as well as any man: how to navigate every ancient oak and boulder; all the trails worn by wildlife; the sites where the deer turn up mud to wallow in for coolness and safety. The beaters are enough in number to sweep around the whole forest, and he can hear them from afar. They make themselves known with wood on wood, thrashing bushes with rods to drive on the game. A better chance than this he'll never see again.

Now he catches their scent, weighty and sharp, alluring and repellent at once. All around lie their droppings. They were here not long ago, and soon he can see their traces all around him: hoof marks in moist ground; tufts of fur on the branches' barbs. Large animals they are, and many in number, but their world only in part overlaps with that of man, for like ghosts they make no noise in their movements, and it's nigh on impossible to set eyes on them until you're already upon them. Bengt stands still in wait, turning his head this way and that, the better to hear. There, perhaps—a single breath, fast and heavy. Soon he sees her, a hind, lying on the edge of the clearing. Young, but without a calf. Perhaps she will bear her first this autumn. From a distance her eyes are black, shrouded by long eyelashes, animate. But she's not the game he covets, and slowly he backs away, choosing another path toward the clearing, to near what he knows awaits him.

It takes time, but Sir Bengt is a seasoned hunter, and he knows that without patience there is naught to be won. Soon he finds himself rewarded. The trees part and behind them lie hinds in their dozens, and there above them he stands, the stag, his crown turning this way and that as he tries to determine where the danger lurks. But he can't choose one direction, for the threat is advancing in a ring, and for the first time in his life the old beast is powerless. He can but stand still, await what is coming, and hope that it will pass him unnoticed.

For the hundredth time Sir Bengt turns his cheek to search for the wind and is once again assured that his scent won't be carried ahead of him, betraying his presence. The rest lies in the hands of higher powers. If the wind changes they will bolt, beaters or no. With a silent prayer he steps closer—slowly, slowly—until he is near enough to begin raising his weapon. Never has he lifted a heavier burden, inch by inch, and suddenly it is as though he is holding an unfamiliar object, its purpose unknown. He blinks foolishly to counter the sweat that is streaming from his forehead, feels his heart pounding in his throat, and has to remind himself of how the bolt is fired. He slowly fumbles to prepare, here in the backwaters of the course of time itself. Once everything is ready it is as though the stag already knows, as though he can feel Death's finger choosing the fatal point on his fur-clad skin. He turns his head, looks Sir Bengt straight in the eye, and gives a deep snort. For a moment Bengt is stupefied before the stag's majesty, never previously beheld this close: heavy as a warhorse, his neck wider than Bengt's own waist, his crown of antlers branching off into spike upon spike. For the first time Sir Bengt feels fear eclipse his own titillation. This beast is not like the rest; if Bengt misses his only shot and the stag lowers his antlers, his own life will be at risk.

An alien sound dispels the moment, and Sir Bengt totters on unsteady legs, unable to fathom what he is hearing and seeing, certain that his chance has slipped from his grasp. Behind the stag something happens; a crimson bird takes flight and whirrs off through the leaves on the other side of the grove, faster than the eye can follow. The stag takes a step closer, and then one more, and only then does he bend his knee and let his crown sink, though his back legs are still straight. Bengt looks around for the other hunter who must have stolen his glory, but there is none to be seen, and when he lowers the crossbow to relieve his tense shoulders he sees that the groove is empty, the string slack. It was his own bolt that flew, running straight through the stag and out the other side. Now the wound is revealed in coursing streams of blood, more than should be possible. Strength fails the stag, his hind legs can no longer bear him, and when they buckle his body twists until he is lying on his side. Bengt staggers in among the trees, taking no notice of the hinds in flight. He kneels down beside the old creature and places a shaking hand to the veins in his throat, which bulge like ropes yet, while the heart still pounds. The mortal wound is gaping, even more so on the back where the bolt took flight than on the breast where it won its entrance. Life fades in the eyes of the stag, and he blows his last breath onto his assassin's hands. Bengt sits there unmoving, tears on his cheeks of sorrow and of happiness, of joy at life and awe before death, until the beaters reach him and his brothers lift him up onto his feet with cries of triumph.

᎒᎔

Six men must cluster around a bier to convey the forest's king, his legs bound to a freshly stripped birch that is long enough to fit them all beneath its load. To lug the stag all the way back to Cuckoo's Roost intact is beyond them; instead they must make a stop at the nearest farm. Bengt delays the butchery, laments being forced to see the kill of his life stripped of its beauty. Anyone and everyone who can be summoned must first see him, feel him, lay a finger on his crown's every spike; must impress the moment so firmly in their memories that they can recount it to children and grandchildren to come. Back in the forest men are still searching for the bolt that flew, to hang on Sir Bengt's high seat upon their return to Cuckoo's Roost.

A glowing bed of fire is lit in the yard between the log cabins. The farmer fetches what drinks he can muster and sends word to the neighboring farm for more, while those who are skilled in the task set to flaying and butchering the stag. They gut and retrieve from it all that can be saved, and find there alone food enough to feed man and guests for a week, even two. Soon enough they'll be sick and tired of venison. Most of the meat will have to be salt-cured for winter. But first a feast for the hunting party of the cuts best devoured fresh. All in the best of spirits. Bengt's shoulder is sore from all the claps and hugs, his cheeks red from all the praise, his voice hoarse from his endless tales of the shot that flew, and with each new telling of the story he hones its phrasing, establishing the right pauses and melody, well aware that this is a story that he will come to repeat until his dying day. Only later, once everyone is full and the drink has tempered the blood that earlier ran hot, on that summer's night by the rattling glow of the fire, do Nils and Sir Bo exchange glances, stand up, and take a seat on either side of their brother, whereupon Nils chooses his words as only Nils can.

Sir Bengt seeks out Stina at Cuckoo's Roost the next morning, loath and dragging his feet. Having washed on his return, he smells like a lord again, much as he misses the scents of the hunt, of blood and smoke and moss. Dutifully she listens when he tells her about his game, but with her as his sole audience he finds his words fall flatter than back in his circle of friends. It is as though the stag itself shrinks in his memory, his feat instantly diminished. Larger looms the melancholy that already weighed heavy enough.

"I want to talk about Magnus."

Only now does he have her full attention, and the sharpness of her gaze makes him all but recoil.

"My Stina, I've been thinking. How much we've loved that boy, you and I, from the very start, like a gift from above. Never a thing have we denied him. Others send their sons to be raised by firmer hands in the homes of strangers, or to the south, to be apprenticed beyond this kingdom's borders. But we didn't, and I don't regret that, not for an instant. For seventeen years and more Cuckoo's Roost has been his. I'd like to think it an upbringing as good as any. But perhaps it's time he saw more of the world."

Her face divulges nothing; she simply watches him with cold eyes, waiting. Bengt feels his cheeks flush, and curses his own weakness in tasks such as this. He hears his voice stammer when he goes on.

"Look what he did. He's no child anymore. Manhood is upon him."

She crosses her arms.

"This isn't coming from you alone. Others have put words in your mouth."

"That doesn't make them any less true."

He gives up, never crafty enough to keep secrets from her. His head lowers as he confesses.

"I've been speaking with Nils and Bo. They want to send Magnus north. To Engelbrekt."

For a moment she is speechless, a silence of a new kind.

"You know it yourself, Stina: what one man thinks, so does another. Far more houses than just ours have been put out by King Eric's follies, and they are just as weary as we are of having to bow down to the Germans and the Danes. The nobility will rally around the northmen's banner, band with them in the hopes of winning back all that they have lost. But we can gain ourselves an advantage. Nils has been north and met Engelbrekt in the flesh. He swears that if Magnus goes to him and offers him his service, Engelbrekt won't turn him away—he couldn't, even if he wanted to. This is Magnus Bengtsson of blue and gold, from Cuckoo's Roost, he whose blood courses unbroken from the Kings over the Headland, from Saint Birgitta and Saint Eric himself. Having a squire of blue and gold at his right hand gives Engelbrekt Engelbrektsson all the dignity his campaign has lacked; overnight he becomes more than a simple rabble-rouser. And us? Not only will we gain a pair of ears in the tents and halls where every discussion is being held, but perhaps even a voice, too."

His words give out. From Stina there comes nothing, least of all the wrath he was braced to meet.

"Nils has nothing but praise for Magnus. A willful youth, certainly, but no one with greatness in reach should be lacking in that quality. The boy doesn't curry favor with others, he knows to keep his own counsel and has courage in spades. Better sense may well come with the years. It's Nils's guess that Magnus and Engelbrekt could see eye to eye, should destiny so will it."

Without a word Stina turns her back on him, and the arms that she has crossed climb higher to embrace her shoulders. She walks away, toward the dwellings, leaving him to call after her raspingly, hoarse of voice after all the previous day's crowing.

K ARI SHARP COMES to her next, knocking at the door that Stina has kept firmly shut behind herself.

"Don't sit here alone while the sun's shining, Sister. Let's walk, you and I, far from men and all their trappings."

Together they cross the bridge and follow the road up into the forest, where shade and coolness reign. Stina knows the land. Soon she turns onto paths so narrow that only familiar feet will find their way, and before long the trees cede to a clearing where a summer meadow holds sway, awash with sparkling flowers. Kari stops at its edge, sighing at its beauty. But beside her Stina has seen something else. She walks through the flowers and ears to an area where the grass has been stamped flat, around a puppet of twigs raised on a post.

"It's been a long time since I was here. This was my childhood refuge. I should have known Magnus would make it his own. This is where he trained."

Kari draws level with her, sees the puppet's wooden limbs marred by slashes and pricks. Stina points farther into the forest while holding her other hand out to Kari.

"Come, I'll show you something."

At the bottom of a slope waits a stream, a chain of silver forged through the forest, clean and clear. Stina lets go of Kari's hand and crouches, then cups a fistful of water in her hands and raises it to her mouth.

"Try some. The water's good. It springs straight from the rock farther up among the trees."

Kari does as she is told and finds Stina's words to be true. The water is sweet and cool, with a smack of fresh earth. She makes a bowl with her hands and dips her face into it before sitting down beside Stina on a log beneath a gap in the foliage where the sunlight falls through. She waits for Stina to break the silence.

"It would've been better had he more time to practice."

"What is it about Magnus, Stina? Why have you kept him at home so long, you and Bengt?"

Stina closes her eyes, turning her face up to the sun with a long sigh.

"I was eleven when I saw my father buried. A malady took root in his chest one winter and his coughs hacked all the worse, clawing blood up out of his throat that he would spit into a cup. He lost all appetite, lay in later and later in what everyone could soon tell was his deathbed in the making. One matter alone was he keen to attend to: his daughter's marriage, her security and keep. Bengt Stensson of blue and gold was his choice, a boy of good blood, with silver in abundance to fund his pretensions. But he made it clear to me that my wishes came first, and that the choice would be mine the day he, Bengt, came to meet us. He was twelve. A boy who did what he could to stretch himself taller than his legs allowed. Plain of looks, plain of speech."

She nods downstream, where the slope turns steeper and the water gathers pace.

"We were young enough to be allowed to play together. I brought him here. He whooped at the sight of the water, no longer a young squire but a mere boy, and he was soon barefoot with his tunic rolled up. He wanted to whittle me a boat from bark as a gift. He found a piece of pine and carved a hull, then used the tip of his knife to gouge out a hole for the mast. But he was far too eager, and I'm sure having me as an audience flustered him. Few have launched as many boats here as I, and I could see well enough that he was making his ship too narrow, his mast too big, a clumsily rigged maple leaf for a sail. It was to be a short maiden voyage. She started to list, then toppled and capsized. Disappointed by his failure, he suddenly tired of the forest and wanted to go back, sulky, quiet, and shamefaced. I had to show him the way, for he couldn't remember it himself.

"Once Bengt Stensson had gone I was shown into my father's chamber. Increasingly it was as though a ghastly weight was tugging at his features; as if his eyes, the sides of his mouth and cheeks were all collapsing in upon themselves, melting down toward the floor. As if the grave itself hungered for him and was sucking him down toward it. When he caught sight of me he lit up and smiled. A warm glow of hope blazed in those beloved features beset by tremors. He didn't need to ask his question. Do you know what it was that I told him, Kari?"

"What?"

"That Bengt Stensson of blue and gold was the best and most able boy whom ever I'd met, and that I wished for nothing more than to be his wife."

Kari laughs.

"Sorry."

Stina shrugs.

"The promise was made that we would stand before the priest five years later. And with that Father could die with a smile upon his blue lips. Bengt and I met again at the altar. He was a young man by then, though not greatly changed."

She squints at the gnats dancing above the stream, now in one shape, now another.

"Father had so dearly longed for a son. But he got only me, and I had to be both son and daughter in one. Above all else I longed for that which my father had been denied. A son. Perhaps I would see my father in him, returned to earth clothed in new flesh."

Above them wings clap. A pigeon makes its sighing flight, scared by some predatory bird or misgiving.

"No children came. Many years we were forced to wait, though we did our duty as man and wife, and it wasn't always to my pleasure. But in the end a seed took root and my stomach began to grow. I was so sure it was the son I felt I'd been promised, the one I'd fought for. But in the end it was a daughter. Bengt was often away on King Eric's errands then, and I was left alone with the little one. She drank so much; my milk quickly ran dry, and we had to send for others, stout lasses from nearby villages, unfailing as cows just back from pasture. The babe never lay sure in my arms, was never calm against my shoulder. She would scream all night long. When it became too much I fled the nursery to shed tears of shame. Me, who had flourished in all else before. I was the lady of the house, with maids and old women alike used to heeding my needs, and without me having to voice it they grasped what it was that ailed me. The girl was never left alone, and someone was always kept at hand to keep the cradle rocking. No one reproached me, though perhaps that would have been better. Their silence spoke well enough. I could never bring myself to return their looks of wonder and pity, however much they stung my skin. Instead I threw myself into matters of the household. I made sure that few estates could compare to Cuckoo's Roost: our farmers satisfied but never headstrong, those incapable of working their land quickly replaced with someone more worthy; the accounts kept in order so that it was clear for all to see that each year had surpassed the one that came before; the pantry always stocked for winter with that which can't be found before spring, but which brings great comfort in the darkness that cloaks half the year. Sir Bengt may have been the law-speaker around here, but everyone was well aware of what was to my credit, that at Cuckoo's Roost it was the Lady Kristina who presided over matters great and small, and that she was both exacting and just. Still, I'd have sooner felt that love in my breast, love of the kind that forgives all. But my prayers went unanswered. At least with that child."

Sir Bengt came home with the spring, in good spirits for once. In the south, the newfound peace still reigned between King Eric and the Counts of Holstein, brittle though it was. Sir Bengt had been there to pour wax on the treaty and stamp his seal, and through the negotiations with the Hanseatic League he had been able to forge new ties that benefited both himself and those of his brothers with privateers in the Baltic. For the moment all was good, and if the peace were to last just another few years, then the kingdom would be able to thrive, and with it his family; nor would his time at home be spent galloping around trying to fleece the farmers of additional taxes to fund more wars, which only ever led to court sessions and seizures. And so the king had granted him permission to return home and see to his own household. Sir Bengt arrived covered in road dust with an unruly beard and went straight to the bathhouse to wash. He emerged a different man. Healthy, slim from all the hours on horseback, his skin tanned by the sun and wind. It was like getting a stranger home in her husband's place. She, too, was a different woman from the one he had left, the baby weight gone, her flesh firm. He had just turned thirty, she a few years his junior, each with appreciative eyes for the other, as surprised by themselves as by finding those feelings reciprocated. They found each other that summer, delighted in sharing a bed for perhaps the first time. Two good months. Then King Eric returned to the battlefield and toppled Castle Glambek's ramparts with cannon fire, resuming the war that would rage on for decades, its undulating front shifting now north, now south over the most fertile of soils ever seen, nourished by young men in the hundreds of thousands having spilled their heart's blood, yet where only weeds could grow. She would never see her husband returned to her the way he was that spring, but as the trees' crowns yellowed it became clear that their lust had borne fruit, and by Epiphany she lay in the birthing bed for the second time. Finally he came, her son, and the very instant she took his little body in her arms and looked down into his cloudy newborn eyes, she knew that this time everything would be different.

She knew well enough that Sir Bengt was keen to name his firstborn son Sten, after his father. *Stone.* A good, strong name, one on which to lay the foundations of greatness, one that had served the house well for as long as anyone could remember. Sir Sten's memory would likely still live on when the lad would come to set out into the world on his own. But duties that couldn't be denied forced Bengt to leave his seat beside the birthing bed empty, and when the babe was carried to the priest Stina chose another name. Magnus. Magnus, after her own father, the only man she had loved. Magnus, a flame lit by a sudden desire, now a beacon to warm her autumn years, the joy and pride of a father who had long feared he would never pass on the name of his house, and had instead had to content himself with the hope of his brothers faring better. An heir to Cuckoo's Roost and its vast estates.

"You should have seen him when he was younger, Kari. Like a vessel turned to hold all of our love. Such a beautiful son, well built and fine of feature. A prince of legend to breathe life into the world that was ours, filling that which had previously stood empty: building huts in the forest, a dam to stem the stream, nooks enough to play hide-and-seek in the keep's shadows. He was a comfort to us when the fire that we had once felt for each other proved difficult to nurse back to life. As the years passed, we could look upon Magnus and in him sometimes glimpse the parts of one another that we liked best. When I was at Vadstena the mere thought of him was a priceless treasure, his absence a pain in my chest."

Kari places her hand on her shoulder.

"But he's something else, too, Magnus. Beyond you and Bengt. The boy has a will of his own. You can see that in the clearing, and you saw it at Midsummer. How many hours must it have taken for him to trample that grass flat? How much resolve to stand on his own with a cudgel among older lads? His wings have grown big enough to reach the sides of his cage. Sooner or later you'll have to let him spread them."

Stina turns away to hide her tears.

A LONE AGAIN, STINA moves as though through a fog, her senses deadened. The world seems distant, close as it may be. Up on the ramparts she finds herself a seat, a planed board propped between two stones, and there she sits for a long time, alone in thought. She rests her palm and ear against the wall behind her, the stones warmed by the sun, stones that sing of her own blood, of her father and grandfather and great-grandfather under the lion and the lily. She has always felt the firmness of these walls at her side here, grounding her with its silent promise of stability, of permanence. A lie that she has been fool enough to believe until now. Those who raised these foundations have gone to their graves every one, but the stones still stand, as indifferent as if they had been left to brood in the earth, unmoved by humankind and its anguish. The keep may well stand strong and still, but all the while her own little life is quaking. All now falters that once stood firm.

By and by she stands up, walks down to the dwellings and the outlying buildings, and observes the housefolk at work. Midsummer is passed, and all that was brought out must now go back away, the effort just as great. They bustle everywhere, each one occupied, seeming to grasp what must be done without her. Out in the meadow a group of men are cutting down the garlanded pavilion, the ones best suited for heavy loads, who are otherwise to be found forging iron, felling trees, and hauling stones. One of the men towers above the rest, and she knows his name. Lars. Many believe him to be mute, but Stina knows better. He merely prefers silence. With robust arms he unearths one of the supporting posts, raising it from its hole though it must weigh more than himself, then tips it over and walks on placidly to the next. He sees her out of the corner of his eye as she observes their work, but knows to hold himself in check. He waits a long while before walking over to the watering trough to drink and rinse the sweat from his face, then sends her a stolen glance. She gives him her nod, undiscernible to the rest. He needs no more to understand. She receives no response, and both turn and go back to their business.

It is late when she comes to him. He lives alone, of his own choosing, in the hut he built himself down by the forest's edge. She knows the way, needs only the summer night to light her path. A single flame stands in the window to guide her, blown out the moment she scratches on his door. The darkness is a part of their silent contract, perhaps in bygone times out of a sense of guilt, but also in the knowledge that that which is deprived one sense is made up for by others. When unseeing they are split from their personage, can become all the more themselves. The cloak slides off her shoulders, and her tunic joins it when she passes it over her head. Neither of them speaks: he seldom does, and there is nothing that she wants to say. She wears her hair loosened from its bands, shakes it down over her back. She hears him before her, and when she reaches out to touch him she meets bare flesh, warm. He is no young man, albeit younger than she, but he is of another ilk, born of a world that is foreign to her own. He steps toward her, places his big hands on her hips, searching for her bosom. With caresses they give form to each other in the shadows. He strokes the years off her, making her young once more, young and just as desirable as she has ever been. He smells of work, of earth and timber, of toil under sun and rain. Stina lets her hand follow his flat stomach downward, where his manhood is ready and waiting. From there she leads him to the stamped-earth floor, where the clothes that have fallen make them a bed, to a play of shifting forms that lasts the night long, one as old as time itself yet with each instance new. What sounds escape their lips are words from a language older than man's.

Dawn finds her in the bathhouse, alone in the dim glow that only the fire imparts. She has often asked the servants to light her a fire at night, as a refuge should sleep fail her, and it has been many a year since anyone found this habit unusual. On the hot stones sits a simmering cauldron of water to mix with the cold for washing, and with it she rinses everything off: his lingering scent, and her own beneath. She pours what is left over the stones, and the steam scours her skin even cleaner. Outside everyone is asleep, the girl who had tended the bathhouse hearth having also been sent to bed. Tears spill down Stina's cheeks, tears of a kind that she has never known before. The pleasures of the flesh are fresh in her mind, but this time she had sought them not only for their own sake but rather to put a thought to rest. Now, afterward, she finds the thought proven. She doesn't need them anymore, the men. Not in the way that she once did. And while she has enjoyed their bodies, there was always more to it than that. A longing for affirmation in their presence, a strange urge from deep within her own being. She won't bleed anymore, never again. Is it a wound that has closed and can now heal? How she had feared this time before it arrived. But now that it is here she finds that she can welcome it, that it brings with it new possibilities and may even allow her to be another than the person she has been, one that she herself can shape instead of allowing others to cast. With change comes many things, perhaps freedom among them.

For a long time yet Stina sits on the bench. Abbess Ingegerd comes to her in her thoughts, and nor does she seem so frightening anymore. A simple woman with simple woes, she, too, fettered to the world of men, and, nun though she was, incapable of breaking those chains. What does a father's name matter in the end, when he has long since gone to earth? Ingegerd's thirst for love was the scourge of her life, a bitterness fomented until it rose up and out of the grave. Just as dead now as Stina will one day be. Nils was right; her curse must be proven powerless, and in that instant it will shatter like a troll in the rays of the sun. Where once there was nothing, nothing shall return.

And Magnus—Magnus first, last, and always. Her beautiful boy, marked by another's cudgel, marred now with a blemish for evermore. Even in his rebellion she finds cause to love him. Kari was right; he must be his own now, claim himself, and seek fortune in the world that awaits him. As must she.

Dry and dressed, she makes for Sir Bengt's bed, where she perches until he wakens, listening to his snores, his restless tosses and turns. It takes a while for him to become aware of her presence and blink the sleep from his eyes, and when he asks his uncertain question it is with a voice that barely carries.

"Stina?"

So small he seems now, Bengt Stensson, laid bare in a tangle of wrinkled linen. And yet he is the father of her son, the man she chose. For the son that she has, she knows that that choice was the right one. Laboriously he raises his body, his paunch heavy. Sitting beside her in his nakedness, he clears his throat.

"Troubled dreams I've had, my Stina. I've been thinking. You're right. This morning I'll go to my brothers and tell them to get sons of their own to send north for their schemes. They took me in with fair words, knowing exactly how to put me in a pliable temperament. The stag, the crossbow. Beer."

"Magnus will go to Engelbrekt."

He blinks drowsily at her while her words gather meaning. Then he shuts his eyes and heaves a great sigh, entreaty in his voice.

"Is that your wish, Stina? Are you sure?"

Ever since Midsummer's Eve, Bishop Knut has lain awake at night, tossing and turning on his bed without catching a wink of sleep. Though age has long since cut his nights short, it has never been as bad as this. Instead of infirmity and affliction, it is the anxiety that now pierces the awls in his gut, ever since his nephews made him party to their schemes. Bo is enough like his father in mind and temperament to be his specter. Bengt, too, shares a number of the same traits, though he hides them better. But Nils, Nils Stensson, he is the worst, that snake, for in him Knut sees something alien, something worse, something he cannot fully comprehend and yet cannot keep at bay.

Knut was made bishop more than four decades before, the very summer Saint Birgitta was laid to rest in her gilded box, his appointment a means of strengthening his father and brother's chokehold on the kingdom. Six hundred and sixty florins was the cost of his office, for no bishop is given the blessing of the Pope and cardinals without paying his due. Parts of the debt were paid on his behalf, but much was left to him to bear. Once the crosier was in his hands he held the keys to the church's coffers, and what choice did he have but to plunder from them enough to acquit himself? Only later did he see that that was precisely his father and brother's aim from the start; that, having embarked upon his bishophood with embezzlement, he could never be tempted into loyalty to the church from which he had stolen. What property and land he had been given as his own lay near the coast, and it needed fortifying to withstand the threat of the pirates of the Victual Brothers. Every bulwark and trench came at a high cost, several sums of which obtained in the borderlands between borrowing and theft. And then came Queen Margaret, that she-dragon, bidden by his brother. The foremost among thieves, she was, taking everything and everyone to task, not least the church. Knut found himself trapped between two iron wills: on the one hand, the clergy's fury at seeing the Lord's alms packed off Denmark, the threat of his own removal never far away; and on the other, his blood relations on Margaret's side, greedy to soon be rewarded with their share of the spoils. It is a gauntlet that he has been running his whole life, and now he has reached his seventy-fifth year. Many a year has it been since he met a man of his own age. And in those years he has learned never to commit his name to paper, never to make a firm promise, never to step too far toward one side that he can no longer claim ties to the other. This has served him well. All the old schemers have gone to the grave, their puffed-up ambitions rarely satisfied. Old Gryphon, his father, his brother. Knut wishes that he could have found some satisfaction in their defeats while reading their requiems, but the truth was he wasn't even capable of that, for in their pride had lain the only security he had ever known. Cocksure and enterprising they had lived their lives, until the moment their folly mined the ground beneath their feet so thin it cracked. His inheritance? Doubt and nothing more.

And now that restless blood courses through the next generation. Their turn to set their sights high and grasp for the crown. Knut curses the fate that saw him survive his peers, wishes almost that he could be dead himself, cold and safe under heavy fathoms of soil. Yet there is something else at play, too, and that scares him all the more: that tickle of ambition and possibility, of his own desire. Perhaps they will see it through this time. Perhaps this venture will be met with success, success for blue and gold, and that with his help. Just think, then, of the looks on all of their faces—Bo Bosson, Sten Bosson, the Gryphon, and Queen Margaret herself—when he meets them in whatever afterlife the Lord has prepared.

Still, the fear torments him, likewise the knowledge that ambition has led many another to ruin and a futile death. And the young, they have so many years ahead of them, years to put right their mistakes, years to try again, and at that with better odds. Knut knows that he is not long of this earth, as impossible as the thought may seem. In his eyes he alone is putting the most at risk, for the time that he has is all that remains him, every moment thus worth all the more.

"I've come to thank you for your hospitality."

Bishop Knut has come up to the keep to take leave of his nephew, climbing the mound and every step on aching knees. Over these Midsummer days he has spent many an hour with his nephews in the chamber, offering his counsel. All the men the house has at its command must be rallied and sent where they are most needed. They must anticipate every conceivable development and agree as to how each of them would do best to act, what orders will be sent when necessity demands and how. Knut's road leads him back to Linköping, where his bastion and diocese lie, and from where the church must be bent to his will. That much will not be difficult. Of the kingdom's seven bishops he is the eldest and enjoys high rank, and King Eric has already plowed much of that furrow for him: Ever since the Archbishop of Uppsala rejoined their fathers two years earlier, church and crown have been beset by quarrels over who should succeed him. Each party has pestered the Pope with official letters and entreaties that the verdict be declared in their favor. Knut has held off putting his own seal to paper, as always wise enough to endeavor to see which way the wind is blowing first. Therein lies the difficulty of his current task: to wield an invisible sway, take risks while sitting safely. So far nothing is decided; King Eric may soon be made aware of his betrayal and hit back hard against the traitors, and, if given the choice, a natural death is always to be preferred over the executioner's axe.

Knut clears his throat, casting into his old-man voice all the confidence he by no means possesses.

"I harbor good hopes for our cause."

Bengt Stensson rolls his eyes, at home in his role of doubter among the brothers.

"Good thing one of us does."

"Before I depart, there is one other matter, Bengt, that I should like to raise with you, and not only as my nephew, but also as the law-speaker in these parts."

The bishop lowers his voice, maintaining his grip on Bengt's arm.

"Some time ago I sent a man north on business, the thrust of which I'll leave unsaid. Olof was his name. He was expected back in Linköping before Midsummer. He was conveying with him a large sum, all the income yielded from his travels."

Bengt's curiosity is piqued, as is always the case when silver is mentioned.

"How much?"

"Silver pieces, pennings and örtugs, and all those other peculiar coins that change hands in this kingdom now that our own are sent off to the king's coffers in Copenhagen. To the value of a thousand marks."

Such magnitude calls for a moment of gravity. Bengt wonders what kind of webs his uncle has spun that allow him to send men upcountry empty-handed and expect them to return bowlegged under the weight of such fortunes."

"How can you know so exactly?"

"Traveling alone with such sums isn't without its dangers. At every church that Olof passed he left word, to be sent forth to Linköping as soon as a cart with a respectable driver passed heading south. The idea was exactly that, that should anything befall him we'd know where to start looking. A rider came to me earlier today, sent by one of my clerics. The last letter arrived on Midsummer's Day, but no Olof, and had all gone as expected he should have arrived long before the letter itself."

"From where was it sent?"

"Some hole by the name of Askersund. I came here by the same road, but had no cause for concern, and the parish priest's nose was so far up my smallclothes that I was disinclined to extend my visit any longer than strictly necessary."

Bengt rubs his beard while pondering the matter.

"This Olof, is he to be trusted? Such a treasure would prove a formidable temptation. Perhaps he sent word from Askersund before setting off in another direction entirely?"

Bishop Knut gives his nephew a cold look.

"You've known me all your life, and you know well enough that I sprouted in the same grove as the Gryphon and your own father, two of the wiliest foxes to ever afflict this henhouse of a kingdom. Have I ever given you cause to take me for a fool?"

Bengt need not respond.

"Naturally I had assurances. I would have entrusted no man with such a task without ample assurance. Take my word that he can be trusted."

"Well, perhaps a tree root ensnared his boot, and now he's lying at an inn with his leg in a splint."

"Would this splint prevent him from sending others with word? Besides, my men were under orders to make inquiries on the way here. I'm telling you, the man is gone. He left Askersund, never to reach Motala. Between the two the forest grows large and lawless. The coins are gone, too. And, while the man is easily replaced, it would seem we'll be needing that silver now more than ever. Once the church has made our cause its own, that sum could arm many a soldier, or pay an avaricious bailiff out of his castle."

Sit Bengt gives his beard a tug.

"I'll see what I can do."

"Swear that this will remain between us. No one else. My other nephews least of all."

After a reluctant nod Bengt makes the sign of the cross, then kisses the fingers that have just sanctified him in length and breadth. Knut impresses upon him the inviolability of his vow with severe eyes.

"Good. Then farewell. Where's Magnus? I'm the eldest among us yet living, and I should like to share a few parting words of wisdom before he's sent off into the wolf's den."

⁂

Together they walk a slow ring around the walls of the keep, Knut with a gnarled hand on Magnus's shoulder for support.

"Do you know the old tale? Three nobles lost in a forest, where they happen upon three dead men. *As you are now, so were we once; as we are now, so shall you become.* I could say the same thing to you now."

Knut stops, halting the boy, too. He takes in his nephew's son. Pleasing to the eye, the boy bears all of his father's merits but all the more of his mother's. The wound he sustained is already exposed, to better dry out. It runs along his hairline, and will soon be scarce visible at all. The boy who stands before him shall soon learn what it means to be used for others' purposes, as all are who are young, weak, or gullible and in possession of that in which others place value. Just as he was, once. The Wheel of Fortune lets you try your hand at all walks of life; first the victim, then the violator. Knut should be too old for surprise, but he can't help himself. So this, too, shall be taken from him before the end: the right to blame those who stand guilty before him. Knut sighs, for a moment humbled by the wealth of life's cruelties.

"Much have we in common, you and I. I, too, was once a young man in my eighteenth summer, sent out into the world from the bosom of childhood at the behest of my relatives. To the south first, beyond the kingdom's borders and farther still, bearing witness to the war along the way. First came the stench, borne on headwinds for hours before we reached the place itself, a meadow where men had clashed days before. The dead lay everywhere, and the ground was crawling with feasting crows and vermin. Two men did I see who were still on their feet. One was walking with a skin full of water to offer refreshment to the dying, with a cross for them to kiss for the salvation of their souls. The other was after gold. He pulled the rings straight off the corpses' fingers. For the most part it was easy, for their blood was already spilled and their limbs pale and slack, but occasionally he would find one whose hands were still swollen with life, whose leg had broken under a fallen horse, or who had been downed by a blow to the helmet. For them he had a knife, to swiftly cut loose his booty. Deaf to their cries."

Bishop Knut sighs.

"War, son of my nephew, will show you the best and worst of humanity. More than I should wish it upon anyone to see. All that man otherwise hides is brought out into the light. He is shown precisely as he is."

Knut reaches his wrinkled hand up to Magnus's forehead, to run it along the wound. The clotted blood forms a longish scab, the bruising around which is now fading to yellow. It suits him in a way; something ugly to enhance that which is beautiful, lending a sort of a resolve to features that might otherwise appear too soft.

"The world is vast. It is neither good nor evil, but indifferent and fraught with danger. In youth it is easy to feel chosen, or protected, but that is vanity. Some hold themselves in good stead, learn to bend life to their will by destiny and force of character, while others get preyed upon. Be there a God in Heaven then he looks on in silence, without interceding on behalf of the weak. No one can be trusted, not even your own flesh and blood. Each one looks out only for themselves. It pains me, Magnus, that I must teach you this lesson here and now, but I'd rather it come too early than too late."

Knut leans in closer and lowers his voice, catching the stench of sour wine on his own breath when it bounces back off Magnus's face.

"At Midsummer you did a foolish thing. You are to be congratulated that the cost was not more than you alone could shoulder. But from this day forth greater things are at stake, and you can no longer afford any foolishness, for your actions will bear upon more than just you. Don't mention my name before Engelbrekt Engelbrektsson. If you speak of Cuckoo's Roost, then I was never here, and I have no part in our house's designs. On my own terms will I make myself known, and then only when the time is right. I wish that your word were enough for me, Magnus, but I don't know you, know not from which part of our trunk of blue and gold your branch has burst forth. Which is why I will say the following, and I want you to take heed. That other boy, Finn. He came with your mother from Vadstena in my company. The two of you are close in age, and as I understand it he's like a foster brother to you, one who drilled you in the ways of the sword and kept counsel on your behalf. I can see that he is dear to you. Well, something precious that belongs to me has recently been lost, and along the same road and at the same time that young Finn walked to Vadstena, at that. Betray me and I'll ensure he takes the fall for it. Nothing would be simpler: all it would take is a few pieces of silver found in his bedstraw. So long as the correct approach is taken, a search will always lead to a confession, be the party guilty or not. And then it'll be his head on the block. Your silence will save him. Understand?"

The bishop fixes his eyes on his nephew's son. The boy's eyes are blue and dark, like those of so many of their blood. The blackness of their center within. Knut tries to plumb their depths, glimpse the boy's essence, but he finds no footing. This disturbs him, for his own words have left him exposed, and now he meets with little response. Eventually Magnus nods and looks away.

"Yes. I see."

For a while they stand there with nothing more to say. Knut places his hand back on Magnus's shoulder with a tender force. He is dejected now, wearied of the world and all that it has forced him to become, he like everyone else.

"Bid farewell now to your carefree childhood. Your youth will be passed and manhood come as soon as you leave Cuckoo's Roost behind. Look at me now. If you like not what you see, then at each fork in the road choose the path that seems to you to lead elsewhere, and pray to whatever power you most believe in that it not lead you here in spite of it all. May you fare better where I strayed."

"WHAT HAVE YOU to say for yourself?"

Sir Bengt leans back in his high seat, his legs wide, arms on the armrest. It is the best chair the manor has to offer, in its most opulent of halls, and it is laden with myriad painted carvings, each one telling a new tale of pedigree and property for those allowed close enough to discern them. In Finn Sigridsson the panic rears, for he can't know for certain for which of his crimes he stands summoned. That he had a part in Magnus's disobedience must be clear to all, but he has worse things to answer for, and part of him yearns to confess with the same vertigo that strikes when standing by a precipice, upon hearing that whisper that urges you to jump. His conscience racks him. He daren't go to bed until he has nettled his body into weariness with useless tasks, for if he lies awake in the darkness he is returned to the forest of his misdeed, at first in the throes of the tussle and then alone, under the staring gaze of the corpse. He can see no other way to wash his hands clean of it than confess, but he doesn't wish to atone for it with his life. When he finds himself at a loss for words, Sir Bengt leans forward.

"When I found you and your sister you were more like mongrels than people. But rags over skin and bones, your speech little more than whimpers and barks, frenzied with hunger and cold. Before leaving the village I found your mother's house, Finn. She'd locked you out, barred the door, and put shutters before the windows. A clear-sighted woman she must have been, and strong of will, to boot. She must have herded you out the very instant the first boil reddened on her loins, and in doing so she saved your lives. I didn't know her name, and so Sigrid was the name I gave her, a name common in my own family. I found you, restored you to God's mercy, gave you names and a roof over your heads. But your sister couldn't get away fast enough. And now you: This is how you repay all my labors. By teaching my son swordsmanship behind my back so that he might put his very life at risk, instead of coming straight to me and averting the madness."

Relief and disappointment battle for dominion within Finn. He can but bow his head, in the hope that only the shame will be visible. Sir Bengt is on his feet now, his hands clasped behind his back as he paces restlessly back and forth before him.

"I know many a man who would flog you to your bare bones and then consign you to an outlaw's life in the wilderness, or drop you in the dungeon and hurl the key out into the lake with all his might."

He says more besides, but Finn barely hears it. Though guilty of the crime of which he stands accused, he couldn't have acted any differently. Had he no more upon his conscience he could have met with placidity the destiny that has been his from the start, but which has nevertheless brought him further than he ever could have hoped. His years at Cuckoo's Roost are a gift that should have been out of reach for one like he. That it should end now is no surprise, greater is the wonder that it didn't happen long ago. With his sister dead he will leave nothing behind in his banishment. He will soon be forgotten, and to no one's trouble anymore. Now Sir Bengt falls silent and steps closer to him, and Finn shuts his eyes to the blow that must come, but time itself must have stopped in its tracks: the strike is far too slow, the hand that eventually lands on his cheek entirely without sting, the voice that now reproves him another.

"I'm not saying it was right what you did, Finn Sigridsson. But punish you for staying true to my son rather than me I cannot. Magnus is to travel north. You shall go with him. I can't imagine a better companion. May you remain just as faithful to him for the rest of your days."

Finn totters toward the door, giddy as a drunk. Sir Bengt's voice follows him away.

"Magnus shall have a worthier sword to take with him. It would be good if he could learn better to use it before he must draw it next."

Finn's relief at going free blends with the fury at being compelled to go on bearing his guilt in silence, but Bengt stops him with a cry, and every feeling is suddenly turned to its reverse.

"Oh, one more thing, Finn. Bishop Knut's missing one of his men, vanished somewhere between Askersund and Motala. An Olof Jonsson. Did you hear mention of his name on your travels?"

Finn clears his throat, tries to wet his dry mouth so that he can answer.

"There was talk of a highwayman, a thief and man-killer who's the bane of lone travelers. They called him Tor the Walker."

Many farewells, each their own, a lifelong closeness summed up in mere moments. Around Cuckoo's Roost the forest glimmers, the vapor rising from the tree crowns as the sun dries the night's rain. Beyond the farthest outbuildings Magnus sees the bridge across the ditch where the gnats swarm, sees where the board joints give way to paving, which in turn gives way to gravel and earth. The road is wide at first but soon narrows, a pale band through the green that lopes in under the shadows of the trees before fading from sight. It hums its siren song for him, and, though impatient to heed its calls, he has still some farewells left to say, each one more burdensome than the one that came before. His father, Britta. The housefolk are all gathered, those who have known him all his life, and few are those who haven't slipped him tasty morsels in secret now and then, blown the sting out of grazed knees, helped him to mount a horse, or joined him out in the woods. Each has something to say, but the words are too many and Magnus hardly hears them, giddy from all this pomp. Now his mother, out of nowhere. Her arms around his neck, her lips to his ear. Her embrace is tight enough to muffle her quakes, and long, as if holding him like a shield against her sorrow.

"I've kept you with me too long. I've denied you the world for my own sake. I was wrong."

His arms tense in response, as stiff as her embrace is close. She steps back and cups her shaking hands around his cheeks.

"Now my only wish is that it could be longer still."

She holds his gaze, pale, then lets go and quickly turns to hasten away with head bowed, the arms that held him now wrapped around herself.

Down by the bridge stand three horses, one each for Magnus and Finn, and one for their luggage. Bridle and harness gleam, shiny and oiled, and the horses are groomed, their manes in plaits. Finn is already in the saddle, wearing clothes that Magnus hasn't seen before, ones that are as much beholden to beauty as to power, a coat of arms on the pommel. Magnus's own horse is the same, one of his father's best, its coat a shimmer of coppery gold. They tread their hooves, as irked of the wait as he is himself. Aware of every eye watching him he puts his foot in the stirrup and mounts, then hesitates a moment before turning one last time to take them all in, those who have peopled his entire world for seventeen years and more. His father raises both arms to lead them in cheers, and the salutations have scarce stopped ringing out when Sir Bengt swiftly strides over to the horse. He doesn't look up, the corners of his mouth held tight in a stiff mask, and Magnus has just enough time to glimpse the tears in his father's beard before Sir Bengt gives the horse a hard clap on its flank. Reeling, Magnus fumbles for the reins to get control as timber clatters under hoof, and by the time he has calmed the steed and turned his head the people are already out of sight, the keep of Cuckoo's Roost all the smaller with each step. Before him lies the world. He adjusts himself, nudges his heels into the horse's sides, and shouts with joy into the oncoming wind.

His freedom is short-lived, for ahead of him on the road Nils Stensson awaits, he, too, on horseback. Magnus feels a rub of disappointment in his heart.

"I didn't know you'd be joining us, uncle."

Nils laughs.

"Don't fret. I, too, am setting out, but at the first fork we'll go our separate ways. I'm off on a treasure hunt. Your father's told me of some lost silver, in quantities great enough to assure our fortune in battle for all that is yet to come. I'm riding south, toward Askersund. I just wanted to say a few last words on my way."

Nils tosses his head, urging Magnus to ride with him. They let their horses trot along abreast at an easy pace.

"Get close to him, Magnus. To Engelbrekt. Be obliging and at his service, but don't stoop to fawning, for that he's sure to see through. Find a way to be yourself, be wherever you can bring the most benefit. Your strength lies in who you are, and I wouldn't be sending you if I didn't think that was enough. Win his trust and get to know him, stay close when matters are being discussed, listen, and remember all that you hear. You're our foothold, the one who has to show Engelbrekt Engelbrektsson that our house is best placed to stand at the head of his allies. I've had clothes packed for you that I selected from your wardrobe, ones whose magnificence hints at all that we might offer. Wear them when you first meet. Are we understood?"

"Yes, uncle."

Nils gives his shoulder a squeeze.

"Good. Now this."

There is a sack on his lap. He lifts it to unveil its contents, then steers his horse close enough to hand the birdcage over to Magnus.

"What am I to do with this?"

"You know that best yourself."

"Do you know how much she cost my father?"

Nils tilts his head to one side.

"Does the price seem to you too high?"

Magnus raises the cage's hasp and offers the goshawk his hand. At first she hesitates, then cautiously she steps through the opening and onto his arm one wary foot at a time, her head twisting this way and that. Magnus sees the uncertainty and concern in her eyes when she looks at him with jerking tosses of her neck. Then, perceiving something beyond the reach of human senses, her dark eyes widen and the predator within enters her gaze, dousing every spark of hesitation. Magnus seizes the moment and throws his arm, casting her up into the air. On practiced wings she takes to the wind, finds her balance, and gathers speed. No bell tells of her course anymore. Both men sit still, watching her flight up over the meadow and above the trees.

Now come the sounds of swift hooves from the forest's edge. Magnus turns to the road but quickly regrets it and twists back to search for the bird, in vain. She is but a speck on the clear sky, once gone impossible to find anew. With that she is lost to the moment, and Magnus looks back down the stretch of road, trying to make out who approaches. The rider is in haste, whoever it is, driving his horse hard. Soon he emerges from the forest, reining the horse in when he sees them in his way. He is covered in road dust, the haste and strain of his journey written across his face, foam on the steed's flank. Nils holds up an empty hand in greeting while the man frowns.

"I'm a messenger for Sir Bengt, and I've no time to lose."

"If it's news from the north, then give it to us first: Nils Stensson, his brother, and Magnus, son of Bengt, heir to the house."

A mere moment's hesitation before the man makes a stiff bow.

"The northmen are on the march. They head for Burg Hill Castle."

For a while Nils is speechless. Rarely has Magnus met anyone who so scrupulously keeps his true mind hidden, but for a moment he sees his uncle exposed. The feelings flow through his face in quick succession: expectancy and joy; doubt, dread. His horse treads impatiently, sensing his master's mood, and Nils only takes command of himself when the reins demand his attention. And with that it is gone, all that Magnus saw, just as quickly as the chink of light through a door slammed shut. Nothing remains to be read, and instead Nils brightens up, laughs out loud, and turns to Magnus.

"Engelbrekt's impatient this year. Last year he only took Burg Hill toward summer's end, before marching onward to Västerås and eventually making do with the Council's fair promises in the king's stead. That means he's decided to start his march on roads well traveled. We have no time to lose."

Nils urges the horse to go, drives it on with a kick of his heels. The messenger stays where he is, confused as to rank: despite being young, Magnus is still Sir Bengt's son. To be on the sure side, he waits until he receives Magnus's nod, giving him leave to ride his horse on toward Cuckoo's Roost. Finn takes the messenger's place, bringing his horse up to Magnus's side.

"What is it?"

Magnus gazes down the road on which his uncle is galloping away, as though it were different now from the road he has known all his life, as though the gravel itself could bear witness to tidings from distant tracts.

"The war's begun."

Finn squints in the sun, shades his face with his palm while waiting for Magnus to go on. Magnus turns his head. The moment harbors a gravity, and both sense it, but they know each other too well to need to put their thoughts into words. Around them the meadow lies empty and wide, the silence great. It is but the two of them now, and the world stretches forth before them, full of everything there is and ripe with promise. Magnus gives him the crooked smirk that Finn knows well, one that puts off all troubles into the future and finds solace in the moment. Finn responds in kind.

"Come, let's ride. First to the forest's edge. Leave the packhorse, it'll follow us on its own."

And so they are off, hard at each other's heels, the sun in their eyes. Summer all around them.

PART III

HIGH SUMMER 1434

SANDER BECK SCRATCHES where the sweat has been beading for hours. His thighs feel leaden under the weight of his paunch, burning with their burden. The rest of his body aches in much the same way: his neck under his helmet, his shoulder under his spear, his swollen feet in their narrow shoes. Above him the clouds float past, and though he knows he would regret it the very instant it should come to pass, Sander wishes that one of them might unleash a cooling shower. Whenever the sun is out the heat becomes a torment, while in the shadows the midges lurk, waiting to lay siege to every inch of bared skin. He pants open-mouthed, feels his eyes start to blacken as soon as the road starts to rise. His fellow men-at-arms exchange knowing looks, their own pains lessened in the face of his. Sander almost wishes he were less of a devoted eater, but changes his mind at the thought of that night's supper, when he'll have space enough to scoop the cauldron empty with third and fourth helpings once the rest have eaten their fill, wipe his bowl clean with bread, and slake his thirst with beer. Long have they been on the road, collecting what taxes have been late. In these post-Midsummer days the farmers are fuddled and compliant, having lapsed into heathendom and drunkenness amidst the festivities.

"Wasser. Bitte wasser."

Sander gestures for the skin that they all share when he hears another's lusty glugs. Long has he held out in his thirst, for the last to drink must carry the skin, and another burden is the last thing he needs, however parched his throat may be. He must pause to drink so as not to spill, for woe betide he who wastes a drop in the road's dust. Though he doesn't fall far behind, it still takes him an age to draw level, and with each step he curses the weakness of his flesh, the weight of the skin. All under the wrathful eye of Black Vins, their man in command, who gets skittish as a sheepdog whenever the group scatters, a sullen curmudgeon who followed Giovanni Frangipani all the way here from whatever southern backwater it was that bred them. Sander has heard that it was Venice, but to him the name bears little meaning, not that he even cares. Sander himself is from the Anglian peninsula, though that was many a year ago now. His father chose to flee north to escape the shifting battlefronts that required them to call themselves

Danes one week and Germans the next, each time the lie the greater. Sander regrets this bitterly, for the force of that first flight appears to have kept him hurtling inexorably north, ever closer to the world's end, though his father is long dead and he himself a man grown. And now he is here, in this godforsaken kingdom with its gibberish that, though intelligible with some effort, still sounds like the garbled mumblings of children or fools. Only behind ramparts and bulwarks are refined folk to be found, and even they are a motley assemblage. Giovanni Frangipani himself a mere adventurer, whose path crossed with the king's on a pilgrimage to God knows where, and whose luck then brought him all the way here, to fill his own coffers for a few years. The rest of them Danes and Germans by turn. Some have all the luck. Sander wishes he were a more orderly sort, capable of saving what he earns in pay so that he might return south a rich man. Weak he is instead. No temptations can he resist: good wine, good food; a woman willing to go to bed and pretend him fair for the sake of a few coins.

A man of the plains is he, used to wide prospects. He avoids the forest that grows here. Given the choice he always prefers the road that lies barren, vain endeavor though it is: the trees are everywhere in these parts, and sooner or later beneath them he must go. It's worse in summer, these loathsome northern summers where night refuses to set in. The darkness he remembers from his childhood was another, as if the whole world would melt away only to be cast anew at dawn, a black embrace in whose depth each man could find calm and surety, for not even fiends would try their luck without sight to aid them. Here everything is different, the night miserly in summertime, the sleep he has always loved so dearly less agreeable now. He is woken by the light and must turn for hours on his bunk, while outside the sun is already risen, its rays rendering his sleeping body exposed and open to danger.

The forest looms closer with each step, dim in the evening light. Through it they must go if they are to sleep in their own beds back at Köping Fort, and Sander isn't the only one who is sick of being billeted in farmers' barns. Homeward they are bound, though they have many an hour left to trudge.

Sander stops to catch his breath with an eye on the edge of the trees, sharp teeth grinning at the sunset. He shudders. As always he is wary. These tracts may be known as Lawless Köping, but he fears the place itself more than the outlaws. With tree crowns over his head it's as though every sense in his possession urges him to flee. A stench of rot in his nose, noises all around like the footsteps of an unseen stalker, his skin clawed at by branches. Prayer and profanity make wards under his breath.

"Scheisse. Gott geht mit mir."

He crosses himself and clutches at his pike, in the hope that it might give him solace.

~*~

It's just as he remembers, only worse still, worse now than ever before. They are a dozen soldiers in all, but their footsteps over the trail's dead leaves and fallen branches seem too few to account for all the racket he hears. The cracks and snaps seem to come from all around, the sound of movements hidden behind trunks and bushes. What manner of beast it is Sander couldn't say, but many are the tales that he has heard. Wiser men than he say that the north is neighbor to Hell itself, its hinterlands afflicted by all that is evil. The dead haunt its tracts, while trolls and goblins glare covetously at man and all that he has made of himself. The shadows should offer some respite from the heat, but Sander doesn't feel it. Instead he feels a weight, a stifling malevolence that closes in around him. He hobbles up to one of his brothers-at-arms, a taciturn Schleswiger of the kind he feared as a child.

"Herman. Wartet mal. Wieviel weiter? Hört du das?"

He receives only a grunt in response, a shrug of the shoulders. Sander's fears are not unknown to this company. Anxiety catches, and rather than pay him any heed they are wont to pretend he isn't there. But Sander suspects there's more to it than that: Herman is just as weary as he is, full of sulky lassitude of the kind that banishes all thought. Now up ahead comes a cry. Black Vins commands them to halt, in his distinct hodgepodge of words of the ilk that sound alike in every tongue. Something is happening farther up the track. Sander steps forward uncertainly, ill at ease yet powerless to silently sit out the unknown. He lets out a sigh of relief: up around a bend two trees have fallen across the track, thick spruces with coats of needles several perches deep. At first he doesn't see why Vins refuses to move, but as he stands there it dawns on him. No storm could have felled those trunks, for they have fallen in opposing directions, and no gales have struck since they last walked this road.

The thought has hardly crossed his mind before he crouches down with his arms around his head, for now more trees are falling, behind them this time. The timber builds to a deafening demon-choir, the trunks crashing and branches howling as the wood is buffeted together. Then silence, as he and his brothers-at-arms stiffen in figures of horror. On the banks that line the sunken path now stand men, men in great numbers, each with a weapon in their hands. Some bear cudgels and flails and diverse implements for breaking ground, but many also have bows. A crossbow he sees, two, three. All of them are drawn, arrow and bolt with their chosen quarry. All of a sudden Sander Beck knows that he is going to die. The feelings abound, conflicting: First the knowledge of the inevitable; some hitherto quelled part of him has always known that this was exactly where his road must end, slain in muck and mud; and yet that he has taken step upon step toward this very grave, without sense enough to veer from it while there was still time. Regret and reproof at all the stupidity that he shares with life itself. Then comes the wrath, powerless in all its force. The injustice of it all. His ears flush with indignation: life has been all too hardfisted with him, even in times of plenty; every feast, every excess, every bedding short and fleeting. Before he could find comfort in the promise of new bounties, but now, all of a sudden, this is all he gets. Soon all feelings drain away, leaving only fear. His heart beats quickly, hastening while it still can, and his guts writhe in his paunch, as if to make space for the arrow that will come and spill his blood over the thirsty ground. One of the men up on the banks steps forward and clears his throat.

"Evening, lads."

Standing on the bank alongside the man, Sander sees many a familiar face, though in his terror their names escape him. Several of the farmers are among those who have hosted the men-at-arms in years gone by, while they trudged far and wide doing Giovanni Frangipani's bidding. All with names like Anders, Jonas, and Sven, each face near impossible to tell from the next. Nor has Sander gone to any great pains to commit them to memory. In days of yore the commoners seemed indifferent, a wry smile carved across their furrowed faces, the kind of men capable of shrugging their shoulders at the tax that must be paid, who would sooner make the most of what remained than have those crumbs tainted by bitterness. Nor the kind to deny a simple soldier a place at his hearth to dry off his tunic when the rain fell, a bed of his hay for the night. They show other faces now. Smooth are their features, no wrath to be seen, and Sander feels any hope cast in him by the fact of their acquaintance take flight. Theirs are the looks of men who have put the hard decisions behind them. Sander has never feared them before, no more so than he fears the wolves who howl at the full moon, for they pose a threat only to those who lie exposed. Besides, he has always had helmet and chain mail, pike and dagger, more than enough to defend himself against those armed only with pitchforks and table knives. But now these men bear crossbows of a kind that he has never before seen in this land, steel-rimmed and wound up by hand, with sharp stocks drawn tauter than any man would dare. The man at their head balances his weapon on his arm, a large man with a broad chest and bushy beard.

"You won't know me, though I stand among familiar faces. Harald Esbjörnsson is my name, a man of the mountains from Norberg this way come. Great things are afoot in the realm. Mayhaps you haven't heard. We're sick of breaking our backs under the yoke while the bailiffs grow fat on the fruits of our toils, whether we shed our sweat in the fields or down the mines. Enough is enough."

Another man steps over to him, tall and thin and fair of complexion, his eyes pale as water and devoid of mercy.

"Engelbrekt Engelbrektsson is coming!"

A mumble of approval is heard from the rest. The man goes on.

"He's marching from the north, and the people are rising up to walk at his side. A giant of a man he is, as if hewn from a mountain itself, with gifts that others lack. God is with him, and he is showing his favor more with every step southward."

Others join in the chorus, voices from the ranks whose faces Sander can't see from down in the hollow. He thinks he sees the one who called himself Harald Esbjörnsson send a wearied glance skyward.

"When the doubters spoke against him at the assembly, he proved himself through ordeals. He had a sword heated in the fire until it glowed red, then gripped it with his bare hands and raised it over his head, before putting it down unscathed."

"If Engelbrekt sets up camp in the same place two nights in a row, a fountain will spring forth on the spot where he laid his head, and he who drinks of that water will be cured of every ailment."

"Good thing he's always on the march then, otherwise we'd be wading all the way down to King Eric knee-deep in holy water."

Mirth breaks out, and they laugh. Sander, too, feels the corners of his mouth tighten to a grin, in the vain hope that one of them will mistake him for a friend. His lip splits, and sweat salts the wound. Over the men's gaiety the son of Esbjörn raises his voice.

"Listen up, strangers. We've been unwilling hosts. This day marks an end to our hospitality. Engelbrekt's coming, and with him every northman old enough to lift a sword or draw a bow. Lawless Köping stands with us."

The tall, fair man raises his crossbow and takes aim. Silence falls like an axe, enough for his quiet voice to carry.

"Let's kill 'em all. Leave the bodies here. First the crow will come, then the raven, and last of all the wolf. No trace will be left."

A warmth runs down Sander's leg when he lets out his waters, shame and relief in one. He drops to his knees, his head bowed and his arms crossed, to shield him from the arrowhead that has already chosen its mark.

"Ich bin Sander Beck. Gott steh mir bei. Gott steh mir bei. Mein Name ist Sander Beck."

Their ride takes them east first, Magnus and Finn, with Nils Stensson up ahead. The lake accompanies them on their left, glimpsed in flashes between trees and hills, its scent carried on the north wind. When the road nears the shore they pass many a rickety fisherman's cottage in disrepair. What people they detect keep themselves out of their way, shy as forest animals, for even from afar the horses' hooves betray that these are riders of note. Squires with costly saddles on rare steeds, those from whom few around here can hope for anything good. Watchful faces are seen from afar, but never close enough for talk or questions, and the places are empty by the time they reach them.

By dusk they are halfway to Strängnäs, and find a larger farm where the farmhands can offer the horses water and keep. They are still on Sir Bengt's lands, and Magnus is known by name without having to show the emblem that he was given to wear on a strap around his neck. Nils has a way with words, and with flattery and wonder he soon has their host satisfied. The farmer is a tenant of Sir Bengt's and is thus eager to be of service, for four years remain of the seven for which he has undertaken to work the soils of Cuckoo's Roost. An experienced host he is, too, and not seldom for Sir Bengt's men, who find his plot a suitable resting place at the end of a day's march. Everyone bustles to be at their service. On the table they place fish from the lake, a pike boiled in a spiced broth, with sausage and ham that has been cured with care. The men are soon left alone to dine, once the farmer himself has stood with them. Magnus wonders whether he is one of the guests who sat at Bengt's table at Midsummer, for he feels the man's gaze searching for the scar atop his forehead. The bunks that belong to the master and his family have been bedded anew for their guests, soft linen in wait, the floor swept with birch brooms and smoked with leafy twigs so that they might sleep undisturbed by gnats and midges. At daybreak they are given bread from the bakehouse oven for their onward journey, and find their saddlebags filled with even more food for the road than what they need. Before they mount, the farmer emerges to see them off, felted cap in hand, his scalp shining beneath his thin hair in the sun.

"Would you do me the honor of joining me for a moment, before you set off?"

He leads them a short way thence, past the farmhouse where they spent the night, to a storehouse raised on posts to keep vermin at bay. A simple ladder leads up, and the door is open for them. The farmer climbs inside first, and he takes care to warn them not to hit their heads. The storehouse boards bear no openings, and it takes time for Magnus's eyes to adjust to the light. Not much to see: unleavened bread in flat loaves threaded on wooden poles, a few clusters of sausages hanging from a beam, ham, beer in barrels. The man falters when he speaks, his voice bleating and dry, as though he has long been rehearsing how his words should best be weighed yet has failed at the moment of truth.

"If their stay has been to their pleasing, the gentlemen might . . . I would be grateful if the gentlemen might mention as much to Sir Bengt."

Nils looks at the farmer for a while, then responds not in words but with a nod, to confirm that he has understood his errand.

※

Hours pass, and Nils Stensson reins in his horse at a point where the road forks. Before them stands a thick post, grounded in a cairn. He points at the markings hewn into the wood.

"Here ends your father's land, and here part our ways. My road takes me south. Wend your way toward Västerås, Magnus. There you'll find Engelbrekt at the head of his hundreds. The castle walls are thick, so the siege may take some time. I'm sure we'll meet there again, you and your father and I."

Magnus wipes his fringe from his face, surveying the land that lies before them.

"Whose lands are these?"

His uncle sits up in his saddle to stretch his sore muscles, waves a hand to fend off the midges that can sense warm blood from a healthy heart.

"The king's. He has his bailiwick at Gryphon Rock, from where he collects his taxes from the peasants."

"Uncle?"

Magnus looks down at the arm held out before him, on which two midges have landed undisturbed to eat their fill.

"Yes?"

"Do the people fare better on Father's lands than the king's?"

Nils sighs and leans back in his saddle, leaves the midges be. He thinks carefully, weighing his words.

"Your father knows better than to drive his tenants to starvation. More does he stand to gain from keeping on good terms with them, and not just today, but tomorrow, too. When you take over, the people will know who you are and who raised you, and know what they can expect. The foreign bailiffs don't know the people, don't speak our tongue. And they don't stay long. From one day to the next they'll be replaced by another man cut from the same cloth, then ride south with hacks limping under all the silver they've amassed. That the people they leave behind curse their memories, or that the village children raised on bark bread never grow to their full height, hardly moves them."

"But then why do the farmers stay? The kingdom is wide and its people few. Why don't they go elsewhere? Wouldn't they prefer to work their own land?"

"With us they enjoy protections."

From Magnus's bare arm rises one midge, then the other, both swollen to red beads against the light.

"Whom from?"

At first Nils is silent. Then he laughs.

"From someone stronger who would take more."

"Uncle, why did the farmer show us his storehouse?"

Nils smiles at the memory.

"For he's a canny tenant, that's why. Think of the day he had yesterday: guests come plodding in out of the wilderness, one of them brother to Sir Bengt of Cuckoo's Roost himself, the other his very own son. Now, this farmer, being an enterprising sort, sees that what awaits isn't mere duty but an opportunity besides, a chance to vaunt himself and his farm to him whose land he works and on whose goodwill his future depends. He gives us a meal of the likes his farm won't see other than at weddings or funerals, so that we might go to bed contented. But he doesn't want to send us off with a memory of extravagance, for if we were to speak of that feast back at Cuckoo's Roost, then perhaps Sir Bengt would think he's been taxing his tenants too lightly. So instead he shows us his storehouse, emptied for our sake, at the cost of him and his workers having to pinch and scrape all winter long. Thus he proves his loyalty, making it clear that our comfort is dearer to him than his own. But he wants to see a value for what he has staked. He wants us to give word to Sir Bengt, in the hope that it might help him line his own pockets in the future. That's good, Magnus. You want sharp folk on your land."

Nils scratches a midge bite on his temple, where the veins lie close to the skin.

"Though not too sharp, of course. A wily enough man might keep two storehouses, one meager to show the squires, another packed to brimming on the forest's edge, where he hides all that he has wrongfully kept. Someone like me might say that whoever's crafty enough for one is crafty enough for the other. It's a dangerous game that he plays. Anyway, that farmer's not my concern. With people come trouble. Now do you see why I choose not to keep any land?"

He looks around, back whence they came, and forward, to where they are heading.

"The difference between our land and the king's is invisible to the naked eye. The trees are the same, and the boulders. And everywhere the same is true: All that the weak have in abundance is taken by those who can. The world is home to those who pray, those who work, and those who fight. To each their own place. If God wished it any different, the world would be another. It's God's will, all that happens."

Finn hears this, though Nils is speaking to Magnus alone. The words send a jolt running through him as he sits, and he must calm his horse with well-tended reins when his unease proves contagious. God's will. Those were his mother's words, her very last. Shuddering in the sun, he lets his horse trudge across the boundary to the crown's land while Nils Stensson takes his leave.

"Farewell then, Magnus. Hope and destiny."

T H E W H E E L O F life seeks out familiar tracks, but for Kristina Magnusdaughter of the lion and the lily nothing is the same. Everything seems distant, every voice heard from afar, every person at a remove. She tries to lose herself in the many duties that she has made her own, all the tasks great and small required each day for the running of the estate. It is as though she has been cleft in two; as though her body wanders around, fulfilling its tasks and performing its role, while her soul stands beside it, deadened and still, her mouth gaping in a cry that no one hears.

By night come the dreams, and in them the abbess Ingegerd, a wizened corpse crawling with worms and rats who holds up the bodice of the dress that Stina wetted with her own waters, points at the stains and sneers at the affront with her gaping grin. Stina will awaken to a flush of heat, and must kick off her bedclothes and nightdress to go sit by the window, letting the breeze cool her hot skin. The night is doubt's domain. Perhaps she was wrong, that old nun by the door. *All your love shall end in blood.* Perhaps the curse does have its own power in spite of it all, a spell with might enough to break into their world unaided by man, Ingegerd a specter whose rancid bones extend beyond the grave. But Britta was born healthy, as was Magnus, and Stina herself was allowed to live. All of this is a comfort to her.

The tenants of Cuckoo's Roost prepare for the harvest, and with them Stina. All that the soils yield will be to the house's gain. Sir Bengt wants to know how much they expect to reap, so that he might sell the ears unharvested to the merchants in Örebro and have silver at hand for when the war comes. To Stina it falls to deal with them on price, to meet with buyers and be plied with polite phrases, though both know well that their sole interest lies in how many örtugs more or less each bushel is worth. This wearies her. So meaningless it seems, this dance around the trivial for the sake of appearances.

One of them is different. Mild of speech despite being German, he speaks their kingdom's tongue well, and if his concern for her comfort is feigned, then he disguises it better than most. He grants her the best seat in his house and, upon seeing her cheeks redden, lets a draft air out the room. He has a young wife who is with child, his first. She is teeming, her belly great, but still she pours the wine in her servant's place, out of deference to her guest. The man's hand reaches for her stomach when she passes, strokes its roundness. They share a wordless smile before the wife leaves them again, to speak no more of silver pieces and the value of rye, but of the child soon to come to the house in which they sit, and of those already born to Stina's.

"Lady Kristina, are you all right? Did the wine not sit well with you?"

Suddenly it is clear to her, the riddle's answer. *All your love shall end in blood.* None of her children were born of love, and thus they were born healthy. But Magnus she loves now, loves him so dearly that her heart could burst, loves him all the more the farther he is from her. He's fair game now.

STRÄNGNÄS IS A lively city with a reek of fish. Merchants abound, each vying to shout the loudest, to be the first to buy or sell the goods coming in from farther inland and the coast. Others underbid each other to transport the timber and iron on to Stockholm, where they will fetch a higher price. From behind the abbey walls they hear the monks chant, the cathedral's tower casting its shadow over them all. Magnus and Finn find a stable that knows Sir Bengt and the way back to Cuckoo's Roost and leave their horses there, taking only the saddles and harnesses with them. A groom takes the packhorse, weary under its increased load, and leads it down to the port, where he helps them to find a vessel and drives down the cost of their passage through a knowing fury at the first price named. The boat is open, five fathoms long and two wide, and it has a crew of only three; one at the prow and one at the stern, with a boy of ten years huddled at the mast. The helmsman spits superstitiously into the water, cracks his hands, and, after a meaningful glance, leads them in the Pater Noster.

"You're in luck, lads, for the wind's with us. If the weather holds we'll see Västerås by evening."

With a long pole to the lake floor they push off, until they can raise the sail, patched and mended but free of holes. It can hardly be hauled up the mast before it's filled, for the southerly wind is eager. It comes from straight behind them and takes hold of the boat, and soon they can hear the water lapping against the boat's outer planks as the timber cleaves the lake. Neither Magnus nor Finn are used to being on the water, except for in the rowboats back at Cuckoo's Roost, and only then when stillness has rolled the waves flat. Involuntarily their hands seek out sturdy beams to which they cling tightly, knuckles whitening. But from the seamen's countenances they can see that their voyage has been blessed, for the former can't hide their good spirits. The man at the helm hums tunelessly to himself, between approving glances at the angle of the sail and the direction of the stem. As time wears on hunger makes itself known.

"If the gentlemen don't mind, could one of you relieve Leif at the prow so that we all may eat? The work's easy enough. We're on deep water now, but occasionally you'll find the odd drifting log that's escaped. We need to keep an eye out ahead, for if we run into one of those it could end badly."

They take turns keeping watch. Finn and Magnus share of the food that they were given by the farmer, fare in greater quantities than they alone could consume before it spoiled, much to the seamen's gratitude and an additional lift in spirits on board. The ship's boy's ravenous appetite is to everyone's amusement.

"They say even the lake has a bottom, but Bjarne has none."

Above them the sun sinks lakeward, until the summer's eve leaves it hovering a few handsbreadths above the end of the world. Scents that were alien but hours ago now settle, made safe through their newfound familiarity: tar, hemp, soaked timber; all the other unknowable things that give the water its smell. The boat rocks them to sleep for short spells, until the helmsman peers out beneath the sail and points beyond the prow. The cathedral's tower pierces the sky, while the castle is its earthly counterweight, a brooding heft. The port is thoroughly fortified on its lake side, the lakebed strewn with boulders, forcing every vessel to enter through a narrow channel that is easily swept by a rain of arrows from the ramparts. The helmsman raises a seasoned hand in greeting at unseen defenders, and though he receives no discernible response, no one seeks to hinder their approach. The three seamen together take charge of the sail, making the most of every last puff of wind before letting the cloth fall while the boat glides on. It is well done. The ship's boy steps onto the jetty and bears off with a light touch before fastening the rope. They moor alongside. Once the boat is secured, the helmsman gives them the same glance as a few hours before and sweeps the hat off his head. Together they say the Ave Maria, before each helping to lift the cargo to dry land.

"Thanks for the food. Such easy passages we see all too rarely. God grant you the same good fortune wherever you travel."

A man in bailiff's attire comes to meet them on the dock, inquires after the fare agreed for the voyage, and demands the part owed to the crown. Upon receiving payment he studies Magnus and Finn.

"My liege, his lordship the count Hans of Eberstein has impressed upon me that I'm not to leave gentlefolk out on the docks at the mercy of all and sundry. Would you be so good as to accompany me to the castle? Melker's my name. I perform the bailiff's duties in the count's absence. As it stands now my tasks are few and slight.

I'm sure the count should like to greet you himself. And supper you shall have, and each your own bed in good chambers."

Finn and Magnus exchange glances, united in the same thought. It is to no siege that they have landed. The castle stands unmolested. Wherever Engelbrekt Engelbrektsson has led his army, it isn't here.

H‍ECTIC DAYS. SIR Bengt all but forgets to eat in his eagerness, goes thirsty in his work. He must send word to every one of his aides on one matter or another. Should war come to pass, each will defend what is theirs. So with his right hand Bengt calls in every debt he is owed, while with his left he requests deferments on all that he must pay. Then he writes to borrow more, borrow all that he can, pledging everything of value as security, for every öre in hand now promises soon to be multiplied. Seldom has he ever been granted such a view over his properties as now. Farm upon farm, field upon field; some on lands that extend unbroken as far as the eye can see from the highest treetops, others displaced elsewhere, lonely shards of old estates, an inheritance from blood ties so dilute that no one living can call them to mind. Land with value measured in gold, silver, petty coins. It recalls the view he's had from the top of the keep, at the times when he was drawn too close to its crest. Now, as then, he hears its vertiginous siren song: *Spread your arms like wings and fly! The journey will be worth the landing.* It's a risky game that he plays, and if the dice roll ill it could all come to naught, leave him cursing his brother Nils's silver tongue and his own folly. At times the fear threatens to overwhelm him. It is the bounty of many lifetimes that lies before him: that of his father, grandfather, and great-grandfather, and of all the lost generations before him that have faded from memory in antiquity's mists, great men the lot of them, who each left lands more bounteous to their descendants than what they were born to themselves. Still, the house motto brings him comfort. Hope and destiny.

Other messengers must be sent, too. The household's most trusted must go out and muster all the forces the house can summon. Every horseman promised in service to the king in exchange for exemption from tax dues must be marshaled, weapons and armor primed, only this time for the house's own benefit and not for the crown's. And more still must be added to their ranks. Farmers' sons must be enticed by loud-voiced men in every village square, and from every pulpit in every church that his house favors with coin. They must be made to see the glory of that which is come at last to this generation racked by peace: war! War, on whose battle-fields the Wheel of Fortune spins the fastest, where each and every man who dares to play the stakes can return home with glory and riches of a kind otherwise beyond him. That ten others will pay for his fortune as feed for the ravens doesn't bear mentioning: everyone already knows. But each man considers himself chosen, immortal in the light of his own delusions. They believe they have little to lose, unaware that any old man in the world would exchange what riches he has amassed over a lifetime for that which is theirs: youth, health, a future. Sir Bengt sends the heavens his thanks; if there is one constant in this world, may it be young men's stupidity and overconfidence in their abilities.

Long does Sir Bengt sit with abacus, papers, and parchment, counting and recounting, tearing at his hair. When the accounts get too much for him he summons his closest men, mounts up, and does the rounds of his tenants with the deepest pockets, to renegotiate the terms of their leases. He wants to see every pound of salted meat, every tub of butter, all the leather and beer in their store-chambers, anything that can be taken to the nearest market town and quickly turned to silver. He waives that which is due to him in the years yet to come, makes new agreements for the use of his land, anything to squeeze any advantage for today that tomorrow can fund. Then back to his chamber, with new numbers to work with.

"Damn it all to hell, it's not enough."

Fury rises within him, something great and unseen that builds until his ears are ringing and his throat is choked of breath. He slams both fists onto the table, savors the rush of pain along his arms, then sweeps the tabletop clear. Papers and sheets in a short-lived cloud; the clang of the inkpot on the floor.

With his heart pulsing through sluggish veins, he gropes for the back of his chair and sits down until sight is restored to his darkened eyes. He pants, deep breaths through his open mouth, until the calm slowly returns and only pitch-black disappointment remains in a mocking emptiness.

A knock at the door. Bengt's voice croaks in his attempt to reply commandingly.

"Yes?"

Britta's pale countenance in the doorway, her eyes quickly downcast to spare her father's dignity all that a mere glance sufficed to see. Sir Bengt cannot recall when he last laid eyes on his daughter. Often enough, yet he can't summon a single instance to mind. Ever since her return from Vadstena she's been like a ghost, Britta Bengtsdaughter, a white lady aged out of time who haunts his halls, always with that same anxious face. A walking bad conscience.

"Something's amiss with Mother."

Sir Bengt should have seen this coming, of course. For a brief moment he'd made the mistake of taking Britta for an asset as opposed to a burden, thought that perhaps she might finally be able to do some good, be a comfort to her mother. But no. Instead she brings her troubles to his door, he who already shoulders the heaviest burden. Come to think of it, he hasn't seen much of his wife, either. He's glimpsed her up on the roof from afar, gazing watchfully first one way, then the next, but whenever he ventures up there to find her it is empty. Shuffling steps through the halls by night, though he too wearied to take up the chase. Mealtimes she has avoided, while Bengt has had so much to deal with that these days he often eats on foot, or elsewhere. Now, as he surveys the disorder, vexation takes root. She should have been here, Stina, she who knows these numbers better than he, she with counsel that could have been to all of their gain. Then the papers would not be on the floor but on the table, and in better order at that.

"Well?"

Britta wavers, searching for the right words.

"I can't say for sure. She moves and does as she ought, but slowly. It's like she's not really there. Like she's walking in her sleep."

Bengt knows his daughter. Ever stricken, she is, something always weighing heavy, and rarely is it something that others can see. If that girl's in possession of a single gift, it's her ability to find gravity in even the most trifling of things. He sighs, feeling his attention already wending its way back to all that he has been brooding.

"Magnus is gone. I suppose it'll take some time for her to adjust. It's no more than that. Time shall mend this wound, too."

He turns to Britta, sees her flush with indignation at being thus dismissed, all that he lacks as a father painted red on his daughter's cheeks. On unsteady feet he steps closer and raises her chin, only to feel her neck stiffen in resistance. He curses his stupidity at having made matters worse, a girl's consolation unwelcome in the grown woman she already is. How fast it all went. Too fast.

"She's fortunate to have you at her side, Britta. There's not much that your mother does that you can't already do."

Britta nods silently, leaves him missing Magnus, too. He is all alone in this house full of womenfolk and the invisible troubles that seem unique to their kind, beyond men's ken.

As they near the castle, Magnus understands what Nils meant by his words about the citadel. Modest as it may appear from afar, the closer they come, the higher its ramparts rise. Its construction is simple, and from a distance this simplicity belies its true scale. But when Magnus finds himself at the castle gates, open at even this late hour, any remaining doubt crumbles. The walls rise to four times a tall man's height, with merlons at every few yards in its battlements, to see the archers safe from enemy arrows. The timberwork that looms above them as they pass through the castle gatehouse is dotted with hatch upon hatch, ready to make way for falling stones, bolts, or cauldrons of boiling pitch the instant an attacker should breach the gate. And, beyond the gatehouse, a bailey cradled by the ramparts, four floors tall.

"How long will you stay with us?"

The bailiff's man, who is one step ahead of them, half turns to ask his question. Magnus clears his throat and replies, with the lie that he has been pondering ever since they left the port.

"Overnight, if there's space and Count Eberstein doesn't mind the trouble. Our travels take us north, to Nidaros, to offer prayers at the grave of Saint Olav."

The man gives a curt nod, struggling to feign greater interest than etiquette requires.

"We see many here on the same purpose. You can reach Lawless Köping and Monktorp on horseback, and if Count Hans takes a liking to you, then I'm sure you'll each be granted a horse to borrow."

A staircase joins the bailey and the castle keep. Inside the house it is dim, for the openings in the wall offer enough light to leave the torches unlit. They are ushered up a level.

"Let's see if one of the family is here to welcome you."

A great hall opens before them, empty but for a girl, a few years Magnus's junior. She sits on a bench in complete stillness, with both hands in her lap, as though in wait. She is wearing a simple dress in bleached linen with embroidered hems, its sleeves so long that they all but veil her hands. Her hair is red, with white ribbons plaited through it. At first she looks afraid, momentarily bewildered, but then she rises to her feet. Magnus and Finn's guide gives her a cursory bow, he perturbed, she at a loss.

"Hebbla is the daughter of Albrekt Bydelsbach, one of Count Hans's fellow countrymen and King Eric's bailiff in Bergen. She's staying with us for the sake of her education."

Hebbla Albrektsdaughter edges closer, uncertain in her steps.

"Hebbla, I present to you Magnus Bengtsson of Cuckoo's Roost, of the house of blue and gold, and Finn, his page."

She curtsies, eyes downcast. Her hair is red as copper, and her eyes flash green against her pale skin. Her words bear the peculiar twang of many countries but are nevertheless easily understood.

"Is he come to take me away from here at last, Melker Göts?"

The bailiff's man gives an apologetic laugh and shake of the head.

"Magnus is headed for Nidaros, on pious feet. The gentlemen must forgive Hebbla: her world is her own, and she is wont to blurt out that which someone wiser would know to withhold. Hebbla, would you be so kind as to entertain our guests while I go and see if his grace is amenable?"

Melker Göts leaves them. For a while Hebbla stands motionless, before inviting Magnus to take a seat with her on the bench by a sweep of her arm. He follows her, while Finn finds himself a spot by the door. Hebbla adjusts her skirts beneath her in neat folds, and sits silently for a few moments before turning to Magnus.

"May I see your hand?"

At first Magnus doesn't know what to say, but when she leans in toward him he places his right hand in both of hers.

"I never know the right questions to ask. But a hand says so much about a person."

Her fingers are long and pale, cool in their gentle touch. The hand he gives her she holds carefully, as though it would break easily if allowed to fall. She turns it slowly to inspect it. It is as though Magnus now sees it for the first time, and he is ashamed to have let it go so long unwashed. Dirt weaves a web of lines where the skin creases.

"You've been at the reins for a long time."

Her fingers sweep his sleeve aside and wander up his forearm, where they find three white marks from wounds long since healed.

"A falcon on gloves too thin?"

"She was a goshawk."

With her fingertips Hebbla feels the softness of his palm, and when they stop at its calluses Magnus senses a shift in her, her breaths now altered. She looks straight at him with concern in her eyes.

"You've been fighting."

She searches for the scar on his face, then lets go of his hand and leans in closer to stroke his hair aside. He allows her to turn his head so that she might better see.

"No one should be allowed to blight something so fair."

She removes her hand from his cheek and goes back to his palm, tracing its creases with a gentle touch.

"My grandmother told me that this one shows life's path, from the wrist toward the thumb. And here's love's. Look, they cross a quarter of the way through your life. Perhaps love will come to you, and soon at that. Perhaps even before this summer's end."

She gives Magnus a long look and holds his gaze until he looks away. Then she returns his fist.

"They hate me here. That's why I asked what I did when you arrived."

A long breath turns to a deep sigh.

"When Mother died, Father gave me to Count Hans and to Ermegård, his wife. Germans both, like my parents, and we enjoyed each other's company. But now Ermegård's dead, too, and the count remarried, and this time he chose a Dane, Lina. To Vadstena abbey she had soon packed off Count Hans's own daughter, who was like a sister to me, but since the count is bound by his promise to keep me here I was allowed to stay. In days gone by the two of us could at least laugh at Lina's wickedness and find new names to use behind her back, but now I'm alone. I have no one left."

She leans in closer, lowers her voice, and whispers in Magnus's ear.

"Sometimes I waken at night to find that someone's been in my chamber and opened all the casements on my windows, letting in all the vile fumes that pass outside at night. She wants me dead."

Hebbla Albrektsdaughter shudders. She wraps her arms around herself, as if shielding herself from a sudden draft.

"When I was little, Mother used to sing for me, long ballads of knights and adventures and princesses. She sang well, and I believed the words. I remember wondering what sort of song would be sung of my life when I grew up. It's turned out to be the song of the evil stepmother. I never liked that one, not even then. In the song the children shed tears of blood on their mother's grave, until she rises up and goes to have words with her husband's new wife about all the wicked things that she's done."

Slowly she sings the words.

"*Though I left them quilts blue as sky, on beds of hay my young must lie. I've cried enough, but no one's coming to save me.*"

A tear spills down over her freckles. She dabs her cheek with her embroidered sleeve.

"Forgive me. I wonder which song will be yours. A beautiful one, I hope."

She gives a start when the sounds of a latch and hinge break the silence. Finn steps away from the door, and in walks Melker Göts with a smile upon his lips.

"Follow me, my lords. The count is presently dining and shall receive you at his table. Mistress Hebbla: a singular pleasure, as always."

Magnus doesn't know what to do: he hasn't had a chance to offer Hebbla any response, but it wouldn't do to keep the count waiting. He gives a stiff bow in departure, and Finn follows his lead. Hebbla watches him as he goes, her eyes red and wet around the green.

"Farewell, Magnus Bengtsson of blue and gold. Our time together was short, but I'm glad that we met. Come back to see me again sometime."

E VENING NOW. SIR Bengt has been drinking, too fast and too much. On tottering legs he trudges back across the courtyard in the warm summer's eve, toward the tabletop of his reckonings. Outside the stone keep he wavers for a moment, glances down at the manor house, and wonders whether he shouldn't instead go to his wife's side tonight. Perhaps he might even be rewarded for his support, if her sharp edges have been tempered by hardship. He might even be welcomed into her bed and treated to her goodwill, kisses, and caresses. He shakes his head to chase the thoughts away, not yet drunk enough to be fooled by wishful thinking, for even if it were possible it would hardly be worth the pains, not in the state he's in. Instead he staggers one floor up, using the wall of the keep for support. In the chamber all is as it was, though now in a dimmer light. He makes to gather up the papers that he scattered before, but, feeling a stab of pain in his back, instead sinks onto his seat. There he sits, trying to summon comforting thoughts from his insobriety. Perhaps Nils will fare well in his endeavor, return home with the bishop's lost treasures. No, Bengt knows his brother well enough: every last coin that Nils finds is bound to end up wherever he thinks best, and Bengt can hardly count on more than an acknowledgment of debt for his share in what was promised. But even that thought is vain, for in all likelihood neither of them will see a single piece of silver. The bishop's errand boy is no doubt busy squandering his loot in some unknown place.

 Sir Bengt heaves a great sigh and lets his gaze fall to the ground, defeated. One of his quill's barbs is making a narrow voyage in a puddle of ink, its middle still shiny and black between drying shorelines. Out of his memory rises another little ship, the bark boat that he whittled the very first time he met Stina. How easily her admiration was won then, all those years ago. An eddy in the stream had dragged the ship under, seaworthy as it was, but his talent had already been proven, her heart already won. Then the thought strikes him, as suddenly as a blow to the head from an unseen beam, his heartbeats suddenly as fast as after a quick march. He clenches his fists around the arms of his chair, terrified that this gift will take flight before he can clothe it in words to remember it by. He roots around in his memory for his brother's words: *King Eric's privateers are already pursuing merchant ships from here to the Kattegat Sea.* At once he has his solution. Salvation suddenly within reach, the future that so recently lay black as land under approaching thunderheads replaced with a dawn full of promise. He gets up, feels the triumph saturating his being. Something must be let out or else he will burst. He bellows into the air, at a solution that promises not only riches but also a welcome break from this house of troubled womenfolk.

The next morning he is on his feet early, his good mood a curative to his nausea. Their roles are reversed now: his heavy knock on the door to the chamber where Britta sleeps, she muddled and confused, he sprightly and sober at the end of her bed, already dressed for the ride that awaits.

"I'm to ride east, Britta. Don't expect me back for some weeks. Tell your mother the same. If a messenger comes for me, send them to my brother at Oakwood."

He kisses her on the cheek before she can reply.

"I know Cuckoo's Roost is in good hands. Your mother's. And what she misses you'll be sure to catch." And with that he is off.

WOULD THE GENTLEMEN like to wait here? I'll inquire as to whether his lordship is ready."

Melker Göts opens a door just wide enough for him to slip through and shuts it with the same care, leaving Finn and Magnus alone in the gray light of a dark passage. Finn seizes the opportunity to step closer, leaning in so that he can keep his voice low.

"We'd do best not to stay long with the count. It won't be easy to win Engelbrekt's trust if he finds us behind the ramparts of a castle he wants to raze."

"I agree. But Hans of Eberstein's hospitality can't be refused lightly."

They are kept waiting for a good while before Melker returns.

"His lordship will see you now."

They are led through an antechamber to where the count has taken his meal. On the wall a tapestry bears his coat of arms, a silver lion rampant with red claws and a red tongue, crowned in gold against a blue background. The count himself sits alone, in a high-backed chair on the side of the table that faces into the hall, a corpulent man of around fifty dressed in ostentatious garbs. Around the table lounge a half dozen hounds, each as heavy as a grown man, black of coat and rife with muscles. Before them the floor of the hall lies empty, ready to make way for clerics, suppliants, or jesters. The count's undivided attention is directed at a just-snapped bone from which he is scraping the marrow, and Melker takes the opportunity to hiss at Magnus from out of the corner of his mouth.

"How's your German?"

"Good enough for simple matters, hardly for more."

"In that case better that the questions and answers go through me. His grace has little patience for slow guests or blundering language. Though I was born and raised here, my family is German, and it's men of such lineage that the count tends to choose for his service. I've already mentioned your name."

Once Hans of Eberstein has finished his meal he looks up at his guests, allows Melker to bow obsequiously, and then begins to speak. Once he has finished, Melker nods and translates what has just been said.

"His Grace Hans Ludvig, Count of Eberstein, Lord of Neugarten, and King Eric's Protector of Västerås, Gryphon Rock, and Oppenstone, bids you welcome. His grace knows your father and many of your father's brothers, even if they are so numerous that he can't always put the right name to each face. He was also acquainted with Sven of the Sharp line, father to your uncle Bo's wife. Likewise with your grandfather Sten, whom he met often as a guest at the Gryphon's table. On the subject of family, the count has been apprised of the fact that you met his ward, and he should like to extend his apologies on her behalf, while avowing that he took her in only for the sake of his sins, although the punishment would now appear excessive. The count ventures to use certain profanities, and he wishes that womenfolk had been granted even a dog's sense of reason, for on a puppy a hard rap bestows a lesson that will last their whole life, while a woman will endure a lifetime of beatings without ever growing any the wiser. The count wishes you both better luck in that regard, and urges you to learn from his mistakes."

Magnus bows and Finn does the same. The count eggs Melker on impatiently while he translates their words of greeting. He seems bloated after his meal, whatever interest their arrival had piqued soon gone. He is fidgeting in preparation for a hasty departure when Magnus plucks up his courage.

"Has his grace heard of any unrest among the northmen?"

Once he has heard the words in German, the count leans in over the table and for a while peers thoughtfully at Magnus, then proffers a bone from his plate to the dog sitting nearest.

"The count should first like to know what you have heard yourself."

"Nils Stensson, my father's brother, returned from the north for Midsummer. He'd heard the rumors on his travels, and recalled that it was this time last year that the men of the mountains marched on Burg Hill, and after that all the way here to Västerås."

Hans Eberstein strokes his beard, listens carefully before he replies.

"As you are no doubt aware, the count came here last year to replace the previous bailiff, Jösse Eriksson, precisely because the miners had complained, and the Council of the Realm had, with time, come to bear out their grievances. The count doesn't suppose that Magnus Bengtsson has ever had the misfortune of meeting said Jösse in the flesh?"

When Magnus responds in the negative, Count Eberstein speaks at length, his speech growing ever faster.

"The count calls bailiff Jösse Eriksson a dolt, and he questions his lineage, conduct, good sense, and manhood. The count considers him a Danish money-grubber devoid of sense and honor, one for whom any form of chivalry has remained a mystery. The count recalls that it was with a certain unwillingness that he assumed this northern bailiff's post, though as ever he was anxious to accommodate his king's wishes. When his lordship arrived it was clear that Jösse had been an unwise bailiff, one who had little grasped the task entrusted to him and who, further to that, had vexed the northmen with his avarice and unwholesome methods."

Eberstein makes only the briefest of pauses for Melker, who is instead compelled to speak at the same time, his face growing all the redder from the strain of having to interpret while taking note of the new things being said. The count rises from his chair with an agility surprising of one so portly, and starts pacing this way and that with his hands behind his back. Their master's anxiety catches on in the pack of dogs, who move restlessly back and forth.

"The count urges Magnus Bengtsson to take heed, for soon enough he shall inherit his father's estate and be called upon to preside over people and property, much like the count does in the king's name. Jösse Eriksson ill reckoned how deeply a man can be subjugated. Much can a bailiff seize, but not all. Some part must always be left to the people, even if it is greatly diminished. With a few small coins left over, our subject might buy himself some painted glass beads or a better horse, add a lean-to to his humble abode. He'll love his scant possessions, measure them against his neighbor's in the hope of stirring wonder and envy, thick-wittedly believing himself rich and superior. So concerned will he be about his property that he'll be grateful for the city walls whose gates are locked at night, likewise the soldiers' sharpened pikes, believing the prison built at his own expense to be all that defends his liberty. An obedient serf he'll become. The count says that Magnus, eldest son of a wealthy house as he is, would be astonished at how little a man will make do with while counting himself lucky to have so much."

Closer and closer he draws, Count Eberstein, until his large face is close enough to Magnus's that Magnus can smell his breath, the wine just quaffed, and the meat's spices. His beard is shiny with grease.

"But in these parts, the wilderness lies both outside and within, and, while the rest of the world has long since been christened, the Swedes are but a few generations from heathendom. Though pious on the surface, at the first sign of a meager harvest they traipse off to groves and boulders to make offerings to the old gods. The men of the mountains lurk in the forest, and what they do there no one knows for sure. The count supposes that they fornicate with the livestock, when they aren't busy scheming to evade paying their taxes. Among such types an uprising can easily germinate, without it being possible to root it out in time. The count declares that he would happily avail himself of thumbscrews tighter than even Jösse Eriksson did, but that the conditions in this high north call for other measures. The importunity of paying one's taxes must always be weighed up carefully against the importunity of taking up arms and the risk of losing all on the quagmires of the battlefield. The former must always win out. In his avarice Jösse Eriksson was feckless with his scales."

Finally the count pauses, though he holds Magnus's gaze until the last word is translated. Then he steps back and gesticulates at the walls of the great hall.

"But if the northmen wish to come, let them. His grace will welcome them, just as he welcomes Magnus Bengtsson, to each their due. They aren't numerous enough nor strong enough, nor sufficiently quick-witted. The castle cannot be taken by the kind of might that the northerly peasants possess, mere brute force with fools at the helm. Even if they breach the ramparts, a handful of men-at-arms could defend the house. The store-chamber is full, and the well deep. No dinner given here would be lacking until long after winter has come and the frost has made icicles of the besiegers' manhood."

And with that he is done, the count, and he exits the hall with dignified steps. Immediately his beasts are on their feet, trailing him in a long line according to rank and strength. Melker maintains his low bow until they are alone. Relieved, he shows them to the table.

"All that the table contains is yours. Eat your fill. I'll share in your supper, if you don't mind, and once you're sated I'll show you to your lodgings."

The bailiff's lackey is hungry, but his thirst is the greater, and once he's drunk enough the bands of his tongue loosen with a readiness that betrays his gratitude at being able to unburden his mind, before guests who will soon be conveying that confidence far away.

"She's strange, that girl. I hope she didn't upset you. If you see enough of her it's easy to forgive his grace's wife her dislike. It would be better all round if the girl could be raised elsewhere. The count's in hot water there. Hebbla's a stubborn girl at odds with her stepmother, and all too often he must resort to the switch. He's given his word to provide her with a home, but at the same time he wants to please his wife. For him being a good foster father is no easy task."

Melker Göts pulls a piece of gristle from his mouth, having chewed it clean.

"He may sound sure in his speech, Count Hans, but I think the anxiety still rankles, and if he became rather testy just now I suspect it's because you happened to ask him about precisely that which is keeping him up at night. Jösse Eriksson may be back in Denmark, but if the retribution comes it'll be the count who'll have to answer for the man's sins."

V IPER HATES THE waves, hates the sea, hates the damp and the seaweed, the wind on open waters, the sudden flat calm. Most people forget his father's name and instead know him as Viper Saltlock, in a nod to his many years on deck and his fading tendrils of hair. In every dispute about currents, steering, and knots it's his voice that men seek to have the last word, and while he always gives the answer that is right, when it comes to his own thoughts he makes sure to hold his tongue. He despises it all: the ship, the sea. From fear's soils spurt springs of hate. So many has he seen lost to the deep, seen washed up afterward and what the sea did to them. Fierce she is, and without mercy. She suffers not a man on her waves, but will seize every opportunity she can to pull him down. With every year he feels her longing for him grow, he whom wiles and luck have saved from her clutches for fifty-odd years. She's impatient now, loath to see him rest in peace in the dry grave that is hurtling all the closer, would rather rock him in her embrace and shape him to her pleasing: silent and cold, swollen and spongy, and pale of flesh.

Younger men are drawn to him to hear his tales, and many does he have to tell. Of his years under Sven Sharp, back when the Victual Brothers had every merchant from Gotland to Foxholm Castle quaking in their boots; of plundering the merchantmen's moneyed ships; of Visby as it once was, the pirates' bustling seat in the bosom of the Baltic, through which every man who knew the Brethren's watchwords would stride like a king, while the small folk would cower and stoop. Of honor and heroic feats of the kind that only the sea can play host to. He knows his words reel them in, that along with the beer they drink, and they'll soon let themselves be conscripted to row his oars. Inwardly he whispers the words intended for the sea alone: *Take them and not me.*

Yet still he can't keep himself away. Restless on land. For she does other things, too, the sea. When his men sail into the wind, her splashes over the stem wash the years off his shoulders and give him power and a sense of self, all of that without which no life seems worth the pains.

His ship is small, but the times aren't what they were. Queen Margaret crushed King Albrekt, drove the Victual Brothers off the waves, and paid the Teutonic Order for their help to sweep Gotland clean. It is said that the Victual Brothers still sail, but now in distant waters far west, along Norway's coast beyond the Kattegat Sea, dried fish their spoils instead of pig iron and silver. As for him, he counts himself lucky, one of the few. The lords inland are keen to keep in with their privateers, for when the winds of war change the lucky ones will make a fortune by plundering ships whose crew were friends yesterday but enemies today. Viper keeps to the waters between the islands and the mainland, his boat one without mast or sail, rowed by six pairs of oars. He knows every shoal and every breaker, knows better than any pilot which firths open wide enough to give the cogs room enough to steer. But King Eric has granted them peace, and so Viper can do naught but watch the merchants' fat ships sway back and forth to Stockholm, stuffed to the gills with silver on the way there and iron on the way back, slow and listless like bloated sows wallowing in mud. His own vessel is slight as a dagger by comparison, quick as a thought and with lively men at the rowlocks, albeit now to little use. He is promised his share in all that he plunders, but with the boat growing leaky on land no booty is won, and the wages he earns for his patience are poor.

Viper sits on the shore to cool off, stroking his beard. Skällvik is the name of the village that he has made his own for want of better, small and dull. When the tedium gets too much for him he might booze himself silly and go to the priest to confess. Only for the pleasure of getting to see the lad, who's a few years and twenty and still wet behind the ears, tremble and quake when he hears Viper recount how he and his brothers herded three dozen of Stockholm's free tradesmen through the streets with strikes and blows, until they were so racked by their torments that they had to crawl on all fours like cattle. Into a barn they were driven, one that the brothers then set alight, before dancing outside to the tunes of their screams. The tale is one that Viper has only heard told: he can't have been more than ten years old when it happened, and never in his life has he herded any more than his father's geese. One fable among many. But he professes to other things, too, ones that he has drawn from memory. Blood that he has spilled, girls he has forced himself upon. Merchantmen whose purses he filled with weights and thrust into the deep, his own mocking grin the last thing they saw before the water over their heads grew too cloudy for their wide eyes to see. When it happened the sight had seemed to him worthy of ridicule, and he had laughed at their anguish, but in memory and nightmare his laughter has fallen flat, and their gazes now strike terror into his bones. The little priest's dutiful absolution is but feeble consolation.

"Viper."

Quickly he is on his feet, for the voice he hears is that of Sir Bengt of blue and gold. He shouldn't be here. At first Viper feels disquiet that something is wrong, but then something else, too. A flutter, a promise in the air. Viper bows his head when they take each other's arms, his master's excitation all but palpable, his sinews taut like strings on a harp. Sir Bengt sits down on the log where Viper was sitting, pats the seat next to him.

"How are the Hansa ships? Do they still pass here?"

Viper nods.

"A week scarce passes without a cog, and if they're coming from the south it's easy to count the days till their return, so laden with goods that the slightest ripple threatens to wash over their decks."

"Do you see any ships under other flags?"

"What do you mean?"

"Dragons and lions and crowns and whatnot. King Eric's flag."

Viper shakes his head, spits in the sand.

"Not one. Not since the peace."

Sir Bengt strokes his stubbly chin. He had suspected that his brother Nils's words might not have been the whole truth. Either Nils lied to lend more weight to his words, or the men of the north are spreading untruths. King Eric isn't at odds with the Hanseatic League, and the merchantmen still sail unmolested. Peace still reigns in the south. Not that it matters anymore.

"Tell me, Viper, have you ever lain with a seamstress?"

"There's plenty of women in the villages with needle and thread."

"Put them to work. Make flags. A red cross on a gold base. That's the Danish court's banner, and it'll do for our needs."

Viper doesn't dare put words to his hopes. Sir Bengt peers out at the water, as if already hoping to see hulls on the horizon.

"Gather men to row and to fight. Do the usual: Scour the coastline, choosing from fishermen's sons. Promise them a homecoming with gold and glory, enough that they'll have their pick of maidenhood's most beautiful blooms. Hint at bloodshed clearly enough to scare off the conscientious and God-fearing. Once you've mustered enough of them, put them to work tarring the hull. Teach them how to row to time. Then go after the merchants. But you'll do it as King Eric's men and not mine, and under his flag."

Still, Viper sits in silence, in contemplation of the good times come anew. His body rocks back and forth, as though he were already on the waves. Bengt gently elbows him in the side.

"Well say something."

"Long live King Eric."

"I'm heading farther down the coast, to speak to others on the same business. But first it would be good to rest my rump and quench my thirst for a day or two. What the future holds no one knows. Let wise men celebrate their wins ahead of time. Coming?"

"Give me a while to stretch my back. I'll be right behind you."

The footsteps disappear up the wooded hillside, leaving Viper alone with the sea, his gaze on the ripples on the water. He feels her gazing back at him. In the breakers he hears her whispering her promises, that temptress: silver, riches. But he can hear her laughter, too, hungry and expectant, rapacious. She doesn't wish him well, him no more than any other. He shudders and crosses himself before following Sir Bengt, silently promising her other lives in exchange for his own; those of men younger and fairer than he, more beautiful consorts to adorn her throne in the depths, naked and firm of flesh, with each day swelling and quick to putrefy.

F INN SQUINTS DOWN the track, where he makes out a distant stripe of forest, a longwise band of shadow that quivers in the heat off the ground. He points, and Magnus reins in his horse. The borrowed mount hesitates, unsure of its new master. Both steeds bear the bailiff's mark and have the manner found in animals who have often changed hands, rarely meeting one who strokes rather than beats. Gestures of a similar ilk have taken on varying meanings with changing riders, making the creatures often confused; they stop when enjoined to walk, turn one way when another was meant. With the animal now stilled beneath him, Magnus shades his eyes and looks the way Finn is pointing.

"How far to the fort at Lawless Köping?"

Finn squints at the sun, counts their hours on horseback, and compares it with what he knows of the lay of the land.

"Can't be far now. Perhaps beyond those trees."

Finn hesitates before posing the question that's been nettling him.

"What makes you think Engelbrekt headed there?"

Some of Magnus's long hair is bound up with a strap, to keep it off his eyes. Now he unties it, shakes his head, and combs his fringe back with his fingers, to better secure it in place.

"Perhaps the messenger was carrying lies to Cuckoo's Roost, peace still reigns in the north and we've sallied forth to no avail. Or the king's men held their ground in Burg Hill and nipped the rebellion in the bud. Or Engelbrekt chose to stop here first on the road to Västerås. In any case, we can't wait him out with Count Eberstein."

"But why would he march on Lawless Köping? That place has nothing to do with the mines. It's with the bailiff in Västerås that he has his bone to pick."

Magnus waits before replying, holding the leather strap in his mouth while gathering his hair.

"There's one reason I can think of. But let's see first."

The wind turns. At first it's visible in the tree crowns, a shaking of the leaves. Both Magnus and Finn take a firmer grip of their reins, ready to calm their horses before they shrink back. Soon they see it in earnest, a sharp gust, warm and damp.

Immediately they turn to each other. Finn peers in the direction of the trees, trying in vain to see over the treetops.

"Smell that?"

"Smoke."

Soon they have entered the forest, shaded by branches that shroud the sun. The track is straight and wide, and it leaves no room for doubt. Finn is uneasy but keeps his own counsel, suspecting that the feelings he harbors belong in another forest, one between Cuckoo's Roost and Vadstena.

With time the track winds in among trees that spread their foliage all the higher and all the thicker, passing boulders, mounds, and oak trunks so ancient that against them axes have fared ill. At the other end of a sunken path a spruce lies felled across the track, and both men stop and search each side, trying to find the best route around.

"Stay where you are."

Finn turns. A man has stepped onto the track behind them, large, bearded, and broad of shoulder and chest, with shaggy hair playing under the rim of his hat. His hands are on his hips. There isn't even a knife on his belt, though Finn senses that other men lurk unseen, surely with arrows poised.

"What business would two youths have in the forest at dusk? Haven't you heard the name given to these parts? Lawless Köping is a fitting title."

Magnus has turned his horse, whose neck he pats in a calming caress.

"We're headed for the fort."

"Your hacks bear the mark of the bailiff of Västerås. Do you mean to pay a visit to Giovanni Frangipani, too?"

"It's true that we ate at the bailiff's table in Västerås, though we didn't seek out his hospitality. We've been granted his horses on loan, for we had to leave our own on the southern shores of Lake Mälaren. They trot just as well as another's. Had Hans Eberstein known where we're headed he'd have sooner kept them."

"Well?"

"We seek Engelbrekt Engelbrektsson."

"Do you now. Well that's one name. Now let me hear yours."

"I'm Magnus, of Cuckoo's Roost on the shores of Lake Hjälmaren, son of Bengt Stensson, our shields blue and gold. The man at my side is Finn Sigridsson, of the household."

The man swipes his hat off his head, scratches his scalp with a sheepish look.

"Off you get, lads. You'll lead the horses where we're going."

They do as they are told. The man leads them a little way back along the track, to where the brushwood has been piled to conceal another path. Others join their ranks, numerous men from within the forest, all armed. Before long the trees open up into a ring around a meadow, its summer blooms folded down to beds for an encampment. Stones make circles around several fireplaces, and simple windbreaks of willow branches clothed in spruce have been raised. Fires are lit in the dusk, enough to warm men in their dozens. As Magnus and Finn cross the meadow, many a gaze traces their path. With an outstretched arm their host bids them both to take a seat, while with his other he shoos away those who have already made the campfire their own. He leans in to better stack the kindling on the fire, casting occasional glances at Magnus, who is sitting cross-legged.

"You seem calm as the water in a well, Magnus of Cuckoo's Roost. What makes you think we're anything but highwaymen who mean to take all that's yours, sling you naked into the nearest ditch, and bury you alive?"

"If you were a highwayman I'm sure you'd have people enough to rob closer to home. Your words sing when you talk. My father's had northmen at his table before."

He gets a laugh in response.

"Well is that so. Of what do they sing?"

"Mountains and forest, mines and furnaces. An end to bailiffs' theft."

A gravity comes over them. The man gives Magnus a long look, then leans back in his seat.

"Harald's my name. Esbjörn my father's. The men here are from these parts, just as wearied under the yoke as we are in the north. They've joined our cause. But I'm from Norberg, as is Engelbrekt, and I'm here on his business."

"Where can we find him?"

Harald shakes his head.

"Not here and not tonight. But let us eat. One of our men has felled a roebuck, and the meat promises a fine meal. Stay seated, let me fetch you some."

"Our saddlebags are full of food left over from Hans Eberstein's table, which his man sent with us. Let everyone share in it, if they can stand to eat what's been cooked over such fires."

"What would be more befitting? They're the ones who paid for those morsels."

The food is shared, and the mood changes as hungry stomachs are filled. Silence retreats from around the campfires. Amidst the babble they hear small talk of the eternal kind: old memories of droll things, theories that prove or refute matters of opinion and taste, weather and midges, prognostications over all that the future might hold in store. While the men bicker, Harald Esbjörnsson eats in silence, and Magnus and Finn follow his example and find that he spoke the truth: the meat is flavorsome and tastes of game felled quickly and without suffering, diligently carved and roasted with patience. On flat stones bread rolls made of flour and water are rising, as simple as they are tasty. As he savors the food, more so than anything he ate at the count's table, it strikes Finn that it tastes of a home. But not his, and not Magnus's. Still, he sees the same thoughts reflected on Magnus's face. Once fed, Harald goes still, his gaze lingering on Magnus.

"He's not like the others, Engelbrekt Engelbrektsson. Never have I met a more farsighted man, nor anyone I'd rather risk life and limb for. He said that this time the nobility will rally for our cause. He asked me to keep an eye out for fine folk on the roads I was posted to, though you're hardly what I thought I'd find."

"Who did you expect in my place?"

"A knight of the kind eager to see his image carved on altarpieces and church pillars, swathed in gold and scarlet with little bells on his sleeves and belt; one whose belly bulges like the bailiff's own and who wears a look on his face like he's doing the world a favor just by resting his eyes upon it. But you're scarce more than a boy. What are you, Magnus—sixteen, seventeen? It makes me wonder if your house is very foolish, or else very shrewd."

Harald leans back, half reclining against a sack. Above them the stars light up out of the nothingness, one by one. Finn stretches out his sore legs and kneads his calf, where a cramp has set in. Magnus doesn't move, but observes their host with stillness in his eyes.

"Won't you tell us of the north?"

Harald raises an eyebrow and thinks for a while before replying.

"Others'll know more. I've only been on the mountain these

ten years, while many were born and raised there. Engelbrekt's line have been breaking rock for generation upon generation. But the mines make a refuge for people of all sorts, and many venture up there to leave the past behind. But you're welcome to what I know."

He makes himself more comfortable by beating his cushion with his elbows, then thinks for a while, choosing the right place to begin.

"Up there the mountain reigns supreme, and the lone man fares ill. But with others he has a chance, with strength and thought and patience. There are fourteen smeltworks in all on the mountain in Norberg, each one its own, but we all share the same mine, all roll the dice on the lot of each vein of metal before changing posts, so that in the end each party has an equal share in all, provided that their toil is the same. Each smeltery has two bellows to melt the ore. We're at the mine every waking hour, and while one man rests another toils. By sunrise each morn the fire that's been burning all night dies off, and the ash and coal are raked from the rock. Then we take our picks and break loose whatever ore the heat has fractured, hoist it up into the light of day, and drag it to the furnaces. Once all the ore is loosed, new firewood is laid underground, stacked against the rock, and lit. Sooty and coughing we scramble from the pit for a few hours' rest. Then all begins anew. The mountain loves us not, and it lays snares in its pits. From the depths it rumbles in rage, and every man must learn its ways or pay for it with his life. With an unseen hand it can choke you, leave you dead in the pit without a mark to your body. Others are dealt tougher blows. First a rain of gravel, then larger stones, and anyone who wavers gets a grave into the bargain with his death."

"A hard life."

"No one seeks the mines of anyone else's will but their own, Magnus Bengtsson. There's things that are worse."

Harald stares into the fire for a while before going on.

"I'll tell you about Jösse Eriksson. This happened in the village of my birth. There was a man there, young and impudent, as young men are. Not much older than you are now. He'd seen too little of the world to fathom its size and know how small he was by comparison; that it was hard and weighty enough to crush all that was his just as easily as he'd smite a louse with his thumbnail. He took himself a wife, the fairest maid in the village, she whose favor every other lad had curried. He remembered his entire youth being a contest to catch her eye, and though he'd taken great pains to be the strongest and the fastest, he could hardly believe his luck when her choice fell on him. How stupid he felt later, when he finally grasped that such things aren't bestowed in reward but of one's wishes alone. He was eager to prove himself worthy of her choice, so he cleared the forest on a hill where others had deemed the effort needed too great. From the stones he lifted from the soil he built foundations, and on them he stacked tree trunks that crossed at each corner to make a cottage. Soon his field started to grow. The bailiff for his tracts lived far off, and his taxes the lad was in no haste to pay. Instead he bought an ox for plowing, with the promise of being able to pay more the better he worked his land. Every time one of the bailiff's men-at-arms came to his door he made sure to be a good host, babbled on until the man saw reason and let himself be sent back south empty-handed. Winter came and it was long, though scarce long enough for a young man who shares a cottage with his young bride. Soon her stomach swelled, big and bulging even by the spring. One day the man went out to the forest to empty what traps he'd laid, and when he came home again he found his farm thronging with people. The bailiff himself was there, with his men. The weather was beautiful, and Jösse had had them carry the table out of the cottage and place it on the grass where the field began. The smell of good food wafted through the village. A huddle of people had gathered from the neighboring farms; they stood, silent and uneasy, while the bailiff's men-at-arms circled like sheepdogs. Jösse himself sat alone at the table, and with a gesture he invited the man to sit beside him. Soon the food was served. The meat was the flesh of the ox that he had bought, the very same ox that now hung butchered from a tree by the farm, while the tastiest morsels were being grilled over the firepit that had been lit. The man ate of the meat, for what else was there to do? Halfway through the meal one of the bailiff's men, a rare Dane capable of making himself understood in Swedish, declared that the bailiff thought it a shame if the new field would be forced to lie fallow simply for the sake of their feast. Then his wife was led out. The ox's heavy harness was strapped to her back with the plow behind it, and the bridle was bound between her teeth. She started to drag the plow, steadfast at first. What they must have said to her to make her obey he didn't know, and he never found out, either. Such toil is no task for a woman—it's hardly one for a man, however strong—and least of all for a woman with child. Strong hands held the man down in his seat, though he pleaded and struggled, yelled and pledged. The men-at-arms cast furtive glances at Jösse, but the man simply waved his finger and she was put back on her feet, to drag the plow in her bloodied skirt. At long last the bailiff had had his fill and tired of his jest, and he took his men and rode off in the knowledge that the message he had wished to deliver had been understood by all present. And the man ran to his wife's side to hold her in the red mud that was their own, while all the villagers who were still there ate what remained of the ox, for it would be a sin to let such gifts go to waste. Nor could the man blame them, for unlike him they had paid the tax levied and long hungered, and he saw well enough that the meat was salted with their tears."

Harald sighs, twists to relieve his stiffening back.

"That's what drives men to the north. I suppose it's little wonder that it's from the depths of the mines that the sparks of rebellion rise, when the bailiff's fists try to reach even those places where the men have flocked to evade his clutches."

"Your wife. Is she still alive?"

"I wouldn't call it a life. But God the Father alone knows best."

Finn squirms at these words, but Harald sits unmoving, watching the tear trail down Magnus's cheek. The last flames of the fire paint its path, a gleaming streak that ends in a shimmering pearl. He sighs.

"I think I know what it is now, your house."

"What?"

"Very shrewd."

With the morning Harald points them in the direction of the fort.

"Ride there and see. It's not far. Once you have, if you still want to find Engelbrekt, then turn back to Västerås. Not on the road you came, mind, but the wider one that veers around the forest. On swift hooves you'll catch Engelbrekt before the day's out. Mention my name."

As promised, their journey isn't long, and the scent of charred timber grows stronger with every bend in the road. Of the fort nothing remains. Burnt-out walls buckle over the embers, punctured by holes that gape up at the sky. Not a single person do they see. Magnus turns his horse.

"If he's razed Lawless Köping, then Burg Hill will be ash, too. Now I know what he's after."

Finn tugs at his reins to impose his will.

"What?"

"This is no uprising against the bailiff alone, like last year and the year before."

"Then what is it?"

"I think Engelbrekt means to take the kingdom."

PERFECTLY STILL DOES she lie, Stina of the house of the lion and the lily, in the dim light of her bedchamber: still on her back, her gaze on the ceiling, eyes wide open yet unseeing. Instead she sees other things, hears other things. Magnus. His boat has struck against rocks. A gust of wind drives a wave over the deck and now he's in the water, flailing helplessly while his waterlogged clothes grow all the heavier. The seaweed hides gnarled fingers that claw at him from the depths, dragging him down. They are Ingegerd's hands, and her malicious cackle carries to the surface in rising bubbles. Now he's lost in a city, lured down a narrow passage between two leaning houses where his way is blocked by hulking men at either end, their greedy eyes on his purse and beautiful clothes. They close the distance while he turns first one way, then the next, gauging how to best ward off the attack. But whichever way he turns, filthy hands soon shut his mouth and a hold clamps down his arms, while a knife tip finds a gap in his rib cage and burrows in all the way to the hilt, silencing the heart that just before beat young and healthy. Meanwhile Ingegerd stands in the shadows behind the assassins, rubbing her hands with glee. Now a wasp stings his horse on the flank and scares it into bolting. Magnus tumbles from the saddle and onto the ground, where a sharp stone buffets his forehead, and when Finn dismounts to help him the life has already fled the body that now lies limp, a ragdoll of flesh. At the forest's edge Ingegerd lurks with a wasp nest between her hands, her parched skin dead and invulnerable to stings.

Stina shuts her eyes as tightly as she can to force these visions away, but they only grow the worse. Out of the black come words from the past, from earlier this long summer. The curse's greatest afflictions are wreaked through the knowledge of others, that's what the old nun said, and Stina was stupid enough to listen. For that reason she has been tricked onto the same path as Nils, that fortune hunter, the same man who risked the lives of his wife and unborn child to prove the curse powerless. Seduced by the promises of others, Stina has sent her only son out into the world, the big, ruthless world. Worse still, she finds her own pride behind these actions, her own conceit. She has the desire to see Magnus close to power, her own house of birth restored to its former glory alongside the one into which she married. Now she regrets it all, with a force strong enough to entrap her in its whorl of madness, where the same thoughts churn again and again, to no avail. In its midst she now lies, paralyzed in mind and body. Magnus. Magnus: now pus flows from a wound he took, one deemed too small to waste time over, but the rot has set in under the skin and his back and jaw start to seize up, death following with the fever. A branch snaps and cracks his skull. He is offered milk in a village where the plague has passed. She prays, prayers more heartfelt than she has ever said before. That her prayers meet with silence she is used to, but every believer learns to sense differences in the nature of that silence. Now, for the first time in her life, she feels the silence of the God who has turned his back on her, one who has wearied of this aging woman and her quandary born of her own folly.

H ARALD ESBJÖRNSSON'S PREDICTION proves true. Lawless Köping isn't far behind them when they find themselves riding in the tracks of an army, one too great to fit on the road that's been worn by hoof and foot. Their number have burst its verges, trampling down the fields and meadows on either side. Their journey can't have been fast, for often the way is choked by forests and swamps that won't suffer shortcuts, and then everyone must squeeze onto the same track, while those at the back wait for those up ahead to pass. Behind a hill an encampment opens up, where the long grass that was forced to bow to its guests bears the indents left by sitting and reclining bodies, the soot-blackened rings of stones that mark where fires were lit for food and warmth. Magnus lays his hand on one. It is still warm from the flames, the embers extinguished in the night that has now fled. Behind his horse he changes his attire. Finn pours water from the skin into Magnus's cupped hands so that he can wash himself clean, rinse the road dust from his face, and comb the tangles from his hair. From the worn-in comfort of his travel garments he changes into the attire that was packed for him from Cuckoo's Roost, stiffer garments intended for more dignified occasions: A deep blue tunic embroidered with golden thread, a hat of the same color with a beaded trim and feathers on one side, and shoes so ingeniously crafted that the seams are invisible in the leather. The seal with his coat of arms hangs on a chain around his neck, now bared for all to see, and he wears a knife in an elaborate sheath on a beautiful belt around his waist. Then away, ready.

Soon they are on the stragglers' heels. The young and old, those hobbling on sprained ankles or in footwear that chafes badly. Finn had expected wounds of another sort, bloodied wrappings and men being borne on litters made of willow, but not a red stain can he see.

"Engelbrekt Engelbrektsson?"

The question is redundant, more a watchword than anything else. No one questions them. They are simply waved on in the obvious direction, occasionally trailed by the mumbles of those who have ceded them space. Slower and slower their passage becomes, for all the more people must share the road, and most are late to see what is approaching from behind their stooped backs and are thus slow to step aside for the horses. The latter, in turn, shrink back in dismay at the crowd's unfamiliar shapes and smells. Finn lets his gaze drift over the faces of those he passes. Men, of course, from boys to elders and everything in between. The odd woman, too. What colors they wore from the start isn't easy to say, for the road has spread a gray shroud over them all, strewn its dust on hoods and clothing. Each one carries their own load on their backs, in sacks or packs or wicker baskets. That their journey has been long is clear to see from their dogged aspects, their bodies swaying thriftily under the straps of their burdens, on legs that have already walked a great distance and still have a long way to go. Not all of them bear weapons. Among bows and pikes that serve equally well as walking staffs are willow branches that have been sharpened and hardened over a fire.

One by one villages are threaded onto the road's band. Farms are seen in the distance, and, around the churches, clusters of smaller buildings. From belfries and steeples the bells are tolled for Engelbrekt, not by bellringers or priests but by northmen who have claimed the bells to summon village folk to assemblies with the clang of bronze. On the church steps stand tall men whose booming voices sing the gospel according to the rebellion, and it falls not on deaf ears. Superfluous sons and fathers whose children are married off or come of age soon gather and nod at the words, stretching necks tall that once hung bowed, their eyes shining with a newly sparked vigor. The calls ring out: Come, follow us to Västerås, to knock on the castle gates and tell the bailiff all that you have long bottled up, offer him your bark bread to taste. The people reply with resounding cries. Village assemblies gather in the squares, quick to count all who wish to go and fill their packs with food for the road. Rust is scraped from blunt blades, which find homes in new belts. With every village the army's ranks swell. Youths and children join in secret, those already refused for reasons of their age taking to the forest in defiance, running the same paths of their childhood larks toward an adventure that promises more.

Finn and Magnus work their way all the farther ahead, and find the men at the front to be of a different stock: large men they are, tall and hulking and broad-shouldered, some on horseback. All the more often they are asked what business they have there, and Engelbrekt's name is required before they are given a nod in response. Here walk those who carry crossbow, sledgehammer, axe, and pike, with steel helmets of the kind that the king's own men-at-arms use to protect their heads. The sun makes its way overhead, and when dusk begins to fall they hear men from the front loudly commanding them to halt, and the cries are passed farther down the ranks. The road is cleared when the crowds step aside to make camp for the night, forming small groups to build campfires and gather kindling for the sparks beaten by steel on flint. Fires crackle throughout the meadows, their glow chasing the evening into retreat through the forest. Finally Magnus's and Finn's horses have room to trot, until a spire emerges from behind the crown of a hill, its hamlet nestled around it. As they enter the settlement, men on sentry at the side of the road ask them for their names and purpose. They are pointed in the direction of the church, a small, white building with a stepped gable. Its nave is full of people conversing in hushed tones in the glow of candles lit in prayer. A man bars the way to the sacristy door, and it is to him each man must apply for admission. Most are given a mere shake of the head and hover there in listless disappointment before eventually sloping out. The wait is long, and the evening is late by the time it is Magnus's turn.

"Magnus of Cuckoo's Roost, son of Sir Bengt of the house of blue and gold, with Finn Sigridsson, of the household. I seek Engelbrekt."

The northman surveys Magnus's attire from head to toe. Then, raising his hand in a request for patience, he opens the sacristy door a crack and quietly conveys what he has been told. He nods in response to the inaudible reply from within, then steps to one side and opens the door wide enough for Magnus and Finn to pass.

The room is small and bare, save for a worn chasuble that hangs on display from a post on the wall. The air is hot and thick with stillness and men's bodies. Five men crowd on the sole bench, engaged in a hushed exchange, and Magnus's gaze passes from one man to the next, attempting to tell which is Engelbrekt Engelbrektsson. The man who eventually rises to his feet is the one he would least have expected: He was seated not in the middle but on the edge, not party to the conversation but rather gazing blankly at the wall, to all appearances lost in his own world. He is the shortest of the five, and younger than Magnus imagined. Once on his feet he is little taller than Magnus himself, dressed in lax attire that bears the wear of his travels from Norberg. His hair is the color of rye, almost shoulder-length, with a blunt fringe over his forehead, as Magnus has seen other northmen wear it. Smooth of chin. Blue eyes, piercing in their attention, an entreating question in his gaze. Nothing in him imparts power. Now that he has risen, his silence spreads to the others, and Magnus bows as he has learned, sweeps his hat down to his waist, and gives his name. In silence they all stare at him, one or two eyebrows raised while waiting for a response from Engelbrekt, who takes in Magnus from head to toe. For his whole life Magnus has had only the greatest esteem for his uncle Nils, a man who always seems so sure of himself, so skilled at explaining why his way is the wisest and only right course. Now Magnus reads in Engelbrekt's eyes how wrong Nils was. It was a mistake to come dressed in these clothes, garbs of a kind that can hardly remind the miners of anything but the bailiff's pinches. In vain he wishes them gone, for every golden stitch and threaded bead seems to scorch his skin under Engelbrekt's blue-flamed gaze. The moment draws out before Engelbrekt responds.

"An uncle of yours came to Norberg not long ago. And indeed, he led me to believe I hadn't seen the last of blue and gold. I was expecting to meet him and his brothers on my journey, in Västerås or Örebro. Why have you been sent ahead?"

Magnus casts his eyes downward, as befits a supplicant, and tries to keep his voice steady in his reply.

"I was told you might need a squire."

More than one of the men on the bench smirk, but Engelbrekt conveys no derision, instead observing him in silence. Never has Magnus stood before eyes so judicial, so clear-sighted. He senses unseen things being weighed up in a balance. Eventually Engelbrekt shakes his head.

"Your life would be all too great a charge for me to bear. Ride home to Cuckoo's Roost. You'll have two men for your journey, as well as your own, to be safe."

Magnus fumbles for a response but finds none. On the bench a dark-haired man not much older than himself clears his throat, scorn in his eyes. He spits on the floor, crosses his arms, and turns to speak to Engelbrekt, without letting his eyes off Magnus.

"Set me right if I'm mistaken, but didn't you just say you were short a stable boy? Someone to groom your colt of an evening, find him a good stall with oats and water for the night, and who won't forget to muck it out at dawn in thanks for the hospitality?"

Magnus's cheeks flush. Beside him he feels Finn shaking with pent-up indignation, his body leaned forward, as though requiring all his strength to refrain from taking that first step in the direction of the man who spoke. His voice is hoarse with rage.

"Is this how northerners greet their allies?"

No one responds. Engelbrekt lets the silence hang in the air, as though nothing was said, and Magnus looks at the stranger on the bench, whose mouth is now twisted in a grin. Certain of victory, for what else can Magnus do but turn and ride from where he is unwelcome, where ignominy is the rent demanded? Magnus turns back to Engelbrekt, looking him straight in the eye this time, and holds his gaze without blinking. He nods in assent.

"I'll care for your horse as best I can."

The man on the bench squirms at this unexpected turn of events, while one of the others sucks in the air through his teeth with a whistle. Magnus feels his adversary staring, but he doesn't deign to satisfy him with a glance, reduces him to naught in that which is between him and Engelbrekt alone. Engelbrekt opens his mouth, as if to put an end to the folly, but Magnus beats him to it.

"Please, let me."

Engelbrekt stares at him, as though gauging his intent and resolve, and when he next opens his mouth it's with a nod.

"So be it, Magnus Bengtsson, if that is your will. Ask Ehrling where to go, the man who let you in. He'll point you toward the stable. There's much to do there, and the hour is late."

In a haze, Magnus bows to take his leave, while inwardly cursing the cape atop his shoulders that makes a tasteful flourish as he moves, sewn to flatter in dances and chambers, and clean now for the last time.

"MISTRESS BRITTA!"

A small clutch of hands approach her breathlessly in the courtyard outside the bakehouse.

"A bull's stuck in the bog. We don't know what to do."

Britta throws her arms out to her sides, instantly at a loss. What can she do where these experienced cattle hands have already fallen short?

"You'd do better to seek my mother."

The menfolk stand with their eyes downcast while one of the maids replies.

"We've already tried, mistress, but she's nowhere to be found. Mistress Britta is the only one here. Come, make haste."

Britta lifts her skirts so that she can keep apace. Together they race over the bridge and down toward the lake, where the water has doused the meadows along the shore, turning the soil into a quagmire too slack to sustain a large animal on hooves. She hears the bull lowing in the distance, and soon sees its horns tossing helplessly above swaying reeds. Its body is all but sunken. Only its broad neck sticks out, an outlandish plant amidst the wet tussocks. On its side the scar from Cuckoo's Roost's branding iron is still visible, clearly marking the animal as one of the house's own. Around it stand the farmhands, silent and powerless. All of them wait with bated breath. Beneath her the ground sags, threatening with each step to give way. For a moment she stands still, then she makes her decision.

"Have the strongest among you fetch boards and planks and lay a path so that we can reach it. Fetch ropes and straps, anything you can find, and horses to help us pull."

At first they all waver. The largest of them gives her a long look before nodding and clapping his hands.

"You heard Mistress Britta. Let's make haste to get this done."

All of them scuttle away, leaving Britta alone with the bull. Halfway to the underworld is the creature, and she can feel its bellows through her feet, bare now that she has cast away her shoes, which to her had been only an encumbrance. Cautiously she creeps closer, adding even more terror to the creature's plight. The whites of its eyes are showing, and it wrenches in vain with helpless horns, its breaths hot as puffs from a hearth. Kneeling in the mud, Britta extends a cautious hand toward its muzzle. After a few attempts, the bull's resistance wears out. She strokes its forehead, humming a song. Behind her the laborers are returning. Some start laying a jetty out to where she sits, while others weave together all the ropes that they have found. Once a loop is made Britta threads it over the horns, and now the bull appears calm. On dry ground horses are assembled and readied to haul, and soon they throw their weight into the pull. The bull is heaved up in its puddle, lowing all the louder at the violence being inflicted upon it, shaking its head to try to free itself. Time and again the loop slips and must be redressed. As soon as the rope is sitting firmly it snaps, and new knots must be added, and when those knots hold she sees every sinew brace in the bull's neck and fears that they, too, will snap, this time to no knot's avail. An hour passes, then two, three, and more, until the sun hangs low, casting them all in a red hue. She backs away, Britta, must steal herself a first moment of calm. No one looks at her, busy as they are, and all of a sudden the tools lie before her. A club and a pick. No one has fetched them since she has been there. They must have lain there from the start, before she arrived. Cold as she is from the water and mud, at this sight she feels a greater chill from within. For a moment she stops, then she turns and walks back to the man who is once again struggling to make the loop hold.

"Stop."

Even the bull falls silent. Everyone looks at her.

"You didn't come to me because I know what to do. You knew it would never work. You just wanted my leave to slaughter the bull."

Though no one says a word, their silence is answer enough.

"Do it."

It happens fast. The biggest of them, the one called Lars, fetches the club and pick. Another helps him, holding the pick so that the blow will land true. The bull is silent now, so silent that it is as though it knows that mercy is come, calmer beneath the iron than ever under Britta's caress. The strike falls, and all is quiet. Britta clasps her hands to her face, but it isn't enough to conceal the shame that she feels. Their gazes bear no censure, only fellow feeling. Still, she turns her back to them and runs, blinded by a veil of tears.

EACH STABLE IS like the next. The scents are the same, of straw and grass on an earthen floor, of the animals' lather in the heat, of the pungent stench of the waters they shed on old puddles, of their fibrous muck. Magnus remembers the smell from Cuckoo's Roost, but this is a more intimate acquaintance, one forged hour in, hour out. Days find their rhythm: he rides with those who go on ahead, those tasked with warning the next village of what's coming, at times to calm, at times to incite. There he asks around for the best stable, one close to the lodgings but also in an adequate state. The farther away it is, the more burdensome his work. With landowners or nobles he haggles on price, most often paying nothing at all, for the majority soon come to see the value of keeping in well with the man at the head of the army at their doorstep. Still, he does pay for feed, for fair is fair. At dusk he fetches the horse from whatever lodgings Engelbrekt's band have managed to marshal and leads him to the stable. A stallion he is, black as night, like all Friesians, fourteen handsbreadths from hoof to withers, proud and fiery. Soot is his name. Winning the stallion's favor isn't easy, but with time they grow accustomed to each other, and Soot soon learns that where Magnus is, thirst is quenched and hunger stilled, rest in the offing after a long day's march. Magnus brings him water from the well, finds him the juiciest feed. Meanwhile he takes the opportunity to sink his own shirt into the water and rinse his body and hair of the dust of the road. The stables are warm of a summer's eve, even more so with the horse's large mass, and so he lets the heat dry his skin as he grooms. First he takes a coarse brush to the worst of the dirt, on Soot's hooves, legs, and flanks, and sometimes he adds some water, too, to loosen the clumps from his feathered hooves. Then a brush with finer bristles for the coat. Magnus has noted that Soot is partial to being sung to, and when he hums he feels the stallion's mighty muscles release beneath his hands, letting him sweep him clean without objection. Magnus learns where the brush tickles, where attention is required to avoid having to dodge stray kicks.

"You're getting better by the day."

Finn should know, if anyone. Few of his age have groomed more horses. Magnus can tell hollow flattery from honest praise, and what was a lie when the week was young now rings true. Soot shimmers like velvet. With satisfaction Magnus sees the play of muscles beneath his coat, its sleek blackness seeming to capture more light than the evening has in its possession.

"Practice makes perfect."

"You know I'll do that for you if you want."

Magnus shakes his head.

"Let me help you, at least? I'll do the other side."

Magnus puts the brush down and rinses his face with water.

"The task was given to me. If I let you do it in my stead, I'd only prove I'm all they think me to be."

Troubled by that which appears to have been dislodged from its state of fixity, Finn looks upon the clothes that once were beautiful, every golden stitch now matted with dirt.

"I'm not one to stand idly by while others toil. Give me something to do."

"If you like, you're welcome to fetch me some birch sprigs while I get fresh water, and help wash my hair."

Finn nods at a service all too easily rendered and does as he is bidden. With time he finds his tasks, just as the others do. And so Magnus sees to Soot and the stable, while Finn does what he can to find them a suitable place to sleep, procure food for their evening meal, and start a fire to keep them warm through the coolness of the night. In the evening he finds a pail, fills it with water and hot stones warmed on the fire, then draws birch leaves in the water until it lathers and smells fresh. Later he helps Magnus to lean back over the pail, on a cloth placed to dull its edge, and there he rinses his hair and loosens its knots, watches Magnus's eyes close as he drifts off in weariness, but he doesn't disturb his rest.

They find their places, among the horsemen they had seen at the head of the army, those with similar tasks: those who ride on ahead to find beds for the night, gather food and drink, and post sentries to each road to the village. They get to know their comrades, and with time the suspicion first shown them fades to indifference. What coins Magnus carries aren't always of use, for not everyone honors the king's currency and would rather barter for what they need with what they can spare. When Finn is able to procure meat and bread, they share what they have around the campfire, winning favor. But more than that, their comrades can see Magnus's work. They see him trudge in wearily from the stables at an hour when most are already settled around the fire, dozing to hushed conversations, a song sung or a story told, and then they see Engelbrekt Engelbrektsson riding Soot the next day, like a hero sprung from a distant past, the stallion glinting like coal in the sun's rays, his saddle clean and oiled, his mane and tail in beautiful plaits. Inured to toil as they are, they know to appreciate good work. A silent approval it may be, but it is eloquent enough for all to understand.

Västerås nears. Before dawn Magnus is on his feet, having drunk a glut of water before sleep so that he would waken early. He fetches Soot and leads him where he is expected, then returns to the dying embers of the fire, where Finn has their own steeds ready. They ride ahead in a small company, now on the highway, the King's Road itself, which increasingly widens to the ten ells' breadth required by law. What people they meet going the other way they warn to move their carts off the road, to allow the oncoming troops to pass. Behind them the army becomes faster: new, fresh legs are setting the pace, with greater stretches put behind them each day. Toward evening always the same: a stall found, Soot retrieved from the village church, and then to work, late into the night after sunset. It's wearying work, hour upon hour in a sweaty stall, though by no means fruitless. Soot yields more to Magnus's hand the better accustomed he is, and thus the more beautiful he becomes. Magnus hums, feeling the horse's great heart find calm under the caress of his brush. Together they lose themselves in the moment; time passes.

"I didn't expect to find you here at such a late hour."

Magnus almost drops the brush at these words. An unfamiliar voice. He turns: Engelbrekt Engelbrektsson, stock-still at the stable door, a moment of hesitation. Then he steps through the doorway and over to Soot, reaching out to stroke his coat. Soot turns his big head with a flick of his mane, seeking his master's closeness. Magnus steps back, unsure what to say. Best to keep quiet.

"Sometimes I come to see Soot in the night. One can tire of the company of men. All day I hear them speak, while also speaking myself hoarse as a crow."

"Would you like me to go?"

Engelbrekt shakes his head while stroking Soot's chest.

"I shan't be long."

He wraps Soot's neck in his arms, scratches him behind the ears with one hand while cupping the other under his muzzle, to sneak him an unseen treat. Engelbrekt closes his eyes, letting touch prevail as they parley in the language of horse and rider, the snorts and tongue clicks whose meaning is clear only to them. When he looks up it is with the same sharp eyes that Magnus remembers from the sacristy.

"The day after tomorrow we reach Västerås."

"So I understood."

"Have you seen battle before, Magnus of blue and gold?"

"No."

Magnus feels his cheeks flush, grateful to be obscured by the evening's shadows. Before he can check himself the question has passed his lips.

"Have you?"

Engelbrekt observes him for a moment, while the silence rumbles with Magnus's own heartbeats, a thundering drum in his ears. Engelbrekt gives Soot one last pat before stepping back.

"I may be a nobleman like you, but my house is a small one. We have no people to send to do battle in our name. I rode myself, fought with King Eric's men in Schleswig. That was bad enough, but it was made all the worse for being so poorly led. An endless field full of howling men with sharp blades, where you couldn't tell back from front, where the spearhead you found in your gut was just as likely to sit atop a friend's shaft as foe's. None of us down in the field thought beyond surviving each day. From a safe distance on both sides, older men with shinier weapons would bluster that victory lay in slaying the enemy down to the last man, loudly and often enough for all to take it as truth. Never did we see that last man. They kept coming. When my service was complete I was granted respite to ride farther south, not because I yearned to see more young men blubbering their way to eternal rest while bleeding out, but because I imagined there must be men who better knew how war should be waged. I wasn't wrong. I joined the crusades, the fifth of its kind, against Jan Hus's heretics. We besieged the city walls until the relief army arrived, six thousand strong. Many of our brothers-at-arms grabbed their weapons and ran at the first sound of their battle cry, for it was deafeningly loud. Some held firm, bolstered by the rumor that Joan of Arc, the maid of Orléans herself, had sworn to come to our deliverance, the Archangel Michael at her side. But she left us to our fate, and it's hard to blame her for that broken promise, for she'd been burned at the stake three months before. Instead the Hussites flew in like a storm with their painted shields, fearless men with wild eyes and froth at their mouths, and for whom death was but a stepladder to Heaven itself. They had fire sticks in their ranks, men who shot lead from iron pipes with booms like thunder, forceful enough to make wet stains of grown men. They had carts encased with iron, built so that they could assemble them in rings to give the shooters peace to aim. They cut us down like rye. Soon we all took flight, in amongst the trees. Few escaped with their lives. I was one of them. My flight was long, long and arduous. But I didn't return empty-handed, Magnus Bengtsson."

Engelbrekt waits, allowing the unasked question to fill the stable from ground to rafter.

"I brought home the secret of war. If you have courage enough to stand with us the day after tomorrow, you'll see for yourself how we northmen take a castle."

Then, with a pat on his stallion's flank, he turns without a word and is gone.

F OR BRITTA THE duties grow in number with each passing day. Stina rises in the mornings, but she is slow and listless in movement and mind, and by midday she withdraws little by little. First she finds an out-of-the-way seat, where for a while she can both see and be seen. When next someone turns to ask her leave or counsel there is no one there, and her chamber door is shut. Britta has stopped knocking on it, for she knows no answer will come, and although she hopes it's because her mother is sleeping, she knows that in truth she simply doesn't care to do so. Come evening Britta eats alone, watched over by housefolk far too numerous for their tasks. It makes her restless to be so observed, always under someone's eye, and as soon as she can she hastens from the table, back to her own chamber. Her mother's daughter. One sheet at a time the manor's bills have started to amass on her own table, for in her father's chamber they would lie neglected, and now she is posed questions whose answers she must seek in densely worded columns. Harvest is approaching, the most hectic time of year, and however well last year's tools were stowed, they have still been worn by winter: straps gnawed to frailness by rats and mice; iron fretted by rust far deeper than grindstones can reach. Everything must be mended or bought anew, and for all of that coins must be found. The housefolk bring her their questions, and more often than not Britta has no response and must ask for more time, trying the while to hold it all in her memory. She sees them when they look at her, the same gazes as at the bull's death sentence. Though bearing no malice, they nevertheless serve to confirm that she is falling short of all that she must do. She stays awake late into the evenings yet finds it difficult to sleep, wearied though she is by the days that seem to pass all too quickly in spite of the abundant summer light. Every matter left unresolved returns to her in her slumber, disturbs her, and drives her to waking. The next day worse.

One night something else wakens her from her restless dreams: someone is sitting on top of her in the darkness, someone heavy. She doesn't understand, can't see in the gloom behind the window boards. A mistake. Someone must have thought the bed empty and sunk down for a moment's rest, still ignorant of the presence of someone else beneath the sheet. She squirms, and as she does so she finds that she is mistaken, for whoever it is refuses to budge. What is happening to her is willfully done. Where she should be at her safest she is instead at an enemy's mercy. Is that a mocking smile she spies above her, teeth bared at her torments? The weight pins her down, emptying her lungs of air, making each new breath more difficult to take. She wants to scream at her nighttime visitor to get off, but her lips form only mute words. She struggles to summon any strength in her arms, and it takes some time before she is able to raise them in an attempt to hurl the weight from her. But when she does so she finds that there is no one there, no one discernible to the human touch. She is alone. After a while she is able to sit up, arms wrapped around herself for comfort, and breathing fast, as if to take back every breath that was choked, heart racing and skin cooling under waves of sweat. Her eyes that had blackened with exertion now see anew, adjusting to the darkness. Familiar shapes—there a chair, there a table. The room empty save for herself. Tears blind her again. Britta can't fathom what has happened, what sort of scourge has visited itself upon her. As soon as her legs can carry her she staggers out of bed to retread a path from childhood memory, one that leads to her mother's chamber. Through the darkness the way is shorter than she remembers it. Instead of knocking she opens the door and creeps across the room, over to the bed.

"Mother?"

It takes a while before Britta grasps that the silence contains more than a question unanswered. No breaths are there to be heard, no heat to be found among the forsaken nest of summer sheets. Anxiety comes in their stead. Where is her mother at so late an hour? Britta leaves the room, only to find her father's bedchamber just as empty. She is shaking now, even in the warmth of the night. With her desertion comes fear, and she scurries across the floor with small steps, from room to room. Magnus's chamber is last, and there she lies, Stina Magnusdaughter of the lion and the lily, in her son's bed, her face buried deep in his bedclothes, his lingering scent. She is sleeping soundly, too soundly to be woken even when Britta joins her under the sheets, where she lies awake until calm is restored with the light of dawn, when she sneaks back whence she came. Already she fears the next night that will come. Something must be done.

NILS STENSSON DELIGHTS in the open road and in being alone, feeling the wind in his hair as he hears its whispered promise of opportunities aplenty. Southward he steers, with loose reins. His horse is young and healthy, like himself, the sun shining upon his face. Though he meets few along the way, he is tickled by the impression that he makes. A mounted man is a man worth stepping aside for, that much they all gather, but he feels their perplexed gazes trailing him. He has dressed well for his journey, not in ostentation and excess but in supple garments that won't catch the eye from afar. And yet the horse's value and his own bearing suggest otherwise. Farmers and farmhands peer at him, unable to say for certain of what stock he is: A commoner upon whom luck has smiled, perhaps? A man of the king, of the church? All stay on the side of surety, leave the road open for him to pass while waiting at its side with bent necks and a mumbled greeting.

The road is wide and well-trodden, worn by the years in their hundreds. White churches cower along its verge one by one, modest stone edifices with narrow pews, low of roof to shelter simple souls. Around them hamlets, poor, many a house abandoned and in decline, their roof ridges cracked as though a wandering giant has used them for a bench during a break. Nils has bread and sour apples to still his hunger when the sun is high, as well as water that grows ever more tepid in a skin, even though he wears it on his shadowed side. By dusk he reaches Kumla, a larger village with a more appealing church, beside a stone tower raised to house bells in peacetime and parish folk in flight in times of misfortune. He sees the lay of the land, helped by vague memories of other journeys, and finds the rectory before the darkness grows all too dense. The priest himself is away on business, but when Nils mentions his name the housekeeper doesn't dare deny him food and keep. He is granted the high seat at the table, where he sits alone, waited upon by all. The meat he is served is boiled to bits and heavily seasoned, the beer better, the bread not bad. Once he has eaten his fill he asks for more to drink, then sits in thought for a while, relishing his body's rest after a long day's ride, knowing that the sleep to come will be good. One of the maids is fine of flesh, and for a while he toys with the thought of letting her show him to bed. Instead he waves in the housekeeper and bids her to take a seat. She is a sturdy woman, broad of hips and bosom. No doubt she warms the priest's bed in winter, when the winds are biting, the scarcity more onerous than the solace that the gospels can offer. For a while he lets her sit and sweat beneath his gaze, and then he leans in, making her recoil in her seat.

"Tell me, did another guest pass this way, earlier this summer? A man of the church, come from the north and headed for Linköping? Olof by name, Jonas his father."

A nod is all that she can get out.

"Bishop Knut's man?"

"So I was told."

"Describe him to me."

Her eyes widen, as if he's demanded the impossible. She gestures helplessly at the door.

"Ask Lovisa instead. She . . ."

"The maid? The fair, pretty one? Did he bed her?"

Nils chuckles, feeling his respect growing for this Olof Jonsson and his eye for womenfolk.

"Was he on horseback? Is the man who wetted the colt here? Fetch them both."

He waits for them to come, by which point he has already refilled his tankard once and twice. The hand, a broad-shouldered man of his own age, enters with the maid Lovisa. One bows while the other curtsies, their hands clasped in front of them and their eyes on the floor.

"So, Lovisa, you share a bed with rectory guests. Olof Jonsson, was he worth remembering? Though perhaps he went by the name of Olaus Jonae? Nothing like a bit of Latin to light a fire in a wench's loins."

The blood rises in her face, her open shame and well-preserved silence just as good a confession as any.

"Tell me about him, everything you know."

It takes time for him to extract from her all that he can think of to ask. Once he is satisfied, he knows that Olof Jonsson has light hair cut into a fringe, as well as what clothes he wears and how he speaks. He knows about the scar on his shoulder and the birthmark on his hip, knows that his manhood bends to the left, that his moans are more akin to ram than boar, and that he is just as inclined to do the deed from below as on top. Lovisa's blush has faded, her face as blank as someone who has received their death sentence and whose sole wish is now to hasten the executioner's axe. Once he is done with her Nils takes on the hand, and soon he knows the horse just as well as its rider: Its markings, height, mane, temperament, harness, and saddlebags. The weight of their load. Satisfied, he sends them both to bed, watches them slink out in a crestfallen line while filling his tankard anew. He can scarce hold out until the door claps shut before letting out a laugh that brings tears to his eyes, then, imagining the priest returning to a new world of painful silences, he laughs all the more, cackling until he feels a twinge in his stomach.

MAGNUS LEAVES THE stable at a late hour, Soot fed and shimmering, he hungry and tired. The coolness of the night does him good after his exertions. Tomorrow Västerås and an unknown fate. He won't have anyone meet with it unready, not if he can help it, and thus his night in the stable has run longer than usual. In return Soot is resplendent; no commander would snuff at such a mount. Now the stallion is sleeping the short night's sleep of horses, on the straw that Magnus bedded down for him before sneaking out in silence, knowing the creature to be both tetchy and easily woken.

Someone awaits him there, and at first he thinks it's Finn. He raises the simple torch that he has been lent, a lump of tallow kneaded around a strip of yarn, borne in a hollowed-out horn. Only then does he see who it is: The man on the bench, the one who put him forward to serve as stable hand. Black eyes under black hair, and hatred in his eyes.

"You're fooling no one. Anyone with eyes can see you for what you are."

Magnus has no response, would sooner say nothing, but his silence vexes the stranger enough that he takes a step closer, his shoulders high and his arms wide, puffing himself up to incite fear.

"Do you think Engelbrekt a dolt, and us who stand beside him even worse? The uprising has begun, and soon every lord in the realm will be flocking to our banner, scrambling over each other in their eagerness to stand the closest, not for our sake and nor for the people's, but as always with their own interests at heart. Your house is old and full of schemers, and by cunning are you sent. Rather than come in their numbers they send you alone, scarce more than a boy. A little knife to sneak up unheeded where a longer sword wouldn't do. This is Nils bloody Stensson's roguery, isn't it? I saw him up in the north, and I was close enough to hear when he and Engelbrekt first spoke. A tongue of silver he has, but it's cloven all the way to the root."

He gestures at the stable behind him.

"That you learned to groom a horse makes no difference. Tell me, Magnus of blue and gold, what makes your father and grandfather any different from the Dane or the German who drive their people to starvation? The language they speak, that's all. All you want is to swap places with those who fared better. You're like leeches, the lot of you. You won't be satisfied till the last drop of blood has been slurped from the wound."

Magnus struggles to keep his voice steady.

"My name you already know. Would you tell me yours?"

The stranger gives a bitter laugh.

"Names. You're Magnus, your father Bengt, his father Sten. Behind you all a shield of blue and gold. Names matter to you, for on your own you're nothing. Me, I care little for birth. Least of all yours. All it tells me is that your family has ravaged your tracts like the plague for longer than anyone can remember. A snarl of lindworms who've wriggled themselves fat since time immemorial, who've stolen all the land and now force others to pay to work it. With what right? Strength and nothing else, old lies masquerading as laws and customs. And now in your hour of need you seek help from your enemy's enemy. But you're mistaken. We have our own strength. With Engelbrekt the world shall finally be cast anew."

He takes another step forward, close enough that Magnus can feel the words on his own countenance. He turns his face away.

"Eric Puck is my name, and I'm telling you to ride away from here. Ride tonight. Ride back where you came from, home to Cuckoo's Roost, where you can sit safely for now while the storm rages outside. You aren't one of us, never will be. When the arrows fly and blows are dealt you'll piss yourself and cry out for your mother, you who've never so much as stepped out of the shadow of the castle where you were begotten. And for the first time in your life no one will hear you, no one will come to your side. You'll be struck by a point or a blade, or a falling horse, or a rock hurled from the ramparts. It's no glorious death. Humble and unnoticed it will be, among all the countless other deaths of the same kind, all of those willing to die for a higher cause. What remains we can salvage from the field are seldom given names, but are placed in the same deep pit, to wait out doomsday in a sludge so rancid that all the living avoid the site and teach their young to do the same. Why should you fall as a stable boy when you were born to be a lord?"

Is he being tested? Magnus wonders. Has this man been sent by Engelbrekt himself, to plumb Magnus's depths with harsh words? No. His speech is too deep-felt, his rage all too sincere.

Who is this Eric Puck, who knows of Magnus's lineage and appears to bear him such ill will? He tries to count the knotted branches of his family tree on both spear and distaff side, fumbling for some connection, but finds none. From inside the stable comes a sound. Raised voices have woken Soot, who now shows his long head in the doorway. Languidly the stallion extends his neck toward Magnus, rests his muzzle on his neck, and snorts a hot sigh, seeking a treat. Suddenly Magnus is no longer alone. Gratefully he strokes Soot's muzzle, glad of the reminder that, stable hand though he may be, he is stable hand to none other than Engelbrekt Engelbrektsson himself, and thus he enjoys his protection. In this camp he has nothing to fear. He looks Puck in the eye, gives a nod in place of a bow.

"I thought I was friendless here, but my life and welfare appear dear enough to cause you to lose sleep. Thank you for your advice and concern."

A hand is raised at him, shaking with rage, but it stops with a handful of empty air when Finn emerges from the trees, his hand at his side, his knife close. For a moment they all stand still, until Puck lowers his hand.

"A horse and a lapdog you have on your side. How far they'll get you remains to be seen."

The lantern's glow is faint. With two steps back the stranger is returned to the night from which he came.

❧

Finn follows Puck at a distance, bent double so as to make out his figure against the light that still lingers on the horizon. Once they are out of earshot of the stable he quickens his steps to approach him.

"Hey."

Puck stops, turns, and stands in silence. Finn steps closer, so close that with one more step he'll be upon him. Though he would rather yell he keeps his voice steady, knowing that his calm will lend the words more gravity than anger could.

"Come near him again and it'll end badly for you."

Puck laughs.

"Are you threatening me, here, in my own camp? You don't know who you're talking to."

Finn takes that last step, now close enough to feel Puck's breaths on his cheek, see the glint in his eye, and hear his heart pound.

"Your name means nothing to me, and who comes running to your aid is no concern of mine."

He doesn't wait for a response. Within him a door opens, releasing the red mist, all the rage that he has kept under lock and key. At once the world is made simple and easily understood, and any last qualms take flight. He grabs Puck's collar, leans back to gather speed, and then drives his forehead straight into his face, while using his arms to pull him into the blow. In the darkness he must rely on luck, but he can soon tell that he has met his mark. Forehead on nose, right where his face is at its hardest and the other's at its weakest, where he feels the least and Puck the most. When Finn lets go, Puck topples backward like a pine cut at the root. From out of the darkness, wet snivels sing a song of profuse bleeding.

"Now go tell your men what happened. You went to spout abuse at a stable hand by night, for reasons few will understand. Then you got a beating from his servant for the trouble. Much respect must you have among your foot soldiers if it outlasts that story. Better that you tripped in the darkness and hit a branch."

Finn turns and walks away, spitting on his fingers to wipe his forehead clean, while pulling his hat lower to conceal what mark remains.

A SKERSUND IS SMALLER than Kumla, but Nils finds a tavern nevertheless, wretched and low of beam, yet with benches and shelter and taps in its barrels. Afternoon is drawing toward nightfall, but the people are still out in forest and field, kept busy by their tasks for as long as the sun grants them light enough to see. The tavernkeeper's displeasure is clear, and though loath to court a lone guest, he can see well enough that Nils is no ordinary man, so dares not do anything but stay. Nils improves the mood by drinking and eating unsparingly, paying in ready money. He buys two tankards at once and offers one to the keeper, then places a coin on the table between them and asks him his questions: describe the man; describe the horse. Seeing his host reach for the coin, he nudges it closer to the other side of the table while the man speaks.

"Aye, I do remember the lad, though the name he gave wasn't the one you said: Olaus Jonae was what he went by here. He came to the village with a limping hack in tow, just like the one you describe. It had put its foot wrong on a tree root not far from the parish boundary. Hobbling badly, it was. He asked me where he'd find a new one."

Nils places another coin on the table where the other had lain before.

"And what was your answer?"

"The best I could give, but hardly good enough, for it didn't take long before he was back, and on his own two feet, at that. Round these parts there's only one farmer rich enough to broach such matters with: Will of the Wall. Your Olof probably wanted a horse in exchange for his and money to boot, but that Will's a crafty devil who could make a profit selling horses to Beelzebub himself. If I know the man, he'll have given the wounded hoof a little squeeze, passed a death sentence on the hack, and offered a coin or two for the meat. So back here he walked, your Olof, buckling under the weight of his saddlebags, and then he sat around in my tavern for three whole days. He was eager to find someone to take him south, but he had no luck, and his impatience grew. No one had space to sell him on a horse or in a cart. For want of better he tried to find a companion to share the load with, since it was too heavy for him to bear alone."

Nils's host appears to have developed a taste for talking. He gets up to top up their tankards without asking for anything in return.

"I heard him courting one after the other, I did. Fawningly at first, but when that did him no good he tried a different tack, started warning them of a Tor the Walker who stalks Tiveden, a dreaded highwayman who plunders lone travelers of all that they have, then cuts off their noses and pricks as a thanks for the trouble. In the end I suppose he must have struck lucky, for after his fourth night on my bunk I never saw him again."

A turn past Will of the Wall confirms the tavernkeeper's suspicions. Grazing in the paddock is the horse the priest's stable hand had described, a strapping, sturdy piebald, brown over the face and pale around the loins, its withers ten handsbreadths above the ground. No lameness to speak of anymore. The farmer has done a good business of wiles and the healing arts, and the fact that Olof Jonsson can hardly have been much of a horseman. Nils decides to demand the entire purchase price from the farmer; not because he needs it, but for the sake of justice and the benefit of his own mood, and because such lies within his power.

On the outskirts of the city the trees thin out, the roads widen. For the second time Magnus sees Västerås. The last time he saw the city it was from the lake and the south, and now he arrives from the north and the land. But the city is the same. As he takes in the cathedral's tower and the castle ramparts, he feels his own heart falter. Both edifices stand proud, with worldly highness enough to put off anyone who comes with malicious intent. He remembers Count Hans's ardent German, and Melker Göts's translation: *The castle cannot be taken by the kind of might that the northerly peasants possess.* As he looks upon it, these words ring true.

But then something happens: on the wide plains outside the city walls their march comes to an end. While on the move, extended in one narrow column down the long highway from Lawless Köping, the army's size had been impossible to tell, but now the hordes are streaming in from every path, out of every cluster of trees. Of the King's Road there is not a bare patch to be seen. Magnus tries to count their heads, but it's impossible, a hundred crammed into even a small space. If they're all standing just as densely, then the plain will hold many thousands already, with more still coming in. Ever since childhood Magnus has been told of the great death that came from the south, ravaging villages, emptying households, and laying waste to the realm, but here he sees more people than he thought the entire kingdom could contain. Every single hamlet along the way must have heeded the northmen's cries and sallied forth. He's seen people in large numbers before, at mass and on market days in Örebro, but this is something else, one single body of many parts, all united in one purpose.

They have paused by a slope, waiting for midday, but now a ripple runs through the ranks, the rattle of harnesses, the stamping of feet. It is time. Magnus follows their lead, tightens his saddle, and gets his reins in order. Out of the crush of people Harald Esbjörnsson steps toward him, whom he hasn't seen since they parted near the ruins of the fort in Lawless Köping. Harald nods.

"Magnus Bengtsson. So you found your Engelbrekt. Praise be to God."

Magnus's throat is dry and he can't get a sound out, but Harald requires none. Stepping closer, he runs a lump of charcoal over one of Magnus's cheeks and then the other, before blackening his own face. Around them Magnus sees the rest of the men do the same.

"The coal's not from the mine, but it might as well be, for the wood here's probably the same as up north. If you're to stand with us beneath the battlements, we'd best make it clear where you belong."

The men at the head of the crowd start to move. Long must Magnus wait before it's his turn, when slowly they tread down the slope and in among the foot soldiers, who open up their ranks to let them pass. The cries begin to ring out in unison.

"Engelbrekt! Engelbrekt!"

Before Magnus the very citadel contracts the closer they come. The ramparts sink, the fortifications weaken. Together they are too many, too many to quell. A giant coming with seven-league strides. Closer and closer.

"Engelbrekt!"

Magnus turns to see Finn's face looking back at him in astonishment, and realizes that the cry must have come from none other than himself. Over the field they go, toward the castle that now stands cornered where the river flows into the lake, ready to be swept off the rocks and down into the tides with a mere swipe of the hand. The battlements stand empty, and neither arrow nor stone rains forth. Twenty yards from the gates they halt, though the troops keep pressing on from behind, jostling them all the tighter. Soon Magnus is forced into Engelbrekt's proximity, where he glimpses the coat of arms painted on his wooden shield, three half-lilies in a triangle. Still, he sits on his black stallion, Engelbrekt, calm and quiet, unmoved by all the people swarming around him in their attempts to reach out to him, unruffled by their questions. Magnus looks around, and no matter what the people are turning to in their restlessness, their eyes are constantly drawn back to Engelbrekt, every gaze a spoke pointed at the center of its wheel. It calls to mind the fresco of the Wheel of Fortune in the vault at Mellösa church, which depicts the course of each man's life under God: small and lank he is born, where the wheel is at its lowest, only to be raised higher and higher. Briefly he straddles the wheel's crown, before growing fat on all the good things in life, and then, when ponderous enough to force the wheel to swing, suddenly he tumbles, drawing the wheel downward on its creaking hinge while on the other side another man is raised, taking up the position that he so recently held. Out here in the field Magnus sees it clearly: Engelbrekt is forged into the nave of the wheel that bears all of their fortunes. Magnus is astonished by the power that encircles the man, one so great and so strange. Around them all the air thickens, and on Magnus's arms and neck he feels the hairs rise up on end. Is all of this power coursing from Engelbrekt, out over them all like the water from a fountain, or is it coming from the people and using him as its means, like a flame around its wick? Both things appear equally true at once. Magnus pats his horse's neck, whispers calming words in her ear. The mare senses it, too, no more qualified than he to understand. It's akin to trying to fathom the crack of thunder, or the torrential force of a spring flood.

One of the horsemen is helped onto his feet, and he stands on his own saddle while his comrades calm his horse and grab his legs to keep him upright. The man holds his arms out in the air until silence spreads. Booming of voice, his cries carry far over the field.

"Engelbrekt!"

They respond, all of one voice.

"Engelbrekt!"

Nine times does the name ring out before the man covers first his mouth and then his ears with his hands, before resuming his seat on the saddle. Quiet they all stand now, the silence immense after the din that came before. They wait, though for what Magnus can't say. Then the sound of the gate is heard, the clatter of locks, crossbars being coaxed from their fastenings and hinges groaning under the weight of oak beams. In the opening, flanked by two foot soldiers, stands Melker Göts, as pale as if the battle were already lost, the last drop of blood long since shed from the mortal wound. Around Engelbrekt Engelbrektsson a circle widens, until Göts can walk all the way to his side, the heavy keys to the castle gate held out before him. Göts maintains his composure even when he sees that Engelbrekt has no mind to dismount. He simply holds the keys up to him on horseback, then bows and steps aside. Then Engelbrekt's men are on the move, herding the people to either side to clear a path down to the water where a boat already awaits, everything carefully planned. Out of the gate rides Count Hans of Eberstein on horseback, his wife beside him with a veil over her face. She turns back to look up at the ramparts, at the home that they are forsaking, contempt in her gaze. Behind them follow their household. The count's dignity is great, his mantle and garments rife with gold thread, and his head is held high, as though this outing were but a jaunt, to let the horse stretch its legs and show the peasantry what abundance is his. But past Engelbrekt he must go, and there one of Engelbrekt's men steps forth and stops the horse with a hand to its bridle. Hans of Eberstein, Engelbrekt Engelbrektsson: for a brief moment their gazes meet as equals, before the count does what he must. He looks down and gives a jerk of the head, in what will have to pass for a bow. A mere inch does he lower the chin formerly held so high, but it's enough, and everyone sees it. The world itself is dislodged from its seat.

The cheers rise, first from those at the front, and the news spreads back in a wave through the army's ranks. With a face like a torch the count kicks his heels into the horse's sides, commanding it to walk to the lake. His retinue follow suit. The taunts follow them from the teeming crowd, the path that just lay open now closed anew behind them. When the horses turn to resume their places, Engelbrekt rides over to Magnus, looks him in the eye, and holds his gaze, a blue regard above a blackened cheek.

"Now you see how we northmen take a castle."

Forest lines Nils Stensson's way from the moment he crosses the stream at Åmmeberg, where a lone mill watering its wheel serves as man's last outpost. Wilderness thereafter. The shadows of branches are roiling with gnats and flies, and for a long time he flaps his arms in a rising panic, trying to protect his face, before time resigns him to his fate and he makes do with simply blowing away those that come too near. His horse shares in his pain, gives futile whips of its tail, and tosses its mane. As soon as the road climbs high enough for the wind to be felt he rests. There he tries to deduce the forest's magnitude, but he remains none the wiser: in every direction it extends farther than the eye can see. A musty breath of air hits him, blown in from some rancid pool. The place fills him with unease. Eager to get moving, he urges the horse to go on.

Motala next, and people, as many now as there formerly were few. He passes the northern side of the city, crossing its stream southward at the point where stones have been stacked to make a ford. In the middle he reins in his horse to let it drink and cool its hooves, while he savors the air that sweeps over the whirling waters, airing his wet tunic. Thus bolstered, he follows the sun's course westward toward the church spire. Here stands a bishop's palace, one of the many that fell into his uncle's avaricious claws, and Nils already looks forward to giving his name on the threshold and taking a foray into his store-chamber. If he knows Bishop Knut, then the bed will also be soft, and no one will deny it to him. But first to the church, in the hope that he'll have better luck finding a man of the frock this time than last. His prayer is answered. He need go no farther than the porch to find a plump little man arrayed in the regalia of his office, already on his way home. Nils takes his blessing before giving his own name and that of his uncle. As usual, Bishop Knut's name is a watchword for profuse fawning, and Nils lets it go on for a while before raising a hand in the air.

"Olof Jonsson."

The priest is silenced. Suddenly watchful, he limits his response to a questioning look and a raised eyebrow.

"Have you seen him here?"

The shake of the priest's head sets his double chin aquiver, before an insight's light smooths out his aspect.

"Ah. Olaus Jonae he prefers to be called, man of pretensions that he is. But yes, Olof ought to be his birth name. I was told to expect him back around Midsummer, but still no word."

"Walk with me, Father."

Together they walk side by side over the churchyard, full of stones and crosses in honor of the dead.

"How much do you believe he was carrying with him from his journey?"

The priest wipes the sweat from his forehead.

"A great deal, if what we made in this church is any measure."

"And how much did you make?"

Hesitant in his reply, the priest seeks out Nils's gaze, as if to divine his purpose. Nils can all but see him calculating how much he dares misreckon by, so as to pocket the difference himself.

"In ready money, twenty marks and a little more. The bishop has every reason to be satisfied."

"And what do the people think?"

His round face lights up.

"Oh, the peasants are all aflame. Naturally the more money they have the more readily they pay, but we've also seen poor people who place their immortal soul before their worldly body, and withhold that which should be paid in tax to give to us instead."

Frustrated, Nils tries to find a way to make the priest let slip how such money is made without betraying his own ignorance. But, weary from his journey and with an empty stomach, neither his mind nor tongue is girded for the task.

"Won't you show me, Father? It's been a long time since my uncle told me about it, and now that he's getting on in age he isn't always easily understood. I still have yet to see it all with my own eyes."

At once he knows that he has erred. The priest stiffens and turns wary, clearly far more cunning than his countenance first suggested.

"It's already late, and I'm awaited by guests at home. Should my lord wish to return here first thing tomorrow I should be most pleased to be at his service."

Nils knows that the next day he will find the church locked and the priest vanished to some unknown rathole, to return only when he has Nils's departure on good authority. Nils curses his own stupidity but checks himself, feigns a yawn.

"Very well, Father. I'm in no haste at all."

They turn and start making their way back to the church gate. The path takes them past an open grave, the smell of freshly dug earth unmistakable. Using the skills gleaned from a lifetime of petty squabbles with his burly gaggle of brothers, Nils steps to one side and catches the priest's foot with his own, then uses his sudden loss of footing to shove him with his hip, down where there is only empty air to break his fall. Like a sack of wool the priest's heavy body falls into the pit, deeper than what he can climb out of alone. Nils looks around. No one nearby. Taking a seat on the neighboring gravestone, he weighs up his options while a long string of moans and entreaties rises up from the grave. Nils waits for the din to subside, then laboriously heaves up the stone that is lying beside the open grave, inscribed but not yet erected, until it is standing on its edge. Its heft is such that he feels a twinge in his arms and shoulders, but by shunting it this way and that he can slowly edge it toward the grave. He shuffles it as close to the edge as the soil will allow, and sees the priest raise his chubby hands in a futile defense, against a weight that would easily crush him like a ripe strawberry.

"Now will you tell me, Father, or would you rather I drop the stone? No one seems to be searching for you. What a quaint little tale it'll make here in the village, one to tell by the fire of a winter's eve: That fat priest of ours never wanted to be of any trouble. He stumbled, fell into a grave, and pulled a stone down over himself, and then it was just a matter of shoveling the soil back on top."

The voice that rises from the underworld is hoarse but resigned.

"Letters of indulgence."

"Excuse me?"

"In the south they've existed for a long time, and that with the Pope's consent, but only now are they reaching our northern soils."

"What are they?"

"An agreement with the Lord that allows a sinner to buy his way out of penance in exchange for ready money."

Never before has such a thought occurred to Nils, but its opportunities slap him like a pail of cold water to the face. He tries to fathom it: Every soul in need offered a contract that ultimately saves money, for a suspended penance would preserve many a day's work. Normal folk would no longer be forced to choose between spiritual perdition and bodily starvation. And, if the church is wise and patient enough to allow partial payments on the debts due—which he has no doubt that it is—the profits will be all the greater. With interest, too, for surely the Lord's commandments apply only to others and not to He Himself? Poor and rich alike will pay. Men like his uncle will be able to plunge their fists shoulder-deep into their coffers and still adorn their church roofs in gold leaf with what's left. At Nils's silence the priest grows restless. He clears his throat and goes on, valiantly trying to cast courage and authority into his abject voice.

"His excellency the bishop sent Olaus Jonae north with the letters, to have the scribes duplicate them in our churches. He went as far north as the Lord's light extends, and on his way back he gathered what coins had started to ring in."

Nils whistles quietly.

"More than even the bishop dared dream of, and I know his dreams have room enough for many a coin."

"As I said when I was still aboveground: if my congregation is any token, then what you say is true."

"It's perilous for anyone to journey with such riches. He made it as far as Askersund, but never reached here."

"Perhaps he was tempted to keep it for himself?"

Nils bears down on the gravestone, which rocks before finding stability. Beneath him the priest whimpers at the sight.

"What we say of others is a mirror of ourselves, Father. The man's actions in Askersund suggest otherwise. But tell me, why such secrecy around something that will soon be known to all?"

The priest's voice quivers.

"Jonae sent word from the bishop that I wasn't to speak of this to highborn men. He gave me no reason, though I've pondered it much myself. I believe the bishop wants to let the habit take hold among the commoners before it can be prevented by law. Once the people have learned that sins can be bought for money there's no undoing it. I suppose many a lord might otherwise see a benefit to enfeebling the church's power before it waxes too great."

A hopeful tone finds its way into the priest's voice.

"His lordship mentioned that he should like to see the letter himself. With a little help out of here I should be happy to show him the copy that we were given to keep here in the church."

"That's no longer necessary. I can imagine it. Tell me, does it bear the bishop's seal?"

"Yes. Jonae carried an emblem on his belt bearing the bishop's coat of arms, to stamp on each letter."

Nils weighs his scales for a while before making his decision. Rising to his feet, he lets the stone roll back onto the ground next to the grave.

"Well then, Father, I now know all I need. For your honesty I am much obliged."

"Would a ladder or rope be too much to ask in return?"

"I cannot fathom how someone could see a letter of the kind you describe and not have it chip away at his faith; if not in the Lord himself, then at least in his church. The revenues will be great, today and surely tomorrow, but I wonder if the bishop isn't sowing his field with dragon's teeth. I feel it behooves me to at least do your soul a service and leave you languishing here overnight. Use the time well, in devotion. Perhaps God's more likely to be found here between walls of soil than beneath your own whitewashed arches. Say a mass for Bishop Knut if you have the time; he'll need all the help he can get now that the pearly gates are looming."

From the hole comes a sigh.

"As his grace pleases."

THEY ALL DISMOUNT. The relief is great among the northmen, who pat each other's shoulders and exchange smiles from blackened faces, their teeth white as knives by night. They stand now on the same turf they stood on last year. That was where their road practically came to an end, when the Council of the Realm convened and promised on the king's behalf whatever it took to ensure the army's withdrawal, even though it was more than they could uphold. No one has yet passed through the vaulted gatehouse, as if aware that a fate far greater than anyone could have expected awaits on the other side. Västerås is no Lawless Köping or Burg Hill, no stronghold pieced together from timber and mounds of stone in the lap of the wilderness, but a castle in a cathedral city, one of the kingdom's greatest citadels, the realm's last outpost before the northern inlands and the mining districts that they contain. It is here to Västerås that all the tax and customs from those regions are brought, the bailiff greedily snatching up his share before the rest is borne south, toward Stockholm and Copenhagen, to fund distant wars.

At his men's urging, Engelbrekt alone steps forward. For a while he stands still. His face betrays no thoughts, not even to those who know him well. His head is bowed over his shoulders, as though the shadow of the ramparts were bearing down upon his head. No one else moves either, an uncertainty in the air. Perhaps his intent will falter here in spite of it all, before crossing the final limit from which there is no return. As it stands he can still turn and ride home to Norberg and broker peace with the king and bailiffs. But then he raises his head and steps forward in long strides, until he is standing alone on the other side of the gatehouse, where the bailey is visible. The castle's master now, to thundering cheers, a jubilation that refuses to abate.

Finn turns to Magnus, wondering what kind of look he will find on his face. Whatever he had expected, it isn't the anxiety verging on terror that he sees.

"What is it?"

"Hebbla Albrektsdaughter."

Magnus darts ahead, past all the others who are now approaching the gates, and reaches Engelbrekt first.

"Sire, a quick word."

It is as though Engelbrekt doesn't hear. He stands there, stock-still, without turning, and Magnus must go around him to make himself known. But Engelbrekt doesn't see him, either, his eyes wide but sightless. His cheeks are red, his breaths heavy. In his face Magnus reads astonishment but also something else, feelings that Magnus would have imagined foreign to a countenance that is otherwise so calm and decisive. Dread, confusion.

"Sire?"

Others are on their way, and their time is short. When Magnus receives no reply he takes Engelbrekt's hand, only to find his arm stiff as a stick. When he shakes it, Engelbrekt's gaze sharpens, like a sleepwalker called to waking. Engelbrekt turns to Magnus as though in confusion, blinks at him as though at a strange vision.

"What? What is it?"

"Count Eberstein had a ward in his care, a foster daughter. His wife wished her ill. I didn't see her among their retinue."

"And?"

"I fear some ill may have befallen her."

Others gather around them while Engelbrekt masters himself anew. Magnus sees Eric Puck, black-eyed and swollen-nosed, his fists clenched. An older man stands beside him, white of hair and beard, a calming hand on Eric's shoulder. It takes another moment before Engelbrekt has fully composed himself. He rubs his cheeks to rid them of the charcoal marks, then makes up his mind.

"It would be a grave ill if we were left with the blame for a girl's misfortune. You go on ahead, and take your page with you. The castle is unlocked, as are all the doors inside. That was the agreement we reached yesterday."

Magnus is off without a reply, and Finn follows him up the steps, then presses his shoulder against one of the castle doors to open it wide enough for them to gain access. In the great hall await chests stacked in piles, a book of accounts on top of them. Silver in abundance. They pay it no heed and run on.

"MOTHER."

Kari Sharp turns around, making one final, vain attempt to commit the numbers to memory before she forgets her calculations, for she knows her son won't relent.

"Mother!"

She gives up and stands the abacus on its side, sending its beads sliding to its base, ready to be counted anew, then turns around. Her son, Nils Bosson, is standing there, and though she should berate him for disturbing her in a way that he knows he oughtn't, she can't bring herself to do it. The boy is seven years old, tall and far too slim, despite her tendency to coax delicacies down him as often as she can. He knows he is in the wrong but crosses his arms nevertheless, impenitent, never so like her father, Sven Sharp, as when he decides to impose his will. A little lord already, though he still hasn't learned to roll his tongue against his teeth or speak cleanly. Kari can only laugh.

"Mother has a guest."

So many comings and goings in these busy days, this calm before the much-awaited storm.

"Who is it now?"

"My cousin."

"What?"

"She says so anyway."

Kari hastens out. Around her Oakwood Manor extends, in sprawling annexes, a labyrinth of boards and planks that to Kari Sharp serve but as an eternal reminder of the fact that where another woman bore ten children she has only one, and no more appear to be coming. It is Britta Bengtsdaughter who has come, all the way from Cuckoo's Roost no less, and suddenly the hairs rise on Kari's arms, for good news can always wait, while misfortune demands haste. Even had she felt otherwise, Britta's aspect would have been hint enough. Haggard and weary she looks, covered in road dust, anxiety in her gaze. Kari takes her by the hands and holds her there, wishing she were still with her abacus in its world of numbers, out of the reach of earthly woes.

"Britta. What's wrong? Tell me now."

Kari sees Britta's lip knot to stem its quivering and her eyes start to tear up, she who so seldom shows her feelings. She draws her in closer, into an embrace, holds her to her chest until her heart has calmed and her breaths have stilled. Britta's voice comes as a whisper against her ear.

"Something's wrong with Mother. And Father's away. I don't know where. I don't know what to do."

Praise the Lord. No one's dead.

"Come, take a seat. Tell me all."

※

One hundred miles she has ridden. From morning to eve and through the whole starry night, arriving the next morning. Kari grimaces at the mere thought of so much time in the saddle, and on a black track at that. Much can befall a young woman on roads like these, when met alone by rogues with no one else to see or hear. Kari listens to what Britta has to say, sighing inwardly at these fragile inlanders. She is of a different stock, raised on a rocking deck. Much has she seen. Drownings, attacks. Red clouds that bloomed fleetingly where bleeding men were shoved into the waters, quickly lost to their depths. She still remembers being marched out of Visby under German spears, though she was but four at the time. Remembers the empty eyes of her shipmates, bloodshot in death, their heads atop spikes that lined the way from the city ramparts to the shore. Many were those who had let her ride on their knees, who had stolen treats for her from the galley. There they stood, reproving in their throatless disappointment, as if envious that the life lost to them was still hers. To this day she is confronted by their gazes in her dreams, but at least she doesn't let herself get caught up by trifles, she who knows how bad things can get. Perhaps they will learn better, this weak next generation, in the years soon to come, the future that gives her cause to count Oakwood's arrows and muster the manor's men. But whatever Britta Bengtsdaughter may be, she isn't stupid, and it is as though she has read Kari's thoughts.

"Forgive me for troubling you. For coming here. I know I must seem ridiculous to someone like you, but I've nowhere else to turn."

It is Kari who is shamed by her thoughts. Isn't the good of the children the best price to set on one's own pains? May the young ones walk dry-shod past the pools of blood that have lain in her way. She places her hand on Britta's cheek, trying to summon all the motherliness that doesn't come easily to her.

"I spoke to your mother at Midsummer. I did sense that she wasn't content. She was carrying a great burden, with Mara's child lost. And she was feeling her own age, too."

Kari doesn't mention Magnus. She is aware of her own share in the blame: though the idea to send Magnus off to Engelbrekt was Nils Stensson's, it was to Sir Bo whom he turned first, and whatever Bo knows, Kari knows, too. No one was better placed than she to bring Stina to reason. Not that anything Kari said was a lie, but she knows well enough that it was said not for the sake of truth but for their house's best interests. Stina gave her consent. Kari couldn't have imagined where it would lead. Now she wonders what she would have thought of Stina had the roles been reversed, had it been Stina who had conspired to pack her Nils off into the wilderness. Immediately she sees herself riding for Cuckoo's Roost with a freshly whetted knife. Only one solution can she find.

"You must find your mother a diversion. Something to drive her melancholy from her mind. Something away from Cuckoo's Roost."

"But what? And where?"

Kari runs her hand over her face, aware that her advice is worse than it ought to be. She doesn't know, has no more to offer, but she feels her guilt and knows that she won't rest easy until she has helped to undo that which she has set in motion. She curses inwardly, an oath from the salty waves, the kind of invectives that Sven Sharp might have bellowed from his hull into an oncoming wind.

*

They share a meal, terse and awkward, marred by a sense of unfinished business. Kari struggles to play the host. She chastises herself while picking at her food, sees that Britta leaves most of hers uneaten as well. Soon she is off home again, Britta Bengtsdaughter, the same way back but on a borrowed horse, anxious that her absence will be noted and prompt concern among the household. Another hundred miles, and that after but a few hours rest. She wants no company. Kari must send two of her best men behind her, at enough of a distance that they won't be seen, but close enough to rescue her should fate demand. She promises them a lashing followed by a salt bath if they fail to keep up with the girl.

Instinct guides Nils on his journey back. In this direction the light is reversed, the sun in his face by morning, overhead at noon and behind him come evening. He tarries, lets his horse plod along at a leisurely pace, while he pays heed to the road's verges, the condition of the branches. Still, he knows his goal: the hill where he rested on the way south, where he had caught whiff from the forest of something going to waste. It could have been anything: a deer, roe deer, or elk, either riven by other wild creatures or glanced by a poacher's arrow, badly enough that it could do no more but flee the hunter's reach before its lifeblood ebbed out and it was lost to the crows and ravens. But one thing can he say for sure: it's big, the size of a man or even bigger.

He frets more the farther he walks, heedful of the forest's whims. Perhaps it is in hiding this time, the hill he remembers, easily confused with others of the same ilk. As before, the day is sultry. What little winds blow fare ill against the lee the trunks provide. It's old forest, that much he can tell, one that knows neither man nor cattle. Now a slope. His hope starts to stir, and he dismounts. Slowly he leads the horse up the hill, then leaves it to munch at the clover along the verges as soon as he reaches its crown. He peers out over the trees, to little avail; after mere yards the view is obscured. He licks a finger and holds it up over his head to better feel the wind. It's blowing the wrong way, if memory serves him right. No help to be had there. He searches for landmarks: none. Tree upon tree. At random he chooses the tallest among them and sets off in that direction, while silently reciting the rhyme that he was taught in case his feet should ever lead him astray, more out of habit than belief in its wisdom.

Any sense of direction soon deserts him. He must guide the horse behind him, worm his own twisting path at the branches' bidding. What little light that penetrates the foliage is all that he has to go on to tell the position of the sun. Haphazardly he wends his way in the direction of the tall oak he saw. Beneath him the ground is still wet from the spring thaw, sodden and difficult to pass, each depression a basin roiling with the corrupted remains of the detritus from the trees. Soon he is muddy and wet up to his calves, his shoes full of bog water that announces each step with a mocking slurp. His mood soon falls by the wayside, and he curses his own simplemindedness, that he could think himself capable of finding the nail in this haystack, however much it might reek. Reaching a dry patch, he sits down to think and feed the gnats.

Then all of a sudden he hears it, the murmur of the wind in the trees above. Still distant, but on the right track. With renewed hope he is on his feet, hears aspens rustling all the closer, sees the plume of gnats disperse around his warm body. The stench that hits him in the face is enough to make him recoil: sweet and rich, like a ghost in broad daylight who has found him in its path and yet marched straight through him. His hand jerks to his nose in defense, and he crouches down as though evading a blow. Then, taking hold of himself, he lowers his hand and follows the scent. Yet again it assails his senses. Flesh; flesh turned to a teeming host of contagion, one apt only for the small, sharp teeth and beaks of the forest, creatures with diets hardened by age-old scarcity. With each step the stench grows all the worse, and he must bend double to heave, then spit once the bile has passed.

Other senses come into play. First hearing: the drone of flies swarming in their thousands before him. The trees clear, and there stands an oak, one taller than the others, a tyrant whose foliage obscures the sun, whose heavy roots have voided the earth of so much nourishment that the ground lies bare in a wide circle around it. Between the trunks that still stand in his way he sees the air saturated with black spots, a tempest of flies around their feast. Then the beating of broader wings as dark shadows dash skyward: a murder of crows scared off by his arrival. They land in the trees at a safe distance, where they await his departure with greedy coal-flash eyes. Nils prays a silent prayer that he won't find what he is searching for; that he might see a hoof sticking up into the air, anything to avoid having to take a single step farther with his halo of rotund flies, their bodies shiny with fat and giddy with plenitude as they buzz around his eyes, in his mouth and nose when he draws in air. But already he sees. No hoof, but a foot, shod. It is a man who lies here, who has lain here for some time. Baked and leavened in the sun. Nils bends down and grabs hold of a few leaves to roll into small balls, then presses them into each nostril.

The corpse is lying on its back, clothes in disarray. Maggots have started to flay the body, revealing graying muscles beneath. Nils forces himself to look, only to blink and clap his hands to his face in defense. The nose has been severed, the ears, too. On his belt? Something that glints. Nils knows that only the crows can see him, but still he is ashamed when he fails to snatch up the treasure on his first swoop. After another failed attempt he composes himself and forces himself closer, slowly and purposefully, until his fingers close around that which he seeks. An iron seal, the bishop's emblem. And there, among the church's symbols, his own coat of arms, a shield parted per fess in two fields, the upper one blank, the lower half latticed. As close to blue and gold as one can get in the language of metal, where all tinctures refuse to stick. Nils nods thoughtfully as he stands there.

"Good day to you, Olof Jonsson. You'd have probably fared better faithless."

Thoughtless words uttered in the heat of the moment. Nils wonders what lessons they also hold in store for him.

F INN AND MAGNUS run through the stone hallways of the keep, the only sounds they hear the echoes of their steps being cast back upon them like apparitions in their pursuit. On the walls the torches hang cool and extinguished, the rugged walls cold in the midst of summer, the shadows deep under vaults and in nooks. From hall to chamber they pass, then up the stairs to the floor above, seeing all around them the signs of a hasty departure, yet little of plundering. The count must have understood that no covered cart would be allowed to leave the castle unchallenged, and seen no other option but to leave all as it was. Slender candlesticks, sumptuous tapestries, movables in abundance, all left as though a chambermaid just stepped out to the latrines, soon to return.

Finn is losing heart, but Magnus runs on. The castle is even bigger than he remembers it: room upon room on floors stacked high, no doubt with cellars below. Anyone with something to hide here would easily succeed in that endeavor. Yet Magnus appears tireless. Only at the top of the stairs is he forced to pause, and they both stand still for a while, bowed, with stitches in their sides and their hands on their knees, while the taste of blood melts from their mouths and their breaths begin to slow. Beneath them they can already hear the northmen taking possession of the castle: raised voices issuing orders on the counting of goods; groans and clatters as the chests of silver are carried off to safer places. Both of them see it at the same time, the door before them. Shut, where others were left open. When Magnus tries it he finds that it is locked, but a key is left in the hole. He turns it stiffly and nudges the wood inward, but steps back with a sharp gasp when he sees what is inside.

She is sitting in a tub of water, her knees drawn up and her arms around her legs. Her red plaits have been unfastened, her waist-length hair released and draped over herself like a mantel, for she has nothing else with which to cloak her nakedness, no clothes lying anywhere to be seen. The color of her locks makes her skin appear all the whiter. Magnus sees the freckles spilling down over her shoulders, over her back. She is shaking in the tub, for the water has long since cooled. The room is bare, without even draperies on the walls. Magnus gestures at Finn to try the other rooms in search of more fitting attire.

"What's happened? Where are your clothes?"

Hebbla's voice comes as scarce more than a whisper, her head still bowed, her eyes fixed on the water before her.

"Danish Lina. She told me I had to bathe before we left, for it would be our last chance before Oppenstone Castle. She had the maids heat the water and draw me a bath. I fell asleep in the water, as I often do. Once it had cooled and I wanted to get out, my clothes were gone and the door was locked. From the window I saw the northmen with their blackened cheeks make way for the count and the castle household, giving them safe passage down to the water. Lina couldn't help but turn back to look up at me with a parting smile. I pounded on the door, but no one could hear. The castle was empty."

"But why? Did the count know?"

Hedda turns toward him while still clasping her knees. A flash of green between red locks.

"Lina despises me. I told you before. The count was upset, and ever since the northmen came to him late last night to confer, he's had other matters to attend to. He was swearing a lot in German, each oath uglier than the one before. When he finally learns I've been left behind in a place he can never return to I should scarce think he'll be anything but relieved. Lina took my clothes thinking that the northmen would find me as I am and do to me what the count does to her each night. Stripped of my maidenhood, it would be a grim future I faced."

Finn appears in the doorway, breathless, his arms full of cloth. He places what he has found on the floor, then turns and steps out of the room to wait out of sight. Hebbla Albrektsdaughter lets Magnus drape the cloth over her shoulders and help her out of the bath. Slowly and cautiously she steps over the rim of the tub, then stands there in a growing puddle. With the fear now defused she bursts into tears, hiding her wet eyes and runny nose in the cloth.

"I prayed to God that it would be you who came, but never before has any prayer of mine been answered."

They leave her alone in the chamber to dress. Around them the silent castle has found new voices. From chamber to chamber stride Engelbrekt's men, their footsteps heavy from their boots and shoes. Together they catalog what has been left, while assigning the rooms to new guests and new purposes.

"I'll speak to Engelbrekt, ask him to have someone escort you to Cuckoo's Roost, where my father and mother will take you in. They'll find a way to restore you to your father's side. From this day forth the north is at war."

Finn accompanies Hebbla to get her something to eat. Once he has left her to wait in safety he searches for Magnus and finds him near Engelbrekt, who as ever is surrounded by a flock of his men. The wait for his ear is long, and just when Finn thinks it's finally Magnus's turn, someone else pushes past with a more pressing matter. It's the same man he saw at Eric Puck's side, easily remembered by his pale hair that is still thick in spite of its whiteness, like fresh snow fallen over his head and shoulders.

"The people are calling for you."

"What do they want?"

"They seek your blessing. Many have fetched their sick and infirm and carried them up to the castle gates. They want you to lay your hands on them to heal their ailments."

For a moment Engelbrekt stands stock-still, staring at the man as though at a joke made in poor taste.

"What madness is this?"

The elder bows his head and lowers his voice.

"When were the people ever any different? No man with sense is asking you to believe what you do, but it would be just as much madness on your part not to see that their confidence is a wind in our sails. We must tune our rig to catch it."

"That's blasphemy. I'm no saint. My hands heal wounds just as little as the sprigs on a tree."

"But is their faith not God's will? A blessing over our enterprise and a curse over King Eric?"

Engelbrekt has no response. He shakes his head, his face pale.

"Come with me. Believe what you will, but either way you must show yourself before them. Without the people on our side we're nothing."

"And when the lame and infirm must lean just as heavily on their crutches on the way home as here?"

The elder laughs.

"You've never been on a pilgrimage, have you? Never to Vadstena. He who is blessed gets to hear that which he so hotly desires, and if his faith is strong enough, any infirmity will feel sinful. He'll cast away his staff and stand on his bad foot, feigning that the pain is gone. The shame of his lie he will suppress. In return he can bask in the miracle's glow for the rest of his days. Everyone around him will exult in his luck and the Lord's greatness. And yours."

He takes Engelbrekt under the arm and follows him out through the gates. A roar greets them, and Finn and Magnus can but wait. The hours pass. Once Engelbrekt finally returns he is pale and his hands are shaking.

T`HE EVENING IS` late when Nils reaches Askersund, his horse in a lather after many miles at full gallop behind them, every last one of which now smarts in his own thighs and rear. He staggers wide-legged into the tavern, paying no heed to the silence he spreads among the late guests. The tavernkeeper is standing at his bar. Nils grabs him by the ear and jerks him from the beer tap so fast that his tankard falls, leaving the brew running straight out onto the floor. The stream draws in the thirsty like flies to dung, by the unwritten law that needs no explanation: since the keeper has left the barrel's tap open, better that the beer be drunk than wasted. Nils leads the man out to their sounds of mirth, through a door at the back of the building that gives onto an open yard lit only by the light that spills out through the longhouse windows. With a deaf ear to the tavernkeeper's complaints Nils shoves him up against the nearest wall. He is weary after his ride, and this lassitude makes him both slow of thought and spiteful of disposition. An angel on his shoulder whispers that it would be wrong of him to take his feelings out on the tavernkeeper, and that his purpose could be served just as well and surely faster by peaceful means, but Nils can't bring himself to listen. It does a man good to assert himself sometimes, to establish his weight in a world of the kind that leaves men mutilated in clearings. He slaps the man to silence him, and then once more, in retribution for the sting of the first on his palm. He waits for the surrender, catches his breath, and hears his heart start to slow, then sets the keeper down on his feet and raises a finger in the air until he has composed himself enough to pose his question.

"Last time I was here you mentioned a highwayman in Tiveden."

Not one jot of recognition in the tavernkeeper's wide eyes. He shakes his head.

"My lord, peace reigns in these parts, for at least a day's ride hence. Last year the bailiff's men-at-arms came and herded off all the vagrants who had fled to the forest to avoid paying their taxes, and who had taken to imposing their own road tolls upon those too weak to deny them. The bailiff had their tarred heads raised on posts around the city limits to deter others, and it was a message that couldn't be misunderstood."

"Olaus Jonae."

"Who?"

"Olof Jonsson. The man who stayed with you for four nights, the one with the lame hack. You said he was angling for company going south, to help him with his heavy load, and that he only had any success when he started warning them of a robber."

The tavernkeeper has clearly been drinking liberally of his own brew, for he is more drunk than he first appeared, habit alone what keeps him on his feet. Nils can smell it on his breath now, hear it on his slurred speech. Feeling his rage return, he starts weighing up the pleasure that he would take from knocking the man to the floor and stamping his foot where a heel does its worst against the possibility of being able to extract what he wants to know.

"Last time I gave you a coin for each answer. From here on out I'll be taking one back for every excuse."

Unease of a kind that only the value of money can rouse darkens the tavernkeeper's face, once the threat has worked its way through his beery haze to the seat of his reason.

"Come now, pull yourself together. A butcher in Tiveden. One who takes everything and cuts off the prick, nose, and ears to boot."

Only now does the man light up. He fumbles for the words in a newfound joy.

"Tor the Walker?"

Nils gives a quick nod.

"Such was his name."

The tavernkeeper's face breaks into a big, merry smile, his tooth stumps red under his split lip. Then comes the laughter, like water from a spring source in the thaw; at first a mere snigger, then a chuckle, then a cackle. Barking sounds erupt from his gaping gob, like a dog who has picked up a scent. Soon he can no longer stand upright and is forced down onto all fours by his glee. Nils gives him a kick in the side that turns him onto his back, but it scarce makes any difference. In the end Nils gives up and throws up his hands, as if to stress the hopelessness of his cause before an unseen judge. He takes a seat on a makeshift bench formed of a board atop two cracked bushels, and there he rubs his dusty face while the tavernkeeper rolls back and forth across his yard in fits of laughter. It takes some time for the jollity to subside. Nils lets him lie there panting for another little while, then walks over to his side and holds out his hand. More sober now. He pulls the tavernkeeper up onto his feet and helps him to sit down on the same bench.

"Are you done laughing?"

"I think so."

"Well?"

"No more slaps?"

"I've lost the mood."

"I've been drinking, see, otherwise I'd have reined myself in better. It's just that I can see how far you've ridden for this, and what I'm about to say I could probably have told you when last we spoke. But would his lordship admit that luck also has its part to play in how words come out, and, since only God the Father Himself and his only begotten son are infallible, the fault isn't mine alone, and no beating in the world can change what's already passed?"

"Fair enough."

The tavernkeeper is on the brink of another fit of laughter, but checks himself when he feels a twinge in his side. He places a hand to his sore rib cage.

"I think I've laughed one of my ribs off."

Seeing no reason to remind the man of the kick that he appears to have forgotten, Nils simply waves him on.

"Tor the Walker. There's no such man, never has been. Olof Jonsson made him up. I heard for myself how the tale grew grislier and grislier with each new telling, until he found someone who finally believed him. The only sack anyone's had reason to fear losing in these forests is the kind that holds silver, and even that was some time ago now."

Magnus lets his heavy eyelids fall. The skin around his eyes stings briefly when they close, but the feeling lasts but a moment before it melts away, ringing out into a gentle darkness. His neck is resting against a cloth folded over the edge of the pail. His hair flows out into the warm water that Finn has drawn, every smell of the stables soon masked by fresh birch leaves. Carefully Finn pours the water over his scalp, then starts washing his hair with a gentle touch. Magnus feels his furrowed brow start to smooth, the world's troubles falling away into oblivion. He is spent, his body aching, but its complaints are soon forgotten when his mind lets go of reality, allowing itself to be lulled into a light slumber. Finn's fingers are softer now, his touch milder, the cleansing caress agreeable. Magnus drifts between waking and sleep, where the thoughts that roam freely aren't easy to tell from dreams. He hears Soot snorting and stamping in his stall, but since the sound isn't one of discomfort he pays it no heed: the stallion is clean and fed.

Halfway to Uppsala they have come, but ever since Västerås Magnus's feelings have changed. Whereas before he simply saw a wandering horde, he now better understands the army's power, its inconceivable size when gathered in one place, the weight of so many wills sharpened to a spike. Implacable. And Engelbrekt at its heart, their sole leader, his presence what binds them all. Never before has Magnus set eyes upon a king: the throne is in Denmark, the crown but a distant fact, its power felt only through bailiffs like Hans of Eberstein or Jösse Eriksson. Such men now seem to him like little boys in big clothes, bereft of any semblance of majesty. Engelbrekt is something else. A man whose very bearing invites reverence. Deeper into his lethargy Magnus descends, and the subject of his dream-thoughts shifts: Cuckoo's Roost. His uncle with his enticements, Bishop Knut with his threat borne on reeking breaths. Out of the depths of his sleep he now whispers the objection that he withheld then.

Yet again Soot neighs, and Magnus is made aware that the water has cooled, the touch now gone. Finn has let him fall asleep. Blindly he reaches for a cloth to dry himself, gathers up his wet hair while rising to sitting, then rubs it dry and dabs the cloth over his bare shoulders. With a gasp he opens his eyes. Finn is gone. It is another man who sits on the stool in the lantern's glow: Engelbrekt Engelbrektsson himself, straight-backed and with his hands in his lap, his gaze calm.

"Magnus of blue and gold."

Soot's neighing. The gentler touch.

"Did you wash my hair?"

"Am I not to blame for it being dirty to begin with?"

Engelbrekt leans in, placing his elbows on his thighs for support.

"I've treated you worse than I should. I suppose I've done some penance now, but take my apologies as well."

Magnus doesn't know what to say. He lets Engelbrekt go on.

"The blame isn't mine alone. Around me are many who would think ill of every stranger, who prefer to take no risks. No doubt many believed you'd sooner return to Cuckoo's Roost than groom a horse, but how wrong they were. You've undertaken the work with your own hands, have come to know Soot and earned his affection. A proud creature is he, tender of hair. Never before has he let anyone plait his mane. And with blackened face you stood beside us on the field in Västerås, with no knowledge of what was to come. Behind you the crowds pressed forward, and had arrows flown you would have had no means of defense. When afterward you came to me, it was not for your own sake, but with another's well-being in mind. Those who chose to look upon your actions with spite assumed you simply intended to use the girl as a messenger for some tiding borne home to your father, with news of all that you've learned from us and of our next goals. The matter gave rise to a quarrel. Harald Esbjörnsson you've met before, and how you won his friendship I know not, for he's chosen to keep that between you. But he spoke on your behalf, reluctant to see a young girl searched to no avail. The others didn't listen, but Harald was proved right. There was no written message, no tidings that you'd taught her to recite."

The stable is silent. Only Soot stirs on restless hooves, heedful of human moods.

"Eric Puck claims you've been sent by your house to win my trust and assure their favor. I don't believe he's wrong. Sir Bengt of Cuckoo's Roost hasn't sent his only son to fight beside me out of concern that I might otherwise fare ill in battle. And yet you've given me no reason to mistrust you. I can't figure you out, Magnus.

For some purpose are you sent, but none of your actions confirm the obvious."

Engelbrekt tilts his head to one side.

"You were heard chanting my name with the crowds at Västerås's gates. Why?"

Words fail Magnus. He has asked himself the same question, only to shy away from what he sensed would be a difficult answer. Far simpler to merely follow the road ahead, so long as it seemed to be the right one. But how it has brought him to where he is now is no longer so easy to discern.

"I can't say."

Engelbrekt points.

"You have a scar on your forehead. It's barely visible, but it's clear enough to the touch. It's not old. How did you get it?"

"A wooden cudgel out of nowhere. I fought at the Midsummer tournament, against the wishes of my father and mother."

"Why?"

"I wanted to show them that Cuckoo's Roost had become too small for me."

Engelbrekt gives a wry smile.

"Last year I was outside Burg Hill when we took the stronghold for the first time. From the roof an unseen arrow was shot straight at me, from a bad angle as dusk fell. Sensing its shadow in the nick of time, I recoiled without thinking. Its point glanced across my forehead. I still bear the scar, in the same place as yours."

He strokes his hair to one side by his cheek, exposing a red line.

"Rebels the both of us, marked by the same stamp."

He stands up and stretches his back, tired after many days in the saddle. When Engelbrekt takes his first step toward the door Magnus replies.

"When I last fought it was to my loss. But you said you'd found the secret of war in the south. Won't you tell me what it is?"

Engelbrekt stops, then turns to face him with a searching look.

"That's simple. Don't fight unless you know the battle to be already won. For one who has mastered the art of warfare, no combat is needed. The greatest victories are won unseen."

Seeing Magnus's dubious look, he pulls his stool in closer and sits back down.

"I shall tell you. It's no more payment than you deserve. King

Eric and Queen Margaret before him have outdone themselves in their hunger for power. That would be the haughty man's interpretation. Someone meeker might say that both are human, just like the rest of us, albeit placed by birth and Providence atop golden thrones, shrouded in scarlet and jewels. But look at Margaret the child, Margaret the girl. She is unique, far sharper than the rest, and she knows as much herself. But no daughter has a son's worth. She must fight harder than anyone else simply to make the men in power, simple-minded and officious as they are, see the gifts in her whose praises would be sung from border to border had she only been born a boy. Through that struggle she whetted her blade even more, and in the end she succeeded in all that she had set out to do. She changed the world, bent it to her will. But I wonder if it didn't bend her with it. Once atop her Danish throne, the kingdom that she had inherited felt too small. She wanted Sweden, too. And what of Eric? Look at Eric the boy, Eric the young lad. Thrust up onto an empty throne in the absence of other heirs, given a new name in a foreign tongue, one with sounds that his new subjects were capable of forming. All that he had been before, swept aside from one day to the next. As king he could have been far more than he is and still look as though he were wanting next to his grandmother's sister Margaret. And so he is obsessed with winning his war in the south, though there is no victory to be had. Viewed thus, it's harder to blame them for their follies. Can you, Magnus? Which of your vices could be turned to the people's misfortune? Do you dare say that you would have made a better king?"

Magnus can do no more than shake his head.

"Motives aside, they have both made a grave error. The kingdom whose borders they have extended is now too great. Denmark and Sweden can't both be controlled from Copenhagen. And so they must assign their rule to trusted men, Danes and Germans. Bailiffs. Not even Margaret, she who was wise enough to see straight through others, found it easy to find good men in sufficient numbers. Eric never stood a chance. What bailiffs we've ended up with are fortune hunters who see no other purpose to their posts than their own enrichment. Such misrule cannot last. Someone would rise up in the end. If not me, then another in my place."

Magnus remembers the fort at Lawless Köping in ashes, the words he said to Finn amidst the smoke and the stench.

"You mean to take the whole kingdom."

"It sounds like a huge undertaking when you put it that way. But the castles don't have enough men for their defense. Only Kalmar and Stockholm have any strength to speak of. The rest count their men in the dozens. They can't resist us. The kingdom became ours the very instant we were able to muster people in such numbers. From here we'll go on to Uppsala, to attach the church to our cause. That'll be easy, for they're already in a tussle with King Eric over the archdiocese. With our arrival the matter will be settled, and the gratitude of the church will be to our favor. Then on to Stockholm. Her we can't take, but we can render her harmless. Hans Kröpelin rules there in King Eric's name, and I know him of old. A good man, wise and just. He'll parley. Then on southward, one castle at a time, until we see the Danish border."

A veil passes over Engelbrekt's eyes as he speaks. Now he blinks it aside, looking upon Magnus with a clearer gaze.

"All of this is clear to those who can see. But now I shall let you in on a secret. I mean to do more than merely take the whole kingdom."

Engelbrekt leans in even closer, his voice lowered, as if in veneration of the confidence about to be shared.

"I mean to take the whole kingdom without spilling a drop of blood."

Soot stirs fitfully in his sleep, and Engelbrekt stands up and walks over to his stallion's side, to stroke his muzzle with a calming hand, soothe whatever dreams have disturbed him.

"That I've seen enough of in Schleswig, at the hands of the Hussites. Here's another one of the secrets of war: it sides with no one. War bloats into an entity unto itself. Muster an army great enough and it will become a beast that must feed itself indiscriminately. It comes marching under banners that claim to be for the best of the people, but to do so it must plunder their barns, slaughter their animals, and lay waste to their store-chambers. Soon enough it knows no laws and becomes a refuge for the basest of urges, constantly moving in search of new sustenance, until all of the feed is consumed and it perishes of starvation or against a superior foe. My army will be different. Only few are to come south with me. The others will go back to where they belong. The people I need I must muster from the bailiwicks we are destined for, for they won't steal what is theirs already, nor from their neighbors. So far all has gone well. It was with the help of the people of Lawless Köping that we drove Giovanni Frangipani's men-at-arms from their province. I can count the men we have lost on my own fingers."

He turns, still with a hand on his horse.

"Will you follow me south, Magnus of blue and gold?"

Magnus draws his damp cloth closer, over the hairs that have risen on his skin. The night has cooled, a wind caressing the tree-tops outside.

"Yes. That's what I want."

"It's a summer's game I'm inviting you to join, one easy enough to play. But it must move fast, for then winter will come, and only a fool would ride to war once the cold has descended, for its aim is surer and its bite sharper than many an arrowhead. Come spring, King Eric will arrive to take back the kingdom that has slipped from his grasp. Then the drops of blood will be harder to spare."

Sir Bengt strides out into the courtyard between the dwellings of Cuckoo's Roost, stepping over to one side so that the keep blocks the sun. Home again. Not that anyone appears to care all that much, his wife still bedridden and his daughter still shy as a hind, though that might be just as well. Soon enough he'll surely be hearing plenty of women's voices. He tightens his belt around his waist and adjusts his tunic, not yet attired in a manner befitting a man of his station, though he's far too eager to greet the messenger who has arrived to care about that. His march is brisk enough to send sour puffs of air rising from his stomach. Perhaps the message is from Magnus, finally. High time that boy remembered the task entrusted unto him and proved he was ready for such confidence. But the sight that greets him in the courtyard stops him like a wall.

"What's the meaning of this?"

A man from the north, surely, burly and with an unruly beard. So far no surprise. But in front of him stands a girl, red of hair. Sixteen, perhaps. The man clears his throat.

"Harald Esbjörnsson is my name, Norberg my home. I've come from Västerås, from Engelbrekt Engelbrektsson, who has trusted me to convey Hebbla Albrektsdaughter here to Sir Bengt of Cuckoo's Roost."

Sir Bengt shifts weight to appease his sore back and throws an arm out to one side.

"What for?"

"Hebbla is of House Bydelsbach, close allies of Bo the Gryphon, as your own house has been. She was a ward of the count of Eberstein for the sake of her education, but was left behind when he fled the castle. Your son took care of her, and that's why I'm here."

"I fail to see . . ."

Sir Bengt trails off, feeling his eyes blacken when the words hit home like a fist to the temple.

"You lie. Engelbrekt can't have taken Västerås. Even if the Teutonic Order had come sailing in in their glory days, that castle would have stood strong for years."

"One day was all it took. I was there. If you don't believe me then send a man to Oppenstone, where Count Hans is licking his wounds. He'll tell you in his own words, but if there are children present who understand German, it'd be best to see to it that they cover their ears."

"But how?"

Harald gestures at Hebbla Albrektsdaughter.

"Engelbrekt entrusted me with a task, and he hasn't given me leave to speak openly with those whose loyalty is yet to be proven. The girl, however, is bound by no such promise."

Hebbla fixes her green eyes on Sir Bengt, holding her chin up high.

"God Himself saw the righteousness of Engelbrekt's cause and answered his prayers; his as well as mine."

Bengt rubs his weary eyes.

"Jesus Christ."

For a moment Sir Bengt stands there in thought, trying to recall the straightest road between Cuckoo's Roost and the seat of the house of Bydelsbach. Old Albrekt is the bailiff in Bergen. But then it strikes him: better yet that the girl stay here, as his honored guest. When the bailiff's castles prove to hold out better against Engelbrekt's forces than Västerås did and the uprising is quashed, it could be useful for Bengt to have benevolent Germans in King Eric's circle. Albrekt Bydelsbach would likely stay friendly for as long as his daughter remains at Cuckoo's Roost.

"Well, Harald Esbjörnsson, in that case by all means consider your task complete. I'll see to it that the girl arrives where she belongs."

The northman gives a curt nod and no more, then turns to Hebbla and bows.

"Here our ways part, and I wish you every luck."

"I wish you the same."

He turns from her and leaves her side to step over to Bengt.

"Sir Bengt. One other thing."

They both step off to one side, out of earshot of others.

"Engelbrekt Engelbrektsson sends his regards, and requests that you meet him in Vadstena when the month of August has run half its course. You and yours of blue and gold."

Bengt feels himself sobering up as quickly as if he had leapt into a lake on a chilly autumn morning.

"Did he say what the matter concerns?"

"The future."
"Oh, yes. What else?"
"Fiefs."

※

Britta sees her father wander off with the northman at his side. She can tell by his bearing that the tidings concern things that he holds dear, and as a result the opportunity that she has been waiting for to speak to him about her mother turns to dust before her eyes. She walks to the unfamiliar girl's side.

"I'm Britta, Sir Bengt's daughter."

Hebbla Albrektsdaughter looks at her face, as though searching for a likeness.

"You're Magnus's sister. Though he's much fairer than you."

Britta is surprised she isn't more offended by these words. But they don't appear to be said with any ill intent, merely an honesty without regard for the feelings it may stir.

"Have you met Magnus? Is he with Engelbrekt?"

Hebbla nods.

"Would you come to my mother's bedside? She's not been herself since he left. Every day she asks of tidings, and when nothing comes she merely rolls over onto her side and lies there all day and the whole night thereafter. I know that she would like nothing more than to hear what you have to say. Would you come, please, and say something that might gladden her?"

The girl nods, setting her red curls in motion.

"Lead the way."

※

With the evening Nils arrives, as usual seemingly blown in on the same winds that carry tidings of import. Bengt lets his brother pay a visit to the bathhouse and waits for him by the fire afterward, offers him food and drink.

"Engelbrekt wants a meeting at Vadstena."

Nils bares all his teeth, rubbing his hands in front of himself.

"It's going well for us. I'll come with you."

Both sit in silence for a while, their eyes on the blazing fire. In flames and embers they both see the same thing: castles, country manors, and vast lands; perhaps even a crown in the tip of the flame. When the heat grows overpowering Bengt leans back in his seat.

"And those thousand marks? What of them?"

"I found Olof, Knut's man. Slain in the forest. No silver. It's a funny story, if you have the stomach for it. To entice someone into joining him on the road, he made up a tale of a highwayman whom he named Tor the Walker, who mutilated his victims in a particular way. Whoever slayed Olof cut him in the same way."

Bengt sighs, his mind on the lost silver.

"I suppose finding the treasure would have been too good to be true."

"Do you know what the silver was from?"

Bengt shakes his head.

"Uncle was tight-lipped on that matter."

"The bishop's started selling letters of indulgence. Ready money in exchange for the forgiveness of sins."

Bengt reels in his seat, dizzy at the mere thought of the market he suddenly sees before him. Knut Bosson, fox in a henhouse. Bengt's attempts to reckon the value of this enterprise dispel every other thought, but on the outskirts of his mind something else lingers, too, a budding suspicion not yet robust enough to make itself known. He pushes it out of his mind when the frustration gets the better of him. He has enough to think about, anyway.

Stina perceives the stranger's presence at her bedside by a sense that lies somewhere between smell and hearing. She lets her spent head roll over on the pillow, feeling the dull pain of this movement in her stiff, unused body. She blinks in surprise. The girl is a stranger, with green eyes and hair like fire. Her own daughter stands behind her. Britta ushers the guest closer to the bed.

"Mother, this is Hebbla Albrektsdaughter, come from the north. She's seen Magnus."

Stina gropes for something to help her sit up, blinking vigorously to see better.

"Where is he? Is he with Engelbrekt? Is he well?"

Hebbla sits down on the edge of the bed.

"He was in good health when we parted."

Stina's voice cracks at the question.

"Is he coming home?"

Hebbla looks at Britta first, then Stina.

"No. He won't come home. He's meant for greater things. He

walks at Engelbrekt's side. There's no one closer. They go wherever God wills it, ousting the unjust from their seats."

Britta watches her mother, sees her eyes cloud over anew. Stina sinks back down into her sheets, incapable of giving her guest even a word in parting before she rolls over and turns her back to them. Britta can only escort her out, Hebbla, mute in the knowledge that the help she had hoped to extend has only made worse what was already ill, having stripped her mother of a vain hope. Over her own chest the weight returns, an invisible embrace, her breath choked and her heart in tumult.

PART IV

LATE SUMMER, AUTUMN, AND WINTER 1434

AUGUST ALREADY. THE summer is still high, though it will soon be drawing toward its close. Every time the wind blows, nameless senses anticipate the gust that will come at any moment, the one that bears a coolness of a kind that hasn't been felt in months, the scents of autumn in the offing. Magnus is standing on high ground, different now than before. His garbs from Cuckoo's Roost he has swapped for others, ones that fit better with the army's movements. A linen shirt and braies, both left out bleaching in the sun for so long that they still bear the fragrance of grass. A woollen doublet and hose, both tight at the top and fastened together by ties at the front and along the waist, though undone at the back, for give while riding. Laced boots in a smooth leather, and a mantle cut in a three-quarter circle that cloaks his shoulders but leaves his right arm exposed. His hat he keeps on his belt, preferring to leave his long hair free to the wind's fancies. Engelbrekt Engelbrektsson is at his side, both of them in the shelter of their grazing horses.

"This one doesn't want to give in, either."

Engelbrekt crosses his arms and peers out over the water at the castle on the other side. Ringwall Castle, of which Henrik Styke is bailiff on King Eric's behalf. Magnus follows Engelbrekt's gaze. Gray ramparts surround the castle on its islet in the river, leaving no opening for an attacker to gain a foothold without inviting a hail of stones and arrows from the parapets above. The name Styke is one that he has heard before.

"His father sailed with Sven Sharp. Sven's daughter, Karl, is my uncle's wife. She was raised on a ship's deck by the Victual Brothers and has told stories about them for as long as I can remember."

Engelbrekt grunts in response. Thus far all has gone well for them, all save for these two. Uppsala is taken; Örebro brokering its terms. With Stockholm peace reigns, the city's residents safe behind its walls, the trade routes open to the sea but closed to land. Eric Puck, still crooked of nose, has gone north to strike Foxholm Castle and the counties in the far north of the kingdom. Åland island is taken, Gryphon Rock burned down. Only here has Engelbrekt's prediction not yet been proven true. They are brothers, Albrekt Styke at Nyköping and Henrik Styke at Ringwall. German by birth, they bear a shield parted per fess in silver and blue with three red rings. Neither will budge.

"I lost my temper when I spoke to him. I rarely do so, and that fact disturbs me more than the words I let slip. Grown men should be above bickering like little boys. The king and the Council have done enough of that already. The campaign is beginning to take its toll, though this is still only the beginning. I must do better if this is going to go our way."

"What did you say?"

A band of geese flies over them in an arrowhead formation. Engelbrekt watches their flight.

"I swore I'd drag Henrik Styke from the castle by his hair before the week's out."

For a moment they stand in silence, until Magnus can no longer quell his laughter. It rings out over the tracts, clear and beautiful, turning heads down in the camp. At first Engelbrekt looks on stony-faced, but soon enough not even he can keep the corners of his mouth downturned. Once their laugher has faded, Engelbrekt surveys the water and the forest.

"You must have learned some of the wiles of siege from your father and his brothers. How would they take the castle?"

Magnus shades his eyes with his hand and peers down the slope. He sees nothing that he hasn't seen before.

"Fire. They would try to get close enough to put a torch to the bulwarks, and then to the castle roof."

"That's a butcher's solution. I know I did burn Burg Hill and the fort at Lawless Köping, but that was only after they'd been taken. Besides, they were wooden huts in the wilderness, good for no more than night lodgings for a bailiff's men-at-arms. But castles like this one we'll need once the roles are reversed; once the kingdom is ours and King Eric stands where we are now."

He gestures at the coursing water.

"Anyway, we still wouldn't get close. The water protects it from every side. The bridge is too narrow, and easily defended. Boats we lack, and even if we did have them they'd be to no great use, for they're an easy shot from the ramparts."

"That leaves the waiting game. With time I'm sure Henrik Styke will sooner compromise than have to listen to his own growling stomach."

Engelbrekt strokes his chin with a frown.

"First Nyköping Castle stood its ground, now Ringwall. I don't like it. Word travels, and it'll lend courage to others who would otherwise lie down flat. Those who follow us expect to see their faith repaid. We don't have long till Vadstena, and the more victories we have behind us, the better the lords will listen to our cause. It would be no great loss to leave Ringwall to its fate, but that could plant a seed for greater things. No. I'd sooner keep my promise to Henrik Styke. Help me think. It's not so difficult. Don't think like others; think of the things that no one else has thought of before. Where is the stronghold at its weakest?"

They stand in silence, turning their heads to find new angles, so that their eyes might extract the castle's every secret. Magnus bends his neck to better see what little there is to glean.

"The well stands alone, on the other side of the bailey to the keep."

"I see. If we could separate the men from the water, then thirst would be a good ally."

"If only we could shoot over the ramparts."

"Just what I was thinking. Look."

Engelbrekt points up at the trees in his line of sight, on the other side of the river.

"Up there the pines grow in abundance. We'll fell them, enough to build a raft with a wooden scaffold, one tall enough to give our marksmen a view over the walls."

Magnus tosses his head, letting the wind stroke the hair from his eyes.

"Is that another one of Jan Hus's tricks?"

"From him I learned that thought wins battles over strength. I've heard of similar towers before. But don't forget what I told you. Victory should be assured before the battle even takes place. I'm loath to have to waste lives on Henrik Styke's stubbornness. With what you know now, what would you do?"

Magnus ponders the question, then points at a meadow down by the riverbanks opposite the castle, one within view of the keep but beyond an arrow's reach.

"We'll build the raft and tower down there, where Styke and his men can see. It'll take some time before they understand what we're doing, but their minds will build up our works to something far worse than they are."

Engelbrekt nods.

"You're a fast learner."

"I wish I could say the same of you. You say that you have no miracles at your fingertips, yet time and again you only prove yourself wrong."

Engelbrekt retrieves Soot's bridle from where the horse has been grazing freely, and together they walk down the slope.

※

Engelbrekt calls it a belfry, the scaffold they raise on the raft. A master carpenter is easy enough to find among the men, and the grimy wrinkles on his face light up like a torch once he has fully understood the drawing they score into the raked earth. Eager as a boy he paces around it in circles, pointing his own cane at its corners and joints, asking questions and nodding at the responses. Then he hastens off to the troop of men who have already been summoned, those with their own axes, who are used to the forest and the quirks of falling pines. Soon enough the sounds of axes are heard from the trees, and trunk upon trunk is rolled down the slope that was evened out in haste. They drop into the water, to drift downstream to the meadow. Few tools are needed. Simple notches are cut into the trunks, which are then latched together and locked in place by virtue of their own weight, as securely as if they had sprung out of the earth in the intended shape. Five levels are soon raised, one on top of the other, and at the masthead sits the carpenter himself, his legs clasped around a log, a plumb line in one hand and an aiming stick in the other, to measure his scaffold's height against that of the castle keep. He nods. Once it is launched, it will be tall enough to allow not only the marksmen to sweep the bailey, but also others to breach the roof, by stepping over the battlements.

It is two days before Henrik Styke has his men raise a helmet on a spear above the battlements, wishing to broker terms. A five-day truce is what he wants, to prepare his departure and ensure no rescue is on its way. From Engelbrekt he gets a yes.

"Magnus?"

"Yes?"

"I won't be here to see the castle taken. I must leave for Vadstena. Ringwall is ours, for north of the Danish border there's no rescue to be had, and should Styke get any other ideas, then we'll put our belfry to use. The army will stay here until the castle is ours. Only three dozen of us are bound for Vadstena. Will you join us?"

"Do you even need to ask?"

"You'll see your kinsmen there. Your father and his brothers, and your grandfather's brother the bishop."

Magnus turns away, for a moment alone in his thoughts.

"What's to happen at Vadstena?"

"Without the nobility no lasting victory can be won. We need them on our side. Besides, with the Council's backing our uprising will be made lawful. Such things carry weight in the people's eyes. They know that only the written law protects them from the whims of others."

Magnus crosses his arms, sweeps his mantle over his shoulders, and looks around. Beyond the trees lie meadows, and there, behind them, new forests, as far as the eye can see. He turns back to Engelbrekt.

"What kingdom awaits us on the other side of your victory?"

"The Swedes must have their own king once more. A king like Saint Eric was, a good man with the people's best interests at heart. Lords beneath him to tend his castles, men chosen for their good character, who can collect the taxes owed to the crown in the name of keeping the peace, but not a single öre more. With the king at their backs they won't be lawless the way the Germans and Danes are now, no rogues with their sights set only on their own good."

"Will you not wear the crown yourself?"

Engelbrekt shakes his head.

"No. Not me. Someone else. Someone better. I've neither the desire nor wisdom enough to sit on the Swedish throne. But perhaps what desire and wisdom I do possess will be enough to find the right head to crown."

"These lords you speak of. Do you mean my house?"

"No one can rule the kingdom alone."

Magnus makes to speak but changes his mind. He blinks several times, turns away with his face to the wind.

"What is it?"

Magnus shakes his head.

"What if you find that we're all of the same stock? Scarce better than the Danes or the Germans?"

Engelbrekt steps closer to stand beside him and lowers his voice to better convey his gravity.

"How often I have asked myself the question you voiced before. What kingdom awaits us? What are we fighting for? These questions tormented me, time and again, through many a long, painful night. None the wiser did I become. I set to leading an insurrection without a clear direction, and inwardly I lost heart behind a face of resolve. Mere weeks ago I wouldn't have been able to give you an answer. But I know better now."

"Why?"

"Because I met you. The tree can't be rotten that sprouted a shoot like you. There must be more of the same kind. With that there is hope."

Engelbrekt catches the gaze that he has been seeking and holds it.

"Come to Vadstena with me. Lend me what aid you can. Thus begins the road toward the realm that must be."

S IR BENGT REINS in his horse when he senses the crowds. Vadstena is teeming with people, people in droves. Not since Saint Birgitta's return can the city have seen so many. They are peasants, vulgar folk with bodies marked by a lifetime's toil, men and women and children in a single heaving mass, their hubbub like the torrent around a water wheel. Sir Bengt has never been one to fear the people, but in such great numbers they make him ill at ease, and his advisers clearly feel the same, for they close ranks around him without instruction. Six men, dressed for festivities but with swords at their sides and spears in their saddle straps, their steel helmets burnished with sand so that they shine like the sun in a slick of water. Sir Bengt turns his nose up toward the town hall's tower and guides his horse that way, doing all that he can to impart a sense of dignity. He feels the people's looks as he passes, and they aren't of the kind to which he is accustomed. There is power in their numbers. Should they get it into their heads to tear him from his horse, he would be trampled to death on the spot. A long time has it been since he was made aware of how thin the ice is beneath him, him and all that is his. How deep lies the water below.

Sweaty and red of face he arrives at the town hall, where he is admitted through an arched passage to the courtyard where he can dismount. The place is already full of horses, proud animals in beautiful harnesses. Without thinking he scans the colors and coats of arms, counting their number. He sees a red boat on a yellow base, and a shield that likens his own, only parted per pale and not per fess. He sees the House of Sharp's water lily, and the one which is parted per bend in three tinctures, carried by House Oxenstar at Eka. And then his own, a parted shield in blue and gold, borne by horses that he knows. Sir Bo is already here, Bishop Knut likewise. Sir Bengt feels instantly more at ease. Better to meet kinsmen than arrive alone. Soon he sees his elder brother standing restlessly by the courtyard wall, his arms crossed.

"Brother Bo."

"Brother Bengt. All well with you and yours?"

Sir Bengt pulls a face.

"Not with Stina. She's bedridden, refuses to get up. Rare are the times that I see her. She misses Magnus, I suppose. Women's trials and tribulations aren't for us men to grasp."

"With time will come comfort. No doubt Kari will be difficult to deal with the day it's time for little Nils to leave home. Thankfully there's many a year till then."

Bengt nods while turning his head, looking for familiar faces.

"Been here long?"

"But an hour or so. The bishops are already up there, chattering like old ladies. Knut, Sigge from Skara, and Thomas of Strängnäs. If I learn that God's been mentioned even once in that conversation I'll have myself christened anew. I've already heard a few rumors, though. Others have got through to Engelbrekt first, my brother. Nils Gustafsson of Rossvik was with him from the very start. Now he holds Västerås Castle as a thanks for his help."

Bengt grimaces at the thought of the castle and its riches in another's care. And all of the northern mines above it, its miners gathered around their precious pits while the iron and copper spurt from them like waters from a fountain.

"Well then. I suppose that just shows the value of helping Engelbrekt. There's more castles than Västerås to be manned, and bigger ones, too, and richer. But what of our own Nils, is he here yet?"

Sir Bo shakes his head.

"Only the devil himself knows what that fox gets up to."

Bo drapes an arm around Bengt's shoulder, leads him even farther to one side, and lowers his voice.

"I know we're already agreed on the road ahead. We're to go with Engelbrekt. But let's not make that too obvious. He needs us and he knows it. Let's not sell ourselves cheap, but rather hold out until the price goes high. Show a little reticence. The bishop agrees."

The chamber lies up in the tower, extending from wall to wall, its windows so high aboveground that its builders afforded themselves the luxury of making them wide enough for a horse. The voices of those gathered fall silent when Bengt and Bo step inside. Bengt seeks out their eyes, exchanging nods with those already in his acquaintance. Most are his neighbors, familiar faces, allied in one way or another. A handful of them are members of the Council of the Realm, like he himself. He makes his way over to his uncle, who is vestured in all the splendor befitting of his office. The bishop is as he always is, shrunken and leathery and reeking of sour wine, and hunched of back, as though poised to make a quick escape from any sudden demands that debts be repaid.

"Uncle Knut. Blessings be upon you."

"Nephew Bengt. Ditto."

"Besides the crown's lands, I see in this room every landowner within a three-day ride. But who the hell is that?"

Bengt points at a young man who can't yet be thirty, broad of chin and with a snout of a nose.

"Crofter. Karl Knutsson of House Crofter. His home is Birdsfirth. He seems to be the only one who has come uninvited. Tells you something, doesn't it. Don't let his age deceive you."

Bengt furrows his brow.

"I've met him before, but he was no more than a boy then. The years haven't made him any fairer. I stamped my seal beside his on a will. Even then I disliked him. The kind of person who sees and hears everything, but never says what he thinks."

"Remind you of anyone?"

Uncle and nephew say the same name in chorus.

"Nils."

"And the man of the hour, where is he?"

"We're awaiting his arrival. Though he'll probably come soon, now that we're all here. If what I've heard from the priests in the north is true, he certainly knows how to make a memorable entrance."

Knut's words soon prove true. Outside the window the tenor of the voices changes. They grow in strength. The men's deep voices in cheers; the women's shrill cries in invocation; the children in laughter and tears, whistles and peeps. The lords jostle around the windows to see a wave spread through the crowd, as the people back away to cede space to Engelbrekt and his men, granting them passage to the town hall steps. Knut extends his bent neck to see better, holds his unwieldy eyeglasses at different distances from his face in order to find the best position. Then he whispers in Bengt's ear with the voice of a deaf old man.

"Soon we'll see if we've had any use of that son of yours."

All of them flock to the window, shoulder to shoulder, its casements flung open. Fingers point and voices whisper, all attempting to tell the leader from his circle of men.

"Is that him, the one on the piebald horse?"

"Does anyone know his coat of arms?"

"It's said that he's tall, a head taller than the tallest man."

It is difficult to see which of the horsemen is guiding their steps. Closer and closer they come, until the edge of the wall blocks them from view. In the chamber all is silent. Every sound from below heightens the suspense. Many men's footsteps are heard on the stairs. Then they cross the threshold, the northmen, and while the eyes of those gathered flit from one man to the next in the hope of finding majesty manifest, Engelbrekt Engelbrektsson alone steps forward.

"Shorter than you'd think."

A poorly veiled whisper breaks the silence, followed by another's titter. The lords assume their positions, as though for a dance long rehearsed. They spread in a wide circle, each finding the place that most befits him. Before the window stand the bishops in their trinity, with Knut in the middle, eldest that he is. By virtue of his age he is the first to speak.

"Engelbrekt Engelbrektsson of Norberg. We bid you welcome. Much have you done, and we owe you a debt of gratitude. May God's peace shine upon all of us who have gathered here at this pressing time."

Knut receives no response. Engelbrekt stays where he is, halfway to the middle of the circle, in wait of more to come. Knut clears his throat and speaks again.

"The foreign bailiffs are fleeing back to where they belong, and what few remain will soon follow them. Swedish castles shall return to Swedish hands. It's a great service that you have done our realm, you and your men, and you have earned your place in our midst. But now that our strength is proven, the time has come for measures of a different sort. We must seek accord with King Eric to secure the best result, and one who has shown such resolve is surely wise enough to see that such discussions are best handled by the Council of the Realm, men of birth who know how to speak to a king in a language that he will understand. The time for the pen is come when the time of the sword is up."

"Pitchfork, more like."

The words are half stifled under a feigned cough from a hidden speaker, intended to be heard without having to be claimed. Engelbrekt waits for a moment, then steps across the room until he is beside the bishop. Thomas of Strängnäs and Sigge of Skara each step aside, and Engelbrekt places a hand on Knut's shoulder.

"Let me show you something."

Engelbrekt leads him over to the window, which is still open. Beneath them swarm a legion of people, as far as the eye can see. Engelbrekt raises his hand in greeting, and the response he receives makes the earth quake, the tower sway. On the steps of the town hall stand northmen from his retinue, who lead the people in thundering chants.

"Engelbrekt! Engelbrekt!"

Engelbrekt lowers his raised hand onto the back of Knut's neck, and in mounting horror the bishop feels his grip, which from the square must appear conciliatory, tighten around his neck like an iron vise. Despite the best attempts of his feet to resist, Knut finds himself being ushered closer and closer to the window, all the way up to its low ledge. The ground below stretches down beneath him, and, with nothing else to support him, only Engelbrekt's hand is preventing his fall. Engelbrekt mutters over the clamor, quiet enough for only Knut to hear.

"I've heard about you, Knut of blue and gold. An old snake clad in a mitre, one who's held the bishop's office longer than anyone else, yet still can't comprehend how the church can blame Judas Iscariot for taking thirty pieces of silver in exchange for his pains."

He shoves Knut even farther out over the empty space, and the bishop hears the seams start to creak in his collar as the cloth bears more of his weight.

"My grandfather's father was a seamster, you know. He took pride in his work. I wonder if the stitches now holding you up are as strong as his were."

Even farther out now, on tiptoe above a certain death.

"He knew to take payment for his labors, and he sewed enough stitches that my grandfather could travel north with his inheritance and buy a share in a smelting-works in Norberg. My generation is but the third that is of the nobility, and my birth isn't much to boast about next to yours. But just look down. Hope and destiny, that's your motto. I wonder what destiny you'd have left to hope for were you to take this leap? Where would you land if I were to let you go? There, I think, in the middle of the steps, the fourth or fifth from the ground. Or perhaps you would strike that balustrade first, with its sharp edge. But perhaps I'm wrong. Yours is an old house in these parts. Perhaps the very ground around here holds you in such reverence that it would cushion your fall. Perhaps you'll land safely on top of your heritage, just as softly and as comfortably as onto a bearskin atop a stuffed mattress."

Knut gropes around in the empty air for deliverance, forgetting that he still has his eyeglasses in his hand. They drop from his grip, and it seems as though they fall for an impossibly long time before landing on the very spot that Engelbrekt pointed out. The clink of glass shattering isn't loud enough to be heard over the chorus of voices, but he sees the shards scatter, capturing the light in their final leap.

"That's not what I think. I think you'd break every bone in your body. And I don't think a single soul would lift a finger to stop it. The world will go on without you. But that's not to say that I count kinship for nothing."

He leans in closer, his mouth right next to Knut's ear.

"You threatened Magnus, Knut Bosson. That much I know. For that alone I'd happily let you fall. But you're his grandfather's brother nevertheless. His blood is yours. For that you may live. But when next you open your mouth here today I'd prefer to hear a different tune from the one you just sang."

And with that the bishop is back on firm ground. Engelbrekt leads him back to his place in the circle of men and, standing at his side, addresses those gathered for the first time.

"God goes first in all things. Among this kingdom's men of God, none is held in greater regard than Knut Bosson, bishop of Linköping, and so, before sharing my thoughts with you all, I wanted to ensure that they had his blessing. This has now been granted. All allegiance to King Eric must be renounced, by all of you, here and now. A letter shall be drawn up to that extent, and every man who intends to walk at our side shall put his name and seal to it. Despite his age, the bishop has decided to do his own part to protect the realm, and has thus agreed to accept the rule of Stepstones Castle and all its lands, once delivered from King Eric.

Cold sweat drips under his shirt and cowl while Knut's thoughts flit this way and that, each one burdened by its own feelings. His entire life he has done the wise thing by never choosing a side, never taking that leap from the stone on which he stood before ensuring that his feet would stay dry wherever he landed. Now he is turned to a traitor in King Eric's eyes, as much a rebel as Engelbrekt himself. Then again, the bailiff's post at the Stepstones does come with a high income. It was one of Giovanni Frangipani's castles, and in the Danes' clutches before that. Its people have been worked to the bone; they'll sing his praises with the slightest reduction in tax. Knut can come sweeping in as their savior and still line his pockets. Old debts repaid, and plenty to pledge for new loans. Still, he hesitates. A mere glance around those gathered helps him to make up his mind. Nothing but faces in envy, lips twisted in undisguised jealousy over the fortune that has just slipped through their fingers. He clasps his hands in front of his waist and bows his head in piety.

"Praise the Lord."

One by one they press their seals into the letter written to King Eric, then greet Engelbrekt, who is standing beside it to witness each one. A barrel of beer is brought up and tapped, mugs dealt out. The mood shifts. Everything has changed. The hordes outside are no longer a threat but friends every one. Relief spreads, twofold in its nature: those who now renounce their loyalty have been given no choice in the matter but appear to be rewarded all the same. As they file to sign the letter, a belch and laugh are heard from one of the many.

"Never in my wildest dreams would I have believed that a peasant army would take me hostage and not let me go until I'd promised to serve as castle bailiff."

Sir Bo and Sir Bengt exchange dark glances when Knut passes them as they wait to add their seals to the ranks. Bo stops the bishop with a hand to his arm.

"We appear to be late to this banquet, and more have been invited than one would hope. With so many at the table the meal will be small."

In Knut's eyes they find little compassion, only the intoxication of new riches.

"Don't speak so rashly. I should hardly think you'll go begging."

"Easy for you to say, when you're already safe and dry."

The brothers wait their turn in a sullen silence. Once the wax has sealed, Engelbrekt leans in to see the emblems.

"Sir Bengt of Cuckoo's Roost?"

"Yes."

"Would you like to step aside with me, to confer for a moment?"

Together they walk to the beer barrel, where Engelbrekt fills the mugs, hands Bengt a foaming beer, and then nods over at a secluded corner. All the expectancy and suspense has rendered Bengt thirstier than he thought, and he downs gulp after gulp while Engelbrekt sips, observing him calmly over the top of the mug.

"Castle Cut has fallen. It's a vital stronghold, and even more so will it become. It needs someone capable to man the ramparts. Are you up to the task, Sir Bengt?"

Bengt swallows his beer the wrong way, coughs, and splutters. Engelbrekt thumps his back with his palm.

"Shall I take that as a yes?"

Bengt nods, and Engelbrekt holds out his hand to seal their agreement.

"At the Cut a task awaits that is of the utmost importance. We can't be sure of taking Stockholm, and I'm loath to waste time and life on an enterprise that could be doomed to failure. But the iron from the north is too heavy to be borne by anything but water, and as long as the city forms a lock between Lake Mälaren and the sea, we can't count on any silver from the Hansa. Those are funds that we need to further our cause. As long as Stockholm remains in the king's hands, he'll have his thumb on our throats."

"The city is where it is."

"The same could be said the Cut. Do you know those tracts?"

Sir Bengt shakes his head.

"The odd church mass, in passing, a market day, no more."

"North of the city lies a lake. It's called the Mare. By river it feeds into the Mälaren. And south of the city is the inlet after which the castle is named, one whose waters run open all the way to the sea. Just three miles of land separate lake from sea. I want you to clear forest and shrub and dig a furrow between them, one wide and deep enough to carry our cargo. Muster what men you will need. We'll deepen the Cut. All the way to sever Stockholm's windpipe."

Sir Bengt frowns. The thoughts accumulate behind his furrowed skin, too many for him to contain. He can't tell whether

Engelbrekt's fancy is ingenuity or madness. Should it succeed and the new current flow fulsomely enough to carry all the iron of the north to tested waterways, Stockholm would be rendered superfluous overnight. Sweden's greatest city and its richest, ruined, and not by warfare nor force of arms, but by a single idea and spades in their thousands. Whoever sits bailiff of that river will be able to claim whatever tolls he pleases. Bengt tries to reckon the figures but finds the sums too great to count. Much easier to count are those three miles. How little it sounds! But then in his mind he walks the road from Cuckoo's Roost to the church at Mellösa, almost five miles in all, including the bends in the road. Halfway along it someone has built a cairn, by a meadow where he often pauses to let his steed graze. That distance to the lake. Dug by mere manpower. Wide and deep enough to float a merchant ship. With stones along the way, nay, boulders, hidden beneath the ground. How many men will it take? How much earth does a single man shift in a day? He mouths an oath on silent lips.

"Some help may be needed. I've little experience of such things. The closest I've come is having my moat dug."

"Perhaps I might be of better service?"

A mild voice. Bengt turns. Behind him stands House Crofter's runt, an ingratiating look plastered to his squashed face. It makes him uglier than necessary. Bengt feels the blood rise in his face, but Crofter speaks first, lowering his head in a bow at Engelbrekt.

"Karl is my name, Crofter my house, we of a red boat on a yellow base. I couldn't help but overhear. Since I inherited Birdsfirth I've scarce done anything but dig. Our fields lay sodden, the house's groundwork likewise. New waterways were essential in order to draw the moisture back where it belonged. The bay outside had to be dredged, for it was too shallow for even a rowboat to reach land. And the soils around the Cut are of the kind that I'm used to, for my estate also lies by the sea, albeit farther south. In all humility I do believe myself the right person for the task, if Sir Bengt isn't opposed."

Bengt steps forward, as if meaning to defend his property with his very bulk. The castle that was just his is already under siege, its revenues threatened by a common bandit. The mere thought is like a glug of water downed the wrong way.

"I remember you, Karl Crofter. Though it would appear that your memory is the worse for wear. You should recall that young men would do best to keep silent while grown-ups are talking, all the more so when they are conferring on matters not intended for their ears."

Sir Bengt shudders at Karl Crofter's cold stare. A lizard's eyes, one who knows to hide his true feelings behind outward gentry. An enemy of the worst kind. Still, he bows his head in feigned humility, as though it were all but a misunderstanding.

"I meant no harm, Sir Bengt. I was simply offering my best services in that which from this day forth will be to all of our benefit."

Bengt would like no more than to do to Karl Crofter what Engelbrekt was on the brink of doing to the bishop just minutes before, to drag him to the window and show him the fastest way out. But before he has a chance to say the kind of thing that can't be taken back, Engelbrekt places his hands on each of their shoulders.

"Come, we're all friends here. Karl Crofter, for this task Sir Bengt is my first choice. But that's no reason to think I lack tasks for you, or that I don't value your skills just as highly. Your turn shall come. If everyone were so enterprising, the kingdom would be ours before the week was out."

With a curt bow Karl returns to the flock of nobles. Bengt breathes a sigh of relief, the first assault on his newly won ramparts averted. He makes use of the silence that ensues to return the conversation to its rightful course.

"Now, we were speaking of the Cut."

※

Magnus stands unnoticed by the wall, concealed behind the northmen's broad backs, his hood pulled low over his forehead. How quickly the mood has shifted, the promise of land and silver like a sudden breeze over a pigpen, fanning away the stench that so recently smothered. Formerly surly nobles are now chattering expectantly, only with crossed arms and watchful eyes, for all of them covet parts of the same whole, and that which is given to one is another's loss. He sees Karl Crofter turn from Engelbrekt's side, leaving Engelbrekt and his father to continue their exchange. At his side a voice he knows well.

"There he slithers, off to find some less protected skin to sink his fangs into. Let's hope the gentry are wearing tall boots."

Nils Stensson, gray with road dust. He must have come straight from the saddle.

"I daresay it's going well for us, Magnus. Stepstones is Knut's. Bo's been promised Stake Isle, so I've heard. What Bengt is getting we'll soon find out, but I haven't seen him look so pleased since the day you came into this world. I can only take it that your time with Engelbrekt has given him a taste for blue and gold. No house has been favored as much as ours."

"And you? What do you want?"

Nils laughs.

"I'll stay Landless Nils for a while yet. But I do hope to get my own private audience with the people's chieftain, like certain others."

Magnus sees his uncle's eyes seek out Karl Crofter. The corners of his mouth stiffen when he finds him.

"Uncle, I wanted to ask you something. There's a man who's close to Engelbrekt, an Eric Puck. When he first heard my name his eyes were like daggers, and ever since that day he's despised me, though I've done nothing to him. Do you know why?"

Nils strokes his chin.

"Puck's the son of Nils Rossvik, the first of the nobility to join Engelbrekt's cause, his coat of arms a boat and a star. As a thanks for his help, Rossvik sits in Västerås Castle. But Puck's a bastard, born out of marriage. He adopted the name of his mother's family, and flies a black wing on his shield, though he has no birthright. Nils Rossvik did marry later: to your cousin Birgitta. You won't have met her, for your cousin didn't make it out of the childbed alive."

A chill spreads through Nils's gut at the words he has uttered so flippantly. His Mara on her bloodied sheets. Discreetly he makes the sign of the cross.

"Is his father an older man, tall and white of hair? I saw him in Västerås. He went out with Engelbrekt to bless the people after the castle fell."

"Rossvik doesn't distance himself from Puck in the slightest, though everyone knows not to ask how they're related. Puck behaves as though he were a lord himself, and others appear to respect him."

Nils surveys the people in attendance, nodding in greeting when he sees those he knows.

"Do you know what the word means? Puck?"

Magnus shakes his head. Nils smiles.

"A minor demon in service of the devil. I suppose I should have said this before you left Cuckoo's Roost, but each man ought to tread carefully when choosing his enemies. The fewer, the better. The country is small, and grudges can come at great cost."

"I had no choice in the matter."

From a distance Karl Crofter's voice, shrill in its laughter. Nils grits his teeth while Magnus looks on.

"Do you practice what you preach, Uncle?"

"Given the choice I'd take Crofter as my enemy every time. Not for how easy it would be to beat him, but for the sweetness of the victory."

Nils lets the words sink in before going on.

"Where is Puck? I don't see him here."

"Engelbrekt sent him north, to strike Foxholm."

Nils frowns, confounded at first. Then he raises an eyebrow.

"Does Engelbrekt know of your enmity, by any chance?"

"Puck's hardly gone to any pains to keep it secret."

His uncle laughs, reaches out, and gives Magnus a clap on the cheek.

"I think you've fared better in your task than I could ever have hoped. I'm off, Magnus, to speak to others. Take care of yourself. Keep doing what you're doing. If I know your father he'll probably forget to say so, but we're all proud that our house's confidence has been placed in the right hands."

Magnus stays to one side until the meeting reaches its end. On the letter to King Eric they have all placed their seals. One by one they leave the chamber, conflicting feelings etched on their faces. Magnus sees his father leave, alongside Sir Bo, their attention elsewhere. He had intended to make himself known to them, tell them about the time that has passed, but now that he's here he can't bring himself to do it. He watches them go, their apparent unease matched only by their triumph. Now they are traitors all, signed and sealed, and although they have been generously rewarded for the trouble, no one can tell what the future holds in store, nor to which part of the Wheel of Fortune they will swing next. He gives them time to mount their horses and leave the courtyard, loath to speak to any of them.

They all seem different now. When finally he turns to leave, a claw grabs him by the arm.

"So you stabbed me in the back anyway, boy."

Bishop Knut, hunched and low, his frail body impossibly swift when it suits his purposes. He draws Magnus closer with a grip of his mantle.

"Did I not make myself sufficiently clear when I told you the cost of betraying my trust? You were to keep me out of it. You weren't to mention my name to Engelbrekt. And yet you blabbed. He knew everything."

Magnus tears his mantle free.

"I've kept my word, though I regret it. I wish I had told Engelbrekt, but I haven't."

Knut's wrinkled lips fumble for words while his eyes narrow in incredulity.

"What Engelbrekt knew was said between you and me. There was no one else there. Who else would have gossiped about what only two people know?"

"I haven't breathed a word to anyone."

Knut must have taken confession thousands of times and more. He knows how to tell truth from lie, knows every manner of falsehood, knows that even those who avow their guilt will diminish their wrongdoing to buy their forgiveness at the lowest possible price. In Magnus he sees no lie.

"Do you swear by the Holy Trinity, Magnus Bengtsson? At the cost of your soul's damnation?"

"I swear."

No hesitation. Knut doesn't know what to believe. The boy must be speaking the truth. But if not he, then who else? What hidden ears could have heard them and carried the words to Engelbrekt? A cold shiver runs down his spine, along the seam of his cope. Ill that he should have an unknown traitor in his midst in days like these, and, even worse, one with a hidden purpose. But that his brother's grandson is blameless may be a comfort to him. He sees Magnus before him, indignation in his eyes and a flush in his cheeks at the unjust accusation. As it should be. Knut sighs, feeling the burden of his conscience.

"It's clear that I'm mistaken, Magnus. Forgive an old man who, in spite of his years, still hasn't learned all that he should."

A curt nod is all the absolution the bishop is granted. Magnus has an open face, one not yet marked by wrinkles in which his feelings can hide. Moments ago the truth was easily read, just as easily as his contempt is now. And with that Magnus is gone, bounding down the stairs to rejoin the ranks of the northmen.

Kari Sharp arrives at Cuckoo's Roost, riding over the bridge at full gallop ahead of her escorts, with a wolfish sneer at the man who steps in front of her to ask her business and must leap out of the way to avoid being trampled. By the dwellings she dismounts and lets the reins fall to the ground, certain that someone will come to stable her horse. A maid with a basket stands dumbfounded at her arrival, before hastily curtsying with eyes downcast.

"Britta Bengtsdaughter. Point me the way."

The maid is wise enough to do as she is bidden without a peep, and Kari Sharp follows her hand. Britta comes to greet her on the steps. Kari studies her grimly, glimpsing the mud stains on the hem of her skirt and the ink stains on her fingers, her pallor and the rings under her eyes.

"I come with counsel. Summon a cart for your mother, and quickly do what you must to get ready for the road. We shall ride east."

"But the harvest . . ."

"I've a man with me who can both count and chide, one who learns quickly and keeps his own counsel. By God, if he were a good marriage, too, then I wouldn't have given Bo Stensson a second thought. At Oakwood he is wasted, so I'm giving him to you on loan. He'll take care of Cuckoo's Roost in your absence. If he squanders a single coin his next household will be a croft in the far north on the other side of the sea, and he knows as much himself."

"But where are we to go?"

"To the Cut. It belongs to your father now. Engelbrekt gave it to him in Vadstena."

She sees the surprise on Britta's face, while withholding the satisfaction at such surprise from her own. When Sir Bo told her about Vadstena she knew instantly what needed to be done, and how she would absolve her guilt.

"I'll tell you everything. But trust me for now and do as I ask. Have the fire lit in the bathhouse."

Leaving Britta to make the arrangements for their journey, she finds her own way to Stina's chamber. The air in the room is close, the window boards still in place even though the day is hardly young. She lifts the latches, opens them wide, and sees the sun itself run her errands: its unshrouded rays fall straight over the tufts of bedding, while Stina groans from her nest at the glare that disturbs her torpor. Kari perches on the edge of the bed, glad of the late-summer wind that now fills the room, chasing away all the must and closeness. A smell lingers, catches in her nose. She knows what it is. Aqua vitae, clear like water but with a taste like fire, the drink that monks boil from wine, capable of soothing pains of every kind, but only when taken in moderation. There are several bottles here, and all but one are empty. Of what remains there is but a little splash. Stina is already fumbling around for it, and Kari gives her what she is searching for.

"Drink up what's left. It'll be the last in a long time."

She sweeps a cloak over her sister-in-law and, as though she were already decrepit with age, leads her out to the bathhouse, where the fire is roaring in its hearth and the stones have been toasted to make steam. Once Stina is warm enough, Kari tips a pail of cold water over her, turning a deaf ear to her objections.

"Is your head clear yet, or shall I have them fetch more?"

Stina shakes her head sulkily, and Kari can only laugh.

"You look like a cat that's fallen in the lake."

She sits down beside her on the ledge, ladles water over the hot stones, and feels their warm caress fill the air.

"You must come with me to the Cut. You must do it, for Magnus's sake."

On the road from Vadstena Bishop Knut is still in high spirits. His cart travels fleetly over the smooth highway, and his tender lower back doesn't plague him. The sun is shining, and there's wine by the cask at hand to slake his thirst. In his thoughts the castle that just became his. Stepstones. He knows it well. A stately stone edifice with a tower and fortifications, situated just where the gulf of Slätbaken is at its narrowest. In days of yore both the land and surrounding waters had belonged to the bishop of Linköping's diocese, but in light of their position King Albrekt had seized them for himself, raising a castle by the shore where before there had stood only a manor house and bulwark. Much ill is there to be said of the Germans, but they do know how to build. At Stepstones he will be happily placed when winter comes, warm and safe, while others in the south will be painting the snowdrifts red. The strait outside is thoroughly piled, its floor studded with sharpened logs to down any merchant ship that tries to evade the bailiff's tolls. Those coins will now be Knut's, as will the taxes from the nearby town.

The sun rises, the day warms up. His road bears him south, home to Linköping, to oversee the transfer of men and property. Where the forest crowds along the road's verges the air is sultry, and the branches offer no shade in return, for the sun stands straight above the road. The journey is slower than it ought to be. Pilgrims on their way to the abbey jostle at every bend, and when they see that none other than the bishop is passing, they delay him with their reverence rather than quickly step out of the way. The sweat drips under his shirt, his intoxication no longer amusing, instead serving mainly to slacken his thoughts. Around him walk his men, still attired in all the finery purchased so that they might shine in Vadstena. A glance of light leaps from a burnished helmet, stinging his eyes. He has paid for it, that and everything else that they bear, and they aren't just things that please the eye but weighty goods, too, chain mail and helmets and sharp weapons, everything needed to honor him on the battlefield that they had all expected to meet. Instead he was granted a castle as a gift, thus rendering his expenses in vain. Dear money, borrowed against great pledges. Knut takes a swig of wine but, finding it too tepid to swallow, spits it out over the side of the cart in revulsion.

The more he thinks about it, the more bothered he is by the Vadstena congress. The land and property that he was granted are no favor, but what should have been his from the start. It has merely been rightfully returned, and with no interest for the long delay, at that. Who is this Engelbrekt Engelbrektsson to bestow that which belongs to others? That he should threaten violence is one thing—one can hardly expect more of a simple northman but three generations risen from base peasantry—but that he should dare speak for those who are better, that is an affront. Ruling a kingdom is entirely different from hacking at mountains, as proven by the man's churlishness in believing that the goodwill of the peasants would be enough to crown him king. Knut's neck smarts at the memory of his touch. Sullenly he changes his mind, takes a long swig of the tepid wine, and lets himself be rocked to sleep by the springiness of the cart.

He is awoken by flies tickling his lip and a pain in his back as he tries in vain to find a position that will spare him the torment. His head feels thick, the taste in his mouth dreadful. But with sleep has come counsel. The bishop's former property comprised more than just Stepstones. With the same nail he can crush two lice, by sending the men he armed at such great expense out to reclaim that which should have been his. Roan Island and its environs, all the farmland and all the property, all the land. Surely that will soothe some of the pain that he has had to endure. The prospect of what the people's chieftain will think when he hears word of it may well do the same. Engelbrekt Engelbrektsson's attentions appear to be elsewhere, if he hasn't already been felled by a soldier's arrow. But even if everything does go his way, he can hardly afford to go to war against both the king in the south and the church elders who stand at his own back. Knut wonders whom he can find to be his ally in this enterprise. Not Bo nor Bengt, nor Nils; it looks like they will be Engelbrekt's loyal lapdogs until the day it no longer suits their needs. But Knut has other kin; if there was one thing his brother, Sten, knew it was how to make up for the bishop's vow of chastity. One of his sheltered nephews, perhaps, one of the twins the rest of the brood blame for their mother's death? Yes. That road is passable, and it's paved with silver ingots. The bishop can't help but clap his hands together, with a rap that smarts in his swollen knuckles.

F INN NEVER STRAYS far from Magnus's side. He attends to everything that it had taken a whole household to handle at Cuckoo's Roost, even if his focus is on Magnus alone. Still, he is glad for the trouble. Sleep eludes him. If he seeks his bed too early, it doesn't come at all. But even if the hour is late when he rests, and he curls up wearied of body and mind, he still wakens early. He is hagridden, wakes up dripping with sweat, his heart as though hatching from his chest, seeking flight from the cage of his ribs.

Then he goes to Magnus's bed to make sure everything is in order. If he finds him there he might hear him mumbling in his dream, now just as when he was younger.

His thoughts churn. Shame and guilt have been joined by something even worse. This summer he has seen more lords than in the rest of his life, and they aren't what he had thought. Once his eyes have adjusted to the resplendent glare of all their chains and gold thread, there is little majesty left to see. He finds them no better than others. Repulsive shapes in beautiful garments. Petty and greedy beneath their splendor. He wonders now whether all nobles are of the same stock. He wonders whether his sister saw these men for what they are before she forsook the pleasures and duties of Cuckoo's Roost for simpler pursuits. She never did go to confession, Ylva, and God she never feared, instead mocking Finn for his prayers. Now he sees things the way Ylva might have.

If he has a free moment he finds each church that they pass and there roves amidst the shadows of the consecrated vaults, in the hope of some revelation. None comes.

Priests he rarely sees. Uncertain of where the people are wont to next direct their wrath, they abandon their altarpieces and lie low, leaving doors unlocked for everyone to come and pray as they please. In the past Finn could sense the power in their relics. But now he hears Olof Jonsson's ghost whispering to him about John the Baptist's loincloth, and his own faith isn't strong enough to turn a deaf ear. He stares at the sticks of the cross and at the splinters of holy bones, unable to tell them from the rubbish on the ground.

By the sun's course he can tell that they are now moving south and east. He following Magnus, Magnus following Engelbrekt. When the wind is right and their voices carry he can catch fragments of their conversations over the clap of hooves.

That something has gone awry he can see on Engelbrekt's face. He hears Magnus pose the question.

"What's wrong? Has something happened?"

"We had word from Örebro this morning."

"And?"

"The bailiff and I had agreed to a six-week truce. If Mattis Kettilberg hadn't received reinforcements by then, he agreed to leave the castle of his own accord. But now that he knows no rescue is coming, he instead wants silver in exchange for his exit."

Finn veers his horse around a stone in the road, then steers back into place to hear Engelbrekt go on.

"We need Örebro. All the small fortresses we've either taken or burned, but in the great strongholds the king's bailiffs remain, safe in their tall keeps. Kalmar, Stockholm, Örebro, Axewall. Still, I don't have a thousand marks, Magnus. We could probably raise such a sum by taxing the people as we go, or take Örebro by force, once our dead lie stacked in a mound high enough for us to step over the battlements. But along both roads our purpose is lost. Kettilberg is crafty. He's heard about Vadstena and knows I have the nobility behind me now, and that they have money enough to lend. Karl Crofter, for example, rich as a troll. He wouldn't refuse me. But what kind of interest would he demand? It would be like leaving the door to the henhouse open. And the lords from Vadstena will soon know what a snarl I'm in. They suppose me to be like themselves, assume that I've been filling my pockets every step of the way from Norberg, and they respect nothing more than wealth. Soon they'll know that both my hands are empty and my purse, too, and then they'll grow all the more brazen."

Engelbrekt turns and looks Magnus in the eye.

"For the first time since I left the north I don't know what to do."

SIR BO'S STOMACH is roiling. Sour lumps keep rising in his throat, leaving a sting in his gullet and a foul taste in his mouth. Long have they prepared their attack, and today is the day that it shall happen, though he's had his misgivings from the start. No sooner has it commenced than they are borne out. He is standing on a hill overlooking the shore, gazing out over the water toward the castle at Stake Isle, at a greater distance than any arrow or bolt can be hurled from its ramparts. He is dressed for battle nevertheless, for anything else would look bad. Still, he despises it. His bare head smarts under the helmet, and his chain mail shirt chafes against his ribs, pressing him down ever further into his uncomfortable boots. The belt intended to carry his sword, dagger, and pouch cuts tightly into his hips. Underneath, his clothes are already drenched in sweat, though the attack has scarce begun. His paunch feels firm and unyielding. Somewhere within him a rock-hard lump swells up and refuses to budge, and with a groan he must release the sour vapors that seep past it below his collarbone.

He is promised the castle on the condition that he take it. He flatters himself that alone he would have executed it better, but here there are three all keen to see their will done: Nils of Hammersholt, a kinsman he would have found it easier to shout down were it not for the fact that Karl Crofter was appointed the third commander. The mere thought makes him spit in the gravel. Slippery as an eel, he is, one who knows how to fawn and pit others against each other until his own will is done, but without it being clear in retrospect quite how it all came to pass. He promises one thing but does another. But this time his cunning has borne rotten fruit, for Bo can already see that their siege will come to naught. The question is simply how many lives must be wasted before they can say that they have done enough.

After long deliberations among the three of them, a brittle compromise was made. All of them know what's at stake. Though Bo is promised the castle, that can easily be changed, and he whose forces claim the greater part of the victory will likely find it easier to assert his right. The first into the castle will be the hardest to shift from its throne. The others refuse to concede that Sir Bo, as bailiff-in-waiting, should lead the attack. Instead they agree to strike the castle from three sides at once. Three rafts they would build, one each, which on the given signal would pole out toward the castle ramparts in the middle of the strait. As soon as dawn gave them light enough to see they set to work. His own vessel started to list as soon as it was launched, and his men crowding closest to the edge were thrown into the water, luckily no deeper than most of them could stand. When they finally got her back on course she ran aground on what must have been a rock, post, or mudbank. Now his men are stranded in the strait, without the possibility of going either forward or back. From the castle keep the marksmen have already gauged the distance and found it to their favor. His men have but their own shields with which to defend themselves. Thus far few have fallen to enemy arrows, but Sir Bo knows well enough why. From the castle they can see what's going on. His raft is stuck where it is, and it's not going anywhere fast. They can very well save their arrows for those who still present a threat. Then, once the more acute danger has been driven back, they can shoot at the shipwrecked besiegers at leisure, until they have picked holes in each and every one of them who doesn't instead opt to drown. Red Lage is what they call the Danish bailiff, by dint of his red hair, but before the day's end he will likely have a new reason to lay claim to his name.

Now cries are heard from the Hammersholt raft, which has started to split where the current is at its strongest. The two parts hang together like a creature with two tails, sparking turmoil on board. Many have foundered in the fissure that opened, quickly and silently, dragged under by all that weighs them down. In rage Sir Bo tears his helmet from his head and hurls it into the hillside with all his might. He wishes his own men had been less thorough the night before, when cutting the willows that held the Hammersholt raft together. *Enough to slow them but not to sink them*, those were Bo's orders, but clearly in their zeal his men's knives grew all too eager. Now all their hopes lie with Crofter, the only one whose raft has made it to the palisade by the water's edge, to which the men have now hooked themselves, to use the enemy's defenses as shelter from their arrows. The bailiff's foot soldiers flock to thrust their spears through the gaps in the palisade's logs, and Bo grimaces when he sees what the spearheads do to the men at the front, who have nowhere to seek refuge with others crowding them from behind. Their wails arrive on the wind but moments later. The day is wet, the air damp, and what fire there was on the raft must have been doused amidst the confusion. He sees sparks from a tinderbox, vain attempts to awaken new flames, all to no avail. Soon any attempt at attack dwindles. On the raft the survivors huddle out of reach of the spears, trying to build their own defenses from their comrades' corpses, before the archers can descend from the parapets and take aim through the palisade from just a few yards away. They are given a brief respite, for the archers return to Sir Bo's raft first. It takes but a moment for them to find their mark. He sees the water seethe as the arrows pierce it in front and behind, all around the raft. At first every shot that lands true is met with jubilation from the keep, but soon enough no one misses anymore. From the raft the men scream out their death's agonies, sounds that Sir Bo would struggle to ascribe to human throats had his eyes been closed. Like swine at slaughter, or foxes in a trap. In terror some start hacking at the raft on which they stand, trying to release a single log in the hope that they might ride it to salvation. Some succeed, until too many crowd upon it and the log flips over, sending them all into the strait. For a few moments he can see their arms in a row clasping at the log from beneath, a strange sight to behold, before their air runs out and the weight of their own bodies overcomes them. When Bo turns his gaze back to the raft there is no one left. Blood billows downstream, like a long, wet streamer. Newly forged armor strapped to the chests of the dead, stained and punctured. Bo can't help but reckon what it all cost him, and for naught. Farther along the bay he sees Crofter mount his horse, already on his way, no doubt to see to it that he is the first to tell the tale of their defeat and thus place the blame wherever it suits him best. Bo curses himself for not thinking of it before, for not doing as Crofter and wearing light riding attire rather than armor. He hastens away breathlessly, to find his own horse while there is yet time.

Down a muddy hillside goes their path, toward a piece of woodland. Kari Sharp can't hide her eagerness. They were scarce given a chance to see the castle, which is larger than Cuckoo's Roost and stands well protected on an islet in the water, like any good castle should. Kari had quickly urged them onward. Stina is now capable of riding, albeit unwillingly. With Britta, Kari reaches the forest's edge first, then dismounts and ties her reins to a tree.

"We'll leave the horses here. The ground's boggy and full of roots. Best that we go on foot."

Britta looks over her shoulder at her mother. She is approaching slowly, her head bowed in lassitude. Kari winks at her.

"Soon she'll be better. We just need to see to it that a flame springs from those ashes, and then soon enough it'll turn into a roaring beacon. Come, let's go ahead. Let her remember that her legs can carry her."

Britta follows Kari as she strides through the forest like a chieftain, batting branches out of the way with a practiced hand. It is as though the trees themselves bend back from her in fear, certain that any attempt to stop her will merely tempt her wrath. Before them the light shifts: green shadows pale, and the branches thin out. The day is gray, with drizzling rain, a herald of autumn. Once out of the forest Britta stops on the spot, trying to understand what it is that she is seeing. She lifts the hood of her mantle to get a better view.

Beyond the forest lies a broad hollow. Down its middle teem men with spade and pickaxe, so flecked with mud that they look like trolls in flight from the underworld. A furrow has been dug where the earth is at its lowest, a brown gash in the green landscape. Some of them are ferrying wheelbarrows, while others carry sacks and baskets full of damp soil, to lay as embankments along either side of the ditch. They haven't come far, nor particularly deep. From the sides of the ditch the earth tumbles down, forcing them to widen the furrow so that it won't fill up again. As she asks her question Britta hears her mother emerge from the forest, her breaths heavy. For a moment she is just as speechless at the sight.

"What is this?"

Kari points up, at the blue water in the distance.

"Bengt will keep Castle Cut on one condition. Engelbrekt wants a trench dug, from the beach in the south to the bay in the north, big enough to carry iron from the north to load onto the Hansa ships."

Stina is still catching her breath beside Britta, resting against a birch tree for support. At Kari's words she steps closer, raising a hand to shade her eyes so that she might see better. Kari Sharp turns to look at her.

"It's thanks to Magnus that this task has fallen to Bengt. Why else? Any noble in the kingdom would barter his crest for a chance like this. If he fails it'll all come to naught, and all that Magnus has achieved will be in vain. He's already well on his way."

Stina starts to speak, but she coughs instead, must compose herself to find her unused voice once more. The words come out hoarse and rugged.

"How far?"

"Three miles."

"How soon?"

"The sooner it is done, the happier Engelbrekt will be."

Stina steps closer, out into the light, squinting to see the men in their toil.

"The way they're going at it they'll never finish."

Kari bares sharp teeth in a malicious smile.

"Aye. Much good can be said of your husband, but putting others to work in the most effectual way has never been one of his strengths."

She pauses before going on.

"If only there was someone else in the family who could better safeguard the confidence your son has won."

Stina has crossed her arms, paces aimlessly back and forth before them.

"He's no fool, that northerner. If the water flows here, then he won't need Stockholm, not he nor anyone else. It'll be reduced to worthless masonry, a lone island in the stream where the king's men will be mere castaways."

Kari throws a glance at Britta behind Stina's back, raises an eyebrow. They are smoldering now, those embers within. Britta sees her mother attempt to straighten her bent back, only to groan and clasp her hand to her hip when an ailment prevents it.

"I'll do it. Else it'll never be done."

She starts walking down the slope and across the field. Britta calls after her.

"Where are you going?"

"Tomorrow I must find more men, and better. For now I'll tell them to stop widening the furrow, but to dig forward instead. We still have a half day's work until the light fails. It needn't go to waste."

Kari laughs, an unfamiliar sound. She places her arm around Britta, to stop her from going after Stina.

"Let her go. Let her remember what strength was once hers. You'll see it's more than enough."

Kari squeezes Britta's shoulder.

"It worked. Now the fire's lit, and I imagine my brother-in-law will soon feel its heat under his collar, he and anyone else foolish enough to stand in her way. Britta, you'll stay, won't you? You'll give her what help she needs? I know things haven't always been easy between you, but one of these days she'll see that she can't get by without you. Know that there are others who've seen that for a long time."

Britta opens her mouth to reply but closes it again. A nod is enough.

J ONAS JONSSON IS standing on his left leg. He'll have to change soon, for his thigh is already shaking with exertion and his foot is going numb beneath him. Heat is all that he can think of, as the cold gnaws all the deeper into his flesh, bite by bite, up his shin and onto his knees, which stiffen and creak in its clutches. He tries to remember summers in the grass—the touch of sun on bare skin, the closeness of the hearth, the crackle of a fire in an enclosed space—but finds the memories difficult to summon. A groan passes his lips, a wordless complaint that this, too, shall be stripped of him, that the claws of Otto Steer's bailiff are capable even of reaching behind his forehead and plundering his thoughts in exchange for the tax he owes. All around him stream the torrents, the water clear and cold, so cold. The sun rises on his third day on Little Torment. There were two of them at first, he on the smaller stone, and Anders of Backa on the other, the larger one. He had never liked Anders, a deceitful little knave with nary a good word to say of anyone out of earshot. But on these two boulders known as the Torments they had only each other. The two aren't far apart, but the river's roar is loud, which had forced them to shout to be heard. Neither of them had had much to say, but it was nice to have another to share in his fate and anguish, one who saw and understood. A cry, a greeting, a question and answer, goodwill. Anders wasn't long on Great Torment. Jonas has seen it before, he like everyone else. First they stand with their legs apart. Then on one leg at a time, once the cold becomes too much. Then they sit down on the stone. Before long it's into the rapids they go, and anyone who blinks will miss it: suddenly their stone will stand empty in the river, as if no one were ever there. The one so recently lost will already be far away, pale and mute beneath the swift waters, to be carried on wet courses out into the depths, where the lake is at its darkest. Together they stood the first day, stranded there by the same boat, the one winched down one fathom at a time from the bend in the river, on a rope that the bailiff's men-at-arms had wound around the trunk of a willow. First they had put Anders of Backa on Great Torment, then him on Little. To begin with the two of them had kept each other's spirits high, even cracking jokes. *How refreshing! You wouldn't have anything to drink, would you? Any interesting plants on your rock? A nice change from the spade and pickaxe, anyway.* But Anders was on one leg after only a few hours. In the afternoon he sat down. Then the sun sank and left the world dark, and by the time the moon rose, its silvery light fell on an empty stone. Silently he had slipped into the rapids, Anders of Backa, he who seldom kept his mouth shut. He should have known better than to write a song in mockery of Otto Steer.

For the hundredth time Jonas Jonsson casts that same critical eye upon himself. Could he have done any differently? Where were those forks in the road at which other choices would have led him elsewhere than to this godforsaken river and the torture stones under Castle Amneholm? His mistake was to believe that the bailiff wanted to listen to reason. Surely a man of the king must see that no one can go on taxing more than the earth can provide? In that belief he had appeared before Otto Steer with his debt, but to no avail. The bailiff refused to listen. His face spoke a language far clearer than his Danish: He understood well enough, had heard the same entreaties before, all too well aware of the impossible situation into which many men are forced, though they would sooner choose another. Otto Steer simply doesn't care. Not least because he needs farmers out on the Torments, to stand one-legged in the torrents while croaking their throaty afflictions at the shores, the likeness of gray herons. Their warning makes the taxes all the easier to collect.

His gaze drifts toward the castle. Amneholm fills the entire isle on which it stands, as though floating in all its ponderousness on the surface of the river. A wooden palisade surrounds the stone keep. He has heard the rumors, he like the rest. Last year the men of the mountains marched on Västerås to complain about their bailiff's rule, but were persuaded into returning home again. None of the promises given have been met. This year they must return, angrier and more numerous. Perhaps even down to these tracts, bearing justice for all upon whom the bailiff has preyed.

Jonas switches legs, careful not to lose his footing, and with the other vainly seeks the warmth of a raised stone, only to find it cold as wet driftwood. He sucks in the air between throbbing teeth when the movement reawakens the pain that had fallen dormant behind his kneecaps. He fears the night to come, if he lasts that long. He has already had to spend one night alone in the dark without Anders of Backa, and all the more often he fancied he could hear him calling out to him from Great Torment. *How's the leg, Jonas Jonsson? Come on, jump in, too, there's more than enough rest to be had here! It's lonely down here, Jonas, so come link arms and together we'll wander the riverbed to Lake Vänern, to feed the fish with all that was ours.*

Cold. In his body an unwholesome heat sparks up in resistance; a fever, a shake. Worse it grows by the hour. It shows him things that he has never seen before. The river is full of faces. From its murky bed they glare up at him, what he had once taken for stones and logs. Human they are not. Water spirits, trolls, goblins of the sort for which no human has found a name. He may be cold, but he's still warmer than they, and they covet what little heat he possesses. From the currents they whisper, promising him his every desire if he would only come down to see them, bring his heat to their chilled rooms never touched by the light: rest, friendship, beautiful stones. He still has strength enough to shake his head, pretend his tears unshed, say a prayer.

"Ave Maria gratia plena Dominus tecum."

What now? People on the shore. He can't hear them over the water, but their fury is clear. They are carrying what weapons they own, as well as blazing torches whose flames draw gleaming streaks over the river. With leather-bound brushwood screens they block the archers' view while bundles of firewood are stacked against the palisade by the island's dock and quickly set ablaze. The fire is greedy in the dry wood; it licks the palisade's stakes, finds footholds in bark and knotholes, catches. With slingstones they prevent the budding flames from being quenched. Jonas Jonsson sees those he knows among the crowd, men and women alike. Ulf, his brother-in-law, Ulf's wife, Maja. Cousins and their children, his father, Anders of Backa. No, now he's seeing things, for his father is dead and Anders lies in the river. Is all of it a phantom vision? Is the fever showing him that which he most wants to see?

Jonas rubs his eyes as he stands there and says another prayer, only too aware that he who sees the dead is all too close to them. He raises his arms and cries out feebly in support of the army, wishing that someone would see him and winch the boat down from the shore. But they're all taken up with other things, and no one has time to spare. Dusk thickens, but the flames from the burning castle light up the sky as though it were still day. Around the blaze more now gather, strangers. Tall men with blackened faces, a man on horseback who points and issues commands with a radiance around his head, and a young man beside him with the face of an angel. But more and more dead join their ranks, those whom Jonas knows have long lain belowground, who can scarce boast flesh on their bones anymore. They want to dance, they, too, in the warmth of the living and amidst the glow of the fire, their teeth locked in eternal mirth behind lost lips. Now they dance among others. Jonas Jonsson is cold and faint, and he can't tear his eyes from what's happening. The smiles of the dead are contagious, and from his stone he smiles, too, at Otto Steer and the Wheel of Fortune that has made its turn. He was placed on his stone to give the bailiff the spectacle of his downfall. Now the reverse is true. But his legs are shaking; they distort his view, blur the world, smear the glow of the fire over all that is unfolding. As carefully as he can, Jonas takes a seat on his stone the better to see.

AMNEHOLM BURNS. OPEN flames leave embers to finish the job. Even before they arrived the castle was ablaze, for here the uprising is more than just Engelbrekt's: it has grown into a creature with legs of its own, swifter than human feet or horse hooves. When they reached the riverbank the peasantry were already armed and on the attack, the castle under siege and its palisade lit. The bailiff himself had long since fled, leaving only a few men-at-arms to submit to the people's mercy, red-eyed and coughing, rather than be roasted alive in chambers turned furnace. The island is devastation. The stone keep totters where its beams smolder, hot stones hissing when they plunge into the water. Another stronghold fallen on the road south.

The people stand by the river, their wrath stilled, their faces turned up at the heat that flows forth from across the water as at a spring sun after a long winter, the flames reflected in their eyes, rage now replaced with wonder. Farther up the hill the northmen have made camp. With the morning they will muster those who wish to follow the army onward toward Axewall Castle, break up camp, and march on. Magnus makes for Soot, not out of duty but because he enjoys the stallion's company, strokes his coat, and finds him succulent feed. From farther down the shore he hears songs and a fiddle, as new fires are built to warm and brighten rather than destroy and raze, the embers prepared to roast what meat the bailiff left, while emptying what beer barrels could be saved. A crash is heard from a crumbling arch; from the shore come cheers in response. A piece of flat ground is kicked clean by many feet and readied for a dance. Magnus leaves the horse behind him and walks among the people. Many have seen him at Engelbrekt's side and remember him, while others need only a glance to see that he is something different, something special. Everywhere men and women step aside to let him pass, running their fingers along his shoulder as he does, or groping for the hem of his mantle. With reverence they look upon him, as though at a vision descended among mortals. A part of Engelbrekt's radiance is now his. Many smile at him, and he smiles back, sharing in their joy. An old woman comes over to him, takes him by the waist, and leads him in a dance, and he laughs and joins in willingly. For a while they whirl together among the throng of bodies. In parting she kisses his hand.

On a spot on the shore not reached by the light stands a lone figure, dark among the bright, faintly familiar. Curiosity draws Magnus closer, until he sees that it is none other than Eric Puck himself, who has returned from his northern campaign to rejoin Engelbrekt's men. Magnus stops silently and hesitantly in his tracks, but something announces his presence, for Puck turns his head and sees him standing there. He is drunk, his body tense and arms limp, head loose on a slack neck. Spittle at the corner of his mouth, either from spit or vomit that he couldn't be bothered to dry.

"You."

His voice is resigned, the rage barely audible. He sinks down onto his haunches, feeling around for a stone for support, but loses his balance and tumbles down heavily onto his backside. He lets his back keep going until he is lying flat.

"I just got back. Foxholm I burned to the ground, and I took Åland too. All of the north is won, all the way up to the wilderness. I've achieved all that's been asked of me and more. Is my return not worth celebrating? But when I look for Engelbrekt he's with you, and I'm told to wait."

He stifles a heave. His voice rasps in hatred now, as if the words were sprung straight from the poison roiling in his belly.

"What business do you have to be here, Magnus Bengtsson? First my father begets a new son to raise in my place, and now you come to Engelbrekt to steal all his favor. What is it with blue and gold? What have I done to your house to deserve all the ills to which you subject me?"

Bitter is his laugh.

"You know what? I thought Engelbrekt sent me to the north because I was the best he had. But do you know what I hear instead? That he sent me north to keep me away from you. There was no hiding my crooked nose, so it all came to light. I was banished under the cause's flag, and though I return draped in glory, he looks upon me like a stray cat come to his doorstep, bearing a mauled shrew for a gift."

He shakes his head as he lies there. The stones crackle beneath him.

"Go away and leave me be. Go find Engelbrekt, he probably misses you already."

Magnus hears Eric Puck roll over to vomit as he walks back to the camp, to the circle of the dance. The voice that follows him is cracking in its cry.

"To Hell with you and your house, Magnus Bengtsson. I'll have the last word, as surely as Foxholm lies in ash. One day we'll see how well red will match your blue and gold."

Puck gets to his feet and staggers off in search of the company of his own men, those who know him well and will listen to him, whatever he has to say. Drinking more than he ought, he gives voice to his heart without heed. Wicked words they are, and ill-considered.

"Halt. What are you doing with that stone?"

Stina calls down from the bank at two new arrivals who have just heaved a boulder out of the earth, only to turn their backs on it in search of a better task. Both stop short, confounded. In surprise they look around them and see that all the other work has slowed, as the dozen closest men all turn to face Stina with heads bowed. There is no mistaking their reverence, and these new arrivals are attentive enough to cast their eyes down in submission and wait for her to go on. She lets go of her skirt, which by now she holds merely out of habit, for the hem is filthy and impossible to keep clean, its beaded pattern lost under a crust of mud. Stina looks around for any others who ought to hear what she has to say, then holds out a hand, and at once a man is at her side to help her up onto the newly unearthed stone. Another man makes his voice heard.

"Attention, everyone. Come listen when Lady Kristina speaks."

They all come, quick of step, and Stina gestures at the two new faces.

"Your names? I don't know them yet, but I shan't forget them."

Timidly they mumble in response.

"Anders by the lake."

"Vidar Tub."

"You're used to stacking stones in mounds so that they're out of the way of plowshares. Not here. Each and every one must be rolled to either side. Like a wall half buried. They're to be used as foundations for logs and supports, to stop the banks from collapsing. A wall to hold back the earth itself."

She looks around and selects two of the men whom she knows well and can trust.

"Jens, Mikael. Show them what we do."

Both bow their heads and answer of one voice.

"Yes, Lady Kristina."

Britta is standing off to one side. She sees the men all listening attentively and knows that there is a respect that can be demanded, but another that is bestowed only willingly.

They trust her mother. With Lady Kristina the work is now well ordered, and although those who plow this broad furrow have no more to gain from the enterprise's success than its failure, they can all see the difference in progress. For every day's work they advance by the perches. Lady Kristina's daughter measures the furrow herself with a yardstick, carving the numbers into her wax tablet, and when she goes to apprise her mother at the end of each day's work, one of the men will make sure he's doing a task within earshot. By evening they break bread on the ground that they broke that day, the first men to do so since the dawn of time, and while the meat is cooked over an open fire all of them learn just what they have achieved.

"Seven today."

"Yesterday it was five, though we did have bigger rocks in the ground."

"Tomorrow we'll do nine."

"How far left?"

They count using sticks to aid them, sticks in a pile, each one worth ten perches.

"Three thousand perches. A little more."

"How long till Lake Mälaren at this pace?"

"Not long. Devil knows. Well, he and Mistress Britta, I should think."

⁂

For every perch over seven, an extra jug of beer is granted to each man for the evening. No one ever beds down thirsty, and after a good day's work some carousing follows, but never too much, enough to serve as a balm for the soul but not leave them sluggish of head the next morn. Each night they eat their fill, on animals slaughtered and hanged to grow tender in the outbuildings at Castle Cut, and on bread from its bakehouse, the oven of which is already fired up by midnight, to bake its loaves the whole night through. From all around the tracts men flock to work under Lady Kristina. Stina chooses only the best, to join groups of five under one foreman. Only reliable folk, honorable folk who know how to work and keep their own counsel. Each man is given but one chance, and any troublemakers and idlers are sent packing, soon replaced by more able men. Those who can keep their places wear each fleck of mud on their tunic like a badge of honor, a mark that only the best can earn. By night they sing while the fires fall, old songs whose origin no one knows, but whose words they have sung since childhood. Soon all is silent. Everyone knows the value of rest, keen to dig even farther the next day.

꽃

"Any news of Magnus?"

Britta shakes her head at her mother's question, just as she did the day before, and the day before that, and every day since they arrived at the Cut. Tidings of Engelbrekt arrive now and then, and sometimes she is able to contrive them into tidings of Magnus. But nothing more than that; no message, no greeting.

"Let us pray."

Ave Maria. Once the day's work is done they pray to Our Lady, but afterward Stina is straight back up on restless feet, the prayer's peace extinguished.

"How long till the Mälaren at this rate?"

Though Britta knows the answer, she doesn't want her mother to think that she is guessing, so instead she gathers her wax tablet and her notes. So much is uncertain: the quality of the soils could change at any moment, or buried mounds slow the works, or the men could fall sick and illness spread. All she can do is look over the day's work and multiply it into an uncertain future.

"We have two thousand perches to go. It's going faster than expected. If not for the frosts we'd be finished by next spring, but we'll have to wait out the winters, both this one and next."

She sees her mother's brow furrow.

"That's not fast enough. We need more men. If we burn fires on the earth by night, perhaps we'll be able to loosen it by morning, even in harsh colds. Then we won't have to sit up in the castle shivering all winter in vain."

She always says the same. More men, greater toil, new solutions. Time and again Britta sees her faced with new trials and always come up with an answer. Her mother's mind is like a flowing stream; should a stone appear in her way, she will find a course around it. Meanwhile her father would sooner lift it, heave with all his might until his back is creaking and his trousers split, and then seek revenge for his failure's affront by butting his forehead bloody against its rugged edge.

"May I see your tablet?"

Britta hands it to her mother, sees her carry it over to the table where Britta has made her notes, added and subtracted, counted every man's work.

"This is wrong."

Stina points at the tablet.

"Olof Ready and his five dug six perches and not seven."

Britta steps closer to look, and she knows at once that her mother is right. She can see that she has put a line in the wrong place, her eyes blurry from lack of sleep. The right line, but in the wrong place.

"Yes. That notch belongs on the row below. Jens Ericsson's five dug seven, not six."

The tablet is shaking in her mother's grip when she places it to one side.

"How many more mistakes have you made?"

"None. Every night I review the day just gone when transposing the figures from tablet to paper. I'd have caught this one, too, had you not seen it first."

It is as though Stina hears nothing.

"Must I do everything myself? Can I not even give you the simplest of duties? Your mistakes could cost us days, weeks. What'll become of Magnus if the waterway doesn't open in time?"

Britta sees Stina's lips pucker to white dashes, while her cheeks redden with a rising rancor. She feels her own heart beat faster in response.

"I count and recount. Once a week I pace the whole furrow and compare it to the numbers I have. There are no mistakes in what I've done."

"And yet there's one right here. If you can't count perches, how can I know that you can count feet?"

Britta doesn't know how to meet with such unfairness. She fumbles for the words. When they come, she hears them carried on a broken voice.

"Magnus is my brother, too. You aren't the only one who wants what's best for him."

Stina's voice is sharp, every syllable a blow or cut. Too hastily does she say the first thing that comes to mind.

"Had you found yourself a husband and borne children of your own, then perhaps you'd better understand a mother's love for her son."

And so it is done, words said and words heard, let loose into the world, where they can do harm of the same nature as the abbess Ingegerd's curse. Impossible to take back now, and the bitter regret that Stina feels is quickly watered down by her rage, till it tastes of nothing at all. Britta stands speechless before her, as though she has had the wind knocked out of her. Her mother's wrath fades to indifference before her eyes. That's even worse. As though she wasn't even worth the disappointment. Stina's attention is no longer hers. Instead she sits down on the stool at the table, the piles of paper before her.

"Go to bed."

"What about you?"

"I'll check everything that you've done. Perhaps I'll have it worked out properly by dawn."

Another long day's ride nears its end. Always south, toward the kingdom's border, from city to city, village to village. The fortresses are few and poorly manned, hardly anyone in place to offer resistance. The people greet the army with cries and cheers, falling to their knees before Engelbrekt, as though he were sent by the Lord Himself to proclaim that paradise has come. Though he is a stable hand no more, Magnus occasionally visits Soot by night, with treats that he has saved to offer to the horse on his open palm. This evening he lingers there longer, awaiting Engelbrekt so that he might speak to him undisturbed. Engelbrekt comes once darkness has fallen, he, too, with a bunch of carrots to give. He stops in the doorway when he sees his place already taken.

"Magnus?"

"Forgive me. I wanted to speak to you alone, away from prying ears."

Engelbrekt nods.

"Let me give Soot his carrots first. He can smell them, and if he doesn't get them now he'll give us no peace."

With that done, he lifts two low stools off the hanger on the wall, of the three-legged kind that maids use to reach cows' udders. He places them in the middle of the floor, opposite one another, then sits down on one and offers Magnus the other.

"Let the conference begin."

"It's Eric, Eric Puck."

Engelbrekt's aspect darkens.

"What's he done to you this time?"

"He's done nothing to me. Nothing more than spiteful words, uttered while drunk. But when we were in Vadstena I spoke to my uncle and asked him if he knew why Puck might harbor such a grudge against blue and gold."

"And?"

"Is Eric Puck the son of Lord Rossvik? A bastard?"

Engelbrekt hesitates at first, but then responds.

"Many know, but no one says it aloud. If you know what's good for you, you'll never brandish that fact as a weapon against him. Many a man has lived to rue the day they called Eric Puck the son of a whore."

"His father married later, and his wife bore him an heir. Birgitta was his wife's name. She's my cousin. Rossvik's heir is one-quarter blue and gold."

Magnus sees that this comes as news to Engelbrekt; sees the insight that it gave him also spread its light in the northman's face.

"Cuckoo's Roost is my home. Rarely has the name been more apt. To Puck it must feel like a cuckoo has laid its egg in the nest that was his. And now that very same cuckoo has found its way here, and yet another egg has hatched. You can see that he wants for no reason to hate me, though I've done nothing to him."

"What would you have me do?"

"Don't send Puck away. Show him that he's foremost in your estimation, that the place he occupies isn't one that I threaten, that this is merely his delusion."

Engelbrekt leans back and studies him for a long time. He has no response. Soot snorts at their side, the gifts he was given already forgotten. Engelbrekt is quickly up on his feet, stroking his steed by the muzzle.

"Come, let's take a turn out in the fresh air. Soot needs his rest."

Around the village lies forest, trees that have been spared the axe and saw to grant the houses lee from the gales that blow in over the fields. They cross brushed earth outside the stable, taking a path toward the forest's edge. Where it will lead them neither of them knows, but there's space enough to walk two abreast.

"I want to ask you something else, you who have such counsel to give."

Magnus hesitates.

"I'm sure there are others who can answer better."

"My question concerns neither cunning, war, nor tricks. It's about that which is both simpler and more difficult; what's right and true. In that I should sooner hear your opinion."

"I'll answer as far as I am able."

"It's Örebro. Mattis Kettilberg is refusing to budge. He's demanding his thousand marks, and his ramparts are inviolable. I have no silver, and from the nobles I refuse to borrow. But there is another way."

They reach a clearing, where the trees' roots weave a frame around taller grasses that are yellowing but still soft. A brook ripples nearby, fresh and silvery through the colors of autumn. Engelbrekt finds a stump along its shore and sits down, tracing the water's flight with his gaze.

"I've agreed to a meeting with the Hanseatic League. I've had dealings with their merchants for a long time. Money they have in abundance, enough to lend me what's needed and more besides."

"So?"

"Once indebted I'm no longer free. They're not demanding a pledge for the loan this time, which is unheard of. I fear they have their sights on a future service in return, a way of harnessing our cause to further their own interests with regard to King Eric. I won't be in a good place to deny them, then, and with me in their pocket the foundations of the new kingdom will be laid on swamp."

Magnus is seated on the grass with his arms around his knees, gazing downstream at where a raised stone flings pearls of water up over the surface. Engelbrekt throws a pebble at the stream. It bounces off the stone before sinking.

"What would you do in my place?"

"Take the money. Buy the castle. It's for a good cause, and when it comes to loans and favors no one can know what the future holds. Come the time, come the means."

Engelbrekt sighs heavily. Nods in agreement.

"Now you know what others cannot. As long as you're at my side, let me never forget what matters most. Will you be my conscience, Magnus?"

A breeze rustles through the trees, strewing them with red leaves. Magnus wipes from his eyes a lock of hair that the wind has blown.

"Yes. Always."

"If Puck is to stay, at least let me teach you to defend yourself, though I hope you shall never need to."

MAGNUS RAISES HIS sword.

"Not so high."

Magnus does as he is bidden while tossing the hair from his eyes, wet tendrils against his damp forehead. His shoulders are sore from the effort of parrying and countering anew. On Engelbrekt nothing shows. By subtle means he dictates their bout; but a few steps this way or that, the sword now in a new position, always the one least favorable to Magnus and the most taxing for him to fend off, always with a shrewd twist to put the sun at his own back. Engelbrekt holds the sword as effortlessly as if it weighed no more than a hazel sprig, moving on light feet.

Nothing Engelbrekt does appears difficult. He lunges on soft knees, sending the tip of his blade farther than what should be possible, then thrusts from below, forcing Magnus to parry again. Under his open shirt Magnus is shaking with exertion, his every muscle in protest as new feats are demanded of them. He must grip the hilt with two hands to hold Engelbrekt off, grateful that the clang of steel on steel muffles the sound that passes his lips when his fingers are stunned by the violence of the blow. He staggers sideways, toward an opening on Engelbrekt's left flank, but loses his footing when his sword meets only empty air where another sword was expected. Engelbrekt has leapt into safety, the tip of his sword hovering at Magnus's waist, which in all his haste Magnus has heedlessly left open for the death blow.

"Good, but too hasty."

He lowers his sword to let Magnus catch his breath, bent double with his hands on his knees.

"You've had a good teacher."

Magnus shakes his head.

"You put me to shame."

"Give it time. I've seen more than my fair share of battle. When your life's at stake the lessons are learned fast."

Engelbrekt steps closer, suddenly poised to attack. He sweeps his sword in a circle simply for the joy of hearing its blade cleave the wind.

"Let me show you something."

Magnus readies himself as best he can, his feet in place and his blade extended. In surprise he sees Engelbrekt let his sword fall to the grass.

"Come at me like you mean it."

"But you have no means of defense."

"Such things happen in war. I'll show you what to do. Make it a good thrust."

For a moment they stand still opposite each other, on this secluded hill out of sight of the camp. The summer wind caresses the field, rolling in the green grass around them, the ears already waist-high where the duelists haven't leveled them with the ground. Magnus looks into Engelbrekt's eyes, as he has been taught to do since childhood, for in them the opponent's intent is revealed. Engelbrekt stands still, his arms at his sides, making little effort to change position based on the movements of Magnus's sword. All levity is gone, challenge alone in his eyes. Around them the air thickens with the danger now latent in their game, and Magnus feels his body respond with the agility of youth, new life coursing through limbs that were previously so faint. He prepares his attack, shifts weight from one foot to the other, bends his arms, and sinks down deeper to give himself a reach that can't be seen. Raising his weapon high above his head, he moistens his lips and takes a deep breath, feels the power surging behind muscles tensed like bowstrings.

He whips around and attacks, as swiftly as the wind. But Engelbrekt is swifter still, has read his movements with a practiced eye and leapt in close, safe far within the sword's sweeping arc. Engelbrekt traps Magnus's arm under his and locks it by his side, as easily as in a dance.

"Never raise your weapon above your head. Your opponent will see it coming, the blow easily headed off, with no harm done."

Face-to-face, then, for a moment, eye to eye, close enough to feel the other's heartbeats through his skin. Magnus hears his own sword fall to the ground beside Engelbrekt's when he can no longer bear the steel's weight. He feels his knees start to buckle.

COLD RAIN. AUTUMN now. Sir Bengt sees the moisture soaking the banks of the furrow that the men have plowed one thousand perches long, between the fresh waters of Lake Mälaren in the north and the brackish sea in the south. Good work she has done, his wife. Better than he. He searches for bitterness but finds none. Why exchange vows if no benefits were to come of it? He is glad that he has her. The soil is turning to mud, loosening, wont to melt and run back down into the ditch from which it was so laboriously dug, but Stina has had trees felled in great numbers, their trunks split into planks to serve as walls. At every other perch a log is propped against them, their bases driven deep into the earth. With them in place the walls will hold all the weight that bears down upon them. Sir Bengt would simply have dug, would have thought no further than that, and now he would be watching on as all his hard toil was undone. Even in weather like this Stina's trusted men walk from log to log, comparing their positions with the marks carved into the wood to ensure they aren't shifting or slipping, for if one loses its grip, then the load on the others will grow. He glimpses her from a distance, sees her pointing but can't hear her words.

His face is wetted when he turns it up to the dark clouds. Plenty more in store. The autumn promises to be both wet and cold, worse than usual, but with a hot, clear summer behind them that should come as no surprise, for the sum of all is the same. Though the work is progressing, Bengt wonders for the hundredth time whether it wouldn't have been better to stand side by side with Engelbrekt at Stockholm's city walls, weapon in hand, rather than be stuck digging in the bogs of Castle Cut. It's a madcap task that he has been entrusted with, an endeavor beyond all reason. All of this earth, shifted. It feels somehow blasphemous, like the tower raised by the men of Babel before their pride was rebuked. Still, the thought of the castle that he has been granted is a comfort to him, now as always. It's a good house, one that he has settled into well enough. The lake boasts fish, the forest is full of game, and his table knows no privation. In fact, he has grown heavier. Old garments now sit tightly and need letting out, new patches to seal the splits where the seams weren't generous enough. Stina has plenty to occupy herself with by day, and he often struggles to find himself something to do. Perhaps he eats more for the comfort.

He turns homeward, content that others are handling the task that he was assigned. Soon the ground frost will come, and then it will be much worse. His horse knows the path, needs no help from him to find the way. Just as little as his wife does.

In the courtyard new arrivals await him, their horses being put to stables, unfamiliar stable hands among his own men. Then he sees them and their harnesses and hurries inside, glad for the company but anxious at what news it brings. His brother shouldn't be here now, and if he has time to spare it can only mean that something is awry. By the hearth in the great hall Sir Bo is already seated, blowing on warm beer in a mug. They exchange nods, and Bengt pulls up a chair opposite, in the heat of the fire.

"Brother Bo."

"Brother Bengt."

"Has Stake Isle still not fallen?"

Sir Bo shakes his head and turns his gaze toward the fire.

"Your men?"

He shakes his head again, and Bengt can't help the sound that escapes him, of a breath hastily drawn through clenched teeth.

"And Engelbrekt?"

"I've tried to find him, but he's not easy to reach. The man moves like the wind. I'd ridden all the way down to Skövde before I even found parts of his camp. By then he was already gone, far south in Halland province, him and his whole army."

"That's Danish soil. Does he mean to take Denmark, too, bring the entire union under his rule? Wasn't the whole point to reclaim Sweden and redraw the frontiers where Margaret had swept them away? Örebro finally fell, too, and from what I understand without bloodshed. Kettilberg's on the march home, the dog. Even a northman should know that pride comes before a fall."

Bo sips at his beer, gasps when he finds it still hotter than he would have hoped.

"There are others of the same ilk, albeit of nobler birth. Did you hear that Knut's seized Roan Island? Not a little brazen. As they say, the more the Devil has . . ."

Bo nods in agreement.

"It was for another reason that I came, brother."

"Oh?"

"I've heard a rumor."

"And?"

A servant appears with a drink for Bengt, and Bo remains silent, keeping his eyes on the man until he has left the room.

"It's about Magnus."

Bo Stensson shifts forward on his seat and lowers his voice.

"As I was saying, I got to Skövde, where I took lodging for the night. Engelbrekt's followers were everywhere, great throngs of them. In the end I found a seat among Eric Puck's men. I spoke to those around me, shared their table without mention of rank, parched and ravenous as I was after a long ride. Soon enough I was one of them, and drinking loosened their tongues."

"So?"

"What I heard was that in the beginning Magnus's place wasn't at Engelbrekt's side, but as his stable hand."

Bengt frowns in perplexity.

"What are you saying?"

"You heard. Engelbrekt took him on as a stable boy, to groom his horse, tend to its stall, muck it out afterward."

Bengt shakes his head in disbelief. He takes a swig of his beer, his brow furrowed in thought.

"Even if there were any truth to it, it's absurd. Why would Engelbrekt reward our house so generously if it were merely for the sake of his stable boy?"

His brother sighs and half turns away, dark of aspect.

"It gets worse, brother. Magnus wasn't long of the stables. It's said that your son and Engelbrekt are closer than two men should be."

Sir Bengt feels a cold jolt running through his stomach, one that appears to drive every jot of heat and blood upward, until his heart's drumfire is pounding in his ears.

"Say it better. Tell me how the words fell, exactly as you heard it."

"It's said that Engelbrekt took an injury in Schleswig, a wound to his gut, perhaps even to his very manhood. Rumor has it that's why he's childless, despite having a wife back home in Norberg. Now they're saying that Engelbrekt's manhood isn't in such a bad way after all, it's just that he'd never found the right tongue to lick his wound. And that the tongue that's licking his wound belongs to Magnus Bengtsson."

For a while Bengt sits in silence. Dismissively he flaps his hand.

"Spiteful words and nothing more. Obviously it's not true."

"Obviously. But I wanted you to know."

Over in the hearth the flames sink their teeth into a knothole, and one of the logs in the stack crumbles. Bo reaches through the sparks to take another one to place on the fire.

"We suffer no shortage of enemies, brother, and each of them has plenty to say. Jealousy will make people voice whatever they most want to hear, and Eric Puck may have more reason than others. Engelbrekt Engelbrektsson has favored blue and gold far beyond other colors."

Bengt Stensson can't help but sweep his gaze around the walls of the great hall. Vadstena is still recent in his memory. All that they were granted; himself, his brothers, the bishop. Favored so far beyond the rest. That's it. That's just it. And he can see from Bo's eyes that his brother is thinking the same.

Autumn comes over the kingdom, reaching even its warm southern tracts. Nils Stensson gives up any thought of sleep. He lies uneasily where he made his bed, while all around him come the sounds of men who have readily found that which eludes him. They are asleep. Snores, sniffs, coughs; the muted rumble of wind broken under sheets. Eventually he tires of lying there in the darkness, tossing this way and that in his vain search for rest. He gets up, puts his clothing in order, buttons up his doublet, and drapes the heavy woollen roundel of his mantle over his shoulders. Slowly he crosses the chamber floor, so as not to step on those who are asleep, or stumble over outstretched limbs. He has slept among the other men for weeks now, and though every night he rues this decision and wishes he had a chamber of his own, he doesn't want it said of him that he's a lord of the old stock. People talk. The country is small. Even among his own ranks there are those who have friends and relatives farther south, and that's all it takes to give a rumor wings. He would sooner have word spread that he's like Engelbrekt, a noble of the kind who hasn't forgotten that all men are sprung of one root. Little good has it done him. It has taken him everything in his power to urge these southern men to rebel. Nils has heard Engelbrekt speak, committed his words to memory, but although he says the same things in the same tone of voice, it's as though his listeners possess a sixth sense that divines his true nature. They seem to see him for who he is, however hard he may try to hide it. The thought nags him, for these are simple folk, the kind that spend their scant years in mud and sweat, believing whatever the priest tells them to, questioning nothing and never thinking an original thought, before going to the grave just as ignorant as they lived. With faces as blank as their very cattle they listen to him and his exhortations: about the people's burden under the bailiff's yoke; the unjust gluttony of the Danes and Germans at the peasants' expense; the taxes that he promises to lower. Once the words have rung out to make way for roaring cheers, silence remains instead. They exchange glances, shrug, and mumble and go back to what they were doing, and Nils must mount his horse and ride on to the next village. There the same thing.

He steps out through the door, shuddering when he feels the

difference between the coolness of the autumn night and the chamber warmed by a hundred men. A watchman leaning against the wall grunts at him without seeing who he is and points at a lone torch that guides the way to the ditch dug as a makeshift privy. Nils takes the road the other way, wandering aimlessly toward the coast. The moon is high and lights his way. Behind him the church at Balk Hill, the place that he has usurped for his own purposes, having turned out the priest, billeted his men in the church hall and strengthened the old fortifications. It's like no other church that he has seen. The walls are thick, their openings clearly narrowed with bricks to aid archers. No sacred place from the start. Its very masonry hums with age-old battles from a forsaken past. A hollow encircles it that once was a moat, easily restored. With a hundred men he can hold it against any army. Shame he hasn't taken it to defend it but merely to use as an encampment, until he leads his men to Kalmar to take the castle. Still, he's hardly mustered a legion of peasants thus far, and the forces Sir Bo promised him are a long time coming, though they were supposed to march this way as soon as Stake Isle fell. With Bo at Stake Isle, Knut at Stepstones, Bengt at the Cut, and Nils at Kalmar, the whole east coast would be painted blue and gold. Once the kingdom is united anew and trade is resumed, they would be able to tax the bulging cogs of the Hansa once, twice, and more on their way to Stockholm and back.

The path leads down to the water. The sea is resplendent, unresting waves forged in silver beneath the moon. A passing cloud brings rain, cold and gentle, its droplets sprinkled with flakes. Nils finds a tree trunk to lean against, beneath a branch that keeps him dry. Soon the moon is obscured and darkness falls, and, as the cloud above him bands with others, the droplets fall all the heavier. Nils curses inwardly and wraps his mantle tighter around his waist, the scent of wet wool now pungent around him. Before long he'll probably feel the moisture on his skin. A white flash casts its light over the sea, and a few moments later comes the rumble. The thunder crackles far off in the distance, late for the time of year. Nils sinks down onto the patch of ground that his body has shielded from moisture, then sits there with his legs crossed, resigned to what bodes to be a long night under the shelter of this measly tree, the hardness of Balk Hill church's floor and the men's noises immediately forgiven. But when another flash of lightning claws at the waves he is straight back up on his feet and out onto the bare ground, heedless to the rain that quickly soaks his clothes. Out there, in the south. Shadows on the waves. He stares wide-eyed out into the pitch darkness, his ears full of the downpour's hiss and his own heart's drum. He must have been seeing things. He prays a wordless prayer that it be so.

Yet again the lightning flares, brighter and closer now, sizzling a few times in quick succession. Under its pale torch he sees them clearly. Black ships. Ship upon ship in a long column, heading north. No merchants, these. They're warships, the kind made to carry hordes of men to wherever the war is to unfold. Nils doesn't need to see the flag under which they sail, for he already knows. A yellowed field, crossed with red. King Eric. King Eric has come. Too soon, earlier than anyone could have suspected, to take back the kingdom that is threatening to slip from his grasp.

"K ARI!"

Britta waves at her and cries out, even though she is too far away for her voice to carry. From the sled she sees a hand raised in response. The weather is mild, though winter lies thick, the days never so short as now. For a long time Britta has been able to follow the sled's course through the slush, while thawing drops fall around her from the castle roof. Katarina Sharp has come to celebrate the first day of the year at Castle Cut, she alone, while the men are all away. Britta hasn't seen her father in weeks; first he was with his privateers on the coast, to witness the arrival of the king's fleet, then in Stockholm on behalf of the Council, once King Eric had ensconced himself on the city's isles and invited the lords to talks. Since then peace has reigned. And yet she fancies that she can hear the sounds of pikes being sharpened from every side.

The sled approaches, braving the ice that lies thick around the castle. Kari Sharp is quickly out of her seat, wearing a bearskin around her shoulders and a hat of the same kind. She pads through the snow to the castle steps and wraps Britta in her arms.

"Britta."

"Kari."

"All well?"

"All is well."

"And Stina?"

"She's down by the ditch, today as she was yesterday, and every day since summer. Not even on Sundays can she keep herself away. I would have gone with her, but, knowing that you were coming, I stayed to meet you. They have fires burning all night long to chase the frost from the ground, and then they break it loose with red-hot picks. We advance less in a week now than we did in a day in summer, but it's something. And it gives her something to do. She's on her feet as much now as she was on her back before. Your idea bore fruit."

"And you, Britta? Are the two of you getting along?"

Britta can't bring herself to look Kari in the eye when she replies, more inclined to hide her feelings.

"It's the same as always. Mother has three yardsticks: one for me, one for everyone else, and one for Magnus. I rarely measure up."

Kari pulls a face.

"It's difficult to see everything that goes on inside your mother. Always has been. Perhaps there's more to it than you might suspect. Anyway, it's something, no? A start."

"It's something."

Britta shakes off her thoughts, smooths out her aspect, and pours the gratitude that she feels into the look that she gives Kari.

"Thank you for coming. I fear this will be a difficult day for her, and I imagine she'll need all the cheering she can get."

Kari gives her a wry smile and places a hand on her cheek.

"One of these days she'll start to do all that she should be doing to deserve a daughter like you. But fear not. If my tales from the sea don't work, I've brought ample help with me in the sled."

They change into dresses that were made to be seen, then take the same sled down to the ditch to fetch an unwilling Stina, who lets them drape an ornately beaded mantle over the clothes that she has been wearing far too long. Their way takes them to the Cut's city center, and to the high mass, the special service held on this first day of the New Year in celebration of the solemnity of Mary, Mother of God. One more year is come to the earth, and on its birthday it is the mother who is honored. They take their seats, on the front pew where everyone can see them, The Cut's masters, the ladies of the castle, each one shimmering like a jewel among peasant winter garb, dyed a dull red with madder root in vain attempts to embellish their gray wool. Around them crowd noble farmers in possession of lands, whose eager flattery falls on Stina's deaf ears. Britta observes her mother with all the greater unease. The priest gives his sermon, recounts how a sinful and simple woman was granted the holiness of God Himself. He speaks of the special bond of motherhood, of Mary's grief at Golgotha. Cautiously Britta turns her head to see her mother better. Black and empty is her gaze, her shoulders sunken, her hands clenched so tightly that her knuckles are white. On the sled home she is silent, led to the table but grudgingly, and, after their meal, to the bench before the fire where the flames roar through the birchwood. Kari has had the cask fetched that she brought all the way from Oakwood, then empties its contents into a cauldron and places it on the fire. A pleasant smell fills the chamber. She pours them each a goblet.

"Taste this. You too, Britta."

Never has Britta tasted the like. It's a wine, sweet and hot and full of aromatic spices, and it tastes of distant lands where the sun always shines. She takes another sip, speechless. Kari Sharp nods at her surprise.

"Yes, I know."

Kari prods Stina in her side.

"Your turn now, kinswoman."

While her mother drinks impassively, Britta fumbles to dispel the silence.

"Where are all the men?"

Kari raises an eyebrow.

"Has your father said nothing?"

"Father hasn't been home in a long time. He has much business to attend to, and we haven't received any tidings."

Kari pours more for them all.

"Then I'll tell you. The schemes continue. Bengt is with my husband. Engelbrekt has summoned them. I hope they don't get dizzy with all the turning they're doing, our husbands, for it makes me faint just to look at them. But such is the game we have joined. They made peace with King Eric at the island of the Holy Spirit in Stockholm, in the hope that it would bring rewards. Now that the king has set sail back home, Engelbrekt is demanding that the allegiance they swore to the throne be refuted anew. He'll have to promise them more than King Eric did to win their favor. And then I suppose the king's counterbid will come. And then Engelbrekt's. And so on."

"How will it all end?"

Kari gestures at the chamber in which they sit.

"You've already got one castle. Two is better than one."

She shakes her head and raises her goblet at Stina.

"Let's leave the fathers' hardships for now. Let us drink to the mothers instead."

Stina drinks, staring into the fire. Then she makes her first utterance since they returned.

"Do you think she thought it was worth it, Saint Mary, all that she did? To sit beneath Jesus's cross and watch him bleed?"

Kari Sharp casts her a watchful glance from over the rim of her goblet.

"Wouldn't you?"

"All the pain. First the birth. Worse than you ever thought possible, and you believe with all your heart that you've known the greatest pain. That is until later, when the children are grown, and you see that your every happiness lies in another's hands, one ill qualified to bear it. That there are places inside you that can hurt even more than the tearing of your sex. The world demands the child as its tribute, and the mother is forsaken."

She drains her goblet, and Kari snatches it up to fill it again, quickly enough to draw her out of her speech, her lapse in forgetting that she has two children and not one. Stina looks up in astonishment to see Britta sitting there. She meets her gaze for a moment, then turns back to the fire without a word. The smoke has gathered under the ceiling high above them, drawn listlessly to the hole in the wall where the draft makes itself felt. Behind its cloud the painted tendrils on the beams appear like living things, coiling and twisting.

"You've got a good castle here. My Bo was promised Stake Isle, on condition that he could take it himself. They fared ill. There was more than one wolf circling that prey, but they couldn't bring themselves to hunt in a pack. Men. What would become of them without us? They'd slay each other, that's what, put the kingdom to ash. We make them see reason, still their blood as best we can. Bear their children. Daughters, if we're lucky. But if they're sons, we can only do what we can to make them better than their fathers. It's as though there's a curse upon their kind."

Stina puts her goblet down on the bench, turns to Kari Sharp, and looks her in the eye.

"*All your love shall end in blood.* Have you heard those words before, Kari?"

She hesitates, her sister-in-law, hiding behind her goblet. But then she puts it down, next to Stina's.

"Bo couldn't keep a secret from me if his life depended on it."

"I found Karin Stensdaughter's grave in Vadstena, where Mara lost her child. The bishop gave me the whole story, that snake. Sir Sten had ten children, enough to seed the earth. And yet there will be no descendants."

"There's Britta, and your Magnus, and my Nils. All were born healthy."

"Do you love him, Kari? Bo. Have you ever loved him?"

The color rises in Kari Sharp's face.

"What kind of question is that? A conceited old goat, he is, no doubt getting worse with the years. Though a handsome man he never was, so at least I won't see him decline. He's the father of my child, and I won't deny that I found pleasure enough in making him. I've met many a man who's worse, and whom I could still have married, had fate willed it. And I've met just as many men who are better, yet who would have made a worse match. Do I feel affection for him? Yes. Share my life with him? Yes. But it's never been more than that."

Rather than look at Stina, Kari has spoken to the fading fire.

"That's just it. In the childbed there was no love to end in blood. Nor for me. But now there is. Our sons are in danger, Kari. You shouldn't have left your Nils, and Magnus should never have gone to Engelbrekt."

In the silence Britta is left to a bitter thought: *But I'm safe*.

PART V

AUTUMN, WINTER, AND SPRING 1435-36

N ILS SEES THE ships return, in daylight this time. He can count them. Four dozen, perhaps five. More than last year. He is standing on the same spot as last time, by the same tree, on the same shore, a half hour's march from Balk Hill church. Almost a year has passed, though it feels like more. Nils remembers the first time they came: how the fleet had anchored and how the boats with shallower hulls had started rowing back and forth to the Småland beaches as dawn broke, putting men to land. Meanwhile Nils had run all the way back to Balk Hill, tasting blood in his mouth, to gather his men within its walls and prepare their defences. The next day they saw the king's foot soldiers passing from afar. They never came near Balk Hill, for with armed men they sought no conflict. Instead they continued farther inland. For three days Nils Stensson waited ensconced in his church, before the king's men went marching back the same way they had come, back to the warships that were waiting in the bay. Nils sent out scouts to follow them, who soon returned to declare the field clear, the ships having all sailed north without leaving anyone behind. Nils spent the next week tracing their steps. They had gone from estate to estate, village to village, dragging the men and boys from their homes, to hang them in trees from their necks or their heels, burn them in barns, or slit their throats in town squares, leaving them lying wherever they fell. Dead bodies everywhere, left to defiled mothers and daughters to bury, their eyes just as empty as those of the dead. With blood Eric's message was written; in the ashes of burned estates; in the tattered shreds of women's ripped garments: See the return of the king! Fear his wrath, pray for his mercy, and repent your disloyalty! All will be as it has been! The king made no more forays onto land; his ships sailed on toward Stockholm from which his power had never swayed, and to its island of the Holy Spirit the Council of the Realm were summoned for talks. They bound themselves to a one-year peace, and the Council swore to leave the king's bailiffs unchallenged in their castles. And with that Eric returned to Denmark, vowing that the leaders of the rebellion would be tried by Swedish law, Engelbrekt Engelbrektsson foremost among them, and Eric Puck next.

The Council had made a pact that they couldn't keep. Engelbrekt called the men of the Council to a parley in the king's absence, where he persuaded them to renew their promises made in Vadstena, renounce the loyalty that they had just averred, and declare Engelbrekt commander of the kingdom's forces. Nils was there, and so stirringly did he bear witness before the Council of King Eric's march of devastation among the peasantry that Engelbrekt rewarded him with command of all of Småland province. It has proved no great blessing. The truce has remained, each side preparing for the clash that must eventually come. And now here comes the king again, as if time were moving in a circle.

Nils thinks back over the year that has passed. A strange year. The king wise enough to see time as his best ally, holding out in his hope that the delicate threads that bound the northmen and the nobles would snap. Engelbrekt Engelbrektsson everywhere, constantly struggling to tighten their knots. The time that has passed feels longer than it should, for slow was its course. In that time Nils has done little more than drill men and whet blades, make Balk Hill even stronger, and whittle himself a likeness of Kalmar Castle and its fortifications, in readiness for the siege that will never come. This fallow period has drained him, aged him before his time, kept him awake at night. A lost year. A year of his youth that he will never get back, one that failed to bring the adventure that life so recently seemed to promise. No glory has he won, and his Mara has had to go home from Vadstena on her own, to the manor where she wanders alone with the ghost of the child who never was. No more are likely to come for as long as he sits in Balk Hill twiddling his thumbs. He misses her with body and soul, a longing embittered by bad conscience. With every passing week it grows all the harder to persuade himself that every one of his sacrifices is made for her best.

He is better prepared this time. For months he has imagined this meeting. Now he lights his beacon for the ships to see, beside a helmet that he raises high on a stripped birch trunk. He has painted his shield in patterns of blue and gold; if the king doesn't know the coat himself, he'll have courtiers who do. Nils's patience is gone, and he's sick of waiting in vain for the chance to run errands for Engelbrekt. The time is come to speak to the king himself, and this time on his own terms. He sees sails being reefed and rudders swinging out on the waves; a boat is launched, oars beating in their efforts to reach him where he stands. Soon he is sitting on a foamy deck beside soaking-wet Danish foot soldiers, ready to stand before his king and offer his future services with an ardency that will make his past disloyalty forgotten.

MANY TIMES HAS Sir Bengt sent for his son in the months that have passed, always to the same response. A horseman will seek out Engelbrekt and his army at their last known location, to summon Magnus home to Cuckoo's Roost, where father and son can meet and talk. His man always returns alone, and with the same message: Magnus Bengtsson does not wish to come. He's staying put. There is nothing that Bengt can do. He has no one to whom he can vent his anger, nor the growing disquiet that feeds it: Nils is still in his godforsaken Balk Hill, Sir Bo wherever the crumbs from Engelbrekt's table promise to fall most amply, and Stina at Castle Cut, so spattered with soil and mud that no one can tell her from a simple farmwoman in sowing season.

The trench is slowly being dug through its intractable soils, by turns too boggy and too hard. A wider road has been cleared beside it, from the shore in the north to the shore in the south, for oxen and men to haul by land the iron floated down from the north, which is then loaded onto the ships of the Hanseatic League that moor in the seas outside the Cut. A laborious trade route, but better than none, and it makes the work easier for Viper Saltlock and his privateers, since Sir Bengt can tell them to where the cogs are bound. An ease that goes hand in hand with danger; if Engelbrekt isn't to discover that he posted a fox to guard his henhouse, the raids must be executed with wiles, four ships allowed to pass unmolested for every one taken, and from that one only a small chunk bitten before it is allowed to go on its way. All without revealing the allegiances of the privateers. That alone would be enough to keep Sir Bengt up at night. At least the silver is some consolation.

The summer has been a long one for him, spent between the Cut, Cuckoo's Roost, and elsewhere. It can't be called peace, what has reigned since Engelbrekt was named commander, merely a protracted wait for the king's rejoinder. It's wearing on everyone. To relieve his own weariness Sir Bengt has paid visits to kin and lords within a day's ride, eaten at their tables, and hunted in their forests. All of them bear deep furrows in their brows, uncertain whether they will keep the fiefs that they have been accorded, uncertain of where their loyalty should be sworn in order to make the greatest gains, and of how they can best recant those words on the day the winds should change.

No point lighting a fire for the crows. Cuckoo's Roost is cold now that autumn has descended, just as cold within as without. He remembers last year's Midsummer, the mirth of the great hall when the whole house was gathered, singing and stamping on its floorboards. As distant now as though a whole generation had passed. Now Bengt is alone here, his family scattered. It is tradition that the master of Cuckoo's Roost should attend church at this time of year, to appear before the people and remind them of his humility. Already duty calls. He is almost looking forward to it this time, merely for the change. People in great numbers in contrast to the emptiness of his great house, its chambers yawning caverns starved of society. Simple folk without schemes or covert designs, their positions clear to all: he the lord of Cuckoo's Roost; they beholden to respect him. With a sigh, as his back complains, he exits the manor house, mounts beside his men, and sets out for Mellösa for the mass.

The priest is younger than he is, the successor to the old one, who died. The young man's voice quakes in fear. It is difficult for him to preach, for he isn't acquainted with Sir Bengt, knows not on which toes he risks treading with his exhortations. With a sigh Bengt notes that he has chosen the safest of courses, taking as his subject matter something so tedious that no one living could find in it any source of offense. Bengt stops listening, lets his thoughts drift while the voice fades, the droning Latin lulling in its sameness. He knows not where he gets the fancy; perhaps from the very dreariness of it all. He hasn't confessed in a year, tends to do so around Christmas, for the sins that the New Year promises are best met with those of the past year forgiven. It is time. During communion he drains the chalice, then guides the priest's own hand to fill it again and again until he feels the first flush of the drink. After the service he needn't push or jostle, for even as he approaches, the other partitioners part as though on cue, letting him pass before them with their heads bowed. In the sacristy, the priest looks as though someone has taken their thumbs to his larynx when he sees who it is that has come. Bengt must clear his throat to remind him of his task. The priest invites him to sit down with a trembling hand.

"In nominee Patris, et Filii, et Spiritus Sancti. Amen."

"I've committed adultery. More times than I can count. With maids, laundry maids, peasants, the wives of others. Many whose names I neither asked nor learned. Rarely have I missed an opportunity, though more often it is I who have willfully sought out sin."

With satisfaction he sees the sweat beading on the priest's forehead, though the room is cold. He sees his eyes flit here and there, uncertain of the most fitting response, for on it hangs his own future and perhaps even that of his church.

"Temptation has overpowered many a man; it is a crime just as ancient as humanity."

"I'm a greedy man, too. I take what I can to enrich myself, unjustly and indiscriminately. I fill my coffers at the expense of young and old, strangers and my own blood alike. Fornication and greed are but the first of all the deadly sins that I have made my own. I'm a glutton. I feel wrath. I'm a proud man, proud and envious. In sloth I live, while others must toil by the sweat of their brows. I break my oaths when it suits me best."

The priest turns all the paler, stammers while fumbling for words of flattery.

"It is all too easy for penitent sinners to see but their shortcomings, blinded to that which is good. All the people in these tracts look up to His Grace, and they harbor a daily, constant gratitude that Sir Bengt holds his hand over us, protecting us from the evils of the world. It's good that you have come to confess, so that your sins may be forgiven, my son."

My son. Bengt leans in over the table that separates them, far enough that the gold chain around his neck taps against the tabletop. He fixes his eyes on the priest.

"And if I've lain with another man, Father?"

The priest opens and closes his mouth, like a fish just hauled out of the deep and then laid on the jetty unclubbed. At first there comes but a whistling peep from his throat, before he makes the sign of the cross, clasps his hands before himself in disgrace, and forces the words to his mouth.

"Such things happen, Your Grace; they happen from lack of judgment, or when warriors who've taken up arms must seek comfort where there are no womenfolk to be found, or when the devil succeeds in corrupting a soul in his moment of weakness. But God is love, and he forgives. Now for your penance . . ."

The priest looks down and swallows, and Sir Bengt suspects that he is saying a prayer of his own.

". . . twenty Pater Nosters and twenty Ave Marias."

Bengt leans back, his desire for sport by now exhausted. He shakes his head slowly and thinks of Bishop Knut, of the letters of indulgence that reaped a thousand silver marks in a single spring, and wonders whether it won't do the church a disservice in the long run, for already he finds it difficult to venerate a Godhead who keeps servants such as this. And with that it comes to him, the answer to a riddle long fallen into oblivion, like a slap across his cheek. A highwayman's name, mentioned in passing by his brother: Tor the Walker. But he had already heard mention of the name before. He leaps up so sharply that he topples his chair, distractedly grabs a fistful of coins from his purse, and releases them onto the table in front of the priest, before turning to leave.

"For your diligence, Father."

Nothing compared to the thousand marks of silver that finally promise to reveal themselves. Bengt shakes his head, talking to himself.

"Finn Sigridsson. Did the bishop's man make the mistake of putting a price on your sister's soul?"

F INN SEES THE man's colors in the distance against the wet snow on the ground, and knows that yet another messenger is come from Sir Bengt to invite Magnus home to Cuckoo's Roost. Once the horse has brought him closer he can even name the man. Finn steps out into the road to meet him and pats the horse on his muzzle: a steed he knows better than his rider, one that Finn groomed in the pens of Cuckoo's Roost.

"Johannes. Peace be with you. I hope your journey has been an easy one."

"Finn. And also with you."

Johannes sweeps his hat off his head and rubs his brow.

"I'm glad I finally found you. I've asked every soul I passed the way to Engelbrekt's encampments. All of them gave me an answer, but not one of them was right until now. Sir Bengt will hardly be pleased at the time it's taken me, but at least now I won't return home with my task undone."

"It pains me that you've worn your saddle in vain. Magnus's response is the same now as it was before."

"It's not for him that I've come. Sir Bengt's message I'm to bring to you this time."

Finn shifts weight from foot to foot, now wary.

"Sir Bengt gave me the words to learn by rote. Would you like to hear them straightaway?"

Finn gives a curt nod. Better that way.

"Sir Bengt says thus: Finn Sigridsson is to return to Cuckoo's Roost for Christmas, to answer for what he left in the forests outside Motala. But if he returns with Magnus Bengtsson no questions shall be asked, and what has happened will be forgotten for evermore."

It takes Finn all of his strength to stay on his feet when the dizziness strikes. Long has he expected a message of this ilk, and long has he brooded on it in thought and in nightmare. That it has been so long in coming is now staggering to him: a man slain, his absence a hole slashed through the cloth of the world, the loose threads not difficult to follow. But all the more staggering are the feelings that wash over him in the wake of the accusation. A relief akin to a priest's blessing after confession. A knot that he has borne tightly drawn in his belly, now loosened. The memories of his childhood have tormented him. Sir Bengt's goodwill. The alms wasted on his sister, Ylva, a debt left to him to repay, a trust of which he has proven himself unworthy. Better would it have been to leave them both to starve. Now Finn must return to Cuckoo's Roost, stand uncloaked before the Good Samaritan and win back his honesty, ask for forgiveness and take his punishment. Like a stranger has he felt, but no more. From the shame of his act is now deducted the shame of having to lie about it, at least. Still, the cost will be great: his neck on the block. He deserves no better, and sooner a quick death than a life lived under the bane of his conscience.

Finn hides his feelings ill, for Johannes is out of the saddle, patting him on the back as though he had swallowed a piece of meat unchewed.

"Are you all right, Finn? You look like you've seen a ghost."

A ghost. Out of the distant forest, Olof Jonsson's wheezing laughter echoes from wet, infested lungs with the rattle of ever sparser ribs. A laughter in glee at the looming retribution, for Finn alone to hear. In silence Finn replies: soon. He shall ride to Cuckoo's Roost alone. Magnus's place is at Engelbrekt's side. Finn has never seen him happy before now. A wickedness it would be to drag him away for his own sake. Alone he will ride, at dusk, when Magnus is away from their camp.

THE ISLAND OF the Holy Spirit. For the second time in two years it is to play host to an audience with King Eric, its great infirmary emptied, the dying and abject hurled out to make way for the sovereign himself and the most powerful men of the realm. Nils hasn't set foot in Stockholm in a long time: ever since the rebellion started, the king's troops have manned its walls and kept the city gates locked. Now they are admitted closer, or at least close enough to set their eyes on the royal palace from just a stone's throw away, on the other side of the waterway that links Lake Mälaren with the Baltic Sea. Flags top every pinnacle, while soldiers pack the battlements, in a show of the king's might. The Council of the Realm has convened yet again to meet with Eric and forge an accord, uniting the kingdom and putting an end to the disputes. For the sake of calm they are to meet in the absence of the commander of the kingdom's forces, but Engelbrekt's absence hangs over them all like a looming deluge: on the fields outside the city his men huddle in great numbers, despite the approaching winter. The smoke from their fires hangs like a mist above the capital, tempting coughs from throats.

The negotiations are drawn out, even longer than they should be, for every word must be translated into a language that King Eric understands, likewise his responses into Swedish. Two interpreters have been appointed, and whenever anything is said they confer quietly and solicitously over the correct choice of words, each making notes on paper with their pens, studiously expunging and correcting infelicities, for every mistake made in ink threatens to claim its price in blood.

Nils studies King Eric. He has heard Sir Bengt's account of his coronation on the rune stones at Mora Meadow, of the fearful lad with pimples on his face big enough to rival every precious gem around his neck. The king he sees before him is another. When they spoke on the royal ship, Eric was by turns pale and green of complexion, never far from a pail into which to spew should the seas turn rough, blankets wrapped around his shoulders and legs, like a sickly child. But Eric is a man in his prime and is now on dry land, a few years and forty, with a body that only abundance can build. Gold and silver flash from his mantle and doublet, and he wears a gilded band in a halo over his thinning locks, to impress his majesty. Chains around his neck, rings on every finger. His gaze is sharp and alert, his chin held high enough to float his thin beard like a streamer in the air. Like a fish in water he is here, a man of power among his subjects. His mere presence is enough to make the knees want to bend, the back stoop. While waiting for his translation he slowly paces this way and that on the floor before the Council, proud as a peacock in mating season. The Swedes look like a flock of famished jackdaws by comparison, the sick-chamber around them just as unworthy of the attendance of such a monarch as the country itself. With some effort Nils chokes his laughter at the sight, hiding his smirk behind a glove.

Leading the meeting is Archbishop of Uppsala, Olof Larsson, the man who beat a Danish prelate to the post and has Engelbrekt to thank for getting to bear its staff and mitre. One by one he airs the propositions, by which everything that the newly deposed commander had instituted is struck out and rewritten. Many a Council member promoted by Engelbrekt sees their post discontinued. The king's castles are his to retain, so say the laws, though he is also bound to appoint Swedish men as bailiffs to those castles where the Danes and Germans were unable to ride out the storm that blew. All that the rebels seized shall be returned. Thus pass long hours of demands and concessions, until only the most important point remains: to keep the king's peace in his absence, a Lord High Steward shall now be appointed, and a Lord High Constable, too; the former to rule in the king's name, the latter a man of war to attend to the kingdom's arms. All of Sweden's power, to be shouldered by two alone. Nils has put his name forward for Lord High Constable, and he knows that he will be the king's choice. On the ship off the coast of Småland province he put his best foot forward and gave what promises were required, and the king clearly nodded his assent, in spite of his seasickness. He entered the infirmary at Holy Spirit the Lord of Småland, a mantle that has now been taken from him. But another he shall gain in return. Soon he will be one of the kingdom's two most powerful men.

From his place he hears Krister Vasa appointed to Lord High Steward, to little surprise. A name that neither the king nor the Swedes are overjoyed by, but one that both can tolerate, a man who has taken great pains to make no enemies. This bodes well: Vasa is weak of both arms and mind, and once he is constable Nils will have no trouble bending him to his will. He adds his voice to the cries in support of the appointment. And now constable. He hears the archbishop read his name before the king as one of those recommended by the Council.

"Nils Stensson, of the house whose coat of arms bears a parted shield of blue and gold."

For a few moments the king stands in silence. Then he shakes his head, in a gesture that needs no translation.

"Karl Knutsson, of the house that bears a red boat on a yellow base, known as Crofter."

The King nods his aye, and a hesitant murmur rises in the place of cheers. Nils searches for Crofter while grasping at the wall for support, and when he finds him among the Council's ranks, Crofter has already found him. Scornful eyes in a brief twinkling say all that need be said, before Crofter leaves his place to step before the king and have his newly won chain of office placed around his neck. With that the conference is over. The archbishop gives God's blessing over the choices made within the chamber and wishes peace upon them, upon the kingdom reunited at long last, which can now rejoin the Kalmar Union under the king who lawfully rules it. King Eric prepares his departure, toward the palace first and then to his ship, to travel back to Denmark. Sweeping his gaze over those in attendance one last time, Eric rests his eyes on Nils for a moment, before he pulls in one of his interpreters and whispers in his ear while pointing. While the king turns up the fur collar of his mantle and takes his leave of the chamber, the interpreter makes his way toward Nils, then bows formally and conveys the king's parting message.

"In the choice between two turncoats, His Majesty chose the one who appeared the more useful to him."

⁂

Outside, where the rain has started to fall with every drop interspersed by a flake, Nils Stensson feels a hand on his shoulder. When he turns he sees his nephew's face beneath the hood of the mantle. He takes him by the shoulders.

"Thank God, Magnus. Good that you're here. Lead me to Engelbrekt. The people's chieftain must be forewarned of all that has just happened. All the good that he's achieved these two years has been undone, and those of us who support his cause must assemble to reclaim the ground we've lost while we still can."

"I came to listen on his behalf, but the chamber was too full."

Nils is in haste, and they beat a swift path down to the bridge across the river, where the stables await. In his mind Nils Stensson is lining up all that he must say to Engelbrekt, which tone of voice to employ. With Magnus he has the chance to try his hand ahead of time.

"Puck and Engelbrekt have both been expelled from the Council, and Engelbrekt stripped of all his titles. In return they mean to give him Örebro Castle as his fief, and Rasbo to Puck. As if the people's chieftain would let himself be bought, when he has only ever had the kingdom's best at heart and never his own."

"Uncle."

"Yes?"

"The people's tax burden, the cause that sparked all of this. Was there talk of reducing it?"

Nils retains the question, feels its weight. A good thing that he chanced upon Magnus first. He's grateful for the reminder about the taxes, about the people. The matter was never raised in all their hours in the chamber, and he had completely forgotten about it himself. It would be wise to lead with that when he speaks to Engelbrekt, and with the very same tone in his voice as in his nephew's.

F ROM THE FOREST they emerge as the afternoon is waning, on a cart drawn by an aged steed, with canvas pulled taut over curved willow branches to protect their load from the rain. Yellow and red leaves fall along their way. October is drawing to its close. On the driver's box they crowd. Harald Esbjörnsson sits alongside the driver, a man wrapped in sheepskin, with a magnificent beard that is trimmed into a point. On his other side is a man in particolored garbs, one side red and the other yellow, with a hat in the same colors and bells sewed to a band across each shoe. In his hand he carries a stringed instrument, and he sings while striking his notes and stamping a jingling beat. The singer's voice is strong and clear, and he knows how to change the tenor of his song, to draw in the listeners and keep them. The song is of a kind that Magnus has heard before many a time, but the melody isn't quite the same, the words more comical and shameless than ever he heard them sung at Cuckoo's Roost. Like many others he has been enticed into following the cart, to find out what will become of the pert farmhand and the coy farmer's daughter who wish to lie together without her father's knowledge. When they reach the middle of the camp, Harald places his hand over the driver's reins and points at Engelbrekt, who is standing with Eric Puck. The man with the beard leaps down and bows deeply, remaining there until he is sure that he has received the attention he sought.

"Your Grace, Commander of the Realm! Far have you traveled, and much you have achieved. No one is more deserving of some rest and diversion than you. Our company offers richly of both, and more besides. Gather your closest men and allow us to offer you a spectacle, in exchange for full stomachs, dry beds, and quenched thirst, and anything else that you feel we may deserve."

Engelbrekt turns around, distracted from his conversation with Puck. At first he pulls the face he normally does when he is about to refuse something, but upon seeing Magnus among those gathered around the cart he instead nods at the man, who responds with yet another splendid bow. Puck has followed Engelbrekt's gaze, and now he is the one staring at Magnus, his eyes black. The bearded man claps his hands, and while the string player in jester's garbs stamps his feet, the canvas is swept off the cart to reveal others in the company, along with barrels, chests, and sacks. In concert they bow and curtsy.

"We shan't give you cause to regret it, Your Grace. Let us get everything in order, and our spectacle shall begin when the sun hangs a handsbreadth over the castle keep."

Stockholm looms in the distance over the meadow that they have chosen for a camp. Rows of masts spread their sails over Saltsjön bay, the Danish fleet heading homeward. Word of the reconciliation has already spread, and in the camp the displeasure is made manifest through furrowed brows and dejected eyes. All that they did appears now to be undone, and if they want anything better than what was theirs before, they will have to start again. But their strength is dwindling. King Eric has chosen his moment with guile: now that winter is approaching he arrives, this year just as last, when the winds are feeling cooler than they ought to against skin so recently bared to the summer sun, causing the thoughts to start to turn to home and hearth. The dwindling light takes the fighting spirit with it. No one wants to go to battle or risk lying wounded on frozen ground. Perhaps this cart of minstrels has come at the right time, no less shrewd than King Eric as to when their seeds promise the greatest yield.

The cart is positioned behind them, the same canvas that covered it now hitched between two posts. One of the minstrels fetches charcoal from a fire and starts drawing strokes over the white. Many gather to watch, and before their very eyes the black marks on bleached linen transform into a landscape of tall mountains and deep forests, a distant castle perched atop a cliff, a churning sea, and a road that winds through the trees. They are all standing in a forest with a castle behind them, but the minstrel's drawing lends the familiar objects a spirit of a different kind, breathing new life into them, turning the cloth to a promise of spring in late autumn. Behind the cart the players change attire, their voices and laughter heard in many a language that no one can name. They ask for fires to be lit around where the spectacle will be held, to offer warmth and light, and by now they have no trouble finding hands that are willing to help. Dusk draws in and the sun sinks, and once the men are all gathered in close ranks, the spectacle begins.

It's comical at first. The man who sang earlier is to sing again, though now wholly altered in manner and bearing, a genteel squire with a nasal voice who means to sing a beautiful ballad. But the strings thwart him, the pegs that hold them taut releasing time and again until he forgets the melody and the words, and the lines that he bungles make a mockery of that which should have been grave. Once the man thinks the audience have laughed their fill, he lets his mantle fall to the ground, revealing his jester's attire, then in an instant sets the instrument's pegs right and sings a song of a horseman who is given cabbage soup for dinner and is suffocated inside his armor the next morning. He bows to the men's cheers, then cedes the floor to another man who can keep many small pouches of grain in the air by throwing them up in ingenious patterns. He finds more and more of them hidden among his garments, with hands so deft that his audience can't keep up. And then, after him, twins who stand on each other's shoulders leap into the air, pick each other up single-handedly, and then stand so still that it is as though they were hewn from rock. Once the fires around them have stilled, the company goes quiet, and their leader takes to the floor.

"Darkness has fallen, the day drawing to its end. To close, we would like to present you with a tale that you can take away with you to sleep, of the knight Tristan and his fair Iseult, both from different worlds and destined for others, yet powerless in the face of love."

They play well. With word and gesture they breathe life into the charcoal landscape behind them. In a wig of long, fair hair stands Iseult, a princess beyond reproach, while the minstrel who previously jested now makes for a noble, valiant knight, albeit wounded in a duel. The king grizzled and bitter, to whom the beautiful maiden is promised. The wider world falls silent around them, until only this little illuminated distortion remains, truer in its moment than reality ever was. Not a sound is heard when Tristan, lying on his deathbed, asks his sly wife about the color of the sails on the ship that is to carry his beloved back to him after a long separation. Voices can't contain their outrage when she lies to him in her jealousy. Though they all hold out hope, they know well enough how it all must end. Death, death to all. What flames still glimmer are reflected in wet eyes when the players stand for a moment's silence, then take a gentle bow. Feet stamped in their hundreds break the spell, in applause at their performance. Magnus turns to Engelbrekt. They have found a small hill at a remove on which to sit, high enough that they can see over the heads of the men standing in the audience.

"What were you and Eric Puck talking about before? His eyes were like glowing coals."

"We were talking about Nils Stensson. I told him everything that Nils had said about the audience with the king; how indignant he was that the people's appeals for lower taxes had fallen on deaf ears yet again."

"What did Puck say?"

Engelbrekt sighs.

"Eric Puck says Nils is a fortune hunter whom he wouldn't trust any farther than he can throw, a man fain to serve any master so long as he often turns a blind eye, and thus won't notice the dagger being whetted behind his back."

Magnus looks down and away.

"What I believe you already know."

"I can't stand alone. I must have the nobles with me. If they won't give me their loyalty out of love, then I must take it as it is. But I need Puck, too. There was a time when I dreamed of making everyone happy, but now I'd be glad if just one person could be, even if for but an instant."

Magnus nods over at the minstrels.

"How did you find the players' performance?"

"A good tale, ably performed."

"What was it about, for you?"

Engelbrekt smiles in response.

"About a love that can find no other course than its own, and that nothing but mean luck is capable of stopping."

Both sit in silence, Engelbrekt's face now grave.

"Where have your thoughts gone now?"

Engelbrekt gestures with his hand at the players, who are bustling to gather up their property and pack it away onto the cart.

"I'm thinking about the parts we're chosen to play, whether we wish for them or not. I knew as much from the start, but I did believe I'd get to write my speeches myself, play the person who I wanted to be. Instead I must be the man who others would have me be. For more than a year I've walked among folk who would soon risk their lives at the foot of tall ramparts, yet would believe the danger slight if I would but stand beside them, deliver them through my counsel, through destiny itself. And afterward I would walk among the lame and disabled, to bless them by the grace of God and heal their wounds. A saint they would have me be, though I am but a man among others, and never have I asked to be anything else. For all the power they grant me, I'm powerless to be the man I am."

"What would your part be in the tale we just saw?"

He shrugs.

"I know who I'm afraid of being. The old king, lonely and selfish, ready to misuse all his power for his own purposes, just or not."

Magnus laughs.

"What are you laughing at?"

"I'm thinking of how my father and uncles would describe the tale. That it's about power and not love. About an old king who finally succeeds in prevailing over all, and that only his ungrateful subjects begrudge him his happily ever after."

"Perhaps you judge them unfairly, you and Puck."

"You don't know them as I do. In their eyes power is worth any defect. But you needn't fret just yet, even less so after the king's audience, for a rebel you are still. The part of Tristan the knight."

Engelbrekt shuts his eyes for a moment, turns away from the scattering crowd of men before them.

"The Hansa had men at the Holy Spirit. I spoke to them. They're pleased with the reconciliation. The war has cost them, and now trade can recommence. They want me to go back to Norberg, dig them iron to send south rather than wield it in beaten swords. They lent me those thousand marks in silver, and now they're demanding that I repay the debt. I promised them a service if I couldn't repay them, and I'm loath to break my word. Who else would take it otherwise?"

Engelbrekt hears the bitterness in his own voice and shakes it off, unwilling to see it spread. His eyes wander over those who remain. He catches Eric Puck's eyes, soon turned away. Yet their gaze met long enough for him to read his feelings.

"How about you, Magnus? Who are you in the tale?"

"Neither king nor knight. But my hair is long and fair."

F INN RISES EARLY. Few are up on their feet. After the spectacle many took a drink or two, and now they are sleeping late. Nothing more is asked of them. He left Magnus lying where he was, deep in a slumber of long, peaceful breaths, one by one, like smoke from spruce needles. Alone he makes his way to where his horse is stabled, to saddle and bridle him and ride off unobserved. By the time Magnus wakens he will be far off on the road to Cuckoo's Roost. Only one other man does Finn see, and he is walking straight toward him. As they draw closer he sees that it is Engelbrekt himself and bows his head in greeting.

"Finn Sigridsson. What luck that I find you here. You're just who I was looking for."

Engelbrekt takes him by the shoulder and leads him by his side.

"I have a service to ask of you."

A tree lies fallen at the forest's edge, the moss on its trunk dried out in the cold. Engelbrekt takes a seat and invites Finn to sit beside him.

"Eric Puck holds a grudge against Magnus's house, and it's become worse than ever since Nils Stensson came to speak to us. Eric is both strong and devious, and he enjoys great respect among the men. In the past I could send him off to wherever he was needed more than at my side, and without him questioning my motives, but it's no longer as simple as that."

Engelbrekt looks him in the eye.

"I know that you're the one who taught Magnus how to hold a sword. I've taught him a few things, too, and at least now he knows enough not to wield his weapon overhead, so that his strike is easily parried. But that's not enough. Puck's a born fighter, and he's had a sword in his hand all his life. Magnus has nothing to counter someone like him. Eric's easily offended and quick to draw. Should the right opportunity present itself, I don't doubt that he'll seize it."

"What can I do?"

"I'm trying to find a good reason to get Magnus away from here, for a while. It hasn't escaped me that Bengt Stensson has sent many a messenger this way, and I'd hazard a guess that he's keen to see his son, but that Magnus would rather stay here. You're his friend, perhaps you could persuade him to change his mind? I want him to be where his life is safe. I'll speak to him, too, give him a reason to stay away for a time, but without your help I'm afraid it'll fall on deaf ears. Help me to keep him away from our camp this winter, until summer is come and Eric Puck has other things to think about."

Finn feels his heart sink. He wonders whether it is God the Father Himself who is speaking to him through Engelbrekt's voice, issuing him an ordeal by which he must wander the world like a lost soul a little longer, his crime unatoned for, his conscience more mortifying than any of the instruments of torture he used during Ylva's penance. Engelbrekt takes his silence for chariness.

"Will you help me, Finn? For Magnus's sake. How I don't know."

Finn nods.

"I do."

"Get him to safety, Finn. Keep him away from here."

THEY SLEEP WHERE they can, the hundred-odd men who remain around Engelbrekt once the army's thousands have dispersed, the peasantry returning homeward when their strength was no longer of the essence. In farms and barns they make camps, those owned by wealthy farmers and lords in whom they can place their trust. The air grows colder with each passing day, the water frozen in its pails by morning. When required, they sleep on the ground under the shelter of trees, as now: Finn lies awake on his bed of spruce twigs, a mantle swept around his body, a warm stone baked by the hearth wrapped inside it to keep him warm. Around him the camp's fires are dying. Magnus arrives later, as he often does, returning to his resting place only toward dawn, when the light is spreading along the borderlands between the night just passed and the day yet to come. Finn lets him make his bed and get himself comfortable, until everything goes quiet and all that he can hear is the pounding of his own heart, hard and anxious.

"Magnus?"

Out in the blackness of the forest a nightjar chirrs. Someone swears and throws a stick at the trees, and the bird's shadow swoops over them in flight beneath the bright, starry sky. Magnus hesitates a few moments before replying.

"Yes, Finn?"

"I've done something terrible. There's nothing I wish more than to undo it, but it's no use."

"You can tell me anything."

Finn swallows, wishing himself deaf rather than have to hear his own confession.

"I slew a man. We met in Askersund. For many days I'd been doing Ylva's penance and suffering torments for her sake, and he mocked my pains, said that the church would sooner take my coins in payment, as if God the Father were holding her soul hostage merely to enrich Himself. The rage got to my head, and in our fight his life was spilled. Afterward I marked his body, to pass the blame to another."

Magnus lies in silence. He lets the confession sink in before responding.

"Why are you telling me this now, having held your peace for so long?"

"I kept quiet out of shame. I've no other friends, no family. Don't think I'm anything but thankful that your father saved my life, but at Cuckoo's Roost I'll never be anything more than what I was. Nor do I blame them, for I haven't made myself deserving of anything else. But you never saw me that way, Magnus. In your eyes I so dearly wanted to remain better than I am. Now I'm made to speak for the basest of reasons. Your father has learned of my guilt. He wants to get you home, as you know, and he's sent a messenger to tell me that if I can't find a way to get you there, then my sin will be brought to light. When I leave for Cuckoo's Roost alone I doubt I'll return, and I wanted you to know why."

He can hear Magnus turn under his mantle, twisting his head. For a long time he remains silent, while Finn's heart is a thundering kettledrum. The night is dark, but he can see Magnus's open eyes catch glints from the flames still burning. His voice is quiet when he replies.

"I'll go with you to Cuckoo's Roost."

And so the words come, as Finn knew they would. He lies still in wonder at the cruelty of the world, that which forced him to twist a snare from his confession and accorded him a mercy that he hasn't earned, thus depriving him of any right to take it as a gift. Inwardly he curses Engelbrekt and Eric Puck both, and God and the Blessed Mother. At least one thing can he give in exchange.

"There's something else. He was one of the bishop's men, the one I slew, come from the north where he'd been gathering in the coins that the churches had collected in payment for the remission of sins. He was carrying the entire income with him, though he'd told me it was iron ingots. I helped him with the load. Only afterward did I learn that I'd been shouldering a more precious burden. I hid the sack in the forest. Would you like to take it, Magnus, and do with it what you deem best?"

"Do you know how much it is?"

"A thousand marks, at least. The coins belong to Bishop Knut. I'm sure he'd use it to further your house's interests."

Silence falls. Magnus thinks for a long time, long enough for Finn to wonder whether sleep has seized him. Then comes a soft voice, one that sounds firm and steady in its choice.

"Between us there are to be no more secrets. Are there, Finn?"

Finn would sooner have the words carved into his very skin than hear Magnus ask them of him now. In the darkness that divides them Finn takes Magnus's outstretched hand and squeezes it ardently. His other hand he places between his teeth, then bites down with all his might, to stop himself from screaming out in pain of a worse kind. With the blood swallowed in a glug of hot iron, he lies in response.

"No. None."

☙

Come morning Magnus searches for Engelbrekt, and he finds him alone, sitting partway up a cliff that affords a view over the camp and forest and the lake that flows behind it, and beyond that Stockholm, whose city walls rise up where the water is at its narrowest.

"My father's invited me home to Cuckoo's Roost to celebrate Christmas. I'd sooner stay here, but I know how keen he is to see me again. It's been over a year."

Engelbrekt nods.

"You're right to go. It's ill to neglect one's flesh and blood."

"What will you do now?"

Engelbrekt shakes his head, shrugs with a sigh.

"I'm trapped, like a fox in a burrow where every entrance is being watched. On one side are the Hansa, on the other King Eric, and the third hole is guarded by the nobles. Until one of them opens up there's little I can do. I shall wait, for come the time, come the means. Isn't that what you said?"

"What would you do, if you could?"

"I'd summon the twelve members of King Eric's Council to Arboga, along with his Lord High Constable and Lord High Steward, and the eight lords who own the most land in the realm. The Archbishop of Uppsala, too, as well as bishops Knut of Linköping and Thomas of Strängnäs. Two dozen lords, the most powerful the kingdom possesses. Together they can repeal all the promises they made to the king, renounce their loyalty and obedience, and make everything as it was before."

Magnus shakes his head in indignation.

"It all just goes in circles. What'll be different this time? An alliance is scarce forged before it's deserted. Every lord assembled in vain, no oath too sacred to be broken. Then the next one, and again."

Engelbrekt traces Magnus's gaze. A gust of wind tears through the crowns of the trees, clawing at the ripples on the lake. Perhaps a winter storm is in the offing, the first of the year.

"This time I'd summon the free men of the realm, too, the peasantry, farmers, and merchants, and not to have them stand shivering outside, but to give them pride of place in the chamber, so that they might make their voices heard as equals. As many as the room will contain, and if they still don't fit, then we'll stand under the open sky. They're just as much Swedes as the rest. That has never happened before now. In the past the lords of the realm have always made decisions over their heads. But they'd have a hard time forgetting the question of taxes then. The king would be stripped of his authority, and each man in service of the crown presented with a choice: either swear themselves free, or face us in battle."

"And then?"

"Then we'd take back all that remains to be taken."

Magnus stands still in thought for a while, weighing up his choice.

"I'll ride west with Finn this morning. Would you give us two trusted men for the journey? They'll soon return, and with a gift in tow."

"Magnus? Since you must leave me anyway, I have a favor to ask of you."

"Anything."

"Spend the winter at Cuckoo's Roost. Stay home over Epiphany. I don't want you on the roads. It's a bad thing to travel in winter, I know that more than anyone. It's injurious to spend too long on horseback when the cold is harsh. I speak from experience. It gets inside your very bones, your very marrow, and your limbs will freeze, and if you're unlucky they'll never quite thaw, never fully regain the keenness they once had. You know I care about your health, Magnus. Do me this favor. In spring we'll meet again, and the longer we're parted, the happier our reunion shall be."

Magnus's shoulders sink, his face darkens.

"I'd rather return as soon as I can."

"Do it for my sake if not for your own."

He stands in silence for a moment, then nods in agreement.

"If that is your wish."

"Do I have your word?"

Magnus hesitates in his response, unwilling.
"Yes."

※

Finn saddles up their horses, to ride south. Two northmen ride with them, to convey back to Engelbrekt the load that is to be found between Motala and Askersund, while they continue on the road that will take them to Cuckoo's Roost.

A BOAT IS SENT to meet Engelbrekt on the beach, where he has lit a fire to better make himself seen. The ice lies like a ledge at the water's edge. With his heels he kicks enough loose to prepare a landing stage on a sandbar. He hears the rowers mutter their approval at not having to wet their own legs. One of them waves him closer and gives him his arm to help him heave himself aboard. From land Harald Esbjörnsson hands Engelbrekt a bag, then puts his shoulder to the stem and pushes the vessel out to sea once Engelbrekt has sat down.

"Warte hier auf mich. Eine Stunde, nicht mehr."

Harald speaks little German, but he's sharp-witted enough to grasp that, although directed at him, the words are intended for other ears. He gives a firm nod in return. Engelbrekt anticipates no sting in the Hansa's tail, but it doesn't hurt to make it known that he is expected back on land in an hour.

Skilled oars turn the boat. Water purls around the bow as it swiftly cleaves through the stillness of the bay. The evening is dim around them, the air cold. While Engelbrekt can only wrap his arms around his waist and sweep his mantle even tighter, the men at the oarlocks work harder than they need, rather than have the sweat freeze on their backs. The last rays of the setting sun cast Stockholm in shadow: its sea-facing wall and palisades, the merchant ships that are still sailing. Fewer now than ever. Although the king and the Council are recently reconciled, the future is still uncertain, and for two years the city's ties to the rest of the kingdom have been severed. No iron comes in from the north anymore, and no goods sold here can be sent to the rest of the kingdom. A long time has it been since any items that spoil have found a buyer here. The Hanseatic League don't think in years, but rather in decades and centuries. The Baltic is theirs, as it has been for as long as memory can recall. In Stockholm the League owns warehouses and guildhalls, keeps offices and docks, more even than the king would care to count, lest he learn that in the kingdom's largest city he scarce owns more than the palace itself. Despite the promise of good food and drink, Engelbrekt has no wish to set foot in the city that has resisted him ever since he took to arms. Instead it has been agreed that their meeting shall take place on the cog that for almost a generation has lain at anchor just within the sharpened stakes at the approach to Stockholm's port, a broad freight ship that lurched all the way up to these northerly climes in the days when the Victual Brothers were coloring the waves red. Here it has remained, the Hansa's northern seat for whenever they wish to make themselves unreachable, or when the pest is raging within the city walls. She most resembles a floating fortress, having long since given up any hope of being released from the hawsers that hold her in place. A rope ladder gives Engelbrekt a foothold to climb aboard, past the downward-facing spikes that are rigged along the sides of the ship to prevent boarding. The forecastle has been extended, swallowing up the once-open deck to make way for chambers for accounts and dining. A firepan warms the air, placed on metal plates to protect the timber from sparks. Engelbrekt is shown through to a room with furnishings of a kind that have no place on a boat, its floor and walls alike clad in woven draperies. A table stands nailed to the floor, with chairs on either side. Engelbrekt smiles inwardly at the League's well-known ruse: the legs of the chair intended for the guest are shorter, while those of the merchant are taller, to establish their positions from the very start.

He remembers his first encounter with one of them, still only a boy at the time, yet old enough to watch and listen. His father had taken him along to a meeting in Västerås, where the prices were to be determined for the entirety of the coming year. Before they entered, a determined Engelbrekt the elder had pulled him aside, and with a low voice impressed upon him what he had said so many times before.

"You think you're striking an agreement with one person. Don't think like that. Think of each and every one of them as hairs on a head, fingers on a hand, heads on a many-headed dragon. The Hanseatic League have ruled the seas for longer than anyone can remember. Even your grandfather could recall sitting on his grandfather's knee and hearing words like the ones I'm telling you today. And never have the League had more might than now. A hundred cities all banded together under the supreme deity of commerce, rich enough to keep their own army and fleet, with the strongest walls that human hands can build. They'll write down your every doing in their books, and scribes will copy them for posterity. The

League never forget, and they have cunning and means enough to forge plans whose spoils only become clear after those who made the transaction have left this earth. Beware. You may think you've bargained well, when instead you've made the mistake of reckoning for your lifetime alone, unknowingly pledging away the future of your descendants. Now there, boy, don't look so afraid. By the time it's your turn to speak for us among the League you'll be older. More suited than I. And better prepared, too."

Engelbrekt the elder's words proved true. Engelbrekt Engelbrektsson has been trading with the League his whole life, and he has learned to speak and understand their language as well as their ways. They never say what they know, and would sooner be broken on the wheel than reveal the going price of iron farther south, where they sell on the bars. Engelbrekt has learned to read into their faces and gestures that which otherwise goes unsaid, for it's the only way to guess how good a bargain they have struck. Only one thing does he know for sure: if the League conclude an agreement, you can be certain that you have funded their profit.

The man he has agreed to meet is seasoned enough to make his features smooth and indifferent rather than betray the slightest affect, but the scents of roasted meat, of soup and pickled vegetables, can't hide the air of disappointment that already hangs thick in the chamber. Dietrich Möller has grown heavier since Engelbrekt last saw him. Engelbrekt tries to count the years. Five? Seven? Weight is a weakness. Most Hansa keep trim with a fastidiousness verging on superstition: a fat merchant gives the impression of all too great a wealth, which invites haggling. But if that is a weakness betrayed, then it is his only one: Dietrich wears simple clothes with no outward signs of prosperity, no rings on his fingers, no chains around his neck. A monk of Mammon, he is, ready for the sacrament of commerce.

Though his face is now wider, his eyes bear the same calm artfulness as before. Few words are actually needed: Engelbrekt has come bearing a heavy load, and it can't be anything but silver, silver enough to repay his debt. But the sum was given to him not to be repaid, rather to fund acts of service over time. Engelbrekt imagines what shapes such schemes might have taken: Örebro Castle in pledge. Over the years they might demand more land by way of repayment, on which their own people would then build warehouses and trading houses. Soon they would control all trade in the city, the work of local merchants either assimilated into theirs or undermined. Only Hansa boats on the waves of Lake Hjälmaren. When the time would come for a new bailiff to be installed in the castle, they would make their case to whichever king then sat on the Swedish throne, get a well-disposed man in place, and find him an equally well-disposed wife to cradle their babes. And so on. By the dawn of the next century, Örebro would be yet another jewel in the Hanseatic crown. Such is the game that they play. From among their own ranks the sharpest of each generation are measured up against each other, and only the best sifted through to claim a seat like Dietrich's, ready to conclude a transaction such as this, the changing of hands of a thousand silver marks.

"Dietrich. Steht alles gut mit ihnen?"

Dietrich Möller can't take his eyes off the bag in Engelbrekt's hands. Just as Engelbrekt knows Dietrich, Dietrich knows Engelbrekt. With a sigh he changes his seat, offering Engelbrekt the higher one in order to take the lower himself.

"Es war besser. Take a seat."

Dietrich speaks Swedish like a native, though he usually prefers to transact in German, to maintain his advantage there. Now he knows that the language will make no difference.

"My time is little and my errand short. Would you like to weigh the silver?"

"That can wait. We go back many years. You're trusted here and have always been an honorable man, though shrewdness would perhaps have served you better."

The chair complains under Dietrich when he sits down, staring at the bag that Engelbrekt has placed before him like a rat that the cat has dragged in.

"One thousand silver marks. Just think what you could do with that sum now that King Eric and the Council have made peace. For your own sake—or for others, if you wish."

"Are we on a boat's deck or the Mount of Temptation?"

"I'm no Devil."

Dietrich makes the sign of the cross, and Engelbrekt regrets his words as soon as they pass his lips. He blames his short night's sleep.

"No more am I the Son of Man. Forgive me."

"So why not keep it? There's no haste in repaying the loan."

"You said yourself that we go back a long way. You know where I stand. You hardly need ask. For the loan I am grateful. Now here's the full sum by return."

Dietrich gives him a long look, then heaves a heavy, reproachful sigh.

"Peace is coming, Dietrich. But it won't be the kind that the king and the Council want. Have patience a little while longer. You have my word that the League won't go without."

He holds out his hand in parting. Dietrich shrugs and takes it.

"You make my work harder than it should be, Engelbrekt Engelbrektsson. None of the masters who drilled me in the merchant's arts taught me how best to deal with someone who won't allow himself to be bought. To them you would probably seem as outlandish as those people far off in the east who bear dog heads atop human bodies: everyone says that they exist, but no one has yet seen one. I wish that they could have met you, wonder if they could have struck a better deal than me. And, as if it weren't enough that I stand here the worse merchant, I also wish you luck, much as I shouldn't."

CHRISTMAS DAY IS come, and Sir Bengt is losing heart. His messenger has returned, saying that he found Finn and gave him the message as instructed, but still Sir Bengt is alone. The day is short, but the wait is long nevertheless. He makes his way up to the garret in the frigid house, where he paces back and forth before the openings that afford a view of the only road that leads to the estate, stopping and squinting through each one as he passes. The fields lie white and windswept, the path scarce discernible. No horsemen. He shudders under his layers of wool and fur, remembering his own childhood Christmases at Oakwood: Siblings and kin as far as the eye could see, and tables brimming with more bounties than anyone had room enough to taste. Joy and mirth and few troubles, his father cheery in the company of friends, as though replete with all the dreams that hadn't yet been crushed. Bengt swears at the cold stone chamber, then leans out of the window until he sees a maid braving the cold with a basket of washing in her arms, and roars down to her at the top of his lungs, so that his voice will carry over the wind that whistles around the house.

"Wine!"

While he waits he drags a chair across the floor, placing it so that he can keep a lookout while seated. Soon mulled wine arrives in a cauldron, and he ladles himself a mug and drinks, feeling the warmth spread throughout his chest. He drains one mug and then two, but still finds himself cold. Strengthened in vigor by the wine, he tears a tapestry from its rod and wraps it around himself. Making sure that he has provisions within reach, he sinks down in the seat, firmly resolved to stay there until the sun has set and obscured all from view. An accursed Christmas.

He must have fallen asleep, for he wakens with a jolt from a dream that he remembers not but that leaves him with sweat dripping under his tunic. He wrestles with the tapestry to disentangle himself, and is just taking a fistful of snow from the ledge to rub over his face when there they are: two horsemen, flashes of color in the white, illuminated by the sun that has found a gap between the clouds just a finger from the horizon. Magnus. Finn. He is startled by the stab he feels in his gut, all of a sudden wishing the wait were even longer, at once prepared to forgive every misgiving and in fear of knowing the truth. Sir Bengt shakes, rousing himself. He takes the stairs down two steps at a time, wondering whether there will still be any warmth left in all the food that he had served in the great hall.

※

He hears the door open, hears the floor creak, and for a moment all doubt is gone. On swift feet he walks toward Magnus, but when he reaches him on the threshold to the room he stops, suddenly uncertain of what kind of welcome is befitting. The last time they saw each other was Midsummer. One and a half years have passed, and not unnoticed: Magnus's face is the same and yet different; either that or their time apart has allowed Bengt to see anew that which force of habit had previously obscured. He blinks to make the image sharper. His son is still handsome. No, more handsome in fact, his beauty as though heightened by his newfound worldliness. His cheekbones sharpened, his hair left to grow. The scar that streaked his forehead on his departure from Cuckoo's Roost has healed, no longer visible at all. But most of all it's in his eyes. Their deep blue color is as he remembers it, the same as his own, but they bear a different countenance now. Not a boy's anymore but a young man's. They return Sir Bengt's gaze as though he were an equal, and Bengt is startled to find himself as much the observer as the observed. Suddenly he is uncertain, unsure how best to greet this apparent half stranger.

"Magnus."

"Father."

Although the chairs have been placed out around the table, the two of them stay standing.

"All well with you?"

"As you can see."

Bengt clears his throat and nods, breaks eye contact and half turns away.

"I must admit that when your uncle Nils first wanted to send you to Engelbrekt I was loath to do so. My other brothers and I have a whole lifetime of Nils's plots behind us, and God knows they haven't always borne fruit. But everything has gone well for us. I have the Cut for a fief, Knut's at Stepstones, Nils is in command of Småland province, and Bo would have had Stake Isle had destiny willed it. Soon enough there won't be a single Danish or German bailiff left in the whole kingdom, and finally we'll be the ones sitting in those castles, where we belong. No other house has been favored as much as ours."

He feels his heart pounding all the harder through the garland of veins that encircle his temples, his face hot. It is as though his tongue has a mind of its own, swollen with wine in the roof of his mouth.

"Of course, there are those who ask themselves why."

Magnus stands still without responding, and Bengt swears a silent oath that in his quest for knowledge no help is being extended. He swallows loudly, takes the spit the wrong way, and has to cough.

"People are envious creatures. Anyone who wins advantages must learn that wicked tongues will find ways to explain away their success. In so doing the small-minded justify their own failings."

Bengt feels a slight tremor in his hands, likewise in his arms and knees. He lets out a mirthless chuckle, shakes his head, and wipes his forehead with a coarse hand, while the chamber walls cast the sound back at him like a taunt.

"Do you know what they say, Magnus, the backbiters? Would you like to hear?"

"What do they say, Father?"

The voice, too. Now another's. Mature, more dangerous. Bengt turns back toward him, as though not of his own choosing, his eyes widening and afraid to blink, compelled to see the accusation received.

"They say that Engelbrekt first had you as his stable boy."

"That's no lie. I was given the choice myself."

Bengt knows not how to respond; he stands still, feeling the fury rock him on his wine-shaky feet. Magnus looks him in the eye, his gaze black, his cheeks red, and his lips pursed. Defiant.

"I've naught but pride for having groomed that horse."

He straightens his back, holding his head up high.

"I heard your message to Finn. He told me. It's for his sake that I came here with him. I shall hold you to your promise to let the matter lie. Finn told me about the silver, too, the coins the bishop demanded on God the Father's behalf, in exchange for a splash of water over Purgatory's flames. Olof Jonsson's load. We lifted it out of its crevice on the way here."

This is too much, these abrupt pitches of emotion. One thousand silver marks, suddenly found. The mere thought leaves Sir Bengt breathless. Who was stable boy to whom pales in comparison.

"Where's the treasure now?"

"With Engelbrekt. To repay the loan the Hanseatic League gave him to buy out Örebro from under Mattis Kettilberg a year ago."

Like an axe the silence falls. Sir Bengt feels his eyes blacken, and he grasps for the table's edge, if not to keep himself upright, then to confirm that the world is still steady, still full of things that are worthy of trust. But then Magnus starts to move, walking away from him, toward the threshold and the door. Like a bout of vomiting the words pass Bengt's lips, a force he isn't capable of stemming.

"Do you want to know what else they say, Magnus? Would you like to hear that, too? They say that you and Engelbrekt are closer than two men should be. That with your tongue you woke new strength in a manhood that was previously to little use. Are you as proud of that, too?"

For a moment Magnus pauses, stopping midstep before turning to his father. The blood has risen in his cheeks, and for a while he says nothing. But then his response comes. Though scarce louder than a whisper, it carries like the screech of a blade against a whetstone.

"Prouder still."

And with that he is gone. Magnus's steps echo down the stairs, growing all the quieter, until he is soon out of earshot. Bengt fumbles for his seat, and from it he stares blankly ahead, into the dying glow of the fire. The cold comes quickly in its place between these thick walls of stone, and he wraps his tapestry tighter around his shoulders but can't bring himself to get up. Outside the snow has started to fall, dampening the hooves of horses that are soon heard leaving Cuckoo's Roost along the same road by which they came.

LEFT ALONE, BENGT reaches for the chair arms for support, then feels his way into his seat. The fire still has heat in it for another hour or so, before the embers die and the cold worsens. It has no effect on him. Maids and hands tiptoe at the door, eager to be of service, but they can see from a distance that something is awry, know that Magnus took his leave just as quickly as he came, and suspect misfortune afoot. Better to leave the bear to lick his wounds than step too close and be mauled. Sir Bengt stays sitting there amidst the chamber's thickening gloom. Late at night he traipses to his bed, but sleep eludes him, leaves him lying awake on his back, blind eyes open to the imperceptible roof beams above.

He rises early, as soon as he hears dough being kneaded to be baked, life being blown into the embers left smoldering under ash overnight. Feeling no hunger, he simply shakes his head when offered a bun. Instead he wishes to have his horse saddled up, and for the men in his retinue to prepare to ride to the Cut forthwith. He meets them in the courtyard, their cheeks still full with whatever they could guzzle in their drowsy surprise. Porridge in their beards. The snow has fallen all night long, crackling when he breaks its crust with plodding steps. It will probably tarry their journey. Such would have troubled him before. Not now.

Mile upon mile over white terrains, unfamiliar under snow. He has mounted into a world cast anew. Sir Bengt drives them disconsolately, resting only when the horses need to and with no regard for his men, who sense his mood and are wise enough not to ask any questions or show their perplexity. By instinct they give him space, allow him to ride a few horse lengths ahead lest they offend him by their mere presence. Every word they must utter feels like footsteps on thin ice.

Castle Cut lies a two days' ride from Cuckoo's Roost. Preferably three or four. They ride through the night. Sir Bengt's men exchange glances whenever they pass a village or inn, farm or barn, but their master rides past each one, following the road ahead while the sun sets, lighting up the stars in the sky. The snow gives them light enough to see, and the way of the road is visible all night long, in the strings of footsteps left by wanderers who have long since sought shelter for the night. Not long after noon on the second day they set eyes on Castle Cut. Stiff and sore the men dismount. Sir Bengt goes on alone, until he reaches the trench. He follows the canal's broad furrow along the road laid to ferry iron to the Hansa's cogs that anchor in the roadsteads of the Cut. For one year they have been digging. Only a narrow bank has been left before the Baltic's brackish waters, and to Lake Mälaren fewer than three hundred perches remain. How long would it have taken before the waters could meet? A month or two. A few thousand spadefuls more and Stockholm would have been brought to its knees.

He smells burning firewood, hears picks and digging bars in the distance, in their stubborn battle with the frozen ground. The lake is visible between the nearby trees, so close that he can catch its scent, hear the wind caress its surface. His wife he doesn't see, nor his daughter, and he is pleased to avoid that fight for now. Instead he searches for the foreman Stina appointed in her place, whom he finds standing on the bank with his arms crossed. He bears a look of dogged satisfaction at the work that will soon be complete, that will see their toil carve its scar onto the face of the very realm, to be seen for all eternity. When he claps his eyes on Sir Bengt the foreman takes a few steps back, in response to a face that looks like a stranger's.

"What's going on? What's wrong, Sir Bengt?"

"Where's my wife?"

"Lady Kristina's been in bed sick for the past week. I fear she's taken her task in hand with far too great a zeal, outdoors in a season like this. Be sure that all of our prayers are being said for her swift recovery."

Bengt points at the rows of logs extending farther than the eye can see, those placed to prevent the walls of the trench from tumbling in.

"Those logs. They're all that keep the earth out?"

The man nods eagerly, keen to be of service.

"Yes, Sire. It was Lady Kristina who suggested them, and without her counsel we'd have dug in vain."

"Gather your men. Tell them to fell every brace. Put the earth back where it came from, roll the boulders back."

"But—"

Bengt silences him with a single look, then steps forward, grabs his collar, and pushes him back, until his heels are hanging over the edge of the bank.

"Any objections, Master Digger? At the injustice and needlessness of seeing lengthy toil undone? Let me hear them now. I'm all ears."

He presses even closer, forehead to forehead, suddenly red in the face, his breath hot and rank, his teeth bared and his voice a low rumble at the foreman, who has now understood that he has never been so close to death.

"Fell them. Now. I'll be back a week hence, and then I'll be less forgiving. If the ground isn't flat and even enough for my liking, then I'll flatten it with you."

※

Sir Bengt turns and rides back, past Castle Cut once again. Then on toward the coast. It takes some time for him to find his way, for the fresh snow blankets all the landmarks. Under a snowdrift the beacon lies prepared, a bundle of oily rags at its base, filled with split wood and birch bark that's easy enough to scratch alight with a tinderbox. The smoke that issues from the moist wood is profuse, but the air is thick and pushes it down. Only once the fire is roaring does he see a boat coming from the sea in response, rowed by a few pairs of men, and soon enough he can make out Viper himself at the stem. He holds out his hand to stop the boat once it's within earshot, near the icebound shore, then cups his hands to make himself heard.

"When did the last Hansa ship pass here?"

Viper has the wind at his back, so he can afford to give a longer response.

"Not long ago. They finished loading this morning, filled the cog with iron. She lurched off low in the water just hours ago. They can scarce have rounded the point by now, with winds as low as these. We haven't made ourselves known, just kept an eye out, as agreed."

"Take your men and go after them, with all the vessels that you have. Hold the ship. I'll take the road. Send a boat to fetch me once you have her in place and the sail is reefed."

※

In two hours it is done. The Hansa captain knows Sir Bengt by name, if not by face. Castle Cut has shielded the trade done behind King Eric's back, and in the shadow of its walls the Hansa have lugged their silver inland and returned with iron-loaded carts. The man can scarce conceal his vexation, unable to see why their voyage has been cut short. His men are all standing in a row on deck, restlessly fidgeting like cattle before slaughter. Viper's men surround them, their knives still sheathed but visible, their mere presence enough to cow the crew. Bengt has scarce hauled himself aboard before the captain is in front of him, endeavoring to make himself understood in the borderlands between Swedish and German.

"My name is Hans auf der Mauer. I'm told these men answer to you, Sir Bengt. What is the meaning of this?"

"Which district mined the iron you loaded?"

"The mine is in Norberg."

Bengt nods and turns to Viper, who is leaning against the bulwark.

"Get the men in your boat, all of them. We'll row the crew to land."

Viper shows his confusion with a questioning look.

"Once everyone's off, burn the ship. The last man lights."

Viper and the captain both speak at once in a joint protest that falls silent when one of them finds the word they both seek.

"Why?"

"Do as I say."

Hans auf der Mauer shakes his head, any sense of caution thrown to the wind in his turmoil.

"You can't be in earnest. Why burn a ship for no reason? Look."

He claps his palm against the bulwark, then grabs the crossbar and shakes it, to show how sturdy it is.

"Fräulein is her name, and she's as beautiful a dame as has ever flown the League's pennant. This is her seventeenth year at sea, and the timber's still good. She's served me faithfully, has saved my life and my riches many a time. Take her instead. Take her in pledge. I'll redeem her if I can, if I can't find others to lend me the sum."

Bengt shakes his head and waves his hand at Viper, who is still standing silently, in the hope that his master will listen to reason.

"Burn the ship."

"We've iron worth seven hundred silver marks aboard. Take them as yours. We'll help you to unload it. That's more than she's worth. Let us sail her home to Lübeck, and you can take the iron as her ransom. An expensive toll, but one I'd sooner pay. I give you my word before God that I'll never mention it as anything but a fair trade."

"Burn the ship. The iron stays where it is."

The silence is deafening when both Viper Saltlock and Hans auf der Mauer understand that they are dealing with something that they have never seen before, something that defies all reason and rests upon motives far beyond their own field of vision. With skittish eyes they look upon each other and upon Sir Bengt, and Viper hears a voice that has called out to him many times before, concealed behind storms and tempests. An icy whisper over spume and wave, the very voice of the sea. She laughs at them, at these abject beings who have ventured out upon this thin film that serves as canopy to her vast underworld, dry-shod on paltry scraps of board. She would sooner take flesh and blood in sacrifice, the heat of dry bodies an affront to her coldness, or perhaps a brief comfort in the darkness of her depths. Viper sends a prayer of thanks that it is only iron that she will get to consume this night. With a shudder he rouses his freezing body, then places an arm on the Hansa captain's shoulder and leads him away, mild in his quiet address.

"Come with me, Captain. Let's find places for your men on the thwarts."

Viper lights the fire himself, belowdecks, easily enough. In the galley he finds smoldering embers in an iron cauldron hung from a chain. Famished flames latch on to a pile of rope and cloths when he ladles the embers upon them using a battered tray as a spade, scoop upon scoop of devastation. Once he's sure the fire has taken hold, he hurries back onto deck, coughing and spluttering in the billowing smoke, then hand over hand he climbs down the twisted ropes to his boat, where he pushes off against the cog's hull until his oars have space to row. Bengt stops them from a distance.

"Wait here till she's sunk."

They sit in silence on the still water, all facing the bonfire that flares up on the waves. The fire comes clambering over the deck, a greedy idol that claws at the masts, sets fire to the shrouds and ropes, and gnaws holes in the hull. For a while she retains her shape in spite of the blaze, a ship of old legend built of flames. The heat reaches them where they sit, turning the winter night to a summer's eve. Hans auf der Mauer is sobbing openly, as powerless as anyone else to look away. Then she starts to list, and the bulwark goes down under the weight of the mast, which plunges into the water. His blubbering is heard until the hull splits, the weight of the iron ingots worth seven hundred silver marks eventually overpowering her charred boards. With fire it was mined from the mountain and melted, but now the fire sends it down to the depths of the sea. The ship is soon to follow.

Horses in the courtyard, hooves on crusted snow. Margaret hears her household go out to greet the guests and hastens to her feet with a flutter in her belly, sweeping her woollen mantle with its wolfskin trim around her. The estate is cold. The wooden house is drafty, and the fire kept burning day and night sucks the cold air in through the gaps in the heavy logs, before blowing it out again through the smoke hole in the roof. If she ventures far from the fire, then she does so in thick clothes, layer upon layer. Her body takes on unfamiliar shapes, every movement made sluggish and slow. Like a dungeon it becomes in winter, this little estate on the forest's edge. The snowdrifts press up high against the walls, and window boards must be placed over every opening to keep out the cold. A rare day is it that she goes outside, and if she does so, then she must follow the narrow paths that have been shoveled from one building to another. The sun she rarely sees on its brief passage through the sky. Everything is dim. There's nothing to do, every week an insufferable mist, its beginning and end marked by the mass at Nyköping convent, which lies just over the hill. Between she sits by the hearth with needle and thread, but it's not an occupation for which she harbors any great pleasure, nor for which she is well matched. Her husband promised her that she wouldn't have to spend her winter here. Yet another in the long line of promises that he has broken. Longer and longer it grows. Every time he takes back his word he gives her new ones in return, beautiful and numerous, the essence of which is always the same: what sorrows she has today are but water for the harvest that they will soon reap together. One day they will look back on their hardships and laugh at the doubts they once had. In castle chambers, then; tended on, respected, rich. So easy is he to believe, Nils Stensson, for it's clear he views every promise as a truth in the making. And in the twinkle of his eyes she, too, catches glimpses of the future that he sees so clearly. She nods and smiles, again and again.

At night she always lies awake. Rest is made scant for she who lives each day in still restlessness. She blames him then, thinks ghastly thoughts, finds wicked names to call him. It always seems to be of her that waiting and patience are demanded. Nils's life seems so full by comparison, always on his way somewhere, always in company. She imagines their roles reversed, only she not as little Margaret of House Beam but the other Margaret, the one after whom she was named. The queen for whom one kingdom wasn't enough. She fancies herself constantly traveling, always busily widening her borders through wars, cunning, or silver, while Nils sits alone in a hut in the forest somewhere. Neglected, left on the side like an object on its shelf, waiting to be used. Would he have waited for her? She knows the answer, and it stings. No, Nils Stensson would not have waited. What's worse: he would have fought tooth and nail to reap whatever he could for himself using the power that was hers.

Is he faithful to her on his adventures? Doubt racks her, and it sparks her yearning for his body, too, for his touch. He is older than she. She was but fifteen years old when they were first betrothed, and he already a man, but he was handsome then and still is now, and well have they entwined. He was her first, of course, and he swore to her that she was his, though she sensed a falsehood there. All too sure did he seem, all too skilled in the art of pleasure. But if indeed it was a lie, it was easily forgiven, for she couldn't begrudge him such skill, however it was gleaned. How she savored those sensations that she had previously only sensed from afar, the depths of which she had never even conceived of. The sudden knowledge that this, too, was what she was created for. And so she writhes in longing, alone in her bed, the bitterness close at hand: Was she not ample for him, in the same way that he was for her? Why is it not enough for him, all that she has to give? The thoughts of lust came easier before. Now a shadow is cast over them. The child, the one who never was, so weighty in her slightness. On the occasions when Margaret does succumb to sleep, she might then wake up sweaty from a dream, believing herself back in the chamber in Vadstena. The agonies a mist. All that pain to no avail, disappointment her only reward. Her own censure bad enough, but Nils's and his conspirator's even worse, their true feelings clear as beacons behind the words that they had chosen for comfort.

But now he has returned, has finally come to take her from this dreadful place and from the bleak weariness of winter. Southward, to where the snowdrifts rise no higher than that a footstep can overcome, and where the light shines brighter and longer; to new chambers swathed in splendor, to good food and soft beds. It has taken him longer than promised, but she has no wish to salt their reunion with resentment. Heavy feet are made light as she springs over the boards toward the future that she was promised. Young she is still, and he, too. The years they have before them are numerous enough to forget all that has been.

She opens the door, and the cold is like a slap to the face. The first of two, for it isn't Nils who awaits her. At first she doesn't know who it is. Young he is, and handsome, too, handsome as an angel, long hair framing the smooth features on his face. He is even fairer than she remembers him, for a change has come over him, his beauty no longer like a caged bird's but that of a freer being. He has always been known as her nephew, and she always as his aunt, though not one year separates her birth from his.

"Magnus?"

"Mara."

She searches for a reason for his presence, in vain.

"Do you come with tidings from Nils?"

He shakes his head, his arms wrapped around his waist, steeling himself to stop from shaking on the spot.

"No. I haven't seen my uncle in a long time."

For a moment she stands speechless, before stepping to one side.

"Come in, out of the cold."

He lowers his head in gratitude, stamps the snow off his shoes, and steps over the threshold. By the stables his page is tending to their horses; she knows his face, but it takes her some effort to recall his name. Finn. She leads them both to the hearth, to the benches placed around it for its heat, and calls for a maid to warm them some beer.

"I wasn't expecting guests."

He holds his hat in his hand, his hair long and wild. With his fingers he combs it smooth. In his gaze she reads distress, and his voice falters when he chooses his words.

"Aunt, I don't know what to do. I was supposed to spend the winter at Cuckoo's Roost, but I can't bear to. Nor do I wish to break a promise I made. I have nowhere else to go. That's why I'm here."

For a while Mara sits in silence, observing him. That face wasn't made for pain, just as little as her own.

"You're welcome here. Stay as long as you wish. Let us ring in the New Year together, and Epiphany after that. I find winter so tedious, and it's good to have some company from kin."

Magnus shifts position and looks her in the eye, and his gratitude warms her more than the hearth ever could.

"Thank you, Aunt."

The beer arrives in mugs, bitter and steaming. Together they drink in silence.

"Would you tell me about Engelbrekt?"

She sees him smile for the first time, his face at once so bright that it is as though a spark has lit a wick within. His smile catches, and she feels a candle of the same sort warming her. The change to her countenance comes first, and only then the thoughts that fit it best. It is Nils of whom she thinks.

"KARL CROFTER."

Eric Puck is standing to one side, far enough to go unseen yet close enough to hear. He likes what he sees. In the middle of the assembly meadow, its grounds shoveled free of snow, stand the dozen men whom King Eric has installed as arbiters over the kingdom after Engelbrekt's Council was dissolved. Each man has just bowed his head in favor of the decision to send a letter to the king cataloging every one of his transgressions, revoking their loyalty and obedience once again. And now each one has voted for a new commander, by writing their choice on hidden slips of paper that were then placed in a sack. All but one have voted the same way, for the man whose name was just read aloud for all to hear. They have conspired ahead of time. Eric Puck snorts when he hears the name. He is not surprised. Nor for that matter is Engelbrekt Engelbrektsson, who stands alone before the members of the Council. The nobility has spoken. The so-called people's chieftain from Norberg has done his bit, and now that his work is all but perfected they would sooner see the realm led by one of their own. They and the Hanseatic League are of one mind: let Engelbrekt Engelbrektsson return to his mine.

But this assembly of the lords is not like the ones that came before it. Long have they spoken, and the hours have drawn on longer than anyone had reckoned. Fires have been lit on the ground to afford warmth and sight as the sun descends, dragging the light with it toward the world's end. Around them the winter night is filled to capacity, for Engelbrekt has summoned not only the Council here to the meadows at Arboga, but merchants and peasants, too, and, while the Council number a dozen, the peasantry around the assembly stand in their hundreds. Puck turns his head and watches on as the name spreads through their ranks like the ripples from a stone in a well, hears it called out from one to another, so that everyone will hear.

"Karl Crofter."
"They chose Karl, of House Crofter."
"Crofter. Karl Crofter."
"All but one for Karl Crofter."
The air is soon seething with rage, vast and indomitable. He

feels it raise the hairs on his arms, at the nape of his neck. The people who have sat down while waiting for the day's conclusion are now back on their feet, closing ranks around the Council. Voices are raised in outrage, each cry soon impossible to discern, though their intent is nevertheless clear. A wolfish grin cleaves Puck's face from cheek to cheek. No more will the many cower to decisions made by the few. A new day is dawning. He sees the Council members, their gazes darting around, their anxious steps pacing the same small patch while the people's discontent mounts to a roar, the air choked with the promise of violence. Even Nils Stensson of blue and gold, a man normally so pleased with himself, looks ill at ease. Ring-clad hands drift uneasily toward sword hilts, and Puck can't help but laugh out loud: ornately forged jewelry for highborn lords. What match are ornamental swords for people in their hundreds, a crowd so teeming that no one can raise their arms up over their heads?

Engelbrekt alone stands calm, his gaze passing from one Council member to the next, his arms crossed. He waits, lets others plead his case, his silence speaking more than any words ever could. It fills Puck with pride to be able to stand alongside one so strong, to be so close to him. The disquiet mounts, the chorus of voices braying all the louder, fingers pointed and fists clenched as they press all the closer. The shiny swords of the highborn lords remain sheathed but for fear of unleashing the inevitable. Then a frail voice rises over the masses, high and hoarse against the rumble of the crowds. It is Bishop Knut of Linköping, standing as tall as his bent back will allow, his feeble arms brandishing his crosier in the air, a futile shepherd's staff for the flock that refuses to obey.

"The people have made their voice heard. Let the Council vote anew. God's peace be upon the assembly."

Puck is almost disappointed, though he knows Engelbrekt's object. But if the Council were to be mashed under the peasantry's soles, little worth does he see that would be lost. Besides, it can scarce be called an assembly of the lords from now on, for no more can the lords claim the sole right to vote. A better name is needed. One by one the votes are read, aloud this time, the bishop raising each slip out of the darkness of the sack. Only half have seen reason. Every other vote is Engelbrekt's this time, the remaining are Karl Crofter's. Each time Crofter's name is announced the people thunder with discontent, and Bishop Knut shrinks back as though from a blow, while each time Engelbrekt's name is heard the cheers ring loud enough to serve as bellows for a dying pyre. The last name is read, and the bishop utters Karl Crofter's name with the tone of someone who has just read his own death sentence. The final votes are equal. Just as the people's hesitancy is about to swing to fury, Engelbrekt jumps up onto the stone from which the bishop just called for a second vote and raises his hands to call for silence, upon which even the crunch of snow can be heard underfoot.

"The people and lords alike have made their will known. May the kingdom have two commanders!"

The relief hits the Council's shoulders like a blow from a cudgel.

Long do the people stay up into the night, gathering around fires to eat and drink and savor life's bounties now that the disquiet is behind them, the wisest among them fully aware of the shift that has happened this day. The people's will, heard for the first time. A glimpse of a future of another kind. Furs and cloths are draped over logs for warmth, and from the forest come the echo of axes on their quest for firewood. To tents or other borrowed lodgings the lords retreat, while Engelbrekt walks among the people and speaks to them, thanking them for the support that he has been granted. Puck resists the temptation to walk at his side, for he would sooner ensure that the Council's defeat doesn't incite an ambush of some kind. He goes and speaks to the men he has had posted to every road and every fork, all of whom with an unbroken view of each other, all around the meadow.

Sleep eludes him, and the whole night he lies awake, one of few. It is as though the power he feels is threatening to burst the banks of his skin. The day slowly begins to dawn, the sun's rays but a faint promise, fulfilled only an hour later in these depths of winter. The stars are still bright in the sky. In spite of the cold, Eric takes off his fur, doublet, and tunic, stripping down to his shirt, and releases his sword from the frost that has lodged it in its sheath. Choosing a slender birch as his adversary, he stamps down the snow around it and makes his attack, slashing at its bark, cutting the branches away. He feels his limbs start to awaken, the blood coursing through his veins as his heart pulses a strong and healthy beat. Soon it is as though his body itself knows what is being asked of it. He loses himself in his imagined duel, finding a deep calm while the steel whirls. It is a good sword, one that he had beaten solely for himself, as a reminder that each man does best to forge his own way. With heritage comes weakness. Better to earn one's property by one's own means. From this day forth this guiding principle of his shall now also belong to the realm.

The birch tree before him stands stripped of its bark, disarmed of every branch within reach. And yet he thrusts harder and harder with his benumbed arm, seeing their faces in the wood. Men who disdained him. Relatives who refuse to acknowledge him. Magnus of blue and gold. Magnus is gone now, and no one is gladder of that than he, but there's something that he's not being told. He saw Magnus riding off, him and his lapdog, with two of Engelbrekt's men. The northmen came back bearing a heavy load. The next day Engelbrekt set out to meet with the Hansa, he, too, bearing a heavy load. It doesn't take much to piece together what has happened, though how is harder to know. Thanks to Magnus, Engelbrekt is released from his debt, free to go on in his endeavor.

Puck cuts harder at the birch, until his enemies are begging for mercy. None does he show them. Now the trunk falls and he dodges out of its way but even then he isn't done, hacking away at the stump with his blade. He has flung his shirt off his shoulders, defying the piercing air with his bare skin, proud of his hard muscles as they glisten with exertion. After more than an hour he stops, once his limbs are flagging and drowsy men have started to rise around him, having given up all hope of the noise abating and of their being able to drift back off to sleep. Eric sits down to whet his weapon, runs the stone along the sword's length and back again. Once the sweat has dried he dresses himself again, and when he wraps his fur around his shoulders it is to the sound of hooves on a winter road. He stands up to wait for the horseman, who is soon in sight, soon before him. The horseman dismounts and bends his knee.

"I come with tidings."

"Well?"

"Bengt Stensson's had the trench he dug refilled. All the work is undone. And he's burned one of the Hansa ships, filled to the brim with iron from Norberg."

Eric Puck turns away to keep his emotions to himself. Scarce could he have believed that a day like yesterday could be followed by one even better. Feeling a flutter in his belly, he takes a deep breath to compose himself before turning back to the messenger.

"We'll ride on Castle Cut, all of us, now, before the sun is high. You're coming with us."

"I was told to ride on, to forewarn Engelbrekt himself."

Eric Puck narrows his eyes.

"I'm telling you otherwise."

With satisfaction he sees the man open his mouth to respond, only to think better of it and close it, bowing his head in obedience. The assembly is to go on for many days yet, until they reach an agreement on all that pertains to the kingdom's rule. Engelbrekt needn't know, not until everything is done that must be done. Once Castle Cut has fallen. Once Bengt Stensson lies slain at the foot of the walls that were just his, the first of many to fall in the name of purging the kingdom of the stain of blue and gold. With any luck he'll find little Magnus himself at the castle, a meeting that he has long coveted. He wonders how many days that face will remain fair once impaled on the stake where it belongs, though he knows that that is not how it will go. Engelbrekt would never forgive him. No, the killing must happen by stealth, in the heat of battle, his body hidden where it will never be found, at the bottom of a pit with others, or plunged into a moat with his belly sliced open and filled with stones. Dead he will be nevertheless, and that death needn't be any more beautiful than Eric has time for. He rubs his nose, the one that was broken and never healed straight, before placing his whetted blade back in its sheath and calling out to his men to hasten their decampment.

IT IS BRITTA who says it first, who comes to her bedside where she lies recuperating. Far too many days out in the cold have claimed their due, keeping Stina in bed with the chills for over a week. Only now has the fever broken. She is finally well enough to hear the news. With dread come the words.

"Father's felled all the braces. The trench is gone."

With Britta's help she dresses, her sickness at once as though forgotten, and rides down to the digging site with her daughter on her heels, to see the truth behind the words. From horseback she surveys all of her toil, undone. The furrow is still visible as a broad rut, a gash sliced through the white expanses. Deprived of the braces' support, its walls have foundered, the snow and earth mixing in the slip. New flakes are already falling, and if much more sticks, then there will soon be no trace of all that the hundreds of men had achieved in the past year. When spring sates the earth with moisture anew, the soils will settle in their former places with all the greater haste. Perhaps the meltwater will carve a thin furrow here. A small brook will it become. But too small for the Hanseatic League, unless they're to take to shipping their iron on bark boats. Stockholm endures.

Slowly she rides along the ditch. Up ahead she sees men hard at work on the banks, with spades and picks to refill that which they had unearthed but days before. Several of them she knows by name. As soon as they see her they cast their gazes back down at the ground, keeping her only in the corners of their eyes. Shame, that's what she feels, and they can sense it, would sooner pretend that she isn't there. A vain woman so rash as to put men to work for naught. For over a year she was allowed to have her way, until her husband quashed it all in mere days. Stina blames herself. Kari Sharp had said as much to her on the Solemnity of Mary a year before, though Stina already knew it well herself: Men. They put everything to ash. She should have known better from the start. Everything that she built was raised on a quagmire. Little right does she have now to surprise that it has crumbled. Behind her she hears Britta, still with dread in her voice.

"Mother? What do we do now?"

She has no answer to give.

Back at the castle, all is life and movement. Men are swarming in the yard, where sleds lie tipped on their sides so that their runners can be rubbed with sand. Outside the castle doors a space has been shoveled clear of snow, where they are stacking the property that can easily be borne. Stina dismounts and drops her reins, letting the horse trot toward the stable of its own accord. Britta does the same behind her and takes her by the arm.

"What's going on?"

"Your father was given a task. He chose to wreck it and has made himself new enemies. The reckoning is on its way."

She stops a man who is carrying a harness over his shoulder.

"Who's coming?"

"Eric Puck and a hundred men. They'll be here before the day's end, and there's no hope of any mercy."

Sir Bengt paces the corridors as swiftly as his sore back allows, sees his housefolk scurrying from room to room, gathering anything of value that can easily be conveyed. He stops by an arrow slit that gives out onto the yard in front of the castle. The horses are being readied, every one, those that carry men and draw sleds alike. The snow lies thick. Castle Cut lacks any form of outer wall, the house itself its sole defense against the enemy, its stonework thick and smooth and many perches high, dotted with arrow slits from which to pick off the more intrusive attackers with bow and arrow. But no one was ever meant to get that close. Like other castles of its kind, Castle Cut stands on an islet in the lake, surrounded on all sides by water, its lone bridge to land easily felled at an enemy's approach. But now the ice lies wide and thick, rendering the water's defenses useless. The besiegers can approach from any way they so choose. The castle isn't easily defended in winter, its architects unable to conceive of an enemy who would be close enough to attack it on ice, in the depths of winter. Bengt has no desire to spill his blood here. Far too little is there to be gained. He won the fief without effort, and the year that the castle has been his has given him little grounds for loyalty, always on the move as he has been. Had the enemy been another, there might have been reason enough to stay behind its stone walls in the hope of bargaining. With Eric Puck it's different. His grudge against blue and gold is no secret. And Bengt knows well enough that he himself sowed the seeds of what has now ripened into a harvest: with spade and tinderbox he has given Puck every right.

Flight, then. No great ado, so long as they can get away before the day is out. The messenger who brought the warning said that Puck was pushing his men hard, but unless they've sprouted wings they won't be here before dusk, and even then they'll scarce be in any condition to take up the chase. Plenty of time. He drains the tankard in his hand, then slings it at the wall to demand the attention of a nearby servant, who is busily gathering up whatever cloths his arms can bear.

"Bring me one more of the same."

The haze is well on its way, already starting to dispel yesterday's complaints. He rubs his temples with a groan, while his foot taps a drumroll against the wooden floorboards in impatience at the servant's idleness. Instead it is another who comes. Britta, red of face, aggrieved.

"What?"

"It's Mother. She says she won't leave."

※

Many months has it been since he truly looked upon his wife. He wonders how someone can appear so different in scarce a year. At Midsummer she was the gem of the household. Now she looks like a tired old crone, aged before her time, some peasant worked to the bone. Lean as a rake, she is, her hair lank and greasy, her skin gray and her bosom sunken. He sighs when he sees her, propped up against the back of a chair. At her silence he stops short, unsure which path to choose. He clears his throat and attempts to summon his most commanding voice.

"Stina. Good to see you up. We must leave."

Nothing about her suggests that she has heard, until her response comes in a hoarse whisper.

"No."

"You don't understand. That devil Puck's on the march. He'll be here before nightfall with all of his men. We can't expect any mercy."

"What have you done, Bengt? Were we not just on the same side, all of us?"

She shakes her head feebly while he blushes.

"Don't answer that. What does it serve? Some folly of the kind that men like you are incapable of avoiding. Best that I don't know. But I'm not leaving this house."

Sir Bengt steps closer, even redder in the face, scratches at his beard until the hairs stand on end. He hears his voice cracking when he tries to yell.

"I should have expected no less of you, Stina. Your madness has grown worse by the day, ever since Midsummer. Are you too weak? I'll carry you out on my own shoulders. There's only skin and bones of you left, as it is. Are you ashamed that others will see the harm you've done to yourself? I'll wrap you in a sheet if you want."

She laughs, a faintly yelping sound, almost a cough.

"You imagine of others what you know of yourself. You never did see why I followed you here, Bengt; why I didn't stay at Cuckoo's Roost, the seat of my ancestors. I came because Castle Cut is our gift from Magnus. The reward we were granted for all of his work. Wasn't that what was intended, the day we packed him off into the world, you and I? I'm not leaving here. Not for anyone."

Bengt opens his mouth to speak, but then closes it again. He lowers his voice, incapable of looking her in the eye.

"He'll kill you. Eric Puck. Castle Cut will be his regardless. The only difference is that his men will have to scrub your blood from the floors before he can make himself at home."

"Blood. You may well fear it, man that you are and unused to the sight. But I've bled every month since the year I turned twelve."

No more, never again.

"Eric Puck will never take Castle Cut. I shall defend her."

"You alone?"

"Let me bid the household farewell before you depart."

※

Early afternoon. The sun is already sinking, and even now the chill promised by the coming night is nipping at whatever it can: cheeks, fingertips, toes. It is a cold winter, even colder beneath the stars. The sleds are ready, the household gathered. Three dozen all counted, bundled up in every last piece of cloth on offer. They stand in silence as she emerges, every eye on her. Bengt is with the men, one foot on his sled, ready to step aboard, wrap his bearskin around his waist, and be carried out of his enemies' reach. Once Stina is close enough to be heard by all, she casts strength into the arm that supports her, stopping her daughter, who has helped her to walk this far. She swallows, to moisten her throat and summon a voice that carries.

"For battle are you trained. Rarely have your skills been put to use, much less to a good purpose. A battle is to take place here, but hours from now. On one side I shall be standing, and I will ask that you stay with me. I could appeal to your honor, for that's as good a reason as any, or ask you to stay out of fellow feeling, for that, too, is good. But I don't stand before you a beggar. I have something to offer in return. Listen well. An opportunity like this comes but once in a lifetime. Whatever choice you make, the rest of your days will be lived out in the shadow of this moment."

She pauses to let her words sink in. A pitch torch hisses when a drop falls to the snow, lit to meet the approaching darkness.

"Brief is life's path from cradle to grave. But even more fleeting is its memory. Three generations later it is as though they never lived. Which of you remembers your great-grandfathers? Their names? The achievements that shaped their lives? What is to happen here shall never be forgotten. In a hundred years and a hundred years more, songs will be sung of how Kristina Magnusdaughter of the lion and the lily, an old woman before her time, stood against Eric Puck and his superior forces, as David stood against Goliath. And of the victory that she won. For I swear it before all of you, before God and the Holy Mother of God: Puck will not win Castle Cut. I'll defend her alone if I must, though I'd sooner do it with good men at my side. Go with Bengt, those of you who wish. Soon enough the sleds will lead you to your own deathbed. Remember then your brothers and sisters who stayed. Know that they won't remember you. And soon enough nor will anyone else."

For a long time all is silent, until a crunch of snow cleaves the air. One of the maids. She has a betrothed among the men, tall, well-built, and broad of shoulder. She tugs him by the hand, and when he resists she lets go and walks over to Stina's side. The man wavers for a moment, in two minds, before lifting his sack and going after the maid, to stand beside her and reclaim the hand he just held. Other men exchange glances, giving each other brief nods before taking what they own and stepping across the yard. One in three leave the sleds. Many number among the house's best, those who find that the words they heard have turned their pride against them. Others the reverse: The ones who have gone unnoticed and have little to commend themselves but who long for change. Those who are too young to know any better. Bengt rubs his face, gesturing at a free seat in the sled.

"Britta?"

She doesn't wish to look at him, turns her gaze down at the snow.

"I'll stay here with Mother."

Bengt steps down from the sled and starts trudging across the yard to take his daughter, unsteady on his feet from the drink and the ice. Stina squeezes the maid's shoulder with her left hand, and she in turn gives her lad a pat on the waist. He steps forward to stand in the way of his master. Others step forward to stand beside him, too, and Bengt has no choice but to stop. He turns back to look at his own men. They hang back on their sleds. Absentmindedly he combs his beard with his hand.

"So the brave all stay with you, while I get nothing but henhearts. Scarce flattering, that."

He walks all the way back, takes his seat in the sled, and sits there for a moment, every eye on him as he gazes out over the snow, out into the thickening darkness. His voice is filled with resignation.

"I fear you mistake courage for folly, every one of you. Know now, as our roads part, that I wish nothing more than that you be right and I wrong."

He gives his driver a pat on the shoulder. The horses are urged into a trot. A pair of runners hiss across the snow. Soon the sled is gone, into the impending night. The rest follow.

꙰

Stina wraps her mantle tighter around herself, shivering in the cold. She closes her eyes for a moment to subdue her feelings, reining in the fear that dulls her thoughts. She turns back toward Castle Cut, trying to call to mind the lessons of her childhood. Her father had so dearly wanted a son, but a daughter was all he got. By way of consolation she was granted a boy's upbringing, full of maps and chalked boards on which wooden blocks were moved in the tracks of old battles. Cause and effect so manifest when viewed from the future, every slip on the way to one's downfall just as easily singled out as the choices that secured another's victory.

Castle Cut consists of two connected buildings: one stone rectangle, with a turret affixed to its corner. The ground has been sunk around the entire base of the building, with a bridge raised to cross the ditch at the castle's sole entrance. Stina counts her people. Fifteen in all, of which a dozen are men. So simple in thought, defending a castle like this. In reality so difficult.

Some of her decisions come easier than others. She chooses the stronger half to address first.

"Empty the outbuildings of everything of value. Then set them alight. We're to leave neither wood for fuel nor shelter for our enemies. Bring all the animals inside. Then tear down the bridge to the doors and stack the wood on the bonfire."

The rest of them she takes inside with her, then sends them from cellar to garret to count and gather anything that might prove decisive. The maid, Maria, she puts to setting up a kitchen out of what was rescued from the cookhouse. A firepan under a cauldron, that's all that they need. A beer barrel beside it, not too strong. Water. Whatever bread there is. Cured meat is fried at the bottom of the cauldron, its broth seasoned and thickened with flour.

"Keep it cooking. Top it up as we go. Someone will always be hungry, and no one should have to fight on an empty stomach. Let everyone in battle smell the scents of food."

Stina counts the essentials on her fingers, time and again, trying to imagine the days to come. Food, water, firewood, weapons. While the people bustle this way and that, she studies the shooting angles, reckoning how close an attacker can come unchallenged. By the time night has fallen all is done. Good news and bad. Stina has had a chair carried in for her, so that she might rest her unsteady legs while she speaks.

"We have plenty of food to last us, especially since we're so few. But in arrows we're less well stocked, and in them our hopes lie, for in close combat we can't win. So listen, and remember: No arrow that is shot can miss. Each and every one must meet its mark. Never shoot from a greater distance than you are able. They will be many, far more than us. Don't let yourselves be disheartened by the sight. You just saw for yourself, out in the yard: But one in three are worth having. Fell the right warrior and two of his friends will start looking over their shoulders. Go for the one who is two steps ahead of the rest, the one with fight in his eyes, who stands straight-backed among those who cower. That being said, the arrows aren't the sharpest of our weapons. We have allies who can't be seen, and there's none fiercer: time, and hunger, and cold. No one is asking that we slay our attackers. All we have to do is hold out long enough, warm and fed inside these castle walls, while they starve and freeze outside."

※

The evening lies long before them, and the night thereafter. They are few, and they fall into a shared existence without any voices having to be raised. In one and the same hall they make their beds. A firepan in the center with benches around it, where the cauldron can be kept warm while they eat, and the beer can be mulled. The meat is good, and the drink quenches their thirst. Around them the house cools, emptied of folk. Only the animals remain in the floors below, making themselves known through howls and appeals, sensing in their bones the coming assault. Upstairs, they feel the heat of the fire on their faces, but their backs are cold. Thirteen of them, in a ring around the blaze. No one wants to break the circle to sleep. In the deep silence, Stina's gaze wanders from one face to the next.

"Some of you I already know. Others less so. By morning we'll be fighting side by side. Everyone will be needed, and much will be asked of us. None of us can be squandered, and each one's value is the same. Let us get to know each other tonight, as equals."

She clears her throat and straightens her back.

"Kristina is my name, of the lion and the lily born, to riches and abundance. And yet sorrow found me late in life, and my mind was wrung. Folly has brought me here. Regret is what I feel now, regret over every fork in the road where I chose the wrong path, only to see my error upon arrival. But staying here with you isn't one of them. With our victory won I shall choose better."

She turns her head to her left, passing the confidence on. The maid is beside her.

"Maria is my name, Torvald my father, Mellösa my home. I'm betrothed, and once the ground lies free of snow we shall be wed. But my husband-to-be is a handsome lad, and temptation has got the better of us. We've already taken what the future promised. I can already feel the life growing inside me. For two moons I've gone dry. I've been one of the household ever since I was a girl. Never would I choose a tomorrow with Sir Bengt when I could have one with Lady Kristina instead."

She places her hand on her betrothed's arm and squeezes it. Sheepishly he stammers his speech.

"Erengisle is my name, after my father. And a father I shall become when the next year comes, and a husband, too. God grant that I stay as loyal to my wife in her choices as I have been today. Never have I seen her choose wrong."

They go around the circle. Stina feels a strength growing between them with every voice. Then the last one comes, and her stomach runs cold when she hears who it is who speaks.

"Britta is my name, Bengt my father, and Kristina my mother. To blue and gold I was born. All my life I've been a daughter unloved. I've gone unnoticed, hidden in another's shadow, and not even hate was I granted in return, for I love him just as much as anyone else. At Castle Cut I have chosen to stay, in the hope that my value will finally be seen."

She searches for her mother's eyes.

"And who in their right minds would follow a man when there's a woman to be had?"

Stina feels the depth of the chasm that opens beneath her, her desire to fight at once undermined. She takes her daughter's hand in hers while tears fill her eyes, reminded of yet another road where she took the wrong turn. Now Britta is crying, too. When the silence between them becomes unbearable, someone starts mumbling the words all of them know. More join in, and then all of them, and then louder. Hands seek hands as if of their own volition, linking together to form a wheel. A prayer that they have prayed thousandfold, but never like now. They admit their humanity and ask for forgiveness, in knowledge of the judgment that soon shall fall.

"Pater noster, qui es in caelis, sanctificetur nomen tuur . . ."

THE SUN RISES. The light reaches for the west, past forests where the trees huddle under white robes, over snow-topped fields. Once it has crept up over the world's end it lights up a sky that is icy-blue and cloudless, a blazing eye with an unchecked view over all that shall come to pass. Eric Puck squints, shading his eyes with one hand. He quickly puts it back in its glove, then shakes it to draw the blood back to his fingertips. The night has been cold, and the day grows colder still. He spits on the back of his glove, holds the little gob out in front of himself, and sees its wave-topped surface freeze in an instant, before turning his hand to release the lump of ice into the snow. He swears a silent oath. The frost will bite deep, dull their grip around hilts and bowstrings, lock the swords in their sheaths. Crossbows aren't made for weather like this: the iron seizes up, preventing the crank from turning. Red icicles from open wounds. Not easy for anyone, but worse still for those who don't have the benefit of a wall's lee, or a hearth to thaw out that which has frozen.

A field lies before him, so luminous it smarts his eyes. Where the land ends and the lake begins isn't easy to say when the snow lies this thick, but that doesn't matter. No one will go through the ice on a day like this; the water must be frozen to its depths all the way out to the castle's isle. Puck is unlikely to reach it unseen, but perhaps luck will smile on him today, as it has done before. If the sentry in the tower nods off for a quarter of an hour, say, or has a tough moment on the privy, that could be enough. Even before dawn he sent one company out to take a long turn around the castle grounds, cross the ice far away, and block the road on the other side, so that Bengt Stensson can't jump into his sled and flee headlong when he sees Eric's forces coming from the east. Eric can't see them anymore, can only trace the furrows their feet carved through the unbroken snow until they fade from view. They must be there by now. Behind him the rest stand ready, their camp already broken, everything they have with them loaded back onto their sleds just inside the forest. Tough men, all of them. No room in these ranks for the untried, those who shy away from arms or soil their breeches under a rain of arrows. He runs his gaze along the row and back, meeting nothing but lively eyes. Beneath him he feels his horse, restless in the cold. He pats her dappled neck, raises his hand

and lowers it soundlessly, then kicks his heels into her sides to set her off at a gallop across the field. The snow lies feathery, offering little resistance for eager hooves. Like riding through mists, over clouds.

Behind him the sleds start to move. The air stands still beneath the sun, but his speed whips up a wind on his face. Happiness is his in moments like these, moments that know neither anxiety nor dejection. Everything so plain, so clear. The rest is for later, once the most prominent of the sons of Sten lies crushed under his heel. Kin to his father's young wife, and until recently the foremost among Engelbrekt's allies. Many words will they have for him, the two men he holds dearest in life, but on one point he shall remain unchallenged: birth is defenseless against power. Eric rides into the light, his path like a tunnel toward the rising sun.

Where the smooth ice meets the slope of the islet he draws at the reins, bringing his mare to a halt, what triumph he had already allowed himself to taste replaced by disappointment. He has been betrayed. Castle Cut has had wind of his approach. The outbuildings have been put to ash, black marks streaking the white snow where the cold has throttled the flames that singed their woodwork. He rides closer. The castle doors hover in the castle wall, some four perches above the ditch around the building. Vexed, Eric sees that they have torn down the bridge. He can find no other reason for this than to cause offense and displeasure, a paltry condition in which to abandon a stronghold. More befitting would it have been to leave the door open and the keys in the locks. The ending would have still been the same, and goodwill costs nothing, after all.

He can't say which sense it is that warns him. A shadow comes quickly, and he recoils in his saddle without thinking. The arrow tears past, close enough for him to feel its flight, followed an instant later by the twang of the string that was plucked. He has already turned his horse, and he bends down low against her protected flank while urging her into a gallop out of range of the shots. Back in safety he sits up again in his saddle and squints at the castle walls. The windows squint back: they have been made even narrower by boards placed on the inside, leaving only slender arrow slits through which to take their shots. People have been left here, the castle prepared to resist. Why, he doesn't understand. Why leave people here if they knew of his intent? Surely they must know what forces he has brought? He scours his mind, searching for hidden circumstances, but finds none. It can't be a trap. But what it is instead he can't fathom.

He rides off, back toward the men who have followed him, stopping them with a hand in the air. He dismounts and searches among them, then beckons to a youngster with a keen look in his eyes.

"You. See the stone there? And the oak? Somewhere between them an arrow struck the ground. Fetch it for me."

Eric watches the boy as he dashes off through the snow, wondering whether he will be made a scapegoat. Doubtful. Not from such a distance, not with such modest reward for a strike. Perhaps he is mistaken. If so, he will know that the defenders have arrows enough to waste. The boy's life is in God's hands. He is gone half an hour. The little shadow trudges back unharried, bent double through the snow. Oh his return he presents him with the arrow with a proud smile.

Eric weighs it in his hand. It is indeed an arrow and not a crossbow bolt, as the sound of the string and the speed of the shadow had already told him. Now he is sure. Good. Had they had any crossbows they would have used them. He turns the arrow in his hands: The shaft has split in the middle upon landing, but it holds together still. The wood is gray, aged, and brittle, the feathers threadbare, the point speckled with rust. He can only assume that until recently this was the best arrow to be had at Castle Cut, chosen by their finest marksman for the shot that alone could have ended the attack. Not a bad shot, either. Mere luck was all that saved Eric's life, blinded as he was. It can scarce be the first shot released from that bow. A seasoned marksman would have chosen a better arrow had there been one to be had. So their supplies are meager. That alone is reason enough to abandon the castle rather than defend it. The riddle remains. He turns back to the same youngster as before.

"Can you handle more? Or have you had enough glory for one day?"

The boy shakes his head, eager to be of service. Eric lifts his helmet off his head.

"Borrow a spear and put the helmet on top. Leave your other weapons. Go to the castle and tell them I want to talk. Demand a promise of peace before God."

All of them watch the boy slink off. The helmet rattles like a cracked bell on the spear when he uses it as a walking staff through the snow. When he arrives, they can see his cry by the rise of his shoulders, too far away for the sound to carry. The lad listens to the response, then cries again. Walks back along the same furrow that he plowed.

"Kristina Magnusdaughter of the lion and the lily says to Eric Puck that he has the choice to either turn back whence he came, or be slain at the foot of the walls that are hers, and shall so remain."

Eric turns his back to his men rather than let them see the fury that he can't stop from stretching his mouth into a grimace. So it is a trap, in spite of it all. He must fight a woman. He no longer has anything to gain, but a great deal more to lose. Reason tells him to turn and let Castle Cut stand unchallenged, but other feelings take root within him when he imagines his return, reproached for his tricks by Nils Rossvik, chided by Engelbrekt. Not only wayward, but worthless, too. He knows as good as anyone that success is the only thing that can justify disobedience. So now he must fight.

STINA SEES THE men preparing. She tries to count them, but it's not easy. Fifty? Seventy? Not much more than that. An advantage of somewhere between two score and five dozen. All men of the right age, all outwardly battle-hardened. And Eric Puck himself, who has already taken Foxholm and has been at war for almost two years. At first they split into two companies: one came over the ice with Puck at its head, and a smaller group from the east. Now all of them have assembled on the inland side. She sees them bedding themselves down, using the snow to raise banks to shield themselves from arrows and create some lee for the night. Others have crossed the ice toward the headland where the forest is at its most dense, to fell trees. In a steady stream they hasten back two by two, with logs in tow and willow branches for snowshoes. Stina can neither see nor hear what is going on behind the banks, but she knows well enough what she would do, and thinks no less of Puck. She can only wait, she and all the rest, keeping themselves occupied as best they can. On the floor beneath them she hears the sounds of furnishings being dragged across the floors, the crash of them being broken down into battens, to better reinforce the castle doors from inside. The cauldron is kept cooking, with food enough for all. No one can bear to stay away from the arrow slits for long, can but stand in the ice-cold draft and look out between the boards in wait of what is to come. One of the older men groans when he stands up, rubbing an aching knee. He responds to Stina's questioning look.

"It does that whenever there's a storm brewing."

Puck's men wait out the evening, the shadow of night their best defense against arrows. Her men need no orders. One in place at each opening. Soon one calls, then another. They're coming. She stands up to peer out, waiting for her eyes to forget the glare of the hearth and adjust to the darkness outside. It doesn't take long. The starry sky is bare and mirrored on the ground, pinpricks in their hundreds of thousands on the white cushion of snow. She guesses its shape, knows what is coming. They have built themselves a shelter from the arrows, a roof to carry on posts, to shield the men who are to build a new bridge across the ditch in place of the one that she had destroyed. They are coming now, as slowly and clumsily as they are implacable. She can imagine the men's feet underneath, poised on two stripped willows, each turned into a long ski that is shared by all, so that they can carry the shield's weight above the snow. One of them calls out a beat, so that their steps are kept even. Between the shield bearers walk other men, dragging bundles of logs behind them. A drawbridge in the making.

"Ready your arrows. Shoot whatever you think you can hit. If they make themselves space to ram the door, we're done for."

One by one they release shots, to no avail. The arrows strike the timber above the men, each plank carefully lapped over the other, leaving no gaps. When they reach the ditch beneath the castle walls, they stop and put down their shield. Stina sees them extend long, straight trunks over the ditch, finding a narrow ledge on which to rest them just beneath the castle doors. The other ends are anchored in the snow. The skeleton of a new bridge. Stina curses the architect who failed to anticipate such cunning and make the surface of the wall smooth.

"Hold fire, but be ready. Once their bridge offers coverage enough, they'll run underneath it."

It is as she says. From either side of the shield they dash out, to slide down into the ditch and under the shelter of their makeshift bridge. In the same instant arrows are unleashed. A quiet chorus of cries; some to summon courage, others in pain. Two hits, three? She can only be sure of one, for he lies in the snow at the bottom of the ditch, a small black human form with hands clasped at his waist, where the arrow must be lodged, unable to crawl to safety on his own. On the slope behind him a dark streak where the blood has spilled. At first his cries for help are tinged with astonishment, but soon they grow all the more pleading: a little drink, that's all, just something to put between him and the snow. No one has anything for him, and no one comes to his aid for fear of sharing his fate. Soon he speaks no more, just sobs and brittle cries. In the castle beneath Stina the animals are uneasy, clucking and whinnying. They, too, know who has come. For a long while all are silent, friend and foe alike, as though in contemplation of the death that has finally reached Castle Cut, heeding all of their calls. An expected guest, though a stranger nevertheless. By the time death has groped its way to the wounded man he lies curled on his side, his arms around his knees. All are grateful that his life seeped away quickly, sparing them more noise. Under the bridge, unseen work begins to support and strengthen the frame. Meanwhile the men who carried the shield slowly start shuffling back whence they came, to fetch more timber, more men. A respite. Stina doesn't know for how long. Not long enough.

"Whose was the shot?"

One of the men raises his hand. It trembles, and not from the cold.

"I think it was me."

No light here. She can't see his face amidst the gloom that must reign to give them sight. She hears the quaking of his voice and imagines him pale and wavering. New to the kill.

"What you did was for my sake. If you feel regret that's a good thing, and from a good man nothing else is to be expected. You're no more guilty than the twig that was whittled into the arrow, the horsehair twined into the string, or the wood bent to form that bow. Mine is the guilt, and no one else's."

Stina gets to her feet to look down. Beneath them the men are raising props, to better bear the weight of the bridge. The next batch of logs will likely pave the way for them to break down the castle doors. None of her childhood lessons have any bearing here. When it came to dispatching a superior foe, fire was always their answer, the men who served as her masters in the art of war. If blade or arrowhead won't help, burn them. But it's too cold. No timber will nurture a flame in a winter like this. She wonders what they would say in her place, the men who knew all that there was to know about war from a safe distance. But no, she already knows. They would have done the same as her husband. Fled. Shaken their beards at a woman's folly. She feels the powerlessness, the resignation. The defeat as though already a fact. The cold cuts her to the quick. Rarely has she felt its like.

A star's light catches on an icicle beside the opening. She reaches out between the boards to loosen it. Why, she doesn't know; perhaps for no other reason than that it offers some beauty on a night as ugly as this. The ice sticks to her fingers, and it hangs for a moment of its own accord before loosening and falling onto the growing bridge. All of a sudden she knows what she will do. Fire may well be the men's solution. But she is a woman.

Quickly she assembles them all and tells them what she wants. The well lies in the cellar, and together they make a chain through the floors to haul the water up from the depths, the pail passing from arm to arm, to be tipped out into a barrel.

It is too slow. In their haste and eagerness water is spilled on the steps. The last in the chain is left with mere drops to pour into the barrel, to little use. At a loss, Stina stares down into the barrel, at the meager mirror of water at its base. She meets her own gaze, and the disappointment that she sees there is an accusation that she cannot face. Then she has company, Britta by her shoulder. Stina turns, and she can see from her daughter's face that she has understood what the others haven't grasped. Quiet is her voice, as befits the words that are to cost others their lives.

"The roof."

"What?"

"The snow. On the roof it sits deep as an arm. We can break the tiles from inside, gather it, and melt it over the fire."

Stina's nod is taken for an order. Axes and picks are quickly found. From above come the sounds of wood being split and tiles being scraped, and in one fell swoop the men are soon running in with snow, cold enough to be whittled into pieces and carried in anything that will serve: pails, cloths, bare arms. Others kneel down around the firepan and blow the flames hotter and taller, feeding them with kindling. The cauldrons hiss over the heat. The snow melts, and the water fills the barrel. And one more, and the next.

❧

Yet again the shield comes shuffling on its many feet. Shapeless from a distance, a cumbrous shadow above the snow with its tail of new logs. It is harder to make out this time than before, for clouds have drawn in, obscuring the stars and strewing scant flakes beneath them. Puck's men make even faster work of it this time; standing in the same place, they slide out the trunks that now rest steady on the supports beneath. It isn't long before they are ready to test their work. Raising their shield above them, they venture out onto the new bridge one step at a time and find that it bears their weight. Stina waits until she hears the first swing of the axe before giving the signal to those who are at the ready. It takes four of them to lift the barrel up to the edge of the arrow slit directly above the castle doors, and carefully tilt it until the meltwater spills over. In a swift stream it gushes out, shaped by the wall's stones into a wide cascade that tumbles straight down over the men beneath. She hears their cries, first in fear, then astonishment. Stina waves on the next barrel, and the last one after that. It takes a while, long enough for doubt. Stina dips her own hand into the puddle beneath the arrow slit, then holds it out into the winter's night. The ice forms immediately, stinging her skin like a live ember. Now the axe falls silent beneath her, and the men stream out from under the shield, lumbering in their freezing garments, whimpering with pain. Her men stand at the ready with their bows, awaiting her orders. She shakes her head, well aware that wet clothes are death sentence enough on a night like this.

"WE CAN'T START a fire. What embers we brought with us have died, and no spark will catch in this cold."

Eric Puck purses his lips. The snow is flurrying all the more in the gusts of wind. He knows that the man who says these words knows of what he speaks, used to lighting fires in every weather. Puck can think of no one who would have fared better. Nor is he surprised. Twenty years he has spent on this earth, and few nights can he remember that were as cold as this one. From his childhood he recalls the old men's fables of harsh winters of yore, while they mocked him for shivering in mild spells; their tales of a withering cold where the frost would eat away at your face like rot, where blackening noses would have to be carved off and frozen toes and fingers snipped, every last speck of iron turned to a sharp thorn against the bare skin that ventured too close. He thought that was all exaggeration. Now he knows better.

"Perhaps it'll be easier by morning. Keep the men going. Don't let them stand still. Anyone who falls asleep in this won't waken."

No bad turn is without its silver lining: the men sense the reaper's breath on the biting winds and know that only Castle Cut's walls stand between them and heat. Just beyond that stonework lies shelter, fire, beer to warm, and meat to roast. Never has he seen them so swift. Scarce has he pointed the way and explained his intent than that a whole forest hill stands felled, freshly limbed trees ready to bridge the ditch and carry them to victory, with a shield pieced together by practiced hands. In the darkness they step toward the castle, where they are met with futile arrows. Only one of them hits its target, and Eric curses at the screams, the harm they do to the mood of the others more ruinous than the loss itself. Of men he has plenty.

Men return to fetch more wood, and axes, too, for once the next batch is laid the bridge will be strong enough for them to breach the door. Eric rubs his hands and jumps on the spot, pleased by what he hears, but also impatient. He hears them shuffle away on their willows, the logs in tow behind them, hears the beating of wood on wood as they put their final touches to their bridge.

Then suddenly there comes a din from the mist, shrieks of pain and surprise. Eric is quickly up on the bank to see better, but between the shadow of the castle and the ever-thickening snow it is impossible to make anything out. The sounds are of a different ilk now, strange voices that babble and stutter, higher than they should be for the men from whom they issue. A shudder caresses his skin, and he jumps on the spot and claps his shoulders to chase it away and bring back the warmth.

Something is coming toward him, a crowd staggering through the snow, which is falling all the thicker, a rustling tapestry. Before him the first man tumbles onto a snowdrift without breaking his own fall, his arms as though fettered in an embrace. He lies there in convulsions, like one with the falling sickness. Eric makes the sign of the cross, as though in the face of black magic, then kneels down to turn him around. No blood can he see, and no wound, but the man's woolen mantle is a hard crust, the chain mail beneath it as though beaten into solid steel. His hair a helmet cast around his head. Frost on his eyelashes over eyes frozen shut, black lips that still send forth fleeing breaths in steaming streaks. But the man is already in a torpor, having fled into sleep from a cold too severe to endure, and although Puck raises him to his feet, screams his name, and slaps him in the face with brute force, the man refuses to stand. Puck squints through the snow, sees other staggering figures in their futile flight toward a camp that has no warmth to give. A wind blows over the ice with a howl, driving a flurry of snow before it. It is no longer the breath of the reaper. Now it's the scythe itself. Eric has no time to lose; he dashes back to the camp to gather what men he has who are still dry.

S IR BO IS woken by a shove to his shoulder, and with an unwilling grunt he rolls over onto his other side, where he is shaken all the harder. Drowsily he blinks in the winter darkness, looks around in confusion to remind himself of where he is. A low ceiling, the gaps in the boards stuffed with bog moss. His body sore from an unfamiliar bed. He is still at Arboga, toward the end of the assembly of the lords, one of the few who have stayed. Nils is already riding south, the commander of Småland province once again. Of the brothers, Sir Bo is still the only one whose cup is empty. What comfort the slumber lent him quickly fades. Yet another day of bickering and cold awaits him, even if the meadow is now behind them, the meeting having been moved into one of the city's churches. He greets the day with a sigh. The man who woke him is one of his own.

"The night felt short. Is it time for the assembly already?"

"No, my lord. Engelbrekt Engelbrektsson asks to see you."

"Me alone? Did he say why?"

"No, but he's here, my lord. He's waiting for you in the main chamber."

"What time is it?"

"Very late or very early."

The house belongs to a farmer, but Sir Bo has borrowed it for himself and his men, leaving the farmer and his folk to cram into stables and outbuildings. He dresses himself quickly in the frigid cell of a room, hits his forehead on a beam while hopping on one leg to thread his clothing over his feet, rubbing the rising bump while sucking the air in between his teeth. His mind scrabbles to find a reason for this audience, with no success. Once he is dressed he steps through the door, knocks on the next one, and goes inside.

Engelbrekt Engelbrektsson is waiting for him by the glow of the hearth, without company and on his feet, pacing back and forth over the beaten earth floor.

"Sir Bo."

"What's going on?"

"A messenger just came. He tells me that your brother, Sir Bengt, has taken one of the Hansa ships in spite of the vows given."

Bo groans inwardly. He can well imagine Bengt letting his privateers engage in some mild pillaging around the islands now that trade is moving again; such is only to be expected when the risk is low and the temptation great. But to do it bunglingly enough to get caught is unforgivable.

"He has also refilled the waterway that he was tasked with opening between the sea and Lake Mälaren."

Sir Bo stands agape. He opens and shuts his mouth several times but can't come up with a single shrewd thing to say.

"I see from your surprise that this comes as news to you and that you don't know his reasons. Good. That's one of the answers I was seeking. But there's more. Eric Puck was the first to receive the tidings. He left without my knowledge, taking the messenger with him as he rode on Castle Cut with all of his men. Only once he was a day's ride away did he let the man return. Puck bears a grudge against your house, and wasn't slow to seize the opportunity to do something about it. I've sent men after him, but whatever's happened at the Cut, it's too late to prevent it now."

Bo finds his bearings, gulps loudly in anticipation of what he suspects is now to come.

"You said you were seeking other answers."

"Are you still with me, Sir Bo? Or would you sooner go with the brother who has made me his enemy?"

Nils and Engelbrekt and the bishop on one side. Bengt on the other. The scales are tipped. It makes his choice all the easier.

"I'm with you. For the good of the realm."

Engelbrekt studies him in silence for a moment, then gives a curt nod.

"We'll ride on Stockholm, all of the nobility and what commoners we can get there quickly. With a waterway opened for trade I'd hoped to leave the city be, but now that's not going to happen. We must take Stockholm, whatever the cost."

Engelbrekt leaves Bo to muster his men for the ride. But first he must sit down. Finding a bench, he tries to piece it all together but cannot understand. And a siege of Stockholm, in midwinter? Madness. Engelbrekt must have lost his mind, too. Surrounded by fools, Bo sways back and forth, asking himself whether he is the only one still in possession of his senses.

SILENCE NOW. STINA peers through the opening, but her sight also finds no footing, sees only a billowing sheet of whirling snow that hurtles around the castle walls, tossed back and forth by the winds. She wonders whether this was all that was demanded of her, whether the night and the cold will do her bidding and the sun rise over a field of fresh snow dappled with low, white boils as barrows over the dead, the bridge they raised to her door the only cross on their graves, until the spring uncovers their resting places, laying on a banquet for sharp beaks. In the hall they all sit in silence. No one wants to be the first to break this peace, of a kind that lies heavy over consecrated earth.

A clatter cuts through the stillness. Stone on stone, from up in the garret. She understands at the same time as the others. Puck is on the roof; he must have raised a ladder the whole way up. They themselves opened up the boards and tiles to melt snow into a weapon, and now the castle is exposed. The men in the chamber quickly find their feet, hasten up the stairs to meet the intruders with axe and knife. Stina hears them die, knows the voices that scream out in pain and anguish. Warm drops fall from the gaps in the floorboards above, hissing in the firepan as they fall. She dashes to the window on the other side of the house and there sees the dark line of the ladder swaying against the white. Slender trunks with rungs bound in place, a quick job but apt nevertheless. On each rung a new man on his way up. Just as moments ago she sat in contemplation of all the men the cold threatened with death. Now she begrudges each and every life that was spared.

Looking around for Britta, she makes her decision. Fire it must be, after all. She takes a stool to use as a lever, but her feeble muscles are capable of nothing. Britta comes to her aid, and together they overturn the firepan, spreading its hissing embers over the dry wooden floor, which soon singes and starts to smoke. She topples a bench on top of them, and then another, and then takes her daughter by the hand and hastens down the steps. The hallway is dark beneath them, the doors unmanned. The animals that were herded inside shuffle uneasily in the shadows, bleating and lowing, their inhuman senses aware of their proximity to blood and to fire. With the crossbar lifted, Stina finds the new bridge steady and well-made, though slick with ice, and together she and Britta dash out into the white, the sounds of battle behind them dampened with every step. Every gust of wind is like a slap to the face. Stina pulls her fur-trimmed hood farther down over her brow to improve her view, to little use. All is but a gray shadow in the winter night, and nothing around her can she tell from anything else. Soon she has lost her way, and she stands there with Britta at a loss, fearful of retreading snow-filled footsteps whence she came, back into danger's reach. Britta cries out and points, then turns Stina to face a blazing giant, its arms flailing in the storm. Castle Cut is burning, its walls a roaring furnace and its roof in flames, puffs of smoke issuing from every window. In each other's arms they stand, for warmth and for comfort, and observe the desolation, before they turn and run on through the snow, certain now of the course that will carry them away. But they don't get far before the bonfire behind reveals new figures in the snow before them. Clearly Puck has posted sentries to capture those in flight. Stina feels her last hope die.

And yet the men remain seated, even though Stina dares to approach one, close enough to touch an arm stiff as a tree's root, or run her finger along a pale cheek streaked with frozen tears. Dead they sit and lie in their ice-lined clothes, men in their dozens, their faces blue and white in the glow of the distant fire. Stina shakes her head in incredulity at the cruelty of the providence that has led her to this place, this frozen grove of other mothers' sons, the ones she killed by the same means that once christened them. Many have chosen to leave the world as they entered it: curled up into balls, as small as they can make themselves, their knees under their chins and their arms clutched at their waists, chin to chest.

Suddenly she sees that she is alone, and that Britta has left her, too, and although the betrayal leaves a stab in her chest, she doesn't blame her daughter. Stina fell in with monsters, and a monster she is become. Her weak knees give way, and she sits down in the indifferent gazes of the dead, her face covered with her hands, ready to offer up her life in their midst in the hope of atonement.

And then Britta is back, shaking her by the arm. She has a horse with her, not one of the household's but one that came with

Puck. She helps Stina to put one foot in the stirrup and then to mount, and Stina bends down over the animal's impossible heat and vigor, weaving her fingers deep into its mane. Britta mounts behind her, takes the reins, and urges the horse into a trot, away through the white whorls. Anywhere better than here.

"WER GEHT DAHIN?"
The snow is falling so rife that the crown of the southern gatehouse at the bridge to Stockholm city is lost in the paleness of the sky. The ice clinks loudly in the bay, but the man who has commanded them to present themselves has been chosen for his strength of voice, and he makes himself heard. Engelbrekt stands with his helmet held aloft on a post, Karl Crofter at his side.

"The Commanders of the Realm, with its Council behind us, to demand that the city be returned from its foreign masters."

Sir Bo stands a few yards behind, alongside the other Council members who have joined them from Arboga. They eye each other up uneasily. Behind them in turn the army is great, though little match for masonry and drawbridges. Even if they were prepared to stack the dead across the water as a bridge, the current would prove too strong. Stockholm can't be taken, and certainly not in winter. In a winter like this even less.

"Wartet mal."

For an hour they are kept standing there, before the heavy chains of the drawbridge start to rattle, lowering it toward the ground. A perch above the ground it stops, and a man is sent out onto the sloping ramp. Bo can't hear what is said between him and Engelbrekt, but nor does he need to. The promises of peace are demanded and given so that the meeting can take place. Soon the bridge is lowered all the way, and the man who was sent out returns to the gatehouse on the other side, where the door is opened slightly to let the city magistrates pass. Germans both of them. Sir Bo should know their names, but in the heat of the moment his memory fails him. Heinz something, or Kreutz. The kinds of names they all have. Of Swedish they scarce speak a word, but Engelbrekt's German is good. Sir Bo catches a phrase here and there. In the name of the people the commanders demand that the city be returned, and hereby declare that King Eric has been stripped of his crown, the Council having renounced all loyalty to a king who doesn't honor his own promises. All of the realm's worldly and spiritual power now stands at the foot of Stockholm's walls, with the law on its side. The Germans don't know what to think, exchanging looks of alarm. They ask for time and to be allowed to go to the palace, where King Eric's bailiff resides, to hear his opinion. Another hour passes, whereupon the same thing, whereupon another wait. For the third time the magistrates emerge onto the bridge, this time with a message.

"Wir können Ihnen die Stadt nicht geben."

Sir Bo and the rest of the Council have slowly edged closer. The cold is biting, and they are impatient to hear the bailiff's words. Nor are they alone. On the other side of the water the city's residents have gathered, in spite of the weather. Bo squints in order to see them better. A grim congregation: for one and a half years the city has been severed from the rest of the kingdom, and every morsel of food has had to come in through the sea routes. Salted herring, cured meats, dry goods that won't spoil. Bo turns his attention back to the bridge, where Engelbrekt has just been refused. He wears a wolfskin around his shoulders, a chain mail coat above his doublet, his sword at his side, and his knife in his belt. Straight-backed and broad-shouldered. Bo feels the sweat trickle down his neck in spite of the cold, glad to be standing on his side even though they have reached the end of the road. What comes next happens fast: Engelbrekt steps onto the bridge with a roar, grabbing one German by the collar and the other by the neck. Karl Crofter gives a startled cry before coming to his senses and darting toward the gate that is still ajar, his sword drawn to stick in the gap. But he slips as he runs, and the city's ever-vigilant foot soldiers slam the gate shut, swiftly followed by the rumble of beams being latched in place. The city may have lost its magistrates, but still she is safe.

The marksmen in the tower keep their arrows poised while Engelbrekt takes a firmer grip of his hostages. Karl Crofter scurries back to safety and joins the Council members' ranks, where Bo silently curses the man's slowness and the heel that slipped. As though he were hauling two sacks of hay, Engelbrekt turns to one side, where he can best be seen from over the water.

"King Eric has given you nothing but famine. I promise you better. Grain and commerce. Welfare and justice."

Never has Sir Bo heard such a voice issued from a human throat. Deep and booming, it carries over the crowds. Bo blinks at what happens next, for he knows that what he sees can't be possible, but rather some sleight of hand that Engelbrekt pulls off in the headiness of the moment. The Germans are both small men, short and pinched, but impossible it is nevertheless. With his bare hands

Engelbrekt places more and more weight on their shoulders, until their legs buckle beneath them and they can do no more but sink to their knees in the snow, one on either side of him. Such eminent lords, suddenly humbled. From the city shores the people cry out their response in resounding cheers. Engelbrekt leaves the magistrates lying where they fell and steps back over to the Council.

"Be ready. Soon we will have the gates open."

Sir Bo would demur, but his mouth is dry and his tongue refuses to obey. It is another Engelbrekt who stands before him, Engelbrekt the warrior, one who appears a head taller than everyone else simply by dint of being the only one who stands up straight. It isn't the predatorial glint in Engelbrekt's eye that scares Bo the most, but rather his command over it; the presence of mind of someone who has been in places like these often enough to feel at home. It isn't customary for lords to risk their lives at the head of an army, but Bo knows that that is precisely what is about to happen. He swallows again and again to slake his dry throat.

"Stay where you are. Let them fire the first shot. Then we'll have justice on our side."

Engelbrekt's gaze wanders from one man to the next, binding each to their spot by sheer force of will. He gives Bo a clap on his shoulder.

"Hope and destiny, Sir Bo."

The Council of the Realm stand in their row before the soldiers' arrows. Bo hears a prayer mumbled somewhere beside him and forces his tongue to whisper the same words. Engelbrekt stands there, unmoving, as though cast from his own Norberg iron. No arrow for him. His mere presence seems such that it would make an arrowhead cower, a sword's blade sag. Suddenly the clang of strings is heard. The shots fall without a strike, and Engelbrekt is the first to bolt across the bridge, toward the gate whose iron-shod boards can't hide the sounds of locks being broken from the other side.

Soon the wood buckles, the gate lurching on heavy hinges as the weight of dozens of bodies strikes it from behind, until the iron gives out and it tumbles to the ground. Blood in the snow on the other side: in vain the king's soldiers have turned to spears to fend off the crowds, piercing holes in the most brazen.

Two are the towers that defend Stockholm to the south: one after the other, the road between them narrow and easily cleared by defenders from both directions. The arrows rain down as quickly as the marksmen can set them to strings. Many have already fallen, dressings for stray arrows. Bo catches sight of Engelbrekt alongside one of his closest men, the son of Esbjörn, a giant from the north with a crossbow on his back and a pick in his fists. Engelbrekt points him toward the door that bars the way to the tower steps.

"Breach the door. Clear the tower to get them off our backs. Don't kill where mercy will do."

Harald Esbjörnsson needs no more and starts swinging his pick at the door's hinges. Soon it is hanging loose, and once he has wrenched it away he leads his northmen up the steps. Bo sees Karl Crofter follow them, bent double and encircled by his men.

"Sir Bo. Bring your men and follow me."

Bo's helmet obscures his view, but he yells at his men to follow him while darting on at Engelbrekt's heels, out between the two towers. He thanks his stars that the marksmen above have plenty of choice: the way is teeming with cityfolk, so much so that he must jostle his way through them. Arrows abound, to the sound of dull claps when their points meet stone, and cries when they enter flesh. Bo makes it to a sheltered spot beneath the battlements of the second tower and presses up against the stone while trying to catch his breath. To his horror he sees that the men who followed him have wavered in their conviction and are now on the retreat back down. Rather than stand alone he hastens on, shadowing Engelbrekt. He is immediately given reason to regret his choice, for three soldiers step across their way. The two at the front bear swords in their hands, and the one at the back a pike, to thrust from behind the safety of flailing limbs. And yet they stand there, at a loss before Engelbrekt's presence. Holding his empty hands out before him, Engelbrekt speaks to them as though he were calming a rearing horse.

"Sie sind auf falschen Seite. Kehren zum Burg zurüch und es wird kein Blut vergossen."

They hesitate, and Engelbrekt's hand slips to his belt to twist his sword in its sheath, ready to be drawn. He shakes his head at them.

"Ihr seid noch junge Männer. Sterben nicht umsonst."

The pikeman nudges his shaft against one of his companion's hips, hissing at the swordsmen.

"Er ist nur einer."

Both step forward with their weapons over their heads, and in that instant Engelbrekt's sword is drawn, his first blow the product of the same movement that removes it from its sheath. A stab follows, and within three steps he is beside the pikeman, close enough to render his weapon harmless. The soldier drops it and makes to draw his dagger, but before he knows it his fingers lie strewn in the snow, and his body soon after, his intact hand fumbling to close his slit throat. Bo feels an untamable force rise through his throat, then bends forward and vomits against the wall. Engelbrekt stands ahead of him, as if on a red carpet in the fallen soldiers' midst. Before him Stockholm lies open, and Bo hastens to draw his own sword and run it through a blood-spattered snowdrift before Engelbrekt can turn around.

"Well fought, Sir Bo."

Others arrive now, ready to take on the marksmen in the tower above, a motley fellowship of northmen and Bo's men. Sir Bo rubs his beard with a fistful of snow, then spits his mouth clean.

"What next?"

"Go along the city walls to the north. Clear the towers. Bargain if possible. Offer the soldiers safe passage to the palace."

"Why?"

"The city is ours. The palace is a palace no more. Now it's just a prison with more splendid walls."

He bends over, like Bo before him, to take a fistful of snow. Spatters of red cover his hands and sleeves. He shakes his head while cleaning himself.

"This is not a road I would have treaded by choice."

NILS STENSSON IS up early, standing by a window. Before him a Småland winter unfolds, wet and raw, with slushy snowdrifts and hail showers that can't tell whether they would rather be rain or show. He shudders at the sight. For more than a year he has come to know these southern climes from within the cold vaults of Balk Hill church, and they offer nothing but wetness and piercing gusts. Now his church days are behind him, the place fortified and manned, and frankly he hopes he never sets eyes on its coarse sandstone again. Outside it may still be winter, but for Nils's soul spring has come ahead of time. He commands Småland province once again, Engelbrekt's foremost in the south. Of men he has plenty, and the people are behind him. Not since his childhood fancies has the world seemed so vast or so welcoming. Now he finds himself amongst dreams come true, old larks turned to reality.

Rarely has he awoken to better days than this. Fort Gadfly at the southern border is now his, his first night spent in the bed that yesterday belonged to the castle bailiff, its posts thick as oak trunks, with a canopy of woven sky above. The girl he brought with him under the bedcovers lies there still. He can hear that she isn't sleeping, that her slumber is but feigned. He must have woken her when he got out of bed, early though it is. Nils walks over to her side of the bed, where he sees her eyelids flicker in their struggle to stay shut. Slowly he pulls back the covers until she lies exposed, with no choice but to pretend she doesn't know it. Beautiful is she, young and pale of complexion, her hair in half-loosed plaits that his hand can still feel in its grip. Her name, however, he has a harder time remembering. One of the usual ones: an Anna, an Agnes, an Alma. Some tradesman's daughter, or a maid from one of the better households. One who responded to the challenge in his eyes with a smile of invitation, took a liking to the victory bells that chimed with his arrival, and needed little wine or convincing to follow him here, to a romping night in a bed wide enough to fit her whole family. He can sense her regret now, though she keeps her aspect smooth. This is only to his amusement, for it makes their differences all the clearer. No pity does he feel for her. Did she not make her own choices, she just like him? Here they are in the after, he dressed and slaked, she naked in her wrinkled nest, filled with ruefulness. How rich it is, his life. His desire is reawoken, and at first he toys with the idea of showing her more of his goodwill, but then he pushes it from his mind. It was good as it was. May their doings be done.

He leaves her to the lot that is hers: To contrive Mother and Father a lie good enough to explain her absence overnight, and pray her daily prayers that she might wake up to blood before the month is out. Of hatching a good story he gives her a respectable chance, at least. The fort fell yesterday, and the night has been boisterous, his victory celebrated in the villages all around, with bonfires and dances and merriment in every taphouse, the bailiff's cellar opened up to quench the people's thirst. Many took him for Engelbrekt himself. Falling to their knees before him, they reached out to stroke the hem of his mantle and asked him to cast his blessings upon them, upon their hardships and their paltry futures. Not so much to ask. Gifts of the kind that cost him nothing. He saw no reason to give his real name.

His victory scarce cost him any more, for the fort was ill guarded. Its moat was easily waded, the guards in its gatehouse taken unawares, the gate itself stormed at the changing of the guard the next morning. After a half-hearted battle the Danes threw down their weapons. Kalmar Castle may still hold strong, but with the Gadfly fallen, the entrance to the Kalmar Strait is locked. When the tradesmen's coins start to dry up and their growling stomachs echo in empty store-chambers, perhaps the residents of Kalmar will listen better when Nils requests that they open the city cates. He lingers for another moment at the side of the bed, giving himself time to commit her beauty to memory. She reminds him of Mara. He feels no bad conscience at the thought, merely all the love that he bears within, in a separate chamber. Had she been here he would sooner choose her, but what else can a man do when his wife is so far away? He shuts the door behind him when he leaves, pausing for a moment to hear the girl immediately leap to her feet, with no time to lose to win back what decency she has lost.

In the light of day the Gadfly disappoints him. How stately the edifice was for an intruder by night, how tall the palisades, impregnable and menacing. Now he can't believe it's the same place. Like a snowdrift melted under scant winter sun. The keep itself squat and pinched, scarce more than a stone barn for its wretched household to rub elbows in, the palisade around it but sharpened sticks, poorly woven. The triumph he just felt melts away, leaving him dejected. From the petty gate that his forces breached the day before he hears a din. The sentry he posted has tried to reach out in his befuddlement for an approaching horse's reins, while the horseman hisses at him to get out of the way. Nils knows that voice, knows whose bald head is capable of glinting so brightly, even in a murky dawn such as this.

"Stand down. This one I've known a long time."

The horseman gives the sentry a venomous look and dismounts.

"Brother Nils."

"Brother Bo."

Sir Bo takes his younger brother by the shoulder, then leads him away and lowers his voice.

"Far have I ridden for your sake, and I've a raw backside and sore balls for the trouble. Even farther must I go before the day's out. I come with tidings that you must hear, for it looks as though this is going to be an eventful winter for us. You always have been a prying fiend, but for once do me a favor and keep your mouth shut till I've said my piece."

Nils nods, speechless at his brother's tone of voice.

"Brother Bengt has turned on Engelbrekt, heaved all the earth back into the canal he promised to dig, and sunk one of the Hansa's cogs while it was full of Norberg iron. Eric Puck seized his chance to attack Castle Cut. Bengt got wind of his intent and escaped in time. Stina stayed to defend the castle. Now it's burned down, and Puck's doing all he can to craft those ash piles into a victory."

Sir Bo halts Nils with a raised finger before he can shape his lips around his first question. He waits for Nils to compose himself before going on.

"Until recently Engelbrekt wanted for nothing more than silver. Now he's rich, with Stockholm in his hand. But that wasn't enough. God knows how he does it. From Arboga to Stockholm, and now on to Kalmar. Now he's on his way here to you. It's like a fever in his blood; scarce does he win one city before he's on to the next. No one knows why he's in such haste. And war, in midwinter? It's hard to know whether he's a fop or he knows something the rest of us don't. He seems to take his rest while besieging castles and outwitting

Danes at the bargaining table. I'm finding it all the harder to blame those who believe him a saint."

Bo scratches his beard and loosens his collar, having talked himself warm.

"I came to warn you. With Bengt's betrayal our loyalty's been called into question, Nils. I've made my choice, I'm staying with Engelbrekt. You'll likely have to make yours, and soon. I'm heading to Castle Beck on his behalf, to sow enough seeds of rebellion so that he can come and reap them. Engelbrekt will be here soon. I'm in haste; I can't stay. If you have any questions, ask them now."

Nils chooses among the many. That Stockholm has fallen without him is hardly good news; victory there makes Kalmar less of the essence. Småland province loses its value, and with it his own commandership. Bo's ride south with Engelbrekt vexes him, too. Nils and Nils alone is best placed to pave Engelbrekt's way to Castle Beck, and if anyone is to shove him aside, then he'd sooner have it not be his own flesh and blood. With some effort he pushes the future to one side in favor of the past.

"Bengt. Why?"

Bo shrugs.

"Who knows? God knows our house has known madness before. Father. Grandfather. We've got more lunatics than the right-minded, if you'll believe what some people say."

Bo is lying. Nils knows his brother, knows to tell truth from lie in his face and his bearing. His eyes are turned away to hide knowledge, his body restless. Much can be said of Bengt, and though buffoon he can be, he's no fool, and nor is he as ambitious as his brothers. Less of an adventurer. Bo knows something that he doesn't wish to divulge.

"Nils, one more thing. Is Magnus with you?"

Magnus. That was the name he was looking for.

"I haven't seen him since King Eric's visit. Isn't he still with Engelbrekt?"

Bo shakes his head, sucking his teeth in impotence.

"That's bad. I suspect Engelbrekt had looked forward to finding him here. Engelbrekt gave Magnus leave to go home for Christmas, but now he's searching for him high and low, for if that devil Puck finds him first, then it won't end well. He hasn't been seen at Castle Cut or Cuckoo's Roost. I had fancied he might have gone to your wife in Nyköping, so we went there first. I wasn't wrong, but on Epiphany he'd ridden on. Where he is now is anyone's guess. I thought Mara might have written to you. Told you where he'd gone next."

Nils shakes his head, showing a troubled husband's face.

"I've had no letters."

Nils hides his satisfaction at his brother's anxious face and fumbling words, seeing through him just as well now as ever he did before. No doubt Bo promised Engelbrekt he'd find Magnus here, in the south with his uncle, to curry favor.

※

Nils bids his brother farewell, then stops abruptly at the Gadfly's palisade. There's an anthill in his belly. But the tickles aren't all bad: Few know as well as Nils does that change is the mother of possibility. Bengt has left a void at Engelbrekt's side, one that must be filled by others. Why not him? It's simply a matter of finding the straightest course there. The first steps he can already see, and he feels all doubt start to bend to his resolve: He gathers his men, drowsy and heavy-headed, and sets them to cleaning up after the night before. The Gadfly is to be readied for eminent guests.

From the roof of the fort a scout cries out that an army is on its way, and by the time Engelbrekt reaches the Gadfly, Nils is ready outside, his men clean and straightened up and bearing spotless shields. He sees that this is an army of another kind entirely, and at the sight of it he is scarce surprised by Engelbrekt's speed. What stands before him is a peasant army no more, but one of the nobility, all mounted on horseback and bearing painted shields. Every warrior once promised to King Eric's southern wars in exchange for tax relief, now mustered to strip him of his throne. Nils knows many of them by name, and they are young, hot-blooded, and ambitious: Herman Beerman with his arm in a sling, Broder Svensson, Arvid Swan. Each man fully aware that every castle henceforth taken must be allotted a new bailiff from within their ranks.

Nils steps forward and bends his knee before the commander, bowing his head. At long last the people have awoken and gathered to watch, and Nils almost thinks he glimpses her there, too, the girl with the plaits, a mocking smile on her face at he who now bows so beautifully before another as not long ago he bowed over her, as humble today as he was proud and virile the night before. Her gaze burns on his cheeks, until he sees that he is mistaken: the girl is another, with similar features. Suddenly the feeling is gone, and he has more important matters at hand. He rises, taking Engelbrekt by the arm.

"A letter came from my wife to Balk Hill. She wrote of Magnus's departure. I'm sure he's headed for friends and kin whose names and estates I know well. In Castle Beck and Varberg. I'll go with you and help you to find him, if you wish."

M ARCH. WINTER STILL holds strong. Magnus peers out through the wind that bears a promise of spring, catches a lock of his long hair, and strokes it behind his ear. With the breeze comes a foul smell, one that he and Finn have known all too well ever since the snowdrifts started to melt, likewise the horse that recoils beneath him: flesh that has lain frozen for months, now gone to rot in the light of day. Along the Småland coast the smell has hung heavy, for on his journey home from Stockholm King Eric decided that the devastation he had wreaked in his foray north wasn't recompense enough for all the indignities that he had had to suffer. On their way back to Copenhagen his soldiers came ashore once again to slay and burn, christening the new-won peace with blood. It has been a harsh winter, and the ground has lain hard: Only now can men venture onto the estates of their neighbors who had uninvited guests over Christmas, and whose properties have stood ever since but as sooty stacks amidst fallow meadows. Only now can they gather the bodies and bury them deep enough to put them out of reach of foxes' paws. Along the roads roam the living dead, those whose lives were laid to waste and whose minds cracked under the burden of all that was taken from them, who survived the winter in caverns and spruce huts, spending many a long night in cold forests with frozen corpses all around. Everyone shuns them, for madness catches like any other pestilence, and just how they have kept the hunger at bay in their frigid hovels no one wishes to know. Some are harmless; they wander idly, asking after a mother, a daughter, a son, or a sister, one who wouldn't recognize them now, even if they stood face-to-face. More often than not they shy away, glimpsed only from afar, hastening away from the road to cower wherever they can in terror, aware of all the evil that man can do to his neighbor. One who doesn't bolt takes Magnus for an angel, come to reunite her with her kin in the fields of paradise. They leave her with only disappointment to dry the tears she shed in gratitude. Others have renounced whatever humanity they once possessed and made themselves as much like their oppressors as they are able; weaving themselves crowns of twigs, they play lord over their weaker companions, enacting raids in all their wretchedness. Bared teeth, knives in hand. Finn must draw his sword and cry out to scare them into flight.

Easily done. They have taken risks before and been burned. Only the resistance of the defenseless entices them now.

South goes their way. At the Gadfly they find no one, just a scant garrison of wounded men, or those wearied by the march there. Outside the nearby town a battlefield awaits, empty and barren. Bodies still lie out as fertilizer for the soils, along with broken weapons and sundry belongings. The plunderers slope back and forth with their necks bent down at the ground, too blinded by the promise of riches to see Magnus and Finn riding past. In the city they speak of nothing else. The battle was small and quickly won, fought by peasants in the pay of the free tradesmen, who for the sake of commerce saw benefits to remaining Danish but were quickly overcome when they attempted to hold a bridge. When the knights came riding in to cut down those in flight, Engelbrekt turned his horse and stilled his men's thirst for blood, demanding mercy for all those who had laid down their weapons. It was in witness to his compassion rather than his violence that the city yielded willingly, one merchant after another renouncing their loyalty to the king. The commander and his men rode off as soon as peace was assured under Swedish rule. Where? To where the sun goes down.

Finn and Magnus follow in their tracks, now heading west, stopping wherever they find people and asking whether they have seen Engelbrekt and his men. Yays and nays by turns. The army's advance is visible all around, leaving all in its wake in a state of change, but most are too taken up with matters of their own to have heeded where the army set out for next. The old borders with Denmark, wiped out. Blekinge province now Swedish. Scania, too, had lain beyond Sweden's frontiers, but wherever Engelbrekt sets foot, King Eric loses his crown. The people of Scania joined his army in their hundreds, to march with Engelbrekt on Castle Beck's walls. Even down in the far south they now answer to him as commander. Magnus and Finn pass a great mound thrown up over all the Danes who opposed Engelbrekt's might only to fall to Swedish lances, the soil so shallow and loose that limbs protrude beyond the crust of ground frost and the fallen snow. Soon they reach all the way to Helsingborg on the west coast, where the bailiff still sits ensconced in his castle, the city around him already won.

Halmstad they find in disarray. The streets are full of revelers, the church doors cast open and its people tottering around as though drunk, though there are no barrels to be seen. They call out Engelbrekt's name, their hands raised to the sky in gratitude and exaltation. Men stand on snowdrifts at every street corner, waving burning sticks and speaking of what their own eyes bore witness to but a week before, and around them all stand crowds with eyes glinting, so warmed by their words that they seem to feel no cold. They tell of how the city magistrate himself stood on the battlements to deny Engelbrekt entry, and scarce had he turned to walk away when both of his legs were snapped with sharp cracks, sending him tumbling all the way to the ground, smitten by God himself. From his remains the fallen man cried out that the Lord on High had punished him for his pride, that the words he spoke must be forgotten, that the city gates must be opened wide and the people welcome their savior with open arms. Only too late had the sinner seen the light: for three days the magistrate languished in his bed, before his life was snatched away. Now all the people are enrapt. A saint has walked among them, to show them that Heaven exists.

Finn and Magnus rarely mention his name. It weighs heavily enough on them both as it is. But Finn can't help but wonder which of Engelbrekt's newly converted instigators pushed his own magistrate off the battlements and dragged him out into the square to cries of astonishment: See the Lord's miracle! Mysterious are His ways!

In the weeks that have passed, Finn has seen Magnus grow all the quieter. The winter weeks with Margaret, snowed in at her manor, were better. Both pained by similar absences, they found support in the knowledge that neither of them was alone, bearing out each other's feelings. That is more than Finn can do now, and Magnus has no wish to eat or rest. Cold and pale, he mounts his horse with his mantle wrapped around him, his hollow gaze fixed on the farthest point of road. By nights he will toss and turn, speaking to the one he sees in his dreams. Often incomprehensible. Sometimes not.

For a while they stop to listen to the gospel according to Engelbrekt. Finn dismounts, handing Magnus his reins.

"Wait here. I'll go into the taphouse, to find someone to ask where the army is headed."

Under the beams inside, the place is all but empty, drink passed over in favor of an ecstasy of another kind. The keeper gives Finn a suspicious look without a word of greeting.

"Did you see when Engelbrekt left the city? Do you know which way he was going next?"

The keeper looks him up and down with the practiced eye of someone who is used to treating guests in accordance with their purse.

"I keep my eyes open. What's it worth to you?"

"I'm one of Engelbrekt's men. Your reward lies in not causing me enough trouble to remember you by."

The keeper gives him one last look before he gives up, casts down his eyes, and raises his empty palms in submission.

"North, my lord. To Varberg."

Finn pulls on his gloves and mounts his horse beside Magnus, who hands him back his reins. His voice is hoarse, harried.

"Did you find out? Where did they go?"

For a moment Finn hesitates in his response, observing Magnus as he now is: thin and pale, black shadows under his eyes. But also alive, and safe, and protected from Eric Puck. He remembers the promise he gave another and points the way.

"East, toward Hylte."

HARALD ESBJÖRNSSON STARES up ahead. Soot, a dark blotch amidst all the white, with Engelbrekt above him, hunched in his saddle. Powerless against the driving snow and biting winds, Harald tries to light fires within, draw warmth from the memories of hearths gone by. Little does it help; the cold pierces all too deep into his person. At first he was shaking on his horse, arms and legs atremble, teeth chattering in his mouth. But with time the shivers faded and stilled, as though he were numbed through his very flesh. That seemed worse to him, like a premonition of death's stillness. In the evenings, when even Engelbrekt's energy ebbs and they must find themselves lodgings for the night, it takes him a long time to feel the warmth again. Though he sleeps in a fur, he is still cold by morning, when they mount their horses, set off for their next goal, and start the whole thing again. The air is so cold that it must be sifted in slowly through clenched teeth with every breath, yet it stings in his chest even so.

He knows that for Engelbrekt it is all the worse. Every day it is as though his body is all the more difficult to thaw, sluggish and immobile, his knees and arms loath to bend. When they set off early this morning the reins slipped straight out of Engelbrekt's hands, his fingers incapable of forming a grip, and Harald had had to bind the leather around his wrists so that he could steer his own horse. He knows that Engelbrekt has made journeys of this kind before, in his youth, through distant lands in the south that were ravaged by war, where his very life was at risk. But it's a bad thing to travel by winter. Engelbrekt knows better. He isn't even following his own counsel.

Harald wanted to say as much this morning, as he was softening the reins' stiff leather so that they would knot. They're lying, these sons of Sten. They don't know where Magnus is. At each new city they claim to have kin who would happily have housed their nephew for the winter, but never do they put eyes on any such men, much less the lad himself. Still, the hope so recently dashed is soon lit anew, through tidings from unseen messengers about dwellings in other cities. And so the song has gone, from the Gadfly to Castle Beck, Castle Beck to Varberg. One siege to the next. One by one the cities have fallen, for Engelbrekt's name is like a spell over the people, who flock to him in such numbers that no one can resist. Around Engelbrekt himself swarm the nobility, young as well as old, each one dissatisfied with their own lot and seeing gains to be made before them, their hunger for land and power insatiable. The sons of Sten always at the head of their ranks. With Magnus's name as their watchword they have kept Engelbrekt close and won favor over others, placing themselves at the forefront whenever it comes time to dole out the fiefs. They know that Magnus's name and a residence is all they need to steer the army's movements to their choosing. And Eric Puck's name, too, which they turn to their advantage, aware of the threat that he poses. They seem to always have news of his progress, keen to warn of the perils of letting him get to their next stop first.

Yet again Harald wants to ride abreast of the black stallion and speak of what he sees so clearly yet appears to have passed his master by, he who always used to sense things more keenly than the rest. *You're being lied to. You're being used.* But whenever Harald takes his reins to urge his horse up ahead, he changes his mind. Such is not his place. Besides, he doesn't want to be the one to strip Engelbrekt of his hope, the only thing that now keeps him on his feet.

IN HYLTE THEY find men who had wandered south to join Engelbrekt's troops in midwinter and now returned from Halmstad having completed their service, not without an assurance that the forces would be heading north from there, to Varberg, to wrest Axel Tott from his bailiff's seat. Magnus immediately turns his horse, and Finn can do no more but follow in his tracks. Relief cools the scalding sting of his failure, for the lies have consumed him, their good purpose all the harder to call to mind the weaker that Magnus has become. Now Magnus spurs his horse on, driving it hard along the northwesterly road, unmoved by the wind that sweeps the mantle from his shoulders and blows his hair back. For a long time he rides toward the setting sun, through a light flurry of snowflakes with Finn on his tail, until the night brings a sky that is clear and black and strews the stars upon them, enough to light sparks in the snowflakes on the ground and illuminate the way before them. Far off in the north a green flame coils high above the earth. In superstition Finn turns away and spits over his shoulder. Rarely has he seen it, but each time he has been told never to look straight up at the fire that billows in such strange colors, for then it can see you, and if it finds you to its liking it will lift you up into the darkness, to dance on black peaks until your marrow freezes to ice.

When the road reaches the crown of a hill, both stop their horses. Along the ditches that have been dug to keep the road dry lurk shadows in rows, peculiar adornments lining the approach to the city, greeting its guests. Only when they come closer do they see what they are. A wall runs alongside the road, and over it people have been hanged, like clothes put out to dry or meat to be tendered. Time and the cold have wrenched them into singular shapes, but when Magnus and Finn step closer they see that it is something else, too: their limbs have been broken by wheels or stakes. Winter has spared them until now, frosted every face with a dusting like that of crushed gems, smoothing out their agonized countenances to make them beautiful again. By force of habit Finn makes the sign of the cross before a man and woman who are hanged beside each other. He wonders whether what he sees is the work of chance in two stiffening bodies from whom the soul has fled, or whether they were still alive when they were placed there and reached out to each other in solace. Whether they were man and wife. Brother and sister.

"What's happened here?"

Magnus sweeps his mantle tighter around his waist and stifles a shudder.

"I don't know."

They go on, slowly and silently, as though in devotion. The ghostly dead in rows around them, all cast in silver under the light of the stars, as though death had just come to them, though they must have been there for weeks. Magnus bows his head, and Finn follows suit.

※

In Varberg, Engelbrekt's men have found shelter where they can: in inns and dormitories; in houses seized from the free tradesmen who stayed loyal to the bailiff; in chambers freed up by the common folk who welcome them. Around the castle, guards are keeping watch day and night, but Magnus and Finn must ask more than one of them before they are pointed toward the house in which their leader is to be found.

Finn is the first to climb the steps and pound on the door, then explain their purpose. A woman takes in the state of them with a mother's groans, then stacks the fire with wood and sits them down beside it, puts on drinks to heat up, and bustles away to wake the master of the house, returning with bread and cold meats. Heavy steps on the stairs, an uneven, slumberous gait. A poorly stifled gasp, a bare crown glinting in the light of the hearth.

"What?"

Sir Bo rubs his eyes, wearing only his shirt. He blinks at them drowsily.

"Magnus? Magnus, is that you?"

Bo hastens closer and takes his nephew by the shoulders, as if to confirm what his eyes say is true. Once certain, he lets go just as fast, then steps back with furrowed brows.

"Where have you been?"

"With Mara for winter, near the convent at Nyköping."

Bo nods feebly to himself.

"Then I guessed right. That was my first thought, when I learned that you hadn't been with your father at Cuckoo's Roost or in Castle Cut with your mother. But when we got there you were already gone. And since?"

"I've been tracking the army, with no luck. The whole kingdom's in disarray, and no one's been able to tell us where to go."

Bo rubs his flushed and puffy face. Somewhere inside him he had hoped that all of Nils's bright promises of where Magnus might be were wishful thinking, rather than the brazen lie that now stands revealed.

"Uncle, the dead outside the city. Who are they? What happened?"

Bo rubs his bony shoulders and steps toward the hearth for its warmth. He spits into the fire.

"Axel Tott. When Engelbrekt took the city last year the bailiff was allowed to stay in his castle, on condition that he leave the county and its people in peace. King Eric restored Tott's authority to him, and he wasted no time in seeking retribution from all the people whose betrayal he had suffered. So. It's countryfolk. With us in place their kin can put them to consecrated earth where they belong, now that the thaw allows. Soon enough the hunger will drive Tott from his den, and when that day comes we'll have something else to hang from the walls."

"Where's Engelbrekt?"

Bo gives him a long look, then shakes his head, turning back to the flames.

"Not here."

For more than a month Bo has watched Engelbrekt ride from city to city at full gallop, and scarce has its loyalty been sworn to him before he's mounting his horse anew. Six hundred miles by horse in winter, and all the worse for it. He sighs.

"I don't know where he is. North, now that our southern border is secured, or perhaps back east, to fortify the cities that have already fallen. But I know where you should be, Magnus. Have you heard from your mother?"

"No."

"Listen to me now, Magnus. Your mother defended Castle Cut alone when Eric Puck rode on it with forces far greater, just as winter was at its coldest. If there's anyone in breeches who would have fared better than she did in a skirt, then I've yet to meet him. She's back at Cuckoo's Roost now. Make haste and go to her, Magnus. Now you've seen the world. Isn't that what you were so keen to show us, that

Midsummer? It's what Nils said, anyway, that devil, when he was bending us all to his will. The adventure must end here. It's high time you went home again. A better horse shall you have, and plenty to eat, and my own sheepskins around your shoulders to stop you from freezing any more. Ride to Cuckoo's Roost. Everyone's searching for everyone, like a dog chasing its tail. Wait there, where you'll be more easily found should anyone come looking."

IN FIELDS AND along the roadsides the flowers bloom. Amidst the browned grasses of last year, still flattened from the melted snowdrifts, the coltsfoot open up their yellow cups in celebration at the end of yet another winter. Bishop Knut lies bedridden, as he has done ever since his return from Arboga. In daydreams and by night he is haunted by the memory of that assembly: Engelbrekt so calm, his righteousness borne like a halo. The Council of the Realm's great lords around him, growing increasingly more reckless by the hour, in their efforts to shroud their own interests in a regard for the realm. Faces like theirs he has had around him for all of his long life, and when his weariness was at its most biting he thought he could see them on the edges of the circle: His brother, Sten. Their father, Bo. The Gryphon himself, that old monster. The whites of his eyes rolling, the red cheeks. And the people around them all, silent for the most part, but the weight of their eyes spoke loudly enough. Like a flock of wolves driven from the depths of the forest by hunger, merely waiting out the first sign of weakness to pounce. Before their ears the tone of the assembly was another, the questions posed differently, the rules of the game rewritten. Beneath the robes of Knut's office the sweat dripped uneasily, for on him and no one else did it fall to keep the peace.

But most of all it's the cold that he remembers. Never has he been so cold. Hour in, hour out, at an assembly on frozen ground, for six days in midwinter. Little did the bearskin that he wore above his vestment help, nor the cloth below his mitre. It was as though the cold spread from within, usurping his lean, old body, knocking his knees together and depriving him of all feeling in his fingers. The deliberations went on long into the night, under the distant sun at first and the cold stars thereafter, and no one dared retire early, for fear of what decisions might be made at his expense. Then a brief rest, too brief for the bed's blankets to warm him, and then the next day the same, and the next.

Now it's the reverse. No matter what he does, Bishop Knut can't cool himself. The shivering fits have him in their grip. He shakes in his heat, like an eggshell rattling against the iron base of a boiling cauldron. He has no appetite, sips steadily at his broth of meat and weak soups. One morning he finds a priest on a chair by his bed and wonders why it all feels so familiar. Suddenly he knows: that's where he used to sit when he was young and healthy, beside the dying at their demise, to cast a few drops of oil over a wrinkled wrist. He knows that he is not long of this world. He tries to speak, but his voice fails him and his lips won't let themselves be shaped. The priest leans in closer, and Knut whispers as best he can.

"Summon my nephews."

Darkness and light do their dance, until he is woken by company. For many years his vision has been clouded, but he perceives them around him nevertheless. Bo and Bengt, the chiefs of the brood. Knut, his namesake, blinder than he. Nils, Devil take him for his restless blood. Magnus and Eric, the twins, their mother's hulking death blows. And so they are, the kin who will survive him. His brother's progeny. Knut fumbles for a cup into which to spit, clears his throat until he dares to try his tongue, and finds that his voice carries.

"A long life I have lived. Longer than most. The Gryphon and my father settled my destiny. No one asked me what I wanted for myself. My brother, Sten, was bound for knighthood, for the Council of the Realm, and little Knut for bishophood. Powers earthly and spiritual united by blood, for the benefit of blue and gold. Sten was given a wooden sword and a Gotland pony before he could walk; I had my nose shoved into a book and was forced to read Latin. They sent me to Prague, bought me all the votes raised in my favor, much to my disadvantage. I've seen well enough how you all look at me, nephews, and when I look back over the course of my own life I see the same thing: a monster's progress, rapacious and ruthless. Such is how I was raised. I've seen others who are far worse. Whether I should count that as success or failure I'm unsure."

He reaches for the crucifix on its gold chain around his neck and strokes the savior's sorrowful face with his thumb.

"God should have been of some comfort to me, since I was forced into the frock. But never have I caught glimpse of him. And now, in the twilight of my life, I find Hell so easy to see before me, but Heaven so immeasurably hard. Down below I'll sit in a cauldron over a silent hearth, boiled alive, and around me will stand my father and the Gryphon, and Queen Margaret and King Eric, and they'll pierce my flesh with sharp pokers to see if I'm tender yet, only to always shake their heads and tell me I'm not good enough."

He pauses briefly to catch his breath.

"Saint Birgitta saw the Lord often enough, the Mother of God even more. Birgitta's blood flows through our veins. Never did I meet her myself, but for my whole life I've been surrounded by those who held her in high regard, and many who were in her close acquaintance. In private they might whisper about how sick her visions made her, their arrival announced by furious headaches, as though her head were about to burst, ones that forced her to her knees not in reverence but to spew. Afterward she would have to lie for a long time in a dim chamber with a cool cloth upon her forehead, and only later could she speak of all that she had seen, of angels and devils and the pearly gates themselves, and the Virgin Mary waiting on the other side. Ingegerd's outbreaks at Vadstena Abbey were of a similar ilk, once she was made abbess in the footsteps of her grandmother. Once I sat with her of a night. We had both quaffed our fill, she so much so that she dozed off. Knowing where she kept the key to Birgitta's reliquary, I took it and went down to the church, then unlocked the case and gazed at the holy bones within. I raised her skull in my hand, brittle and light, the same skull without which none of the walls or tower around it would have been raised, no abbey founded to which monks or sisters would have flocked, with rich relatives to bestow upon it property and lands. No pilgrims taking to the roads by their hundreds, to bolster their faith and offer up their alms. I carried a torch with me, and I shone it inside the hole where her neck had been, and inside the hollow of her skull I saw something strange: a dark stain on its inner wall, vile and rough where elsewhere it was smooth. I stuck my finger inside the saint's skull to scrape it with my nail, and it was like there was a large pit there, as though some rot had eaten straight into the bone until it was as fine as an eggshell. I thought it was an illness of some kind, some caustic tumor that had fattened itself therein, big enough to dispel her reason, causing pain and madness. And I thought: Is this her true face, Saint Birgitta's Holy Virgin? I wonder if we would find the same thing if we were to open Ingegerd's grave and peer inside her skull. One a saint, the other interred where few go to be remembered. One perhaps no madder than the other. The curse she left over us perhaps no more real than the Lord Himself."

None of his nephews respond, and Knut reaches for his eyeglasses, the ones he had made after the others he lost in Vadstena for Engelbrekt's sake. Now he sees the room clearly, and where before there had stood several there now stand none. Alone in an empty chamber, unheard. His right hand slippery with oil. A sigh comes over his lips, a shrill groan, when a grip within him tightens and then lets go. Late comes death to the last in his line.

Sir Bengt rides alone from Cuckoo's Roost to Örebro. Sixteen miles is the journey. Not much for the horse that bears him, but all the greater for him. Now that it's April the nights are without frost, and when the ground softened it left the King's Road waterlogged and boggy. One by one he passes the villages that he knows well, the timber houses that stand along the road and their churches behind, their steeples raised to shame, too poor for stone spires. The sun hides bashfully behind scattered clouds, the air heavy and wet around Lake Hjälmaren, with cold gusts blowing off its mirrored surface where there are no trees to offer lee. He is unmoved. He lets the horse walk at the speed of its choosing, unable to bring himself to hasten its progress. Soon enough he sees the city. Örebro is known for its annual iron market, but none took place this year, for the northmen have held on to their iron for as long as Stockholm has been in the king's hands. Instead they had their ingots stacked high in mounds, in wait of the waterway that Bengt himself was tasked with opening, the one that is now refilled. With Stockholm taken and Lake Mälaren now free of ice, the port is bustling with northmen and boatmen, all eager to make the most of what they have missed out on these two lost years. The city is small, but it's clear that the Germans were the ones holding the chalk when its quarters were drawn: The market square in the center, with its town hall and church. The age-old bridge across the river, leading to the islet on which the castle stands. Bengt steers his horse straight, with a disinterest that sends everyone darting out of his way. Many stop in their tracks, wonder who this knight could be who is come without retinue and what his arrival might bode. He rides across the bridge to the castle and gives his name and business to the man who awaits.

"I know you're who you say you are, for this isn't the first time we've met."

Harald Esbjörnsson takes the horse's bridle with one hand while Sir Bengt dismounts, at a loss for a response.

"I see that you're here alone, and no doubt it's Engelbrekt you seek. But your name's no longer considered that of a friend between these ramparts, and if I let you anywhere near him with a blade or point within reach, then I'd forfeit what trust I've been given."

"I come with neither sword nor dagger."

For a while they stand looking at each other, each gauging the other's will, until Bengt casts his mantle over his shoulder and does a turn to reveal his empty belt. Harald nods in approval.

"I see you speak the truth, though many would say it's unwise to set out on the roads unarmed in these wicked times."

He raises two fingers to his lips and whistles for a hand, then hands him the horse's reins.

"Follow me and wait in the hall. There you'll find people who'll bring you whatever you ask for. Food, water, wine, or beer."

Harald takes his leave of Sir Bengt, walks up the stairs, finds the right door, and knocks cautiously before stepping inside.

"A man's here to see you. It's Sir Bengt Stensson, come from Cuckoo's Roost."

"Help me to a chair."

⁂

The light in the chamber is dim when Sir Bengt is eventually shown in. Engelbrekt is standing in wait by a table, a jug of wine and one mug before him, his hand resting on the back of the chair for support. It has been one and a half years since last they shared a room, in Vadstena's town hall. To Bengt the shadow on the other side of the table appears thinner, though wrapped in thick clothes. The silence grows great between them, Bengt unsure as to how to begin. Engelbrekt himself precedes him, clears his throat, and coughs, hoarse of voice.

"You should know that Eric Puck didn't ride on Castle Cut at my bidding. He was the first to be reached by the news, and he set out of his own accord, compelled by the grudge that he has long harbored against you and yours. I had no knowledge of it until it was already too late. Had it been up to me, I would have acted differently."

Sir Bengt scarce hears him. He licks his lips. White of face he stands, like an apparition, and of the speech that he has been preparing for days and silently rehearsing on the ride here he can't recall a single word. He reaches for the wine and pours it with a shaking hand, then drinks, finding courage therein as so many times before, courage and voice.

"I'm not here to speak of burned ships and filled ditches, of Eric Puck or the ashes of Castle Cut. I'm prepared to shoulder my share of the blame and grant you whatever redress you feel you deserve, give my testimony under oath, and let the Council judge for us, decide what's fair or not. Nor have I come to discuss what has or has not happened. I've come to air a rumor. It concerns you and my son."

The mug is dry in his hand. Was it ever full? Never full enough.

"It is said that you're closer than two men should be."

He fills it anew.

"Your house hasn't been long of the nobility. We who paint our shields in blue and gold have been lords longer than anyone can recall. The Kings over the Headland, that's what we used to be called, before this was a kingdom under any other name. We have land, we have wealth, and we have respect. We laid the groundwork of the church and we raised its spires, and in return we are laid to rest under its stone slabs, to listen to the requiems that will remember our names for centuries to come. Such houses are built by generation upon generation, the new taking up where the old left off."

Bengt drinks again.

"It's strange, how it has gone. Eight brothers and two sisters were we, after Mother and Father. Had each of us bred as they did, our house would have filled the entire kingdom. But few babes were born, and those who made it to birth died young. Bo has one son, but the lad's still a reed in the wind, he hasn't survived childhood, where the slightest fever can be a death blow. Of all the dreams that our father harbored and all of our own hopes there is only Magnus left."

Yet another mug. The jug half-empty.

"My wife and I had a daughter first. For a long time we thought Britta would be our only progeny, for however we carried on, no more children came. We had almost given up. Then, after six long years, a seed took root, and Magnus came to us like a gift from Heaven. A more beautiful boy the world has never seen, one with his own will and a good head on his shoulders. I remember taking him in my arms for the first time, how I held him close and stroked the birth blood from his cheek. He opened his eyes then, bright and blue, and looked right at me as though he knew straightaway that I was his father and he my son and that that was good, and it was as though my heart was about to burst in gratitude. He was a beacon in our lives. The love we felt for him was even abundant enough to spill over onto each other, we who had long walked separate paths. To see him grow was an honor. While other sons were sent away to be hardened, Stina kept him with us, and I couldn't blame her, for without Magnus we would go back to being what we had been before, cold and gray, half-people plodding toward our fates. Far too long did we keep him in the cage we garnished as best we could, but in the end we couldn't stop him from taking flight."

Another one, in deep glugs.

"I'm not asking you to feel any tenderness toward me or my house. Little if anything separates us from those you have chosen for your enemies. We could easily have stood on opposing sides from the very start. I come for Magnus's sake."

He takes a quivering breath, then composes himself before going on.

"If the rumor spreads, it'll ruin Magnus. People talk. His reputation will be tarnished. Soon he'll be shunned by all. I remind you: I'm not here to rake through what has or has not happened. I don't want to know a thing. I stand here for the sake of just a rumor. But rumor is enough. By the mere fact of your closeness you stole my son's future and the life that awaits him. Your doings must come to an end. You must make that clear to Magnus, and you must do so in a way that leaves him in no doubt that such is your true wish. Only in doing so can you save him. If you harbor any love toward Magnus, as I do, then it is to this end that it must be used."

Then he is silent. He sways on unsteady legs, grabs the edge of the table for support and lowers himself onto a bench beside the table. Relieved at having said his piece, he is drained of all strength. He reaches out over the table for more, fills his mug past the brim, drains it, and fills it again.

"Such a treasure I was entrusted with. How poorly I have cared for it. Unworthy of my fatherhood I sit here today. I listened to others where I should have known better. A trap was laid for me around tempting bait, and I reached for it without thinking, and then it was too late. Greed killed my grandfather, and it led my father to his grave. Yet I learned nothing from their example. I'm just as greedy, and as simple-minded, too, and here I am today. I should never have sent Magnus away, never fallen in with my brothers. At Cuckoo's Roost we were happy enough. I wish for nothing more than to get back what I once had, to undo the two years that have passed."

Bengt drains the mug, and when he tries to place it straight down on the table he topples it clumsily on its side, whereupon he leaves it lying in the puddle rather than risk any greater damage. He pinches the bridge of his nose tightly, stifling the sound that rises from his throat, then stands up heavily and staggers toward the door, his task complete.

Harald passes him in the doorway and takes his place in the room, before hastening to Engelbrekt's side to take his arm, scared by what he sees. Engelbrekt stands still, his face in shadow, his voice scarce more than a whisper.

"The hour is late. Sir Bengt shouldn't mount his horse in the state he's in. Show him to a bed and let him sleep, give him everything he desires."

Stina shuns the bed in which she lay for so long, fearing that she will find herself unable to rise from it again. By night she instead takes to the window openings, shooing away those who come in the evenings to put up the window boards. She sees the stars light up in the order life conforms to: The strongest first, the weakest last and quick to die out, fleeting torches in all the black, leaving their more able siblings to greet the blush of dawn. First at twilight, last at dawn. She prefers to sleep while seated, where the weariness can overcome her, steal upon her unannounced. In her torpor a flurry of uneasy dreams. The dead outside Castle Cut, ice statues in the whirling snow. One by one she trudges through their ranks, each face gradually disentangling from all the white, until she sees Magnus among them, his beautiful features immortalized in frost. Her scream is loud enough to ring out through the waking world, and it rouses her, wrenching her lowered head from its resting place on her chest, her neck sore.

The sun rises to yet another day. Longer and longer they grow, for spring is here. Stina wishes for the reverse. She would sooner have them shorter, for they are filled with longing and wait, and in their wake comes the pain. She saw Sir Bengt riding off, asked him neither of his way nor his purpose. Britta is at her side, always helpful. A good daughter, closer now than before. Yet she is still the less loved. How easy would it have been were Stina's children able to change chambers in her heart? Britta the apple of her eye, home and safe, her brother the one whom Stina could more easily go without, astray somewhere in these unsafe lands whose borders change from one month to the next. But the choice was never Stina's, and the world bows not to her will. She could just as well wish that the moon shone like a sun, that the sun were the one put to wandering the night sky in its shifting guises. It is a torment, this, too, for her conscience weighs heavily, and the more time she forces herself to spend with Britta, the more unshakably the nature of things stands. And yet: they pray together, go from building to building, overseeing all the hundreds of tasks that fall to the lady of the house, from the barrels of pickled vegetables and cured meats in the storehouse to the files of bills. One day all of this will make Britta a good housewife, the day she finds a man to her pleasing.

And for Stina it passes the time in wait of Magnus. Rarely does she do anything in a place that doesn't afford an unbroken view of the muddy streak of road through the brown meadows and their dead grass, still flattened from the melted snow.

When it happens, she thinks that she is seeing things. Two horsemen on unknown steeds. She thinks she knows them, but blames wishful thinking till the very last, until she can hold out no longer and runs across the courtyard down to the road. The taste of blood in her mouth doesn't bother her, nor the pangs in her side. She runs to meet them, past the outbuildings and over the bridge, out into the field. The one at the fore dismounts when he is near her, and she wraps her arms around him. All the strength left in her she pours into that embrace. He feels thin and looks pale, harried by his journey, but he is home now, home for good. Under her care any harm shall be undone, until not even time itself will be able to tell then from now. She holds Magnus tightly, doesn't want to let go.

"My son. My beloved son."

The curse, voided. Abbess Ingegerd but a corpse. This love shall not end in blood.

Britta is up early. She wraps a blanket over her nightdress. Every day when she wakes up Magnus is already gone, and he doesn't return to Cuckoo's Roost until after everyone has retired to bed. Having been woken by a dream, she now makes the most of her waking. She climbs up to the roof of the castle keep, step by step, until she has only the sky for a ceiling. Suddenly she sees that she isn't alone.

"Hebbla?"

Hebbla Albrektsdaughter is still at Cuckoo's Roost. For more than a year she has been Sir Bengt's guest. A strange girl she is, but Britta finds her better company than her mother, and better than nothing.

"Hebbla, what are you doing here?"

Hebbla turns, stroking her long, red hair behind her ear. Dawn is nearing, a band of light pulled taut along the horizon.

"The same as you."

She turns back to the slit in the battlement wall that she has chosen for her lookout and gestures at the free space on its other side. Britta goes and stands beside her.

"Wait. He'll be coming soon."

A shadow down in the courtyard, beyond the outbuildings: Out of the stable walks Magnus, a slender figure in the dark. He leads his horse toward the bridge and across it, slowly, so that the hooves won't clap against the timber. On its other side he mounts, urges the horse into a trot, and then into a gallop. Through the meadow, toward the forest, and then he's gone.

"He rides before dawn every day. Not before midnight does he return."

"Why?"

"He's hoping for a message, I think. Rather than wait here, he rides as far as he can, in the hope of meeting it on its way. Then he rides home again."

Britta shakes her head with a frown.

"I don't understand him. He's been so different ever since he came home. Mother wants nothing more than to give him all the love she was forced to save for months, but he doesn't want it. How she suffered in her longing. Now the pain is even greater."

"You said it yourself; Magnus has changed. The one that Lady Kristina loves is the memory of the son he no longer is. No one knows that better than Magnus."

Britta draws a deep breath, taking a better look at Hebbla. A heedful guest, never any trouble, well-mannered and obliging whenever she sees her.

"You've been with us a long time, and we've been such poor hosts. You must be sick of Cuckoo's Roost by now. God knows I am. Mother in pieces, Father rarely home, and I haven't seen him sober in weeks. I'll speak to him on your behalf, ask him why it's been so hard to find you passage to Bergen."

Hebbla looks at her, her gaze empty.

"Arranging passage is no trouble at all. Sir Bengt wants to keep me here because my house is German and my father close to the king. You think me a guest, but I'm just as much a prisoner. A hostage to bargain with whenever the need so demands."

She loosens a plait, combing its locks straight with fingers through her hair.

"It's good to have a value. Even if that's all I have. You must know that as well as anyone."

The moon is a thin crescent in its calm course toward the earth, spilling its silvery light over the forest's trees, over the path that Magnus left empty behind him. Hebbla's gaze rests on it.

"Besides, I don't dare travel. I want to stay here. Don't you feel it? This place is like a string being pulled all the tighter. Something has to snap, and soon."

FINN HEADS FOR the lake, to be alone for a while. At Cuckoo's Roost, one day easily turns into the next, and soon they are difficult to count. He is home, and everything seems as it was before, and yet not. He is restless, Finn, without quite being able to say why. All that they have seen. All that they have done. Around them, out of sight beyond the lake, hills and forest, the kingdom is another now than the one they rode off into. His own crime both uncovered and forgotten, albeit never forgiven. Those thousand silver marks bought a castle, but to what avail? If there is atonement to be found, then he knows not where, however much he may search for it. Down by the jetty the boats bob amidst the scent of fresh tar, applied to keep them watertight for another year. He remembers bailing them, he and Magnus, when Nils Stensson appeared like a creature of legend, to haggle over life and death with fair words.

There is a spot on the shore where flat pebbles tend to wash up, known by every child around the castle. He chooses himself a handful and walks out to the end of the jetty. The lake lies calm, the afternoon neither hot nor cold. One by one he hooks his forefinger around the curve of the stones and spins them in a shallow course, so that they bounce up again off the surface of the water. Every landing forms a ring of small ripples, quick to expand, their patterns simple at first but soon joined in confusion. Another stone's flight crosses his own, and he counts the bounces before turning around. Seven, perhaps eight. A good throw. His first hope is that Magnus has given up with his futile rides, but on the shore stands Britta instead, and he casts his eyes down, as is befitting of a servant. Never has he been close to her. They were never children together, she always above him and a girl. With the years Ylva's betrayal hewed yet another cleft between them, a silence that came to pass that neither wanted to break.

"The most bounces wins?"

He nods sheepishly, throwing only once she has gestured at him to do so. Five. Her next. Nine. They go, again and again, until neither has any stones left and the last ripples run smooth. She replies before he need even pose the question.

"Magnus always had you, but Ylva left me on my own. I had no one. I often came down here to be by myself, and it would be some time before anyone asked after me. Few have skimmed stones as much as me."

She turns toward him.

"Now you're the one slinking off. You can feel it, too, can't you? Everything's wrong."

Finn nods.

"Yes."

"None of us are what we were before. Yet we all keep on pretending that the last two years haven't happened. Father's either away or drinking, of course, more than ever, and I'm sure that's a great help. Mother's worse than she ever was, bustling from task to task in fear that she might happen to stop and see what's right in front of her. Like a hare with hounds in pursuit, she's terrified that reality will catch up with her and tear her to shreds."

"And Magnus?"

"I don't know. In any case, he doesn't want to be here. It's as though he's waiting for something."

"And you, then?"

She laughs, mirthlessly, unused to being asked.

"When Mother and I staggered out of Castle Cut on the run from Puck's men, it was to a snowstorm. We could only see a few yards around us, at most. We stumbled upon the dead, the ones who had frozen in the water we'd poured over them and been taken by the frost. Mother turned just as powerless to move. Without thinking, I let go of her hand and stumbled on myself. Soon she was gone behind me, and it was as though I was in a white chamber, void of life. Alone in horror. I don't know for how long. A few instants, no more, though perhaps in our memories the moments are lengthened that bear a significance beyond their duration. Soon I heard horses neighing, sensing my presence. Puck's steeds. I took the reins of the one that looked to me the strongest and let the rest loose, saw them bolt off into the storm. I traced my footsteps back and got mother up in the saddle. That's how we escaped. But often I still find myself alone in that barren whiteness, in dream and in thought. I didn't see it then, but it was more than just fear. A glimpse of freedom, too."

She turns back to land, where the house stands on its mound, bright in the sinking sun.

"I'm marked by what happened to us, I like the rest. I'm sick of Cuckoo's Roost. Far too long have I stayed here. As soon as the roads have dried I'll harness up the horse that carried me from Castle Cut and ride him away from here. Perhaps my parents will take note of my absence more than they did my presence. It makes no difference to me. Perhaps I'll find myself a husband, keep a household, be a mother to children. As my mother was before me."

"Is that what you want?"

"Hope and destiny."

Feeling a dropped stone underfoot, Finn picks it up off the planks and offers it to Britta, who shakes her head. He casts it himself, half-heartedly, for its shape offers little promise of a good throw. Both trace its flight with their eyes. She is the first to say it, while pointing.

"Boats on the water. Coming from Örebro."

Finn shades his eyes with his hands to see better. Two long, narrow vessels are being rowed over the calm by a handful of men. He knows several of them by name.

"It's Engelbrekt's men. The ones in his closest circle."

"Fetch Magnus, Finn. I'll stay and ready the boats."

※

Harald Esbjörnsson splits more wood for the fire. It's already lit, bundles of bony snags snapped from the dead branches of trees, with larger branches on top. He splits the thick branches, shortening them to just the right length. An armful will suffice for a steady bed of flames, with heat enough to take on the bigger logs. He is careful, would sooner have everything too ordered than not enough, for even though Engelbrekt would never ask him, he knows that the heat relieves the joints that appear stiffer and sorer with every passing day. No one should ride so far in such cold as he did this winter. Harald has also warned him against this journey, even if it is being made by boat at a warmer time of year. Engelbrekt refused to listen. The Council are to meet in Stockholm, and Engelbrekt is the nave of the wheel that will now carry them all away from the Danes and King Eric's wavering scepter. Any absence or weakness on his part can only lead to failure. Without him the lords would be at each other's throats, eager to snatch up more of the spoils than they have been granted. Few say it aloud among heedful ears, but the question weighs heavily on them all: If Sweden is now freed from the Dane, who shall wear her crown? If not Engelbrekt, then who? Harald swings his axe through a sinewy bough. On their way from Örebro Engelbrekt had let them make a bed for him on his boat, then he wrapped a blanket around his waist and lay there pale and still, bundled up like an ancient chieftain on his final journey to pyre or mound. Harald hopes that he finds strength in his rest. Only Engelbrekt can secure the peace.

The point they rounded at dusk gave them sight of a sheltered bay, behind which lay a small meadow in the lee of budding broad-leaved trees. Sand welcomed the boats and Harald was quick to Engelbrekt's side, loath to let anyone else suspect the extent of his ailments. With an arm around his waist, he carried more than led him away from the shore, while the men stacked stones for a fire and beat sparks into shredded birch bark.

Harald rests, sitting down on a log to let the sweat dry before it wets his shirt. A glance at the water reveals an unexplained swell in the midst of the flat, and he follows its course until he sees the boat. Two pairs of men at the oars, and a few others who aren't rowing. He stands up and walks down to the shore to get a better view. A woman. Finn Sigridsson at the bow. And Magnus Bengtsson. He sighs. So this time has finally come, too. Long put off. He walks over to the fire, takes a branch, and carries its flame down to where their own boats lie, holding it high so that the travelers can see where the best port lies. Then back toward the fire, to waken Engelbrekt, who is still asleep.

"Sire."

At first no response, no attempt.

"Sire, wake up."

Engelbrekt turns his head and opens his eyes, and for a moment Harald sees the peace of his dream linger before the world announces itself, and with it his torturous joints. Calm breaths are broken by a sharp gasp when Engelbrekt raises his head.

"I've asked you many times not to call me that."

Harald doesn't listen. He places an arm around Engelbrekt's shoulder to lift him to sitting.

"Sire, a boat's rowed in from Cuckoo's Roost. Magnus comes with it."

Engelbrekt nods to himself, pale and flinty, and Harald can sense a pain of another sort, one that cuts to the quick.

"Help me up, Harald, and lead me to a place where I might speak with him undisturbed."

Harald links a new grip around him and raises him to his feet.

All too light. So much thinner has he become. Only heavy clothing in numerous layers lend him his former shape. Harald reaches out to take the crutch that Engelbrekt has been using ever since his return to Örebro.

"Leave it where it is."

"But how will you stand?"

"I shall stand."

Harald doesn't gainsay him, for well he knows that tone, but inwardly he asks himself how those legs will hold out when they haven't borne his weight in weeks; when they each draw their own furrow in the soil as Harald drags as much as supports him down to the clearing where he was just splitting his wood, close enough to the fire for him to be able to see what's happening, but far enough away not to hear.

❧

Finn has the helmsmen steer them to where the torch was held, and at the shore Harald is waiting to lift them ashore. Strong as a bear he raises the bow until it is resting heavily in the sand, then extends an arm in both greeting and support to help Finn to land dry-shod.

"Finn. Good to see you. You are welcome here, now as always, you and yours."

Finn nods and sheepishly extends his arms toward Britta, to spare the hem of her dress from getting wet.

"This is Harald Esbjörnsson, one of Engelbrekt's trusted men. Harald, this is Britta Bengtsdaughter of Cuckoo's Roost, sister to Magnus."

The name has scarce passed Finn's lips before Harald sets eyes on its bearer. Magnus has little more color than Engelbrekt, his eyes hollow, his mouth a taut line between white lips. Quickly he is ashore, without Harald's help. Harald greets him with head bowed.

"Magnus. Peace be with you."

No questions need be asked, no purpose given. Harald wraps his arm around Finn's shoulder, then widens his embrace to also lead Britta along the right track.

"Come and sit by our fire, friends. We don't have much, but what we have is yours to share, and given all that's happened since we last met, I'm sure there's a story or two worth telling."

He lets them walk a few steps, then hangs back, nodding Magnus in the direction of the forest hill.

"He's waiting for you in that grove."

Then he turns and follows Finn and Britta up the hill toward the glow of the campfire. From the boat follow the rowers, who diffidently exchange names with the men around the fire, who in turn widen their circle to offer them space and search among their utensils to find drinking vessels for all. Harald does what he can to be a good host, makes his merriment known at the slightest chance, in the hope that his laughter will prove contagious. He can hear how falsely it rings. The tautness in the air refuses to loosen, the unease a snake pit in his stomach. Harald can't stop his eyes from time and again drifting back to the clearing and the two men who stand therein, face-to-face. He is not the only one. How similar they look, though so much separates them. Pale figures, glaringly white between the shadows of the trunks. As though harried by the same sickness, or ghosts squabbling over who gets to haunt which patch. That Engelbrekt's legs don't buckle is beyond his understanding.

In perfect silence they stand for a while, Engelbrekt still, on stiff legs, and Magnus restless on fidgety feet, eye to eye.

"Long have I searched for you, in vain."

"Our time had run its course."

"You sent me away."

"Everything ends, Magnus. And far too seldom is that ending a beautiful one. Better that we took our leave as we did. It was a summer's game I invited you to join. Don't you remember? Easy enough to play. And we were granted much more than that. Summer, winter, spring, and summer again. Memories untarnished by bitterness. Wasn't it good enough as it was?"

"Why are you doing this to me?"

"Time passes and things change. For me it is time to turn my attention to other things. The Council of the Realm is being formed anew, and my presence is required all the more. I'm headed for Stockholm, the right place for the realm's commander to be. My wife I'm to bring with me from Norberg and Örebro, she who has waited so patiently for me while I've been away. An adventure like ours belongs in the field. In war and youth men can grow close, before age and peace must part them. The time for play is over. It's time for me to be earnest."

At the fire, Harald is startled by a sudden sound, a strange noise, like the whimper of game caught in a trap, a fox in a snare. Yet it is sprung from a human throat. Others hear it, too, and, casting their gazes down the hill, let him rise to his feet without making a point of noticing. He finds himself a task on the edge of the fire's glow, so that he might peer down toward the clearing. Magnus is shaking enough that he can see it from afar, his slender hands raised to hide his face. Engelbrekt remains unmoving, as though hewn from stone. A twig snaps behind him. Finn has followed, Magnus's sister a few steps behind.

※

The tears are streaming down Magnus's cheeks, the pain contorting his face, every breath drawn as though in struggle.

"And the realm?"

"Magnus. You believe me capable of far too much. No one can change it all. The realm will remain what it always has been, albeit with a crown atop a new head. You let those lullabies get to your head all too easily."

"Everything you said to me. Your fair words. The hope I gave."

Engelbrekt stands in silence for a while, his breath as heavy as sighs.

"Since the dawn of time men with power have said what they must in order to gain what they most covet. Surely you of all people should know that, you who grew up surrounded by your father and his brothers."

※

A jolt runs through Harald, like a stab to his gut. The axe. The one he was using for the firewood, newly sharpened on his own whetstone. It was there when he left it to guide the boats, in the clearing. Leaning against a trunk. All of a sudden it is in Magnus's hands.

※

Magnus's hands are white around the shaft, and he can feel the promise of sharpened iron in the weight at the end of the wood.

"Will I never again know peace on Swedish soil?"

They stand still facing each other. The spring wind caresses the grasses in the twilight clearing, the ears still low around them. Magnus raises the axe, and Engelbrekt stands still, his arms at his sides, making no attempt to move in the face of the blade's menace. Around them the air thickens now that they are joined by danger. Magnus's voice is hoarse and dejected in his cracked appeals.

"You lie. Why, I don't know. This isn't you who is speaking. I knew Engelbrekt Engelbrektsson as well as one can know another. The one standing before me is a shapeshifter, a fraud. Take it back, everything you said. You told me to be your conscience. You asked for my word, and I swore."

Engelbrekt looks at him, sees Magnus blinded by tears, pale as ash with the wind in his hair; sees Magnus now repeat every mistake that he knows better than to make: Shifting his weight from foot to foot, he raises his weapon high over his head, moistens his lips, and draws a deep breath, while the strength swells in his sinews, taut as bowstrings. Engelbrekt remembers how it ended last time. Just as Magnus does. But he can't move, and nor can he take back his words. It was near Amneholm the last time they were like this, on a secluded hill out of sight of the camp. Knees buckling. Grass pressed into the ground, the scent of snapped stems in the languishing summer. Heartbeats under salty skin. So strong in him, that memory. He is close to tears himself. In the eyes, that's where the opponent's intent is revealed. May the axe fall before his tears do. Fearing that his gaze will betray him, Engelbrekt shuts his eyes.

※

Only too late do they start running, Harald and Finn and Britta, and only too late do they arrive. Magnus is lying over his knees, as small as a person can make themselves, his face pressed down into the soil and his shrieks sifted through earth. Engelbrekt felled beside him, at rest. The axe on the ground between them, its destiny fulfilled. They all stand there in silence, with Magnus's ethereal laments the only sounds that carry through the forest, until the premonition of death is borne up to the campfire behind them and the men get to their feet, dash to their side with weapons in hand, and clothe what has happened in words, as if testing this newly forged reality with their own tongues. Anticipating what he knows must come next, Harald steps forward to stand beside Magnus, swipes his hat off his head, and turns back on his own.

"He among you who thinks he has lost more than the slayer himself, step forward and demand what justice you feel is reasonable, here before my eyes."

Britta and Finn go and stand on either side of him, but there is no need, for no one touches Magnus as he lies there. Instead they take routes around him to leave him be. They have come to retrieve Engelbrekt Engelbrektsson. Wordlessly they lift his body between them with gentle hands and carry him down to the beach, to rinse him and wash the blood away, so that he might be borne to his last resting place clean.

※

Finn sinks to the ground beside Magnus, loosens his hands from his face, and dries the soil from wet cheeks. Magnus stares down at his blood-spattered fingers and holds them out toward Finn, as though calling upon a witness.

"Finn. Is this God's ordeal for me? That one sin should lead to a worse one, the second in punishment for the first?"

Finn takes Magnus's hands in his own. The redness spreads.

"My hands bear stains like yours. Often have I asked myself questions of the same sort."

He grips onto Magnus's powerless hands and lowers his voice to a whisper, one that quakes with the enormity of that which he is giving voice, thoughts long brooded upon, finally aired before another.

"I'm no longer sure that there is a God. If he exists, he isn't the one we've been told he is. Perhaps the sky is empty. Perhaps it'll stay blue forever. All I know is that what I doubt is powerless to forgive my sins. Perhaps forgiveness is to be found elsewhere. Come, let us search for it together."

In their embrace he raises Magnus to his feet and leads him down to the beach, where the boats are waiting with their oarsmen ready, impatient to get away from this place visited by death unbidden. Britta turns to Harald.

"Gather your men and follow us to Cuckoo's Roost. No harm will come to you there."

"Perhaps not there. But where else now?"

"Who dares promise anything dearer? Not I."

Together they walk down to the beach, where the boats are already afloat. Oar strokes guide them out into the dusk that has fallen, the light of spring under the moonshine, through mayflies in swarms. Away from the fire that dies behind them, over the ripples of still waters salted by tears.

THE BOATS REACH the shore with the shattered whisper of hulls on shingles. The Cuckoo's Roosters strike land first, followed by those come from Örebro, oarsmen now for a funeral procession, with Engelbrekt Engelbrektsson placed on a bier between the thwarts. In silence they step ashore. Britta sees them peel off into the twilight, Magnus led by Finn, his head bowed and his hands clasped to his face, with the rest of their men behind them. She hangs back and sees the northmen struggling with the bier, their efforts multiplied by their desire to make every movement slow and dignified. She leads them alongside Harald, guiding him up toward the house. The sun sets and the land blackens, but the sky is yet light. Cuckoo's Roost appears behind the crown of the hill, its stepped gables dark against the blush of the clouds. Harald stumbles on a root, and when Britta turns she sees tears falling from his beard. He stops where he is, and Britta turns to the bier bearers.

"You can see the house now. Just follow the path, it'll lead you to the drawbridge across the moat. My mother and father will receive you there. Step carefully in the dark."

A stump stands beside the path, and Harald sits down heavily, drying his eyes on his sleeve.

"The axe was mine. I forgot it in the clearing. I helped Engelbrekt there and showed Magnus the way. It's all my fault."

Britta crosses her arms, drawing her mantle tighter around her waist. With the day at its end, the evening is cooling.

"I could have told on my brother, on Midsummer's Eve two years ago. Then he'd never have fought before Father and Mother, and never been sent to Engelbrekt."

"That's not the same thing."

"It's easy enough to blame yourself. Perhaps we're all to blame for everything that happens in this world."

No more can he hold out against the sorrow. Rather than show his face contorted with convulsions, he hides it in the crook of his arm, where he draws long, quivering breaths through the fabric of his doublet. Britta stands in silence beside him, tracing the path of the bier, now lost in dusk's mists. With time solace of a kind comes to Harald, who eventually stops crying but remains seated all the same. He stares out blankly into space. Britta sits down beside him on the stump.

"What are you thinking about?"

"Sander Beck."

"Who?"

"A man-at-arms from a foreign land. Engelbrekt sent me south, to Lawless Köping, to speak to the people and incite them to rebel. I took a dozen crossbows with me in my cart, and had I had ten times as many I'd have found marksmen enough to squabble over every one. We took to the forest, felled trunks across the path, and sat in wait for Giovanni Frangipani's men. They came soon enough, caught unawares, defenseless. The thirst for blood was great among my men, and I myself had a hard time forgetting the injustices that I'd suffered at his hands. So easy would it have been to kill them all and leave them there in the forest. So close to retribution. Of all those who awaited our judgment, Sander Beck was the weakest. No courage did he have to spare, not even for the sake of his dignity. He pissed himself as he stood there, prayed to God, and babbled on about his family in a guttural German. He kept saying his name again and again, to make us see that he was more than just the colors he bore. I stood on the bank high above him, with power over life and death in my hands; I high and he low, he fat and I tall, he German and I Swedish. A thought struck me as I pondered his fate."

"What?"

"Through our senses we observe this world, but everyone sees and hears differently. For each person the world is their own. Slay someone and you slay the whole world that is theirs."

"What did you do?"

"We spared their lives, as Engelbrekt had instructed me to do. Sander Beck was forced to dry off his breeches on the long march south, and what then became of him I don't know. Shortly thereafter I met your brother on the same road."

He shudders, wraps his broad arms around his waist, and strokes his shoulders for the sake of warmth. He nods toward Cuckoo's Roost, to where the bier is shrouded by night.

"Engelbrekt is dead. I'm thinking about the world that is lost with him. He wasn't like the rest. The world he saw he wanted to make all of ours. A brighter and more beautiful world it would have been, too, with the people's voice on the Council and everyone's good their cause. The low raised up and the high brought down. Those who pray, those who farm, and those who fight, united, and all the stronger for it. A world in which no lord would allow the people to starve while good food was slapped on the muckheap. In which no bailiff would harness up a woman as an ox for the sake of some taxes. One hundred and twenty miles lie between us and Stockholm. That's how close Engelbrekt came. To Cuckoo's Roost's shores, but no farther. Now the world will be another instead."

Around them the forest is still, until a blackbird strikes up its verses from a hidden branch, a yearning for better present in its languishing trill. In the distance another responds with the same tune. Britta remembers her larks with Finn mere hours before.

"For now it's calm, like after a stone cast on still waters. Soon enough the ripples will spread. What will happen next?"

Harald Esbjörnsson hesitates in his response.

"Everyone with strength and ambition will dash to grab any scrap of power within reach. The realm will collapse on itself: The people against the people, the people against the lords, the lords against the lords, the lords against the king. From now on everyone's at war with everyone."

With a sigh he effortlessly rises to his feet, then dries his cheeks and holds his hand out to help Britta up.

"Soon there'll be wolves at play all around. No more will any highborn lass seek to dry a northman's tears and be offered an arm in return."

And Britta:

"Then let's go while there's yet time."

Afterword

THE NAMES BY which the medieval houses of the nobility are now known were often contrived much later. To have a surname in addition to one's patronymic was rare. When genealogical tables started to take hold in the Renaissance—a society that attached great importance to birth and ancestry—genealogists in turn started arbitrarily ascribing names to houses that had, in many cases, already died out, based purely on the appearance of their coat of arms. The house of Natt och Dag—meaning *Night and Day* in Swedish—known since 1280 and bearing a shield parted per fess in blue and gold, is one example of this practice. It was only in the eighteenth century, when the nature of Swedish surnames had shifted, that members of this house started using this name of themselves, among the last of their kind to embrace this norm. It is for this reason that no such surnames feature in *Hope and Destiny*.

The sequence of events described in *Hope and Destiny* happened so long ago that the truth can hardly be asserted. Of the higher echelons of fifteenth-century society few traces remain, beyond the bare-bones dates of weddings and deaths. The advance of men of power can be glimpsed through their participation in the Council of the Realm, distributions of estates, and land deals. The distaff side, however, tends to be neglected. The peasantry is as good as forgotten. Their personalities can only be guessed at.

The many twists and turns of the Engelbrekt Rebellion are well documented, but all Engelbrektiana tends to end in letdown when it comes to the description of his murder, whose motive remains unexplained. The events depicted here bring together a number of known facts through the help of fiction.

We first meet Magnus Bengtsson (Night and Day/Natt och Dag) in fifty or so curiously rhymed lines that were struck from the original Chronicles of Engelbrekt, authored by an unknown hand soon after Engelbrekt's death. This removal was thought to have happened when this rhyming chronicle was incorporated into the more ambitious and politically motivated Chronicles of Karl later that century. Here Magnus figures as a page to Engelbrekt, described as the foremost among all of them in love, one who is given clothes and estates. A strange place for the son of a member of the Council of the Realm, of one of the most powerful houses in the kingdom, to find himself. After a while together their ways parted.

Around the turn of the year 1436, a conflict arises between Magnus's father, Bengt, and Engelbrekt, despite the two having been close allies and Bengt having been granted a fief of Castle Cut (in modern-day Södertälje), located just next to the site where Engelbrekt had undertaken to dig a canal in order to subvert Stockholm's trading monopoly. Bengt Stensson attacks a Hansa ship, in direct breach of the prevailing truce. What motivated Bengt's actions, we don't know. After Eric Puck attacks Castle Cut, which is defended by Bengt's wife, Kristina Magnusdaughter (Leopard), Bengt goes to meet Engelbrekt in Örebro for a conciliation, which is settled.

When Engelbrekt not long thereafter moors on an islet outside of Cuckoo's Roost (Göksholm) in the spring of 1436, on his way from Örebro to Stockholm, he is slain by Magnus. The chronicle makes a point of noting that the murder weapon was an axe. Mats Linday, a relative who chronicled the Natt och Dag line and to whom this book is dedicated, is to my knowledge the first to highlight the strange choice of weapon: no young nobleman would have traipsed around with an axe in his belt. Had Magnus left Cuckoo's Roost with the intention of putting Engelbrekt to death, it would have been more plausible for him to do so with a sword, spear, or bow. My conclusion is that he found the axe on the spot, and that the murder happened in the heat of the moment, based on words exchanged then and there between Magnus and Engelbrekt, formerly so close.

After the murder, Magnus stops bearing the coat of arms of his father's line. For the rest of his life he instead chooses his mother's lion and lily.

Toward the end of his life, Magnus establishes an anniversary in Julita Abbey, a special mass to be read every year on the fourth of May. This was the day of Engelbrekt's death.

After his murder, Engelbrekt's fame grew. For any man who coveted the crown, the ability to position himself as the one to shoulder the fallen mantle of the people's chieftain became crucial, until Gustav Vasa made good on Engelbrekt's intent just under a century later. For a long time I wondered why the verses about Magnus and Engelbrekt might have been struck from the chronicles, stuck in the idea that the censor's focus was on Magnus. A false conclusion on my part: if this removal suggests that there was indeed something about Magnus and Engelbrekt's relationship that the times thought worthy of hiding, the lines wouldn't have been struck for Magnus Bengtsson's sake, but to protect the memory of Engelbrekt Engelbrektsson, so vital to the populism of the time.

It is from Magnus that all the living members of the house descend, the oldest of its kind still in existence. Between Magnus and myself runs an unbroken line of fathers and sons for fifteen generations.

Niklas Natt och Dag, Visby, July 2023

Acknowledgments

MY WIFE, Mia Natt och Dag, went to great lengths to trace family ancestry, not least on the historically neglected distaff side, without which my book wouldn't be what it is. Mia has also designed the family tree of the sons of Sten that opens and closes the book, and interpreted the coats of arms. Thank you for your work and your patience, and for the life we live together.

Thank you to Fredrik Backman, the first to read, for your thoughtful reading, notes, and many years of support. Thanks also to Gunilla Backman for your feedback on the manuscript.

Thank you to Sara Bergmark Elfgren for reading with an author's insight and a friend's generosity.

Thank you to my publisher, Åsa Lindström, and my editor, Andreas Lundberg.

Thank you to my mother, Elisabeth Natt och Dag, for proofreading.